THE CLONE REBELLION
SEDITION

STEVEN L. KENT

(THE) CL8NE REBELLION

SEDITION

TITAN BOOKS

Print edition ISBN: 9781781167236
E-book edition ISBN: 9781781167397

Published by Titan Books
A division of Titan Publishing Group Ltd
144 Southwark Street, London SE1 0UP

First edition: September 2013
1 2 3 4 5 6 7 8 9 10

Printed and bound in Great Britain by CPI Group Ltd.

Did you enjoy this book?
We love to hear from our readers. Please email us at:
readerfeedback@titanemail.com or write to us at the above address.

To receive advance information, news, competitions, and exclusive offers online, please sign up for the Titan newsletter on our website.

www.titanbooks.com

Having grown up during the era of Muhammad Ali, I've always wanted to write a novel about boxing. Last August, I finally put on the gloves, so to speak, and started writing.

Pleased with the results of that particular experiment—a satirical novel that merged real boxing lore with four heavy-weight champions of my own invention—I rushed the first fifty pages to Richard, my agent. He phoned back a few days later to tell me that while he admired my sports-writing abilities, the book was unsellable because no one buys novels about boxing. (For those of you willing to prove Richard wrong, the first third of the book has been released as an e-book called Long Live the Champion.*)*

Richard feared that I had lost touch with my readers. As his advice should always be taken to heart, I decided to spend the holidays working at my local Barnes & Noble... Call it a paid internship. I met customers, stocked shelves, and received a first-rate education about the other half of the book business from people who genuinely know what they are doing.

One thing that I learned is that most people in the bookselling business are smart and well-read. With an increase in online sales and a growing apathy toward the art of reading, however, the business of selling books has become unreasonably difficult.

This book is dedicated to the brilliant, hardworking, and talented crew at Barnes & Noble #2617—Joe, Niki, Todd, Andrew, Sean, Adrian, AnnaLee, Angela, Carly, Cassie, Debra, Dick, Hilary, Jamie, Jason, Jay, Jose, Katie, Lisa, Maria, Mary, Mo, Nina, Renee, Rianna, Roxie, Susan, and Tuesday. Thank you for the many lessons and the endless hospitality.

Steven L. Kent
January 5, 2012

SPIRAL ARMS OF THE MILKY WAY GALAXY

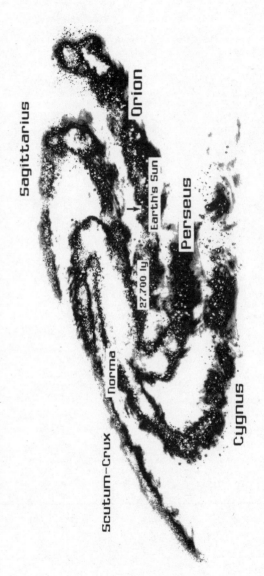

Sagittarius

Orion

Earth's Sun

Perseus

27.700 ly

Norma

Scutum-Crux

Cygnus

100.000 ly

Map by Steven J. Kent, adapted from a public domain NASA diagram

NINE EVENTS THAT SHAPED HISTORY
A UNIFIED AUTHORITY TIME LINE

2010 TO 2018
DECLINE OF THE U.S. ECONOMY

Following the examples of Chevrolet, Oracle, IBM, and ConAgra Foods, Microsoft moves its headquarters from the United States to Shanghai. Referring to their company as a "global corporation," Microsoft executives claim they are still committed to U.S. prosperity, but with its burgeoning economy, China has become the company's most important market.

Even with Toyota and Hyundai increasing their manufacturing activities in the United States—spurred on by the favorable cheap labor conditions—the U.S. economy becomes dependent on the shipping of raw materials and farm goods.

Bottoming out as the world's thirteenth largest economy behind China, United Korea, India, Cuba, the European Economic Community, Brazil, Mexico, Canada, Japan, South Africa, Israel, and Unincorporated France, the United States government focuses on maintaining its position as the world's last military superpower.

JANUARY 3, 2026
INTRODUCTION OF BROADCAST PHYSICS

Armadillo Aerospace announces the discovery of broadcast physics, a new technology capable of translating matter into data waves that can be transmitted to any location instantaneously. This opens the way for pangalactic exploration without time dilation or the dangers of light-speed travel.

The United States creates the first-ever fleet of self-broadcasting ships, a scientific fleet designed to locate suitable planets for future colonization. When initial scouting reports suggest that the rest of the galaxy is uninhabited, politicians fire up public sentiment with talk about a new "manifest destiny" and spreading humanity across space.

The discovery of broadcast physics leads to the creation of the Broadcast Network—a galactic superhighway consisting of satellites that send and receive ships across the galaxy. The Broadcast Network ushers in the age of galactic expansion.

JULY 4, 2110
RUSSIA AND KOREA SIGN A PACT WITH THE UNITED STATES

With the growth of its space-based economy, the United States reclaims its spot as the wealthiest nation on Earth. Russia and Korea become the first nations to sign the IGTA (Intergalactic Trade Accord), a treaty opening the way for other nations to become self-governing American territories and enjoy full partnership in the space-based economy.

In an effort to create a competing alliance, France unveils its Cousteau Oceanic Exploration program and announces plans to create undersea colonies. Only Tahiti signs on.

After the other nations of the European Economic Union, Japan, and all of Africa become members of the IGTA, France discontinues its undersea colonization and joins the IGTA. Several nations, most notably China and Afghanistan, refuse to sign, leading to a minor world war in which the final holdouts are coerced into signing the treaty.

More than 80 percent of the world's population is eventually sent to establish colonies throughout the galaxy.

JULY 4, 2250
TRANSMOGRIFICATION OF THE UNITED STATES

With most of its citizens living off Earth, the IGTA is renamed "The Unified Authority" and restructured to serve as a government rather than an economic union.

The government of the Unified Authority merges principles from the U.S. Constitution with concepts from Plato's Republic. In accordance with Plato's ideals, society is broken into three strata—citizenry, defense, and governance.

With forty self-sustaining colonies across the galaxy, Earth becomes the political center of a new republic. The eastern seaboard of the former United States becomes an ever-growing capital city populated by the political class—families appointed to run the government in perpetuity.

Earth also becomes the home to the military class. After some experimentation, the Unified Authority adopts an all-clone conscription model to fulfill its growing need for soldiers. Clone farms euphemistically known as "orphanages" are established around Earth. These orphanages produce more than a million cloned recruits per year.

The military does not commission clone officers. The officer corps is drafted from the ruling class. When the children of politicians are drummed out of school or deemed unsuitable for politics, they are sent to officer-candidate school in Australia.

2452 TO 2512
UPRISING IN THE GALACTIC EYE

On October 29, 2452, a date later known as the new "Black

Tuesday," a fleet of scientific exploration ships vanishes in the "galactic eye" region of the Norma Arm.

Fearing an alien attack, the U.A. Senate calls for the creation of the Galactic Central Fleet, a self-broadcasting armada. Work on the Galactic Central Fleet is completed in 2455. The newly christened fleet travels to the Inner Curve, where it vanishes as well.

Having authorized the development of a top secret line of cloned soldiers called "Liberators," the Linear Committee—the executive branch of the U.A. government—approves sending an invasion force into the Galactic Eye to attack all hostile threats. The Liberators discover a human colony led by Morgan Atkins, a powerful senator who disappeared with the Galactic Central Fleet. The Liberators overthrow the colony, but Atkins and many of his followers escape in G.C. Fleet ships.

Over the next fifty years, a religious cult known as the Morgan Atkins Fanatics—"Mogats"—spreads across the 180 colonized planets, preaching independence from the Unified Authority government.

Spurred on by the growing Morgan Atkins movement, four of the six galactic arms declare independence from Unified Authority governance in 2510. Two years later, the combined forces of the Confederate Arms Treaty Organization and the Morgan Atkins Fanatics defeat the Earth Fleet and destroy the Broadcast Network, effectively cutting the Earth government off from its loyal colonies and Navy.

Having crippled the Unified Authority, the Mogats turn on their Confederate Arms allies. The Confederates escape with fifty self-broadcasting ships and join forces with the Unified Authority, leaving the Mogats with a fleet of over four hundred self-broadcasting ships, the most powerful attack force in the galaxy.

In 2512, the Unified Authority and the Confederate Arms end the war by attacking the Mogat home world, leaving no survivors on the planet.

2514 TO 2515
AVATARI INVASION

In 2514, an alien force enters the outer region of the Scutum-Crux Arm, conquering U.A. colonies. As they attack planets, the aliens wrap an energy barrier around the atmosphere. Called an "ion curtain," the barrier cuts off escape and communications.

In a matter of two years, the aliens spread throughout the galaxy, occupying only planets deemed habitable by U.A. scientists. The Unified Authority loses 178 of its 180 populated planets before making a final stand on New Copenhagen.

During this battle, U.A. scientists unravel the secrets of the aliens' tachyon-based technology, enabling U.A. Marines to win the war. In the aftermath of the invasion, the Unified Authority sends the four self-broadcasting ships of the Japanese Fleet along with twelve thousand Navy SEAL clones to locate and destroy the Avatari home world.

2517
RISE OF THE ENLISTED MAN'S EMPIRE

The Unified Authority Congress holds hearings investigating the military's performance during the Avatari invasion. When two generals blame their losses on lack of discipline among their cloned enlisted men, synthetic conscription is abolished and all remaining clones are transferred to frontier fleets—fleets stranded in deep space since the destruction of the Broadcast Network. The Navy plans to use these fleets in live-ordnance military exercises designed to test its new, more powerful Nike-class ships; but the clones thwart this plan by declaring independence.

After creating their own broadcast network, the clones establish the Enlisted Man's Empire, a nation consisting of twenty-three planets and thirteen naval fleets. As hostilities continue between the Enlisted Man's Empire and the Unified Authority, the Avatari return, attacking planets using a devastating weapon that raises atmospheric temperatures to nine thousand degrees for eighty-three seconds.

The Avatari attack three planets in December, 2517—New Copenhagen, a Unified Authority colony, Olympus Kri, an Enlisted Man's colony, and Terraneau, a neutral nation. Working together, the Enlisted Man's Navy and the Earth Fleet successfully evacuate Olympus Kri prior to the attack. Following the attack on Olympus Kri, the Avatari accelerate their attacks, incinerating a new populated planet every three days as they work their way toward Earth.

Despite the mutual threat, the Unified Authority renews its assault on the Enlisted Man's Empire.

2517
DESTRUCTION OF THE AVATARI HOME WORLD

The Japanese Fleet locates the Avatari home world in Bode's Galaxy. While the inhabitants of the planet have become extinct, its automated mining and military systems continue their destructive expansion.

After depositing all nonessential personnel on New Copenhagen to establish a new colony, the *Sakura*, the last ship in the fleet, launches a successful suicide attack on the Avatari planet.

2517
FALL OF THE UNIFIED AUTHORITY

Unaware of the Japanese attack on the Avatari home world, the Enlisted Man's Empire divides its military into two groups. One group establishes a colony on the burned-out remains of Terraneau, while the other launches a preemptive assault against Earth, defeating the Unified Authority and establishing a clone-controlled government.

PROLOGUE

Three men were following me, but I only needed one to answer my questions, so I decided to kill the other two.

It was near midnight. It was that rare dry winter night in Seattle. A thick cloudy fog filled the street, making the darkness darker. Only a few lights shone over this part of town at this time of night. When I walked under them, they made the fog glow.

There was a strange odor in the air, a sharp, chemical scent I did not recognize. The smell was faint and becoming weaker. I did not have time to wonder what it was, though. My mind was on the men who were following me.

Ironically, those men might have taken me by surprise if they had not tried to sneak up on me. I was out late, alone, letting my thoughts wander. On empty streets like these, I could hear their footsteps from a block away and read the sounds they made the way trackers read footprints. Three guys, sticking to empty alleys, stopping at corners, walking as quietly as they could—that much was obvious. I had to surmise the rest.

Muggers or assassins? I asked myself. Muggers didn't worry me. In truth, neither did assassins; but that was because death held a certain attraction for me, especially if I could take these bastards with me.

The streetlights glowed white-tinged amber above the sidewalks, but the fog smeared their light into a pastel smudge. I was a block in from the waterfront, in the part of Seattle with the fancy bars and the movie holotoriums.

I was dressed in civilian clothing instead of the uniform of a Marine in the Enlisted Man's Empire, and I did not have a gun or a knife. No problem. I'd use their weapons against them, whatever they had brought. I'd even return their weapons when I was done.

Muggers tended to be big, strong, and aggressive, but untrained, relying on fear as much as violence. I wasn't afraid. I was trained, and I was ready.

I listened to their footsteps. *Not muggers*, I thought. Muggers would come at me from all sides. They would pretend not to notice me until they had me surrounded, then they'd attack.

I came to a corner and looked both ways before crossing, not searching for cars or muggers but surveying the potential battlefield. Seattle's restaurant district butted up against old town. Of course, this was Earth, and not just Earth, it was former United States territory. The old Unified Authority government had considered the United States the cradle of modern society, and they had maintained it like a museum exhibit. When buildings in U.S. cities reached their expiration date, so to speak, the Unified Authority Department of Historical Preservation replaced them with immaculate reproductions. Square walls, glass windows, revolving doors, brick, slate, and mortar façades... whatever it took to preserve "the cradle of society."

The Unified Authority was now every bit as extinct as the United States, but the Enlisted Man's Empire wanted to maintain appearances as well.

Maybe I should run, I thought. Would I stand a better chance of luring them in if I pretended to be afraid?

If they had come after me hoping to mug some random civilian, they would respond to my panic like sharks respond to blood. If they knew I was a military clone, a show of fear would make them suspicious. If they knew I was Wayson Harris, the commanding officer of the EME Marines, my pretended panic would scare them away. Anyone who knew who I was knew I was programmed to ignore fear.

A strange thought ran through my mind. *Anything that can be programmed can be reprogrammed.* I had no idea where the thought had come from or what it meant. It was a stray.

My shadows saw me standing by the curb and stopped abruptly. One scuffed his shoe across the concrete.

If these guys are assassins, I thought, *they're the dumbest specking assassins on the face of the earth.*

Dumb and slated for extinction. Charles Darwin would have said they needed to die for the preservation of the species—the dumb ones and the broken ones are the first to go.

I walked across the street and sprinted into the fog. The hunting party followed my example; but, of course, they had given me a head start.

Now that they knew I had heard them, they abandoned their attempt at stealth and raced after me.

I was twenty-nine years old and in my prime. I kept myself in shape. Apparently, only one of my would-be attackers jogged every day. When I turned a corner and paused to listen, the sound of their footsteps told me that one of my pursuers had pulled away from the pack. He would be the tough one, the athlete.

"Careful, Butch," one yelled.

Butch?

Butch didn't have an opportunity to answer. He came tearing past the corner where I waited, and I stuck out a leg, sending him on a seven-foot flight. He screamed as he tripped and landed face-first on the concrete, dropping his knife.

I placed a foot across the back of his neck and snapped

17

his spine. Then I quietly walked back into the alley, into total darkness, and I worked my way slowly and silently back around the block. By the time I came back to the street, Butch's two pals had found his corpse.

These boys don't know the first thing about recon, I told myself. Judging by the way they ignored me, they might have never heard of the term. One stood with his back to me, paying no attention to anything but his fallen friend. The other was even more stupid. He knelt beside the body, asking, "Butch... Butch, are you okay?"

Using parked cars for cover, I came within ten feet of the bastards. After watching them to make sure they were as stupid as I thought, I stepped out from behind a sedan, and said, "He's with God and the angels now."

That turned out to have been an insensitive thing to say.

The short-term survivors turned and squinted into the fog, trying to find me. The guy kneeling beside the body had a book in one hand and a carving knife in the other... hardly the weapons of an assassin or a mugger. The bearded one on his feet held a two-foot-long metal rod. He grasped it between his hands the way a worker would hold a pickax. All three of them, the two men and the corpse, wore rags instead of clothes. Their hair was long, and they had the dirty, musty smell of unwashed clothes.

Too inexperienced to be military... too dirty to be muggers... too stupid to be assassins. And the book, a black leather book, had gold leaf along the pages. I only knew of two books that people still printed on paper, both were religious texts.

These weren't assassins, they were goddamned—*missionaries?* Had I just killed a man who had come thinking to save my nonexistent soul? But if he came to save my soul, why did he have a knife? The two who were still breathing carried a rod and a blade.

I took a step closer, and asked, "Do you want to talk about this?" in a voice that was civil and reasonable. The one on his feet raised his rod in the air, yelled, "Father, take me unto the bosom of Abraham!" He charged right at me, screaming and waving his stick.

Bold move. I decided that he'd be the one who lived.

He brought the rod down as if it were a samurai sword. I stepped to the side. Blending my motion with his, I caught his hands, twisted the rod, and stabbed its short end into his gut. I gave it an extra shove, pushing it in a couple of inches, then I yanked it out. The guy coughed up a rope of blood and sank to his knees. I could hear him crying and babbling as I switched my focus to his friend.

The third man stood and faced me. He muttered, "The Lord is my shepherd; I shall not want."

"Put down the knife and you might just avoid the valley of death," I said.

The man continued his recitation. "He leadeth me to lie down in green pastures." He spoke clearly but quickly. "He leadeth me beside the still waters. He restoreth my soul."

He swung his knife and lunged.

Trained fighters don't often lunge with their knives because the whole point of using a knife is to lash—quick, controlled, lethal. As this guy sprang forward, I used the rod I'd borrowed from his friend to break one of his kneecaps.

As he screamed and fell, he dropped his knife.

By this time I was in the midst of a combat reflex, meaning the glands built into my brain had pumped so much adrenaline and testosterone into my blood that rational thought was the last thing on my mind. Violence became like air when I had a combat reflex, and I breathed it greedily.

I cracked the man across the back of his head with the rod, knocking him unconscious. Then I picked up his knife and slit his throat with it. Once the combat reflex ended, I'd probably reevaluate my actions and decide I had gone overboard; but at the moment, I felt pretty good about my judgment.

Still holding a knife in one hand and a steel rod in the other, still under the influence of the hormones, I walked over to where the sole survivor lay squirming and crying on the concrete. A steady flow of blood coursed from the hole in his stomach, just below his ribs. Every time he inhaled, he made a squeaking sound.

I knelt beside the man, carefully placing the rod and knife where I could see them. For all I knew, there might have been a fourth or a fifth man lurking in the darkness, one with half a brain who walked softly and sacrificed his buddies in the name of stealth.

The guy tried to sit up. I placed a hand on his chest and pressed down until his back went flat. He stared up at me, tears leaking from his eyes, twin streams of blood running from the corners of his mouth. He whispered, "You murdered me."

"You should have thought about that before you came after me," I said.

"I... I'm dying."

"Don't pack your bags just yet," I said. "Let's chat."

I kept my left hand on his chest, pinning him. Pointing at the hole in his gut with my right hand, I said, "Nasty wound," and I plunged my finger into it, and added, "Deep, too."

It was deeper than I expected. I thought I had driven the rod an inch or two into his body, but I was wrong. Reaching in with my finger, I felt a slippery surface that might have been his liver or possibly his intestines. The tip of my finger brushed against his spine.

The man tried to scream, but he was weak, and the hole the rod had left in him must have grazed the bottom of his lungs. If doctors got here quickly, they might be able to save the bastard, but I doubted it.

Now that I saw the damage I had dealt, I started to come to my senses. The guy was going to die. The question was, would he answer my questions first? I said, "You don't exactly strike me as your typical dark-alley stalker."

He squirmed and managed to inhale a chestful of air. Pain showed in his watery eyes. He breathed quickly, held the air, and spat at me. It didn't work. Flat on his back, weak and dying, he only launched his bloody spittle a few inches in the air. It arced and landed on his chin.

With my left hand still on his chest, I placed my right hand over the wound. I wasn't trying to torture him, but I wanted to remind him who was boss. I said, "That wasn't very nice."

He tried to wrestle free, but he had no more strength than a toddler. His breathing was fast. He whispered, "Damn you. Damn you."

"I want to help you," I said. "I'll show you. Watch." I pulled out my mobile, and said, "You there."

"Base command."

"This is General Wayson Harris."

"Yes, sir."

"Do you have my location?"

"Yes, sir."

"There's been an accident. Can you send med-evac?"

"Yes, sir. I'll have it out…"

I looked down at my victim, and said, "That's a medical-evacuation unit… military talk for an ambulance."

"We'll have an air unit there in five minutes, sir."

Turning my attention back to base command, I said, "You better hurry, this guy has lost a lot of blood." I looked down at my victim, and asked, "Do you think you can hold on for five minutes?"

The guy began babbling, something about Satan and burning in hell. I listened to him for a second, then told the operator at base command, "Tell them to bring a gallon of plasma."

I ended the call, then I looked at the bastard, and said, "There. See, I'm trying to help you."

He shook his head. He convulsed, then he tried to squirm free of me, but I kept him pinned to the concrete. He tried to push my hand away, but he had no strength. Then he started to sob. He took a deep breath, and said, "I failed." He took another deep breath and repeated himself, "I failed." He was dying, and he knew it.

Do you feel guilty for killing this miserable speck? I asked myself. Hell no, I told myself, but I did not believe the lie. These guys weren't killers, they were just pretending to be. Had I broken their legs, these idiots would have told me everything; but no, I had to give in to hormones.

"Hope you're happy, asshole," I told myself.

The bastard on the ground must have thought I was speaking to him. He said, "I forgive you."

I looked down at him. Even in the fog-filtered light, I could see that his face had gone as white as milk. His eyes stared straight into mine, the sockets as dark and empty as the socket of a skull.

"Don't you die on me," I said.

He did not respond.

I placed my knee on his chest and slapped him across the face. "Why'd you come after me?" I asked.

He stared up at me, the trace of a smile forming on his blood-smeared lips. He said, "Legion."

I asked, "Are you part of some kind of militia?"

The son of a bitch showed me the sweetest, most angelic smile, then he coughed up his last jigger of blood and died. Kneeling there on the street, my knee still pinning his chest, I slapped the guy to see if I could wake him up, but I knew it wouldn't work.

Then that alien thought repeated itself—*Anything that can be programmed can be reprogrammed.* It kept flashing in my brain. *Anything that can be programmed can be reprogrammed. Anything that can be programmed can be reprogrammed.*

PART I

THE NIGHT OF THE MARTYRS

1

"What were you doing on the waterfront?" the cop asked.

"This is the hospitality district," I said.

"Not at midnight, it isn't."

"I came for a drink."

"Didn't you say you're staying at Fort Lewis?" he asked.

"Yeah."

"I don't buy it," said the cop. "You drove fifty miles for a nightcap. What? They don't have bars on base? How about in Tacoma? They got bars in Tacoma."

He had a good point. Tacoma, a fairly good-sized town, was located just north of Fort Lewis. I'd driven forty miles to reach Seattle.

I said, "I felt like celebrating?"

"By yourself?"

Granted, my reason for driving to Seattle sounded thin, even to me. I said, "I didn't come trolling for Christians."

I wasn't going to say it, but the person I had come to see was the opposite of the men I ran into. I came in search of a mercenary named Ray Freeman. He never showed.

As a civilian, the police detective had absolutely no authority over me. Even if he'd caught me torturing these guys red-handed, he couldn't have arrested me. My participation in these crimes automatically put them under military jurisdiction. Had I wished, I could have ended this street-side interrogation at any time, but I hoped maybe my cooperation would foster a little goodwill. It wasn't working.

Four hours had passed since the confrontation began, and I was still on the street, standing around in the fog and the cold, watching the crime-scene-investigation unit scour for clues. The police cars' spotlights illuminated a forty-foot circle with a shortwave light that penetrated the fog.

Why, I wondered, *are they searching for clues when they have the confessed killer?*

With the cars here, I could see the scene clearly. Mostly I saw the bodies of the victims, three soft, domesticated types, two of them barely over twenty years old. They looked like college students.

"Why don't you tell me the real reason you came?" the policeman repeated.

"I like the bars in this part of town. I like watching the waterfront," I said. It was a lie, and the detective saw through it.

He pretended to suddenly notice the thick fog shrouding the docks, and said, "Yeah, nice view."

"Are you quite finished, Officer?" asked Travis Watson, my civilian advisor. I had hired him because he was smart, competent, and natural-born. I needed a natural-born aide to help interface with the civilian population. Having recently been conquered by the all-clone military, a lot of people were wary of clones. Go figure.

Watson was also fresh out of college, brash bordering on disrespectful, and easily distracted by women.

No one is perfect.

"You know what I think, Harris?" the detective said, clearly ignoring Watson. "I think these kids came to the bar for a drink, and you lured them out and killed them. You probably had friends hidden out here in the alley. That's what I think.

"How many men did you have with you?" The detective was in his forties, a large, pudgy man in a long coat that kept him warm. He glared at me, knowing that I was above his law.

I said, "That's an interesting theory. Does unsubstantiated guesswork count as police work these days?"

He gave me a wolfish smile, and said, "Listen to you. You've got three stars and a civilian assistant, General, but you don't have an alibi. Does your rank let you get away with murder in the Army, too?"

"I'm a Marine," I said.

"Same difference. Marines are like ants, they're real tough in a group. How tough are you when you're all alone?"

"Good question," I said. "Why don't you ask them?" I pointed to the three dead men lying on the concrete where I had left them.

"You want to know what I think…" the detective began.

"Not really," I said, shutting him down before he blew off more steam. "Look, we know who killed these men, so there's no point investigating the murder. I did it. My fingerprints are on the rod, my shoe print is on that one's neck," I said, still pointing at the corpses. "Now that we know who killed them, the next step in the investigation would be to find out who the speck they are. I want to know why they came downtown and why they were following me, and why they had two knives and an iron rod. What I really want to know is why that asshole over there was carrying a damn Bible.

"Do you get that a lot up here… thugs carrying Bibles and butcher knives?"

"No, we do not have a lot of Bible-toting thugs," growled the detective.

I turned to Watson, and asked, "Is it just me, or do you find his taste in books as fascinating as I do?"

"We'll look into it," the detective barked. Clearly, he did not like taking direction from criminals.

"You might take DNA samples, too. Find out why these

clowns attacked a Marine, and you might even save a few lives in the process," I said.

"Since when did you care about saving lives?" he asked.

"Oh, Detective, my entire existence is about saving lives… both natural-born and synthetic."

He looked back at the corpses, then turned to me. "You still haven't told me what you were doing out here."

"So what were you doing out here?" asked Watson. Like the detective, my civilian adjutant did not entirely trust me. Like the detective, he had been woken by an early-morning call. But the detective had probably woken up on the wrong side of his own bed.

Watson, on the other hand, had been in someone else's. I didn't even let him go home to change. I told him to get his ass over to Bolling Air Force Base, where a plane would be waiting to take him to Seattle. Three hours later, he met me on the street, still dressed in his bar hopper's sports coat.

Watson came across as sensible though I wavered between not approving of his lifestyle and envying it. He was a big, good-looking kid who'd slept in every bed in Washington, D.C., except quite possibly his own. He knew all the bars in town and had a mental catalog of every woman he'd seen in them.

He didn't brag about his conquests. Had I not sent spooks to follow him a few evenings, I never would have known. As my aide, he dealt with sensitive information, and I made a point of knowing what he did in his off-hours.

Nearly a year had passed since the Enlisted Man's Empire had conquered Earth. It was a fight that nobody wanted, but we didn't have much choice.

The government of the Enlisted Man's Empire was really just an expanded military chain of command, a collection of clones. Originally brewed to serve the Unified Authority, the Earth-centric empire that colonized the Milky Way, we clones began our existence protecting natural-born-mankind's 180 colonized planets. The Unified Authority wanted to protect its citizens without sacrificing their own children, so the government amassed a vast military with clone enlisted men to do the heavy lifting. The officers were natural-born, but they didn't stay around when the fighting began.

That system worked just fine right up until an alien army stormed the galaxy, capturing 179 of our 180 colonies. When the natural-born politicians asked what went wrong, the natural-born officer corps blamed their failures on the clones, and the natural-born public took them at their word.

In response, the Unified Authority decided to ditch us. We were shipped out to obsolete fleets stranded in deep space. Two things ended our exile. We figured out how to return to Earth, and the aliens launched a new kind of attack. They started incinerating planets to exterminate the inhabitants. With the Avatari burning our bridges behind us one planet at a time, we turned our sights to the home world.

I led the Enlisted Man's invasion of Earth. We beat the Unifieds, then we dug in and waited for incineration. A year had passed with no sign of the aliens, not that anyone complained.

Ask a dozen people why the aliens never reached Earth, and you'd hear a dozen explanations. The prevailing theories were that (a) God destroyed the aliens; (b) having been turned back before reaching Earth on their first invasion, the aliens now ignored the planet; and (c) a small fleet sent out to track down the aliens had located their planet and destroyed them. I personally preferred the third option, though I could not imagine how they'd managed to accomplish such a feat.

"General?" Watson said, bringing me back to the present again.

"Yes?"

"Why did you come into town?"

That was another of my reasons for hiring Watson, he was

persistent. It was one of those chicken-egg quandaries—did he learn persistence hunting for scrub (Marine-speak for one-nighters) or had his bar-hopping safaris ended in success because he was naturally persistent?

The guy was six-foot-five. He was trim because he had good genes and good eating habits, not because of exercise. As far as I could tell, he had no tolerance for pain. It wouldn't have taken more than a paper cut to bring tears to his eyes. I could not imagine how he would react to a broken bone or a gunshot wound.

Watson had an easygoing nature. Angry detectives didn't bother him, neither did angry Marines. I could swear at him, threaten him, call him out of bed, he never took offense.

When I responded to his question with, "I don't see where that is any of your business," he said, "It is, and it isn't. You killed three civilians. If you want to label the killings as a 'need-to-know-basis Marine Corps operation,' then it's none of my business. If you want to keep on good terms with the local police, you need to give me something."

I said, "Drop it."

The final lingerings of the lustrous night still hung over the city. Streetlights and headlights and the occasional lit window pierced the darkness, but daylight was only an hour or two away. The air was still cold and wet, but the fog had thinned.

We walked in silence for a few seconds, then I said, "I came to meet a friend... well, a business associate, a guy named Freeman."

"Did he show up for the meeting?"

"No."

"So he wasn't one of the three guys back there?" Watson confirmed, sounding a little nervous. Maybe he was starting to take my Marine Corps "killing machine" jargon a bit too seriously.

"No," I said. "He is not one of the corpses."

"Are you sure your friend is safe?" Watson asked. "Maybe we should have the police look for him?"

Worrying about Ray Freeman's well-being was like worrying about the welfare of a shark or a missile. "There's no point involving the locals," I said. "If Freeman doesn't want to be found, the last thing you want to do is find him."

"Would you like me to contact Naval Intelligence? Maybe they can track him down."

I thought about that and smiled. Naval Intelligence had more than its share of smart-ass officers. Assigning a few of them to track down Freeman would send a wake-up call.

Watson had flown to Fort Lewis on a military jet and driven to Seattle in a staff car. He'd parked the big sedan far enough up the street to give us a chance to talk. As we reached the car, I said, "Freeman will find me when he's ready."

Watson asked, "Do you want me to take you back to Fort Lewis?"

"Might as well," I said. "It's been a long night."

I looked back toward the crime scene. The fog had mostly cleared, and an overcast morning had begun. I wanted to end my day, not begin a new one.

As he climbed into the car, Watson pulled out his LifePad and stared at it for several seconds. Then he said, "There's a plane waiting at the base to fly you back to Washington, General. Admiral Cutter wants to meet with you."

"Do you know what it's about?" I asked.

"Apparently, you weren't the only Marine mugged last night. The admiral thinks this may have been the first shots fired in a civil war."

There were 1,723 Marines attacked on the night of January 9, 2519. The Marine Corps lost 108 men and killed over two thousand.

All things considered, it was a pretty good night.

2

It was beginning to look like the opening salvo of the war would also be the final shot. The mystery group that attacked so many Marines on January 9 never announced itself. Maybe they were ashamed. They lost almost twenty times as many people as they killed.

When the police, both military and civilian, found nothing useful, Naval Intelligence took over. Results followed. So did briefings.

"What do you mean they were from Mars?" I asked the officer from Naval Intelligence.

"Well... they're not from Mars. I mean, sir, Mars does not have a native population. They're New Olympian. The men who attacked you were refugees from Olympus Kri."

Olympus Kri was the first planet the Enlisted Man's Empire evacuated during the second alien attack. We crammed the entire population, seventeen million people, into Mars Spaceport, the

32

enormous and superfluous civilian travel center that had served as the hub of pangalactic travel back in the days when mankind traveled the galaxy.

"Lieutenant Colonel, I am well aware who is on Mars," I said. "What I need to know is what the hell six thousand homicidal New Olympians were doing on Earth and how the speck they got here."

The officer had brown eyes, brown hair, and stood five feet, ten inches tall. He was a clone. Every man serving in the Enlisted Man's Military had brown hair and brown eyes. All but one of the men in the Enlisted Man's Military stood five-foot-ten. I was the only exception. I stood six-three. I was a clone just like everyone else, but I was a discontinued model.

The lieutenant colonel lowered his voice, and said, "We haven't had any success answering those questions as of yet, sir."

He was scared of me, I could hear it in his voice, and it wasn't just my rank.

With one exception, the clones of the Enlisted Man's Empire did not know they were clones. I was that exception.

My class of clones was bred for independence and violence. The lieutenant colonel was a newer model than me. My DNA included a gland that released a highly addictive cocktail of testosterone and adrenaline into my blood in battle. The scientists who invented my kind called it the "combat reflex."

I was the final specimen of a distinguished class of clones called "Liberators." Congress discontinued the Liberator Clone Program a few decades before I climbed off the assembly line because we tended to get addicted to the hormones produced by the combat reflex. Once we got hooked, the only way to keep the hormone rolling was through violence, and we sometimes stopped caring who we hurt.

My kind had been replaced by a breed of clones who were tough, obedient, and docile. They made good soldiers, but most of the independence had been jimmied out of them. Instead of a gland that kept them cool in battle, the new clones had a "death reflex," which shut them down as swiftly as a bullet to the head.

Their DNA included neural programming that made them believe they were blond-haired, blue-eyed, natural-born humans instead of clones. When they saw their reflections in mirrors and windows, they saw themselves as having blond hair and blue eyes even if they were standing beside an identical clone whom they recognized as having brown hair and brown eyes.

Anything that disrupted that programming would set off a death reflex. We called ourselves the "Enlisted Man's Empire" because the empire might suffer a mass death reflex if we called ourselves the "Clone Empire."

"General, these are photographs of the men you killed," the lieutenant colonel said as their faces appeared on the briefing tablet in my hands. "They're not the type of people normally associated with violent attacks."

Tell me something I don't know, I thought.

Autopsy photographs and identification documents appeared on my briefing tablet. Why the hell the Intelligence division ran autopsies on these stiffs was beyond me. I knew damn well how they died, I was there.

Granted, I was being obtuse. The men in charge of the autopsies, a team of experts that included civilian policemen, military police, and Naval Intelligence officers, searched for signs of drugs and other oddities. The first reports indicated clean blood and no notable brain abnormalities.

The pictures on my tablet rotated so that the autopsy photo of one of the men came to the top. I had slit his throat. No doubt about the cause of his death, bone showed in the back of the smile-shaped incision I had carved across his neck. Below his pictures, a table listed his vital statistics—Name: Tom Niecy; Height: 5'11"; Weight: 163 lbs.; Age: 37.

"This is Tom Niecy. From what we can tell, he was the ringleader," the lieutenant colonel said. "Prior to the evacuation of Olympus Kri, he appears to have worked as an engineer designing car seats."

"He designed seats for cars?" I asked. *Now there's a terrorist*

34

profile if I've ever seen one, I thought.

"Yes, sir. He specialized in 'smart' seats for luxury cars. The seats he designed read your *posterior* signature and automatically adjusted to your body temperature, spinal posture, and firmness preferences."

I said, "Seats that know you by the spread of your ass."

"More or less, sir," he said.

"Thirty-seven-year-old car seat designers don't strike me as much of a security risk," I said.

"No, sir."

"What makes you think Niecy was in charge?"

"He was ten years older than Grant or Rand."

"Who are Grant and Rand?" I asked.

"Niecy, Grant, and Rand... the three men you kill—who attacked you, sir."

"The other two were named Grant and Rand? I didn't know their names."

"Yes, sir. Tom Niecy was ten years older than the other men. He was the only one with an actual job on Mars. That was one of the patterns we found when we started investigating the 'Night of the Martyrs.'"

"The Night of the Martyrs?" I asked. I had never heard the term, but I understood what it meant. The New Olympians lost more men than they killed, and thousands of corpses turned up the next morning as well. Most of the attackers who got away committed suicide. By the end of the next day, we had six thousand New Olympian corpses on our hands.

"That's what they're calling it on the mediaLink."

"Three of those martyrs came after me with knives and a pipe," I said.

"Yes, sir," said the lieutenant colonel. What else could he say?

"Catchy name." I sighed.

"Yes, sir."

"You might as well continue."

"Yes, sir. As I was saying, sir, there was a pattern among all of the teams, an older member, generally with a paying job, leading two younger men…"

"Was he designing car seats on Mars?"

"No, sir. Niecy worked in the spaceport loading docks."

"He was a stevedore?" I asked.

"Yes, sir, and the assistant pastor of a spaceport Christian congregation."

"A pastor," I mumbled. That checked out. I remembered the Bible. *A Bible and a blade*, I thought to myself.

"Have you contacted Gordon Hughes about this 'Night of the Martyrs'?" I asked. "What does he have to say about it?"

Gordon Hughes was the de facto governor of Mars, or at least the population living in Mars Spaceport, which was the only known population on the planet. He'd once been an important man in Unified Authority politics, then he joined a group that wanted to overthrow the Unified Authority, only to return as an ally in the very same war.

Hughes, who originally hailed from Olympus Kri, used whatever political capital he could muster to evacuate his home planet before the aliens cooked it. Now he and his people were trapped on Mars—seventeen million residents trapped in a revolving-door facility meant to accommodate less than six million transients.

"He says his people are still loyal to the Enlisted Man's Empire, sir," said the lieutenant colonel.

"Do you believe him?"

"We're still trying to piece it all together. I spoke with Colonel Riley before coming here." Martin Riley was the head of Mars Spaceport Security, a detail of five thousand lucky Marines attached to the spaceport as a peacekeeping force.

"What does Riley think?"

"He believes the spaceport is a powder keg with a lit fuse." The lieutenant colonel checked his notes, and said, "His exact words were, 'They're going to start eating their babies and blaming us for it.'"

"It sounds like Colonel Riley and Governor Hughes don't exactly see eye to eye," I said.

"No, sir. According to Colonel Riley, Governor Hughes has become something of a figurehead."

"Really? When did that happen?" I asked. I had not paid much attention to Mars over the last few months. Clearly, I should have.

"According to Colonel Riley, a religious revival has spread across the spaceport. He says the religious movement has superseded the government."

"Does Hughes still live in the administrative offices?" I asked. We had installed Hughes and his provisional government in the spaceport's former administrative offices. We had originally expected to relocate the New Olympians from Mars to Earth right after our war with the Unifieds ended, then we ran into the realities of creating a new government. A year had slipped by, and those people were still trapped on Mars.

"Yes, sir."

"Governor Hughes says the New Olympians are loyal to us and Colonel Riley says they want to start a civil war," I muttered to myself.

"There is no evidence of a popular movement on Mars," said the lieutenant colonel.

"Except that two thousand Marines were attacked by six thousand New Olympians who should not have been on this planet in the first place," I said.

"Hughes says they don't want to go to war with us," said the lieutenant colonel.

"Of course they don't want a war," I said. "The ungrateful bastards can't feed themselves without us. Mars Spaceport isn't a colony, it's a damn homeless shelter. The bastards can't declare war without starving to death."

"Yes, sir," the lieutenant colonel said as he waited for permission to speak.

"What is it?" I asked.

"Governor Hughes says we can avoid further bloodshed by closing down Mars."

"He wants his people repatriated," I said, echoing the last fifty messages I had received from the man. It was a fair request. Earth had enough room for a billion immigrants. Given our current fleet limitations, it would take months to transport seventeen million people to Earth; but we could do it.

After the Night of the Martyrs, we were less likely to relocate those people than we would have been a week ago. Now we had to worry about sedition, which was a highly contagious virus. If we brought the New Olympians to Earth, their unrest could and probably would spread among the general population.

I said, "The locals didn't exactly welcome us back when we overthrew the Unifieds. We don't need Olympus Kri zealots fanning the fires."

"No, sir."

"Anything else of interest?" I asked.

"Yes, sir. Colonel Riley sent over a report about a movement called the Martian Legion."

"The Martian Legion," I repeated, remembering that one of the men who attacked me had uttered the word "legion" as he died.

A picture of a hallway appeared on my tablet. Scrawled across the wall was the word, LEGION. The picture shrank, and dozens if not hundreds of similar pictures appeared. I tapped on one. It showed an ornate archway leading into what had once been a gourmet restaurant. Somebody had carved something into the beam along the top. I zoomed in for a closer look. LEGION IS WATCHING.

"What exactly is Legion?" I asked.

"According to Colonel Riley, the important question is, 'Who is Legion?'" said the briefing officer. "When we received these images, we thought the term referred to the spaceport security detail, but it doesn't fit. We can't even tell if the New Olympians consider Legion a friend or a foe. Some of the graffiti makes Legion out to be a threat, some suggests that Legion is a savior.

"We have been able to determine one thing: Niecy and the

other martyrs were connected to Legion."

The screen on my tablet showed a photograph of an elbow. Tattooed on the soft flesh inside the crook of the joint, in curly longhand letters, was the word, "LEGION." The skin around it was pale and slightly blued, the color of curdled milk. The picture had been taken during the autopsy.

"Is this Niecy's arm?" I asked.

"It could have been any of the martyrs' arms, they all have the exact same tattoo," said the lieutenant colonel.

I'll be damned, I thought, *something useful did come out of the autopsies.* I said, "We need to find out about Legion. Tell Colonel Riley I'm coming to Mars. A job like this could require a delicate hand."

3

I did not need anything new on my plate.

I had Marines playing policemen on Mars. I had a corps to run. I had bases and operations to look after. Now that we had brought down the Unified Authority, the Enlisted Man's Empire was creating a government to replace it. We had laws to write and enforce and two angry populaces to placate. Nearly a year had passed, and we were still trying to round up the politicians and officers who had led the Unified Authority into starting the war. Most of the sons of bitches had gone into hiding. We caught scapegoats during the early days after the war and locked them up in jail. A few kindly Unifieds had even been good enough to fall on their swords, so to speak. We buried them quietly.

On top of that, there was another nagging security issue that needed to be resolved—broadcast travel.

Measured from edge to edge, the Milky Way was one hundred thousand light-years across, give or take a trillion miles. Man had not yet invented a ship that could travel at the speed of light, meaning that a quick jaunt across the galaxy and back would take a minimum of two hundred thousand years.

Enter broadcast physics, a technology that enabled ships to travel to any precalculated spot instantaneously. Broadcast travel, which involved unleashing incredible amounts of energy, rendered questions of distance irrelevant. Once you plugged the data into a broadcast computer, it no longer mattered if you were traveling to Earth's moon or to another galaxy. You vanished from one spot in an eruption of energy and you arrived at your destination in a similarly powerful eruption instantaneously.

The Unified Authority Navy had a fleet of self-broadcasting ships, which vanished during the war. They had broadcasted to a battle in the Scutum-Crux Arm of the galaxy, and no one ever heard from them again.

A year had passed with no sign of those ships. In my book that meant they were sunk.

Officially, the Enlisted Man's Navy did not have self-broadcasting ships. We used a pangalactic highway called the "Broadcast Network," a series of satellites that broadcasted ships from one location to another. Unfortunately, the satellite that connected Earth to the rest of the galaxy no longer existed. We were home, and we were stranded… in theory.

The Enlisted Man's Navy was supposed to have one self-broadcasting ship, a stealth cruiser designed for spying. That ship had disappeared during the battle for Earth. For all I knew, the spy ship might have been orbiting Earth or it might have been parked on my neighbor's front lawn. How do you track an invisible ship?

One of the reasons I missed my former life as an enlisted man was the simplicity of that existence. You take a private or a corporal or even master sergeant, he generally tackles one assignment at a time. That assignment might involve running into burning buildings or facing down mortars; but I liked the life of a grunt. What I never liked was juggling multiple concerns.

Mars was a problem that might evolve into a catastrophe, but it was not the only thing on my plate. There was another hole in our security. Somehow, this hole had become my direct responsibility as well... Smithsonian Field.

We rode out to inspect the site in a staff car. I did not know the sergeant driving the car; Watson and I rode in the back. "Are you taking me to an airfield or a bird-watching event?" I asked. "There aren't any Air Force bases out here."

We had driven forty miles out of the city and were deep in the forests. There were no buildings out here, just trees and rocks. It was a great place to visit if you wanted to go snowshoeing, maybe hunting for deer or rabbits.

I'd been prickly of late. With Mars and natural-born relations on my mind, I snapped at officers and staff. People began referring to me as "sir" more often than needed, a bad sign. Watson did not have that problem. As far as he was concerned, I was either "you" or "General." The word "sir" had not found its way into his vocabulary.

"The Air Force didn't build it, they took it over," said Watson. "It used to be a museum."

"No shit?" I said. "And people drove out here to visit it?" I asked.

"Not exactly. It was top secret under the Unified Authority as well."

We wound around ash-, alder-, and beech-covered hills, driving deeper and deeper into a no-man's-land until we left the paved road and went another five miles over gravel.

We weren't just a million miles from civilization, we were in a high-security forest. We passed four checkpoints before reaching the facility's front gate. Along the way, we drove through acres of trees lined by miles of electrified fences. There were guard towers hidden among the ash and cedars, and I spotted a missile battery as we approached the front gate.

As far as I was concerned, Smithsonian Field should not have existed at all. Since it did exist, I was glad to see the Air Force taking its security seriously.

There, in the middle of nowhere, behind the electrified razor-wire fence, was a series of oversized bunkers that looked like missile silos. Beyond the bunkers lay an unadorned airstrip mostly covered in snow.

"This is it?" I asked.

"Smithsonian Field," said Watson.

Our driver parked beside a jeep in which two officers waited. Watson and I transferred from our staff car to the jeep, traded names and salutes with our new driver, and our journey continued. We drove down a snow-covered ramp and entered a bunker, only it wasn't a bunker. It looked like a bunker from the outside, an underground fortification with reinforced walls. That ramp led down twenty-five feet and wound into an enormous hangar with thirty-foot ceilings.

The place was as clean as an operating room and brightly lit. It looked like a showroom for luxury cars. It wasn't, though. It was a museum with 207 antique spaceships that posed an enormous security risk.

"This is the original scientific explorer fleet, sir. These ships are one hundred years old, sir," said the Air Force major conducting my tour. I heard awe and reverence in his voice.

The spoon-shaped ships had silver hulls. Each ship was about thirty feet long and no more than fifteen feet tall. They had retractable wings and clusters of booster rockets for vertical liftoffs.

The Air Force maintained these ships in pristine condition. These were the ships that had mapped the galaxy. It was on these small ships that mankind eliminated so many astronomical myths. Entering this hangar was like stepping onto a dock and seeing the *Nina*, the *Pinta*, and the *Santa Maria*.

I said, "Destroy them."

"General, these ships are an invaluable treasure."

"And an incalculable security risk," I said. "These ships are the key to the galaxy. Anyone getting their hands on these ships can go anywhere they want. They can go looking for U.A. ships. They can transport Unified Authority enemy troops."

"But... but... General, these ships are our history!"

"We'll let future generations worry about preserving history, I'm more concerned about survival, Major."

"General, sir, these ships have no strategic value. It takes them an hour just to charge up for a broadcast," the major said.

"An hour?" I asked. "It takes them an hour? That means they can travel from Earth to Terraneau in an hour." Terraneau was the last-known location of the Unified Authority's self-broadcasting fleet.

That comment ended the tour. The major must have begun the day seeing himself as some kind of museum curator; now he realized he was a military man and part of a chain of command. He said, "Yes, sir."

Watson did not speak a word.

We returned to the staff car and started the drive home in silence. As we traced our way back along the gravel road, I asked, "What the hell did you expect me to say?"

Watson did not respond.

I repeated myself. I asked, "What the hell did you expect?"

Watson's answer was honest and bigoted. He glared at me, and said, "You probably can't appreciate the value of those ships."

"Yeah? Why would that be?" I asked.

He went silent. Smart man.

"Let's hear it, Travis. I can't appreciate their value because they are part of human history, and I'm synthetic. Is that it?"

He did not answer.

Normally, Watson and I had an amicable, almost friendly relationship. I didn't scare him. I was the Liberator clone, a monster most everyone classified somewhere between sharks and rabid dogs; but he'd never seen me kill anybody. In our dealings, I generally behaved like a bureaucrat.

I said, "Watson, six thousand New Olympian refugees made it from Mars to Earth by means unknown. For all we know, they traveled in those very same self-broadcasting ships." Actually, we knew they hadn't, but I was making a point.

4

Three months had passed since the Night of the Martyrs, and nothing significant had happened, no arrests, no attacks, no further intelligence gathered; but tension was growing on Mars. Mars security reported riots and disobedience. The Enlisted Man's Empire had a time bomb in its closets. We either needed to disarm the bomb known as the "Martian Legion" or detonate it.

"Remind me again, Harris. Why are you going to Mars?"

"I want to find out about Legion," I said.

"As I understand it, the term 'Legion' may very well be their code name for us, isn't that right?" asked Admiral Don Cutter, the highest-ranking officer in the Enlisted Man's Military. He had four stars, I had three. He didn't have any stars when the war with the Unifieds began; but having always been a big believer in a clear chain of command, I gave Cutter three stars during the war and a fourth star after it ended. He generally treated me as his equal. In his mind, the fourth star was ceremonial.

The man had brown hair and brown eyes and all of the other clone features. He was in his forties, some of his brown hair was turning white.

He said, "Harris, the New Olympians are an infestation. Have you actually been in the spaceport?"

"Dozens of times."

"Since we converted it into a flophouse for wayward New Olympians?

"I haven't been there since the evacuation," I admitted.

"It's a cesspool."

"Flophouse" and "cesspool," ancient terms still in circulation even though nobody knew precisely what they meant. Despite the certainty in his voice, Cutter had been no closer to Mars than he had been to a cesspool or a flophouse. I reminded him of that.

He went from authoritative to formal, and said, "I have discussed the situation with Spaceport Security. That's as close as I choose to get to that rat's nest. Colonel Riley says the air is so bad that he sleeps in his helmet."

Cutter was a Navy man, clearly he'd never worn combat armor. He was a fine officer, but his breath smelled like coffee.

I knew Marines who had coffee on their breath as well, but their halitosis did not carry the same connotation. While I and my men were out in the battlefield, he was safe on his ship, never more than a few feet away from his next cup of coffee.

"Hyperbole," I said. "Sleeping in a helmet is like sleeping with your back on a floor and your head on a bookshelf. Next time he says that, ask him if he has ever actually done it."

"Maybe it's time we shipped those people to Earth," said Watson. EMN procedures barred civilians from military ships; but I had brought him along just the same.

"Sure, we can ship them to Earth," I said, "Once we know who's loyal and who's looking for a change of government. They're not going anywhere until we know who is who."

Cutter glanced at Watson, and asked, "Who is he again?"

"He's my adjutant," I said.

Cutter asked, "Why do you have a civilian adjutant?"

I said, "Because I deal with a lot of civilians."

"And you're taking him to Mars as a civilian advisor?" Cutter asked. "As I understand it, this will be a military operation."

"He's not going to Mars," I said. "I'm leaving him with you."

Cutter arched an eyebrow as he said, "I don't remember authorizing that."

Watson said, "Leaving the New Olympians on Mars is a bad idea. The longer they are stuck there, the less loyal they will become."

"If we ship them to Earth, they'll infect the general population," said Cutter, a notion I shared. "I can work around seventeen million angry New Olympians on Mars. If they stir things up on Earth, we'll have forty million angry people on our hands."

"What do you plan to do with them, Admiral?" asked Watson, not showing the admiral proper respect. He was such a damned natural-born. He couldn't help himself. I suppose he was born that way.

Cutter said, "Like I said before, the place is a cesspool, we should flush it."

"Admiral, you are talking about killing seventeen million people," said Watson.

Cutter said, "I don't want to kill them, I want to wash my hands of them."

"Isn't that the same thing?" asked Watson.

"One more time, Harris, who is this man?"

"He's my civilian aide," I said.

"And who gave him permission to come aboard my ship?"

"I did."

"And you plan to leave him aboard my ship? What makes you think he'll still be alive when you come back?"

"Are you going to wash your hands of me?" asked Watson, then he thought about what he had said and gave me a nervous look.

I said, "Give the kid a chance, Admiral."

Cutter ignored me. Taking a step toward Watson, he said, "If

I wanted to kill those people, I would have cut off their food long ago."

He was right. The Enlisted Man's Empire sent an endless supply of freighters between Earth and Mars.

"That would be an interesting way of solving our sedition problem, starving one-third of our citizens to death," I said, knowing that Cutter's neural programming would not allow him to take my bait. On some level, the need to protect human society was hardwired into his brain.

Changing the subject, I said, "I have some ideas about the identity of Legion. Have either of you ever read the Bible?"

We were in the stateroom of the *Churchill*, the fighter carrier that served as the flagship of the Enlisted Man's Fleet. At the moment, Mars was one hundred and fifteen million miles from Earth, meaning we had a four-hour trip ahead of us.

"The Bible?" Cutter asked, barely stifling a laugh. "I'm not a fan of mythology."

"I haven't read it," Watson admitted.

"I've read it," I said.

"You read the Bible?" asked Cutter. He sounded incredulous. "Of all the people I have ever met, you would be the last one I would ever expect to read the Bible."

He wasn't commenting on the content of my character but rather the questionable existence of my soul. All of the major religions of the world agreed that clones did not have immortal souls. "I once spent a month trapped on a transport with no one but Ray Freeman," I said.

Cutter, who had met Freeman, said, "Good Lord! I would have shot myself."

"I tried," I said. "My neural programming does not allow for suicide." That was true though I had not actually tried to shoot myself. My modus operandi had been suicide by grenade.

"Freeman, that's the guy you were looking for in Seattle. What's so bad about him?" asked Watson. "I thought you were friends."

"We are friends," I said.

"He's never met Ray Freeman?" asked Cutter.

"Obviously," I said.

"Ray's not much for conversation," I said. "Traveling with him is lonelier than traveling alone.

"Anyway, the only book I had was a Bible. It was read the Bible or talk to Ray. I went through the specking book five or six times as I recall."

Watson gave me a sly smile, and asked, "Did you just refer to the Bible as a 'specking book'?" The guy read me well. He knew how to kid around and still get along.

"Did I?" I asked.

The term, "speck," by the way, referred to that one particular bodily fluid that Marines and other military men lived to excrete. "Specking" was a gerund, the verb form of a noun. It referred to the act of transferring that fluid.

"I take it you were not converted," said Cutter.

"Oh, but I was," I said. "Maybe not so much by the New Testament, but the Old Testament made perfect sense once I accepted God as a metaphor for the government. The government created all things and the government took them away. It made perfect sense."

Cutter asked, "What does a New Olympian militia have to do with the Bible?"

"The Bible has a story about a guy named Legion who was possessed by demons," said Watson. "Christ banished the demons, and they went into a herd of pigs, and the pigs killed themselves.

"One of the guys you killed in Seattle had a Bible; but if you're saying this is about devils and demons, that wouldn't make sense."

A chilled silence filled the room when I did not answer immediately. We sat around Cutter's desk, none of us quite meeting the other men's eyes.

Cutter said, "The Bibles, the suicides, it has all the trappings of fanatics and zealots."

Watson laughed, and said, "Harris, maybe they think you're the antichrist."

"Maybe they do," I agreed.

Watson attempted to be serious, then laughed. He said, "I can't say that I blame them. I kind of do, too."

"This really could be the Mogats all over again," said Cutter. Like me, he had fought in the last religious uprising and found no humor in the situation. Watson, on the other hand, had still been in school. He didn't see the massacre on Little Man or the ugly battle on a cinder of a planet called Hubble. The only natural-borns who fought on the Unified Authority side of the war were officers, and most of them fought from the sidelines.

"Harris, if it is another religious fanatical uprising, you'll be walking into a real shitstorm when you land on Mars," said Cutter.

I said, "Just like any other cancer. Catch it early enough, and you might even survive the treatment."

5

Providing Mars Spaceport with power, water, and oxygen did not pose a problem. With seventeen million refugees living in a facility designed for six to eight million travelers, providing space, food, and bathing facilities did. The refugees lived as crowded together as termites in a nest; and the once-elegant spaceport now smelled of grime and sweat. Lines one hundred people long extended out of every bathroom. Soup lines shuffled along the halls.

For the first time in known history, Mars had an indigenous species of life—a form of lice. The creatures must have come from Olympus Kri, riding in some refugee's hair; but, as there was no record of a home planet for this particular variety of pest, it was now known as the "Martian louse." With all of the grime and overcrowding in the space station, the little bastards proliferated.

Spaceport Security sprayed chemicals through the ventilation system in an unsuccessful bid to kill the lice, but there was nothing anyone could do to fix the stench in the air. Engineers built shower facilities and added air filters to the vents, but the place still stunk. Because of the overcrowding, the residents of Mars Spaceport only showered twice per month. A black market had formed for shower passes.

Throughout history, relocation centers had always been breeding grounds for crime, dysentery, and insurrection. Mars was no exception.

I was in one of the fifteen transports preparing to launch when Admiral Cutter contacted me from the bridge. He and Travis Watson would remain safe on his ship while I went down among the heathen.

"Harris, are you sure you want to run this mission?" Cutter asked. "The empire might be better served…"

"When I come back, we should have a conversation about renaming our government," I said. "We're not an empire. We don't have an emperor and we only have one planet. I think 'republic' would be a more accurate term."

"Harris, you could direct this mission as easily from the ship," Cutter said, not acknowledging my attempt to change the subject. "You are a general, not a platoon leader. When they talk about boots on the ground, they don't mean boots with stars."

"I want to make sure Governor Hughes gets the message," I said. "If I'm there, he will know we mean business."

"Call him and tell him," said Cutter.

"I don't think it would have the same impact."

"Do you want me to send Watson down once the area is secured?"

"No," I said. We were sending fifteen hundred Marines into a hostile population of seventeen million. Nothing short of destroying the spaceport would secure the area.

If it came down to a fight, we didn't stand a chance. We were going into a battle zone in which tanks, gunships, and air support would be out of the question. Marching like an early-twentieth-century army with only small arms for weapons, we would try to intimidate an enemy that could simply trample us; but we didn't have a choice. The spaceport was a civilian structure, a thin bubble of life support on a planet with a carbon-dioxide atmosphere. Firing a rocket could cause the spaceport to explode; even a grenade might cause enough added pressure to burst the outer walls.

"Have you told Colonel Riley that you are coming?" he asked.

As the head of the spaceport security detail, Riley had a right to know I was on my way. He was an officer in the Marines, which placed him under my command. Military courtesy dictated my warning him about the mission as a formality. Three-stars do not drop in unannounced.

"Yes and no," I said. "He knows that I am coming, but he doesn't know when. I didn't want to spoil the surprise."

"Do you have a problem with Riley?" Cutter asked.

"Not at all," I said. I didn't. "This is a diplomatic operation, Riley and Spaceport Security should not be involved."

Watson asked, "What if you run into trouble?"

"I won't," I said.

"Harris, if things get hot down there..." Cutter began.

"Just be ready to pick us up when we're done. I don't want to bring any indigenous Martian life home with me in my hair," I said. I signed off.

Our transports had two compartments... three if you included the head. They had a two-man cockpit up front. The rest of the bird was all cargo hold. Most people referred to this area as the "kettle" because it was somewhat domed like an oblong teakettle, made of metal, and had no windows.

We loaded the maximum recommended number of Marines in the kettle of each of our birds—one hundred killing machines in combat armor. Some stood, their bodies attached to harnesses in case we came under fire. Some sat on the bench that ran around the wall. Almost all of them would try to occupy their minds with thoughts about R& R as we flew down to the planet. They'd need that, the accommodations were dreary on the transport, and the destination did not give them much to look forward to.

As we prepared to launch, I climbed the ladder that led to the cockpit. Like every man on board, I wore standard-issue Marine combat armor though I did have one additional piece of equipment built into my helmet—a piece of communications equipment known as a commandLink. Using the commandLink, I could address every man, fire team, platoon, and company under my command, or I could speak to each Marine individually. I could peer through their visors or send them information.

As the commanding officer on this operation, I had the commandLink. Everyone else had interLink equipment.

Using the commandLink, I addressed the platoon sergeants and officers in the group. I said, "This is General Wayson Harris. You've all been briefed; but on the off chance that any of you were not paying attention, I will remind you that this is not, repeat, not an invasion. Mars Spaceport is EME-held territory.

"This is not an invasion. It is an inspection."

That much was bullshit, by the way. This was not an inspection or an invasion, it was a damn pissing match. We were sending a small but lethal force into the belly of the beast to prove to the New Olympians that we were still in charge. We were sending a force that was too small to protect itself and daring the bastards to attack.

"We are fifteen hundred men patrolling an area populated by seventeen million hostiles. We cannot afford to pick a fight. Sergeants, do not allow your men to touch triggers or disengage the safeties unless specifically ordered to do so. That is all."

I entered the cockpit and watched as we launched. We floated out of the ship and penetrated the atmosphere.

Below us, Mars Spaceport sparkled on an otherwise dismally dark landscape. The planet's rotation had the spaceport pointing away from the sun. As we descended, I saw the three raised train tracks that ran the ten miles between the spaceport and Mars Air Force Base. They looked as slender as guitar strings from a half mile up.

I surveyed the landscape below. Some people played down Mars's unique beauty by comparing it to places like the Mojave Desert on Earth. To me, the surface of Mars looked like the deepest depths of the ocean, a silent, alien world filled with familiar elements.

I left the quiet surroundings of the cockpit and returned to the kettle, with its capacity crowd. As I came down the ladder, I used the commandLink to eavesdrop on a few of my lieutenants as they briefed their men. The company commander in my shuttle told his men, "Remember, these are friendlies. Even if they act hostile, do not aim or shoot unless ordered to do so."

Good information, though delivered in too timid a tone.

I listened to the briefings on other transports until I heard:

"...you are a grenadier, damn it, you specking better have some launchers on you."

"But sir, we have strict orders..."

"I know what General Harris said," yelled the lieutenant. "I also know how things work in this man's corps. Riflemen carry rifles, automatic riflemen carry automatic rifles, and grenadiers carry specking grenades. If I want you to carry a slingshot, I will call you a slingadier. If I want you to carry a bucket, I will call you a specking bucketier. You are a grenadier, gawdamnit! Hide some specking grenades in your specking gear or I'll throw your specking ass in the brig and call you a specking brigadier! *Do you read me?*"

Using the commandLink, I addressed the entire regiment. "This is General Harris. You have been issued special short-range rounds for your M27s. Any men seen carrying grenades, rockets, or particle-beam weapons will face a summary hearing. Do you read me?"

I then switched to a direct to Lieutenant Geoffrey Bates, he of the "slingadiers-bucketiers," and I said, 'If I ever catch you pulling another end run, Lieutenant, I will place your ass in front a firing squad and tell them you are a *targetier*."

"Sir, yes, sir," he shouted in the very loud fashion of a Marine who has been duly chastised by his superior.

And then we touched down. The muffled sounds of booster rockets rumbled through the walls as we lowered into place. The iron deck below my feet gave one hard bounce as we landed.

The only door on a transport was the rear hatch, a slow-moving metal slab that took half a minute to swing open. Outside, a startled crew stared in at us. On an open mike that the dockworkers would hear, I said, "We do not require your assistance, gentlemen. My men are perfectly capable of off-loading themselves."

Workers rushed out of our way as we marched off the transports, but we still locked the birds tight for safekeeping.

6

I was the first man off the transport. One of the dockworkers asked me, "Who's in charge of this?" as I waited for my men to form ranks.

Each of my men's armor gave off a unique signal identifying his name, rank, serial number, and area of military occupational specialty. I could see those signals through my visor. The man who approached me did not have that advantage.

I said, "I am. Is there a problem?"

"Oh," he said.

He was big, strong, natural-born, and unarmed. I was as tall as him, armed, and wearing combat armor. I had fifteen hundred armed men at my command—all of them carrying M27s with the detachable rifle stock in place. In close quarters like these, the stocks would get in the way if a firefight started, but they made our guns look bigger and more menacing. It was a bluff. I hoped we could avoid shooting our guns by making sure everybody saw them.

Having been built to serve as a pangalactic commercial port, Mars Spaceport had enormous landing areas designed to accommodate freighters. My fifteen transports did not fill even a tenth of the loading area in which we landed, and the spaceport had twenty-five freight docks.

Crews of longshoremen stood still as statues as my men finished forming into ranks. They eyed us warily, not moving, not speaking, afraid to turn away.

In military parlance, this was an inspection, not an invasion; but they did not know our intentions. It was also a show of force, and I would not say anything to change that impression.

Once my various companies had formed into a regiment, we marched out of the hangar without saying a word.

Thanks to our combat armor, we would not need to deal with Mars Spaceport's unique charms. We could see the squalor, but the head lice could not penetrate our bodysuits. Our rebreathers recycled the air inside our armor, allowing us to breathe without inhaling the sweat-permeated spaceport air.

I saw the grime and wondered if Riley really did sleep in his helmet.

We entered a long service hall. Here the floor was only thirty feet across, but rows of families occupied the areas along each wall. The word LEGION had been written in ten-foot-tall letters above their hovels, the letters badly scrawled in runny bright red paint. Beneath the word, the artist had sketched a row of bloody combat helmets, some modern and some that looked like they came from ancient Rome.

"You seeing this, Jackson?" I asked. This mission belonged as much to Colonel Curtis Jackson as it belonged to me. Tarawa was his unit. That had been the nickname for the Second Regiment of the Second Division since the regiment won a battle on a tiny island nearly six hundred years earlier, Tarawa. It was a newly reactivated unit, created over the last month.

"Yes, sir. Hard to miss," he said.

The spaceport's lights were dim, and the floors were crowded. Looking around that first corridor, I saw families living on tattered blankets, their only belongings were a pot for water, a few dirty dishes, and the clothing on their backs.

Like a mass picnic in Hell, I told myself. From that moment on, I thought of the people on their blankets as "picnickers." Assigning names like "picnicker" was a coping mechanism. Thinking of these people as picnickers made the bleak reality of their existence easier for me to ignore.

The blankets were spread one right beside the next. They stretched the length of the hallway. I saw a woman nursing her baby. She did not bother covering her exposed breasts. Living as refugees had forced these people to abandon every hope of privacy. If this woman could not nurse her infant in a crowded hall, the infant would starve.

Walking through that hall, we passed a twenty-foot mountain of trash that touched the ceiling. Flies buzzed around the pile. How flies had migrated to Mars I could not understand. The spaceport must have had equipment for disposing trash into some kind of landfill, but these people had long since abandoned such civilities as burying their trash.

Most of the people we passed just stared at us. One clever fellow, dressed only in his underwear, stood at attention, saluted, and then farted so loudly that I heard it fifty feet away. A little boy no older than three pointed a toy gun at us, and yelled, "Bang! Bang!"

When I passed within ten feet of an old man lying on a blanket, he asked, "Are you speckers invading the spaceport?" Without waiting for me to answer, he added, "You can have this hole as far as I'm concerned."

"Do you know who painted that wall?" I asked, pointing to the Legion graffiti.

"Nope. Must have happened when I was taking a shit," he said.

While my fifteen hundred Marines marched past, I approached a woman with three children and asked her the same question. She ignored me.

My Marines marched with perfect precision down one decrepit corridor and into the next as we made our way to the administrative offices. A woman jumped up from her blanket and threw something at one of my men. Whatever it was, it hit him and splattered across the back of his armor.

We passed a water dispensary. A line of people carrying pots waited for a turn at the water. Lines for food, lines for water, lines to use the bathroom and bathe, no wonder these people were hostile. Living on Mars, these people were no more self-sufficient than newborn infants.

Maybe they were right to hate us; but until we sorted out their civil unrest, they would remain on Mars. In their eyes, the same clone military that had saved them from destruction on their home planet had abandoned them in a dump.

We originally promised them a short layover on Mars. Now, one year later, they were prolonging their incarceration by their actions. The way station had become a quarantine.

We could have turned into one of the spaceport's bigger and more populated hallways, but I wanted to avoid the masses for as long as possible. Instead, we followed the service hall as it snaked around a line of passenger-boarding areas.

I had a copy of the floor plan in my visor, a rotating three-dimensional map that included photographs of Mars Spaceport back in its halcyon days. Using optical commands, I spun the floor plan and viewed it from all sides, looking for detours; but our options diminished as we marched on.

In order to get to the administrative offices, we would need to enter the grand arcade, a two-mile corridor of stores and restaurants. There would be multiple millions of people in the arcade, maybe even a full five million.

I looked back down the hallway behind us at the people lying on their blankets with their belongings scattered around them. They were dirty, and their blankets were filthy and tattered. They'd spent a year like this, with no more dignity than cattle locked in stalls.

Using the commandLink, I contacted Cutter on the *Churchill*. I said, "Admiral, do you have any spare service blankets?"

He asked, "How many do you need?"

"Seventeen million," I said.

"How bad is it?" he asked.

"Dante Alighieri wouldn't have survived this," I said.

"I don't know Alighieri. Is he Marines or Navy?"

"Neither," I said. Cutter was a good officer, but his interests did not extend to the classics. "He's a civilian."

"So what is the situation?" he asked.

"We had no problem landing," I said. "The natives aren't especially friendly, but no incidents. We've been avoiding the main areas, but we're going to need to enter the hub to get to Governor Hughes."

Mars Spaceport had six passenger wings, one for each of the Milky Way's spiral arms, all of which connected to a central hub. We had entered the spaceport through a loading dock in the Orion Wing. Now we were just outside the grand arcade, the hub. The administrative offices were just off the arcade.

"It's not too late to withdraw," said Cutter. "You're sitting on a 'powder keg.'"

I'd never wanted to be an officer. I hated wearing the weight of men's fates on my shoulders. Depending on what happened next, seventeen million lives could hang in the balance.

I said, "It's too late to back out now."

I led my men to the end of the service hall, turned a corner, and got my first look at the grand arcade.

What had once been a glorious atrium ringed by five floors of upscale stores was now a slum of lean-tos and blankets. Sixty feet up, an enormous banner hung from the ceiling. It was not a gleaming, streaming, glorious banner announcing a sale or welcoming travelers to Mars. It was a torn swath of dirt-colored carpeting, forty feet long and twenty feet wide with the words: LEGION: NIGHT OF THE MARTYRS painted across it.

"Check your console, I'm sending you a streaming feed," I told Cutter. Using an optic command, I transmitted the images. Now he could see everything I saw. I stared up at the banner.

"What is that?" he asked.

"It's a banner."

"I can see that," he said, sounding peevish.

"It says 'Legion: Night of the Martyrs,'" I said.

"Yeah, I can read," he said.

"Then why did you ask what it was?" I asked.

No answer.

I looked away from the banner and gave Cutter a panoramic sweep of the area. I showed him throngs of people leaning over the rails of the upper floors. The place was dark and dingy and teeming with refugees. Like I said before, the people crowded together like termites in a nest, and they did not seem happy to see us.

A loud and angry howl filled the air as we emerged from the service hall. People screamed, they shouted, they booed. Teenage boys ran in front of our column and made obscene gestures. One kid dropped his pants and showed us his ass.

Crowds of people stood on either side of us. There had to have been more than a million people crowded onto the main floor and hundreds of thousands more along the railings of each of the upper-atrium floors.

From a tactical perspective, we had walked into an untenable nightmare. I had led my men into a deep ocean never realizing just how helpless we would be against the tides.

"Keep 'em moving," I told Jackson.

"Aye, sir," he said. Curtis Jackson had a temper. He wasn't hotheaded, but he wasn't the type of man who tolerates bullshit and smiles.

"Order your men to set their sound filters," I told him.

"Aye, aye."

Our helmets were soundproof and equipped with microphones for picking up ambient sound. People become paranoid when they cannot hear what goes on around them; it's human nature. So we generally allow the boys to leave their mikes hot.

Having them turn off their external mikes would cut them off from the outside world, a move that would make them tense; but I compensated by allowing them to speak to each other.

"General, sir, should we proceed as we are?" asked Jackson.

"We discussed this route back on the ship," I said. "There aren't any alternate routes."

"You could return to the *Churchill*," said Cutter. I had forgotten he was still Linked in.

"Begging the general's pardon, sir, but what this Marine means to say is that perhaps we should give them a show of force. We don't want them to think we're scared."

"You aren't scared?" I asked.

"No, sir."

"Not even the least bit nervous?" I asked.

"No, sir."

"You should be, Colonel. There are ten thousand New Olympians for every one of us."

Fortunately, we did not need to walk the entire length of the arcade to reach the administrative offices. The alley that led to Hughes was only a hundred yards away.

We passed what must have once been a water garden, a series of ramps, falls, and pools that now sat as dry as the Martian landscape outside. Unlit signs, some shattered but many still whole, identified stores that had long since been emptied of merchandise and furniture. Inside, in their shadowy reaches, people stood and stared out at us. They looked like ghosts.

The people on the upper decks began hurling trash at us. It fell like enormous balls of hail. Articles of clothing, shoes, burning shreds of paper, bits of carpet, a grating from a ceiling vent, and more rained down, mostly missing us. Ceiling tiles, so light they seemed to glide on air currents, tumbled through the air and shattered a few yards ahead of us.

For a moment, and just a moment, I turned on my external microphones. I heard such a cacophony that I could not interpret a word of anything that anybody yelled.

The people seemed to sense that we had not come to fight. Small bits of debris rained down on our heads, but the bigger stuff crashed and splattered fifty feet ahead of us.

Then it happened. Something about the size of a motorcycle

cascaded down from one of the upper floors and hit three of my men. Whatever those people had thrown, it crushed two of my men and grazed a third before hitting the ground and disintegrating into a cloud of dust.

The two dead Marines lay ruptured on the floor, the exoskeletons of their armor broken to pieces and their legs and arms stretched out so that they looked like man-sized insects that had been crushed. Blood pooled onto the floor around them.

That stopped our parade. Jackson told the men to halt and guard their flanks while a medic checked the bodies. We didn't really need the medic, the cracked helmets told the tale well enough. He ran a scanner over the bodies and pronounced both men dead, then he went to see after the injured man, who was struggling to remove his chest plate.

The parade wasn't the only thing halted at that moment. The fusillade of debris dried up. So did the shouting.

"What do we do now?" asked Jackson.

By this time, I was in the throes of a full-fledged combat reflex, lying to myself that I cared about these people, that they deserved mercy, and that I did not want to kill them all.

"We walk," I said, ignoring the way the hormone-tinged blood running through my head screamed for violence.

"They killed two of my men. They don't get away with killing my men."

"Yeah?" I asked. "And what exactly are you going to do about it, Colonel? What the speck do you suggest we do?"

"We find the people responsible and make an example."

"How are you going to find them?" I asked in a silky, serpentine voice.

People flooded into the already packed atrium, gawkers hoping we would put on a show, protestors looking to show their anger, and a small battalion of men in suits. The gawkers and protesters kept their distance. The men in suits walked toward us.

Like any standoff, this one seemed to generate electricity. As many as a million pairs of eyes stared at us, waiting for us to make a move. If we stayed in the center of the atrium, they could stone us to death with their debris. If we opened fire, there was no telling how many people we would kill.

The combat reflex distorted my thoughts. I wanted revenge. I wanted violence. I wanted to increase the amount of the hormone in my blood, and the only way to do it was to attack, to kill. *Think!* I told myself. *Stay focused.*

The men in suits pushed through the crowd. I did not recognize any of them, but I knew who they were. They would be the politicians. *Hughes must have sent them*, I told myself. *Just hold on. Have these men take you to Hughes.*

"General, are you going to let them get away with killing Marines?" Jackson asked.

"The men who dropped that... whatever the hell it was, are long gone, Colonel," I said. The words came out slowly now. I had to force myself to speak calmly. "They're long gone, and I can just about guarantee you that you won't find anyone who saw what happened."

"Somebody saw," said Jackson.

"Sure they did, but they won't admit it."

One of the suits approached Jackson as he stood over the bodies. Speaking over the interLink, Jackson said, "The head assholes are here."

I said, "Keep your men on alert," then I pulled off my helmet and got my first whiff of Spaceport air. It didn't just smell of sweat; this particular potpourri included feces, garbage, and rot.

The men in the suits spotted my dead Marines and stopped walking.

Politicians. I had the feeling that none of these men had ever seen a violent death up close. They stared down at the bodies. By this time, a couple of sergeants were loading the bodies into "ash bags." We would not leave our dead behind, though the locals could deal with the blood. We would ship the bodies back to the *Churchill* in the bags, fish out any salvageable equipment, then toss whatever remained into an incinerator.

As a Liberator clone, I had the same basic architecture as the newer model that replaced my kind. I had the same face, the same brown hair, and the same brown eyes. I stood six-three, five inches taller than any of the clones around me; but, as the politicians didn't bring a sizing laser for taking measurements, they did not recognize me.

"Are you in charge of this invasion?" asked the man in the suit.

"Invasion?" I asked. "Why would we invade Mars?"

"You have landed on our planet with a large body of armed men."

"I have one regiment; that hardly qualifies as a large body."

"Why are you here?" the man demanded.

I said, "Look, I don't mean to be disrespectful…"

"Yes, you do."

"What?"

"You have come here to threaten us. If you wanted to talk, you would have contacted Governor Hughes through diplomatic channels. Instead, you came with your *regiment* of heavily armed men."

After that comment, I almost gave in to my combat reflex. I said, "I came to see Gordon Hughes, not you."

"Governor Hughes sent me. If you have something to say…"

"I'll say it to Hughes."

The man was tall and handsome, in his fifties and distinguished-looking. I could tell he'd enjoyed a successful life in politics, and he did not appreciate my attitude toward him. He said, "The Governor is a busy man."

I said, "Yeah? Well, I'd hate to inconvenience him. Let him know that General Wayson Harris stopped by."

"General Wayson Harris?" he asked. He still wasn't sure it was me. To him, we all looked the same. "Did you say you were General Harris?"

"In the synthetic flesh," I said.

"Would you like to see the governor now?"

"That's why I came."

"Yes, sir. We'll go straight away."

"And my men? I don't think it would be wise to leave them here."

"No, sir," he said, suddenly the cooperative fellow.

He was not in charge. He was just a lackey for Gordon Hughes, who might not have been in charge as well. Hughes was officially the governor of Mars Spaceport, but the people seemed to have ideas of their own.

7

The suits led the entire regiment to the administrative building, then escorted Jackson and me inside while the rest of the men waited in the hall, which was so wide that it looked like a cul-de-sac. There were areas within the spaceport that looked like buildings inside of buildings.

Gordon Hughes could have lived a life of luxury if he returned to Earth; instead, he chose to live like his people on Mars. He lived in this three-story building with his extended family and the extended families of his staff and advisors. Apparently, he allowed himself one luxury—he slept on a bed instead of a blanket; but he did not have a personal shower, bathroom, or kitchen.

The executive offices looked like they must have looked before all the trouble began—bright light shining from the ceiling, a clean beige carpet underneath our feet, and a pretty personal assistant to greet us as we stepped off the elevator.

She was tall and curvy with long blond hair and pale skin. Her eyes were ice blue. She introduced herself as Emily and ushered us to the governor's office.

One of the suits who led us to the building whispered, "That's

Hughes's granddaughter."

I thought, *If Watson gets ahold of this one, Hughes will wind up a great-grandfather before his time.*

Emily Hughes caught Jackson staring at her and gave him a shy smile. The colonel couldn't take his eyes off her.

"Put it on ice, Colonel," I whispered as she opened the door. "We want her grandfather on our side."

Jackson grunted a soft "yes, sir," but his eyes remained fixed.

Hughes met us at his office door. He said, "Good to see you, General," and reached to shake my hand. He and I had met on a few occasions over the last two decades. Some of our meetings had been cordial, but most had not.

I shook his hand.

"Governor, this is Colonel Curtis Jackson," I said.

Jackson and Hughes shook hands, and Hughes led us into his office, which apparently doubled as his home. There was a bed in one corner of the room, Hughes's bed.

The meeting started off on a civil tone.

Once he closed the door, Hughes said, "I suppose you are here about the Night of the Martyrs. I can assure you that my office had nothing to do with that unfortunate event. Colonel Riley has asked me about the incident several times."

"So he tells me," I said.

Hughes said, "I understand EMN Intelligence has had agents investigating as well." Instead of hiding behind his desk, he stood with Jackson and me.

"And you still have no idea who could have been behind it?" I asked.

"No idea." He paused, folded his arms across his chest, and said, "General, these people are loyal to the Enlisted Man's Empire. They are aware of the sacrifices your military has made."

I interrupted him, and asked, "Did you know I lost two men on the way here?"

"Yes, I heard about that. Most unfortunate. I am sure Spaceport Security will find the people responsible."

"Spaceport Security is my people," I said. "What about your people? What are you going to do to help?"

"What do you mean?" Hughes asked. His eyes darted around the room, and he started pacing.

"Two murders have been committed," I said. "Help us bring the killers to justice."

"General, how would you have me help? Your best course of action is to keep me out of this."

"Bullshit," said Jackson. "You know what I see when I looked around the spaceport? I see the beginning of a war. Those Legion banners on the walls out there, they're a call for war."

Hughes ignored Jackson and aimed his answers at me. He said, "I assure you, General, war with the Enlisted Man's Empire is the last thing these people want. What happened in the grand arcade was an accident, a serious and unfortunate accident."

"The Night of the Martyrs was not an accident," I said.

"Those banners aren't an accident," said Jackson.

"Nor are they a call to arms," said Hughes.

"Tell me about Legion," I said.

"There is a religious revival going on," said Hughes. "These people have nothing. They live in squalor. Some of them are turning to religion.

"Look, General, they are refugees with nothing but the blankets on which they sleep. They are impoverished, they are uncomfortable, and they are unhappy. What would you expect?

"It's a common thing. People who have nothing often turn to God. Frankly, I consider the revival a positive turn of events. People in need look for a deliverer. They could have turned to a military figure, but they chose to go with God."

"What does that have to do with Legion?" asked Jackson.

"In order to have a god, you need to have a devil," Hughes explained. "They call their devil Legion."

"What about the Night of the Martyrs?" I asked. "What was that, hybrid military/faith-based salvation?"

"General Harris," Hughes said, drawing my name out, giving it a patronizing tone, "you can't possibly believe those attacks were connected with a spontaneous demonstration in the grand arcade."

He finally stepped behind his desk and sat down.

Even though two chairs had been set out for us, Jackson and I remained on our feet. Jackson said, "I sure as speck see a connection. Those people consider us their enemy. I don't know shit about Legions and devils, but I know war flags when I see them, and those banners qualify as war flags. Those people out there, they're looking for a fight."

Hughes sighed, and said, "They don't want war, Colonel. They know their situation. They know that you feed them and that you rescued them from the Avatari... rescued them twice." He turned to me, and added, "General, they are loyal to the Enlisted Man's Empire. They know what would have happened if you left them on Olympus Kri. They haven't forgotten.

"There are women and children out there... wives and sons and daughters. You cannot possibly believe these men would sacrifice their wives and children."

"Bullshit," said Jackson. He wasn't showing proper respect, but I had decided to give him a long leash this visit. I wanted him to make noise, and I wanted Hughes to see we meant business.

Gordon Hughes may have been a war hero in his youth, but now he was a dried-up old man with white hair and wrinkles. His bloodshot eyes peered out from puffy red rims, and his lips were flesh-colored and dry.

The corners of his mouth drew back in an ironic smile as he said, "What did you expect when you arrived, Colonel, a hero's welcome? Perhaps you were hoping for the red-carpet treatment, Colonel. I'm sorry if we disappointed you."

As a sign of respect for Hughes's office, Jackson and I had left our M27s back with our troops. Good thing. If he'd had his gun, I suspect Jackson might have used it. I saw murder in his eyes. He said, "No, Governor, when I save people's lives I expect them to throw trash at me. Wasn't that why we pulled your people off Olympus Kri, so they could crush my Marines with their garbage?"

Hughes glanced at me for help. When I said nothing, he turned back to Jackson and asked, "Did you happen to notice the way those people are living out there?"

Jackson said, "Maybe they would have been happier if we'd left them on Olympus Kri. They could have died in the comfort of their homes."

I decided to take control of the conversation. "How did six thousand New Olympians get to Earth?" I asked.

Hughes turned to glare at me, the anger he felt toward Jackson still showing in his eyes. He asked, "Do you think I had something to do with it? Do you think I sent them?"

He calmed down quickly. Jackson had riled him, but Hughes knew how to play the game. He said, "If I had to guess, I would say that they stowed away on a freighter."

"Six thousand men... that's a lot of men to go unnoticed," said Jackson.

"Six thousand out of seventeen million," Hughes reminded Jackson.

I had already done the math in my head. "Small fraction," I said. I believed Hughes when he said he knew nothing about the men who came to Earth.

"Would you have stopped them if you knew about it?" Jackson asked.

"They broke the law," said Hughes. "Aside from questions of right and wrong, Colonel, I am against anything that prolongs our encampment on Mars. Just from a pragmatic standpoint, it seems obvious that their actions would be interpreted as provocation, yes? You see those men as seditious, a threat to the stable government you are trying to create, and your suspicions extend to the entire population of Olympus Kri."

Jackson started to say something, but Hughes put up a hand to stop him. He said, "I understand why you have reacted to the attacks as you have. You asked me a question, and that is my answer. I am against anything that keeps us trapped on Mars."

"But you don't care that they tried to kill two thousand

Marines?" asked Jackson, his anger again on the rise.

"Colonel, which answer are you more likely to accept, that I object to the killing of Marines because it is evil or that I object to the killing of Marines because it's politically inconvenient?"

Jackson laughed.

"You still haven't answered the question," I said. "Would you have stopped them?"

"Leaving Mars was a criminal act. I consider them criminals."

"Another dodge," I said.

"What do you want me to say?" asked Hughes.

"Would you have stopped those men if you could have?" I asked.

"I could not have stopped them, General. I would not have tried.

"There are people in this spaceport who wish they had died on Olympus Kri. After a year of waiting, people who would rather have been incinerated than live in this squalor," said Hughes, his politician's veneer wearing thin, the touch of anger in his voice.

Transporting the New Olympians was going to be a long, slow process. Back when we evacuated Olympus Kri, we had a fleet of barges that could carry a quarter of a million passengers at a time. We no longer had those barges. Now we would need to ferry the New Olympians to Earth in warships and freighters, a few thousand at a time. The process could take over a year.

When I mentioned that to Hughes, he said, "That's no excuse." His eyes turned cold and his voice more hostile. "You should have started the evacuation eleven months ago."

8

The regiment bivouacked in a food court, a tight fit for fifteen hundred Marines but probably worse for the twenty-five hundred people we evicted.

I chose the food court because it was in a secluded cul-de-sac. A narrow service hall looped behind the ring of empty restaurants, but that made the area all the more attractive—it might lure the enemy into an attack.

"Do you want me to post guards in the service hall?" asked Colonel Jackson.

"Not a chance," I said. "I don't want to scare visitors away, I want to invite them."

"Yes, sir," said Jackson. "My men can rig a warning system. That shouldn't scare them away."

"Good thinking, Colonel," I said.

"Aye, sir."

"And, Colonel, why don't you place some equipment in the air ducts while you're at it. Set up a wide perimeter. I want to be ready for visitors."

"Yes, sir."

Jackson was hardheaded, but a good Marine with all the commendations and decorations of a vet with ten years of combat experience. I'd never met the man before this mission, but I'd seen his record. The Second Regiment of the Second Division was a newly formed first-response unit. When Jackson requested to join the unit, I placed him in command.

I watched my men set up their bivouac. They set up a manned, chest-high, bulletproof barrier by the entrance into the food court. One hundred men tended that checkpoint.

Technicians filtered out the back doors of the various restaurants. Once they placed their filament-sized cameras and sensors in the hall, not even a Martian louse would be able to slip through unobserved.

Self-guiding robotic sentries now roved the air ducts, patrolling for movement, heat, sound, electrical current, and chemicals. They were our electronic canaries. The size of house cats, the sentries were far from discreet. They were loud and large, but that was their charm. They saw and heard everything; and if the enemy destroyed them, that provided us with an early warning as well.

The mood around the regiment relaxed. Most of us removed our helmets. Some men even stripped off their armor and walked around in their bodysuits. I removed my helmet but kept my armor on.

I'd grown numb to the heavy, sweaty scent of the air and mostly forgotten about the head lice. After a while, I started scratching my scalp and noticed other Marines doing the same. Only then did I realize we might bring some of Mars's only indigenous population home with us.

This particular food court was far from the hub of Mars Spaceport. It was a place for spaceport employees to eat, not travelers. There were no windows overlooking a vast Martian vista, and the unfinished ceiling was crisscrossed with ducts, pipes, and wires.

If it came to a shoot-out, there was no chance we would

breach the spaceport's outer walls. Not in here.

Using the commandLink, I contacted Cutter on the *Churchill*. When he answered, I said, "What I wouldn't give for a private room with a rack and head right about now."

"I can send a shuttle," he offered.

"I'm just bitching," I said. "By the way, you might want to set up some sterilizing lamps for my men."

"Head lice?" he asked.

"Mars's only indigenous life-form," I said. "A lot of my men are scratching their heads."

"But not you," said Cutter.

I said, "No comment."

I told Cutter about my visit with Gordon Hughes, and that led to a brief discussion about the ancient Roman practice of decimation. Cutter asked, "You know what the Romans used to do when their soldiers were attacked in conquered territories?"

I did know. Roman history had always fascinated me. In fact, I had sparked Cutter's interest in Rome when I told him about the Praetorian Guard.

He did not wait for me to answer before saying, "They used to line up the town and kill every tenth person."

I knew Cutter wasn't seriously suggesting I kill New Olympians, he just liked to demonstrate his knowledge.

"There are seventeen million people in this facility; I'd end up killing 1. 7 million people plus change."

"Plus change?"

"Plus change. You may not have heard this, but the New Olympians have not stopped copulating since moving to Mars. Does a mother and a newborn count as a single unit?"

"I don't think the Romans killed mothers or newborns, just men," said Cutter.

"Oh. In that case..." I said.

We were down for the night, and we had a secure perimeter at that point, and I had no idea how much trouble I was in.

9

The sons of bitches tried to gas us. They must have known we would take off our helmets once we set up camp, and they tried to get us by pumping poisonous gas through the air vents.

The killer mist rolled along the bottom of the air ducts like fog on a lake. One of our robot sentries sniffed it from forty feet away, analyzed the chemicals, and reported that the lethal cloud was on its way. The robot then switched into stealth mode and drove straight into the gas, cameras rolling, using telemetry to send back everything it saw as it tried to trace the source of the attack.

The men monitoring the robot called for Colonel Jackson, and he invited me to watch.

"What kind of gas is it?" I asked.

"Poisonous gas," said Jackson, the bastard.

"Chlorine gas, sir," one of the techs answered.

Chlorine gas was an ancient weapon, primitive and reliable. It would not penetrate the breathing gear in our armor. Wearing our helmets, we could nap, exercise, and write poetry in a room filled with chlorine gas.

"After they run out of chlorine, maybe they'll come after us with bows and arrows," Jackson quipped.

"It's easy to make," said a tech. "You can find the chemicals anywhere."

"Improvised munitions," I muttered, knowing that chlorine was one of the few chemicals in good supply on Mars. Any cleaning done on Mars probably involved chlorine-based disinfectants.

The little robot pushed through layers and coils of greenish yellow gas relying on magnetic and sonar signals to navigate through the vents. It detected every turn, every rise, and every weld; and it transmitted its findings back to us in the form of a three-dimensional map.

The robot traveled through sixty-three feet of chlorine gas before it located the open vent and the glass hose that were the source of the trouble.

"Can you transmit the source location to my commandLink?" I asked.

The tech tapped a couple of keys, and said, "Aye, sir. Try frequency 99998."

I came prepared. I brought a small handheld communicator that I patched into the commandLink. The little remote included a four-inch screen and a camera and a microphone. When I powered the screen, I saw the glass hose and the map that the robot had transmitted. The opening of the hose looked to be about four inches in diameter, with gas spewing out of it as thick as sludge.

"Do we know where the gas is coming from?" I asked.

"They must have a geny, sir," said the tech.

"I suspect so," I said, a little irritated by his telling me the obvious. Of course they were using a generator to mix and blow the gas; they weren't mixing it in paint cans. "Can you tell if there are people around it?"

The robot cruised right up to the mouth of the hose, peered inside it, then the world began spinning out of control.

"What happened?" I asked.

"It pitched an eye," said the tech, tech-speak for dropping a remote camera.

On my display, I saw yellow gas and glimpses of glass. The camera must have been tiny, no bigger than the point of a pin, but dense enough that the gas did not flush it out of the hose. It rolled down the hose, all the while transmitting back images of a small space, maybe a closet, in which three men stood.

I handed Jackson my M27, and said, "Keep it warm for me, Colonel."

"What are you doing, sir?" asked Jackson.

"I'm going to introduce myself to our new friends," I said.

He laughed, and said, "Admiral Cutter said you would go rogue at the first sign of action."

"Did he? I bet he told you to send a team with me if I did."

"No, sir. He said not to bother asking."

"He knows me," I said.

"He also said that I should warn you that you will be relieved of command if you continue playing commando," said Jackson.

"Another good insight," I said.

"Do you want me to send some men with you, sir?" asked Jackson.

If I had a team of men with me, we might end up with another grand arcade situation, surrounded by screaming hostiles while the enemy ran away. Alone, I stood a chance of slipping through unnoticed.

I stripped off my armor and the bodysuit underneath. Hoping for a chance to get out on my own, I had come with civilian clothing under my bodysuit. That was also my reason for bringing the handheld remote. The brick-sized device felt clumsy in my hand; but I thought I could use it in the spaceport without drawing too much attention.

I asked Jackson, "Are any of your troops packing civilian gear under their armor?"

"Negative, sir."

I said, "Then I guess I am forced to go alone." Turning to leave, I heard the colonel whisper, "Bullshit." I could have busted the bastard for insubordination. Instead, I quietly laughed.

As I walked to the barrier, a soft voice came from the remote. Jackson said, "General, there's movement in one of the service halls."

"I want prisoners, not corpses," I said. "If someone knocks on the door, you let them in, and you take them alive. Am I clear, Colonel?"

"Aye, sir."

"And speaking of being taken alive, I will signal you if I run into trouble."

"Yes, sir."

"And I will signal you before I return. I don't want your boys shooting me when I come back."

"No, sir."

I looked both ways as I left the court. There were people around, but the hall was dark and crowded, and I was pretty certain that I had sneaked out unseen.

The spaceport had an artificial daylight cycle. During the artificial day, lights shone from every corner. During the night, the lights dimmed down so people could sleep. That was as far as privacy went on Mars, dimmed halls and mass campouts. Moving through the shadows, I saw a man in his fifties groping his equally aged wife. The people around the couple simply looked the other way.

There was nothing erotic about the moment. The man was fat, and both participants were sweaty and grimy. The woman moaned softly, but the people around them pretended not to hear. They carried on conversations as if nothing was happening on the blanket next door.

I was cleaner than everyone around me, and so were my clothes. I wondered if cleanliness gave off a stench that dirty people would notice as I crept through the hall, sticking to the shadows, looking for walls and passages that led away from the crowds.

"Hey... hey you?" a teen yelled as I walked past.

I ignored him and moved on.

As I traveled through the spaceport, I came to see reason

in its chaos. The New Olympians had divided the facility into neighborhoods and districts. I, of course, did not know one district from the next; but there were subtle clearings between the wards. Each neighborhood had its own food service and bathrooms.

I turned a corner and found a street meeting. A priest or pastor stood on a little wooden stand two feet above a large crowd of listeners. Behind him hung a ten-foot-long banner that read, LEGION IS AMONG US.

His flock of listeners provided better camouflage than the shadows. I walked the outside of the throng as if planning to join, all the while thinking about the banner and testing it against the things Gordon Hughes had said.

If Legion referred to demons, then the banner warned that demons or devils had entered the spaceport. Maybe he meant me and my regiment, we had entered the spaceport; but we weren't the only demonic presence while Colonel Riley had five thousand men. *We are the demons*, I thought. *We are the devils. We are Legion.*

I thought about the three men I had killed in Seattle. They were small, soft, nonmilitary types. They would have fitted in with this preacher's flock. I wanted to do a little reconnaissance and listen to the sermon—who knew what messages I might have heard—but I did not have that option. These folks only qualified as religious fanatics; I had assassins to capture.

The lighting in the wide corridor was dimmed enough for families to sleep along the edges. The outlying crowd could not see the preacher's face clearly in this obscure light, but his voice was sharp. He said, "Be ye wise as serpents yet harmless as doves. We are not supposed to live our lives wearing blinders. We are not supposed to lie down to be sacrificed like lambs."

At first I thought the crowd was mostly men; but as I pushed my way through, I noticed teenage boys as well. Maybe as many as two thousand men had gathered to hear the sermon, a pretty big crowd until I saw tens of thousands of people still lying on blankets and trying to sleep.

Some revival, I thought. *Most of these people don't give a shit.* I registered that thought, but I did not have time to consider its meaning.

I pushed through the revivalist flock and walked down the center of a lane, watching the map on the remote. When I reached a clearing between two neighborhoods, I found a shadowy corner and contacted Jackson. I said, "What is your report?"

"The gas wasn't a problem, sir. We threw a couple of pellets into the vent and dissolved the gas."

"Did you test the air?" I asked.

"Yes, sir, we did. It stinks, but it isn't toxic."

"And the service corridor?" I asked.

"They're still out there, sir. It does not look like they want to come in. Per your orders, we haven't gone out to collect them."

I said, "Good job," and I signed off.

The signal from the robot sentry led me through a dark alley. There were no lights on the walls in this area, just a long, narrow corridor in which the light from my remote stood out like a neon target.

If I needed a reminder that I was inside a defunct spaceport, not on a street in a city, I found it at the end of the hall. This area may have been created to look like a city, but the back alley I entered led to a maintenance closet instead of another street.

I pulled the door partially open. Beyond the doorway, I saw a portable oxygen generator, a glass hose that stretched from the top of the geny to a ventilation shaft, and three men. That generator might have been designed to create oxygen, but there wasn't any oxygen coming out of it on that night. The vomit-colored gas belching into the glass hose had an activated chlorine base.

The oxygen geny did not surprise me, but the three men operating it did. I expected Bible-toting dupes, like the men I had killed in Seattle. What I found was a trio of government-issue military clones—Colonel Martin Riley's men.

My first impulse was to strike. I didn't have a gun, but I wouldn't need a gun to kill a trio of G.I. clones. *Take it easy,*

Harris, I thought, reminding myself that I hadn't come to kill little fish; I would allow the little fish to swim free in the hope that they would lead me to bigger game.

What can you learn from a dead man? I asked myself.

Backing away from the door without closing it, I left the alley. Up the hall, the street preacher continued delivering his fiery sermon. This part of Mars Spaceport did not have shops or administrative offices or waiting areas. The hall was long and straight, with no doors or turns except for alleys that probably led to janitorial facilities. I looked for someplace I could hide, but the only cover I could find would be to rejoin the congregation.

"Jackson, what's the status?" I whispered into the remote.

"Same as before. They keep pumping gas, and we keep neutralizing it. Those chickenshit bastards are still loitering in the halls."

I wondered about the men waiting in the halls outside the food court. Were they clones, too? Had Riley joined forces with the New Olympians? It didn't make sense. Why would he join the New Olympians? As I thought about it, I realized that I had not seen any of Riley's men the entire day. He had five thousand troops, supposedly fifteen hundred of whom were on duty at any given time. The combat armor his men wore was different than ours. It was covered with white enamel so it could be spotted from a distance. They belonged to the Corps, but they did the work of policemen.

I hadn't even seen any of Riley's men in the grand arcade, and he should have had hundreds of men patrolling the area.

Somebody had to be helping the locals, and Riley was the logical candidate. The only weapons the New Olympians had were cleaning supplies. Not even Alexander the Great or Napoleon could launch a revolution with janitorial supplies.

Stunned by what I had found, I said, "Speck. Riley is behind this?" I needed to report the defection to Cutter; but before I mentioned this to anyone, I needed to make sure this was Riley's work and not the work of a few rogue Marines.

I had not meant to mention this to anyone until I knew what was what, but Curtis Jackson, who was still on the Link, overheard me talking to myself. He said, "Riley? Colonel Riley? He's working with the Martians? You mean those are turncoat Marines out there in the hallway? We oughta go out and kill those bastards!"

The term "Martians" was a derogatory name a lot of Marines used to refer to the New Olympians.

"Negative, Colonel. Do not engage the enemy."

"General, those clone bastards have attempted to murder my men."

"How many men have you lost?"

"If they had better weapons, they'd use them," said Jackson.

"I'd have lost a lot of men if that gas had turned out to be Noxium instead of chlorine."

"If Riley is behind this, he's got M27s and five thousand men," I said.

"We better inform Cutter that Riley's gone south."

As far as I knew, Colonel Martin Riley was still a loyal EME Marine, and I did not want to blight his record with an unfounded accusation. I said, "Let's hold off on that court-martial until we know what's what, Jackson."

"Yes, sir."

I held the remote right by my face so I could whisper, and I covered the screen with my hand to block the glow. I stood about twenty feet from the edge of the congregation and just a few feet from a row of picnickers. Looking around the hall, I saw people watching me. They did not seem to know who I was, but they knew I did not fit in.

"Jackson, have your techs track my signal and get ready to move."

"Ready to move, sir?"

"I'm going to follow those clones and see where they take me. If I give them enough space, maybe they'll show me who's in charge."

People were looking at me now. The preacher had stopped

speaking and stared in my direction, so did most of his congregation. Along the nearest wall of the hallway, people stood on their blankets and watched me.

It had not occurred to me before that moment, but now I saw it clearly—these people did not have electronic devices. No flashlights, no mediaLink shades, no communications devices, no computers. The muffled glow from my remote communicator might as well have been a spotlight.

As casually as I could, I lowered the remote and continued down the hall, away from the congregation. People watched me, but nobody approached. When I glanced back, though, I saw a group of men coming after me.

There was a T-junction up ahead. I could go left or I could go right, but I could not go straight. I chose to turn left, the direction that took me farther away from the grand arcade.

10

My instincts told me that people seldom crossed neighborhood lines in the spaceport. The picnickers along the walls eyed me carefully as I crossed the clearing that marked the border between one neighborhood and the next. I heard people mumbling to each other, some asking questions about me, some speculating why I had entered their domain.

I slowed and waited to see if the men would follow me.

They did, and they didn't. Three men turned the same way I had, walked a few feet into the hall, and slowed to a stop. They stood at the edge of the new neighborhood, searching the gloomy corridor, looking for me.

Deciding to blend in with the locals, I spotted a vacancy along one of the walls and walked right up to it as if I belonged.

Nobody said anything until I sat down.

The man on the blanket to my right leaned over, and asked, "Who the speck are you?" He sounded angry, but he kept his voice low because it was the quiet hour, and most of the people around us were asleep.

Trying my best to make this look like a friendly conversation,

I said, "Just visiting."

"Yeah, well go visit someplace else. That is not your spot."

"Who does it belong to?" I asked. "Where are they?"

"Sanitary pass," the man said. "Not that it's any of your specking business."

I pretended to lavish all of my attention on my new neighbor while watching the men who had been following me in my peripheral vision. They stared in my direction; but the hall was dark, and I was hidden in the shadows. They might have seen where I had gone, but they did not come after me. As I watched them disappear around the corner, I apologized to my temporary neighbor and told him, "Sorry to have bothered you, I was just trying out the new neighborhood."

"Yeah? Next time go someplace else," he said.

Hostile bastard, I thought; but he was protecting his neighbor's property, something I could respect. I said, "Sorry."

I killed another minute strolling the neighborhood. Had this part of the spaceport been multitiered like the grand arcade, I might have taken the stairs to an upper floor. That would have made my job so much easier. I could have watched the alley from the next floor up; tracking hostiles is always easier from higher ground.

The spaceport was still in dusk mode, so people could not see me clearly. As long as I did not use the remote, I would not attract attention. I wanted to know what was going on back at the food court, and I wanted to radio Cutter, but I did not want to risk giving myself away.

I waited another minute or two to make sure the coast was clear, then I walked back to the alley. If anyone noticed me, they ran their recon a lot more subtly than the guys who followed me up the hall. People tracked me as I left one neighborhood and entered the next; but no one said anything. With the glow from my remote hidden, I had become a New Olympian.

I strode to the alley and entered. The open door was just as I had left it, and I heard the voices of general-issue clones speaking inside.

I hope this finishes quick.

You still nervous?

Hell, yes. I hear Harris is in there.

Harris isn't so scary.

Get specked! The son of a bitch is a specking Liberator.

Bullshit, there aren't any specking Liberators left.

A third man said, *There won't be any Liberators once Harris breathes this shit, I promise you that. This shit makes your lungs blister.*

I'm just saying I'm nervous.

Don't sweat it. If Harris breathed this, he's already dead.

They were clones fighting against the Enlisted Man's Empire; it made no sense. They must have joined forces with the New Olympians, though I was not sure which New Olympians. Governor Hughes would not have sanctioned something like this. Were they religious converts out to kill Legion? If the term "Legion" referred to clone converts, they could have been out to kill *for* Legion. "Legion is among us." What the hell did it mean?

No matter how I tried to fit the pieces together, the end result made no sense.

If I'd been wearing combat armor, I could have recorded their conversation and given it to Intel for analysis; but I had come dressed as a civilian. Apparently, these clones had the same idea. I peered in the doorway and saw they had come in slacks and tees.

The night period ended, and the light around the spaceport started to brighten when the first two members of the trio finally emerged from the alley. The illumination level had not reached daylight levels, only the murky shadows of the early morning.

The third guy must have been in charge of the oxygen geny; his friends left the alley empty-handed. I watched them from across the hall as they turned right and disappeared.

My instincts told me to wait for the final traitor.

A few early-rising natural-borns drifted through the area. The street revival had long since cleared away. A twenty-three-man crew set up food tables where the preacher had been.

A clone wearing white security armor but no helmet drove up in an old-fashioned electric-powered cart with a flatbed for hauling cargo. He parked outside the alley and beeped the horn.

The third clone came out to meet him. They traded salutes, then the new clone drove his cart into the alley. Five minutes later, with the light level just below breaking dawn, the two men drove out of the alley with the oxygen generator in the back of their cart.

They drove slowly, talking happily, not looking back. Staying about fifty feet behind them, I followed as they left one neighborhood and entered the next. The floor was smooth, and the cart glided over it without making much noise.

I followed the cart through a crowded maze of halls and corridors. The illumination hit midmorning levels, and I thought about using my remote to check in with Jackson; but the bastards in the cart kept driving forward. I would lose them if I stopped to chat.

We turned a corner, and there it was... the grand arcade, with its five-tiered ring of stores that now served as a campground for refugees. This time, though, no one noticed me. I was just another New Olympian, walking around the spaceport at the break of another unhappy day. People noticed the clones driving the cart with the oxygen geny, however. I saw a few heads turn to follow them.

We crossed the arcade and continued down a main hall. Arteries such as this one had been constructed to handle tens of thousands of harried travelers at a time.

The cart entered a nearly empty hallway and started to pull away. By the time I reached the corner, it had disappeared. Fortunately for me, there was only one place it could have gone, a doorway with a sign that said, MILITARY PERSONNEL ONLY.

A hand-painted banner hung below that sign. It read, BELIEVE IN LEGION.

11

I knew where I was before I saw the trains and the tracks that led ten miles across the desert from Mars Spaceport to Mars Air Force Base.

The train station was brightly lit and nearly empty—only military allowed, no picnickers. I stood on a large mezzanine overlooking three tracks, three loading platforms, and three trains. An escalator slanted down to the platforms below on one side of the mezzanine and a cargo elevator lowered from the other. Peering over a rail, I saw the cart parked beside the nearest train. The clones had removed the oxygen geny from the back of the cart and left it on the edge of the platform. They stood gabbing inside the train. As an officer in the Marines, I felt ashamed of the bastards, not because they had turned their backs on the Corps but because they had no more purpose in life than a pair of specking ninety-year-old grandmothers. They took a five-minute gossip break. One told a joke, and the other laughed and slapped him on the back. If they weren't traitors, I would have dogged them for goldbricking.

We were alone in the train station. With them laughing and

gossiping and horsing around, I had no trouble slipping down the escalator without being seen. I reached the platform and started toward the train before the lazy bastards started back to work.

The geny was not light. Struggling together, they managed to pull it onto the train without dropping it. Then they surprised me. They paused and gave the platform a security sweep. Had I hesitated a moment, they would have caught me. They entered the train's lead car. I had already boarded the rear car. There were six cars between us.

I sat quietly as the train glided into motion.

The train slid through a tunnel that ran under the spaceport. It rolled along the track as smooth as wind. After we passed what had once been a stop for Norma-Arm-bound passengers, the tunnel went dark. We passed platforms for passengers heading to the Perseus and Cygnus Arms as well.

Bright lights illuminated the inside of the train. I left the last car and walked into the next. It was as bright and empty as the one I had just left. Looking through the windows, I had a blurry, blinded view into the car in front of me. I could not see clearly enough to distinguish between men and machinery, so I checked for movement instead. The next car was empty and the one after that. It soon became clear that my quarry had remained in the lead car with the oxygen generator.

I made it to the second car, peered through the window, and found them sitting on a bench, gabbing.

I made my move. I eased open the door of their car. They might have noticed the door, but they didn't react until they saw me charging toward them; but by that time, it was too late. They did not have time to draw weapons, and they had nowhere to run.

I slammed the edge of my hand across the throat of the first clone as he stood to face me. He gasped and fell, and lay on the floor choking for air.

The second man rushed me. He was young and stupid, I saw it in his brawny gait. I needed to keep the bastard alive, though, and that meant I needed him more than he needed me.

Under normal circumstances, I would have hit him in the nose or throat as he raced toward me. A shot to the crotch or the eyes would have worked as well; but I wanted to chat, so I kicked out his kneecap instead. His leg buckled under him, but momentum carried him into me and we tumbled backward. As we wrestled on the ground, he tried to wedge his forearm under my chin to choke me. He worked his way on top of me, slammed a fist into my face, and tried to pry my chin up.

The blow left me dazed for just a moment, but I recovered quickly. I was in the midst of a combat reflex, my senses heightened, my brain moving in double time.

I wrapped a hand around the man's wrist and twisted it over. He tried to pull the hand free as the smaller bones popped and separated, and he screamed in pain as I pulled him off my body, using his broken hand like a lever. A few feet away, his friend lay on the floor, suffocating slowly, his face turning blue, his hands clenched around the crushed larynx. In another minute, he would die.

With his leg and wrist broken and his friend dying, the Marine forgot he was a Marine. He backed away on his ass and tried to climb to his feet. I grabbed one of his ankles and pulled his feet out from under him. As he fell, he tried to break his fall with his broken hand. He howled in pain when he hit the ground.

I grabbed his arm and wrenched the broken hand out from under his body. I was in full combat reflex now; seductive warmth filled my head. As I climbed to my feet, I placed a foot on his broken wrist and pressed my weight on it.

I might not have wanted to kill them before the reflex; but now, with the hormone running through my veins, murder appealed. I looked at the clone with the crushed throat. His eyes bulged, his mouth formed an O, and his lips had turned blue. He'd die in a few more seconds; only a field-trained surgeon could save him.

For just a moment, I wondered if slicing the man's neck and forcing a tube in his throat would continue my combat reflex. I asked myself if I could possibly keep the hormone flowing with an act of mercy? The notion intrigued me, but I let the bastard die.

The survivor lay on the floor cradling his hand, which had swollen to the size of a catcher's mitt and turned purple. I said, "I need to make a quick call. Don't run off."

Battlefield humor. The bastard was not about to leave; he had gone into shock.

I pulled out the remote. "Jackson, you there?"

No one responded.

I tried again. "Jackson, report."

Nothing.

Thinking I might have broken the remote during my wrestle, I switched to an open channel and listened for chatter. My men had gone silent.

The train had crossed the spaceport by this time. Looking out the window, I saw the automated air locks. Once we passed the air locks, we would enter the Martian badlands. The train slowed as the first door of the air lock slid shut behind it, preserving the breathable atmosphere inside Mars Spaceport. The outer door opened, and we slid into the wastelands.

"*Churchill* command, come in." I contacted the ship to see if the remote still worked.

One of Cutter's lieutenants answered. He asked, "General, do you need to be sent through to Admiral Cutter?"

I said yes.

When Cutter came on, I said, "I have a hot mess down here. Somebody tried to gas my men."

"Do you know who?" asked Cutter.

I said, "I'm still investigating, but I think it was Riley."

"Did you say Riley?" asked Cutter.

"I caught the men with the gas. They're clones. The question is, who sent them? They were on their way to the Air Force base."

"I see a train leaving the spaceport on my monitor," said Cutter. "Want me to stop it?"

"Hell no. I'm on that train."

"What about your men?" asked Cutter.

"I can't find them," I said. "I told Jackson to circle the wagons, now he's not answering."

"You went out on your own," said Cutter, demonstrating a knack for stating the obvious.

I looked down at my two victims. One was dead. The other had pulled himself together. He sat on the floor holding the arm, his face pale. I said, "There is a lot going on here. More than we know. There are a couple of Spaceport Security men on the train with me; one's a bit stiff but the other looks like he might be helpful."

Cutter asked, "General, will you be able to control yourself long enough to have a productive conversation?"

I told Cutter, "I'm sure we will get along fine," and signed off.

I sat down beside the man with the broken wrist. He looked like a scared child as he regarded me. I asked, "Ever wondered about life after death?"

He did not answer.

"You will know the answers very soon, Marine."

He said nothing. No surprise.

I said, "I heard you and your buddies chatting. One of you said I was a Liberator clone, another one didn't believe him. Which one were you?" There had been a third clone, but I was trying to make a point.

He asked, "Are you Harris?"

I said, "In the Liberator flesh."

He surprised me by showing some backbone. He gathered his strength, and said, "Get specked, you alien-loving bastard."

"What happened to my men?" I asked.

The son of a bitch did not utter a word. He might have cowered during our fight, but now he was acting like a Marine. This wasn't a scared little lamb like the idiots back in Seattle; this man had faced death before.

"Listen up, Marine," I said. "It has been a long day, and I am not in a good mood. Now tell me what happened to my men. That is an order."

It should have been in his programming. Post-Liberator military clones followed orders automatically. Tell them to do push-ups, and they start humping the ground before their brains register what they're doing. At least, that was how it was supposed to work. I had just ordered this son of a bitch to answer me, but he wasn't talking.

"You specking tried to gas them, asshole," I said. "You tried to gas them, now I can't reach them. What happened to them?"

He stared at me like a young, scared cadet trying to stand up to a drill sergeant. I said, "Okay, then let's start with the easy stuff. What's that?" I pointed to the oxygen generator.

He said, "It's an oxygen generator."

"What were you doing with it?"

He whispered, "Generating oxygen." He closed his eyes and laughed, but terror showed on his face when he opened his eyes again. By that time I was wringing his shattered wrist like a soggy towel.

I said, "We've got a few minutes before we reach the base. Come clean, and I might even let you live."

He stared at me in silence.

I said, "Maybe you've already made up your mind to play it the hard way. Do you have any idea how much pain I can cause you before we dock?" As I said this, I wrung his wrist a second time.

He did not scream. He whimpered.

I loosened my grip. "Why do you want to kill my men?"

"We weren't trying to kill them," he said. I started to squeeze again, and he shouted, "No. No. Really! We knew you would stop the gas. It was a distraction. We were supposed to distract you."

"Distract us," I said, relaxing the pressure on his arm. The gas was a feint, and I had fallen for it. "Distract us from what?"

The man did not answer. I got the feeling he did not know. I asked, "Who sent you? Riley?"

"The colonel is not in charge," he said.

He turned toward the front of the train. I followed his gaze.

Looking through the windshield, I could see Mars Air Force Base in the nearing distance. It looked like a butte in a desert, tall and flat and deep in shadow.

"Kill me," he said.

I stood, as if I wanted to get a closer look at the base, and then I kicked him across the face. I had probably broken his jaw, which was not my intent, and I gave him a concussion from which he would not soon wake up. I stripped the bastard naked and tied his hands, feet, and mouth with his clothes. I wanted him to stand before a military tribunal. I wanted him tried, interrogated, and hung, so I stowed him with his dead friend in a cargo compartment for safekeeping.

If I was killed while exploring the Air Force base, the bastard would starve to death or die of thirst. Maybe he would develop a gangrenous infection and die in delirium. We both had a stake in my survival.

The train slowed as it approached an air lock that led to the base. The outer door slid open, and we rumbled into the tube. The door closed. There was a soft *whoosh* as indigenous gases were flushed away, then the inner door slid open.

I did not know who would greet the train. The train station was brightly lit. I could not afford to be seen. Because I had a clone's face and stood over six feet tall, any clones who saw me would instantly identify me as a Liberator.

The train rolled slowly as it left the air lock and approached an empty passenger platform.

I recognized the base from the time I had visited it many years ago.

"General?" a voice purred from the remote. I reached down to shut it off, but stopped when I saw who it was.

"Jackson? Where the speck have you been?"

"Right here, sir."

"I have been trying to contact you," I said.

"The bastards must have blocked our signal."

He sounded fine. A security force like Riley's probably did

have "sludging" equipment for blocking interLink signals. Such equipment was not uncommon, but I did not think my regiment's disappearance could be explained that simply. If they had blocked the signal five minutes ago, why had they stopped blocking it?

I did not have time to ask. The train had rolled up to the platform, and I had to move.

I said, "I need to go," and signed off.

Places like Mars Air Force Base have discreet security cameras built into their walls and in the ceilings. They have electronic ears that can detect footsteps, breathing, beating hearts; and thermostats that can detect the change in temperature when a body enters a room. There was no question the security system had detected my presence. Whether or not anyone watched the monitors was another story. Maybe they did, and maybe they didn't. I only knew one way to find out.

I stepped off the train and crossed the platform without bothering to look for cameras. If they had people staring into monitors, they'd already seen me.

The only way from the train tracks to the base was up a steep escalator. I climbed the stairs two at a time as the escalator whisked me up. No one met me at the top.

The base lobby was dimly lit, spacious, and clean. The air was cold, my breath turned to steam; but there were no picnickers, which made this icebox the Garden of Eden in my mind. Moving at a fast creep, I crossed the shiny, black, granite floor. I was not alone.

When I reached the door that led from the lobby to the offices, I heard voices. I stopped, listened, then took a few steps back. I pulled out my communications remote. "Jackson."

"Yes, sir."

"Load your men on the transports, double speed."

"Yes, sir. Are we going back to the *Churchill*?"

"No," I said. "Come to the Air Force base and tell your men to hit the deck running. I think the locals might put up a fight."

"Do we get to shoot this time?" he asked.

"This is not a civilian facility, Colonel. You have permission to kill anyone who gets in your way."

"Aye, aye, sir," he said with more enthusiasm.

I contacted the *Churchill* and gave orders to "wreck the rails and board any ships seen leaving Mars." Then I switched off the remote.

There were people in the base, but not very many of them. No one entered the lobby the entire time I was there. The train still sat idle beside the platform.

I left the lobby and entered the work area, expecting to see clones. I thought Riley might have moved his clones out of the filthy spaceport and into the nice clean Air Force base. I suppose that was what I would have done. A moment later I knew I was wrong when I saw a woman walking down a dark hallway.

Seeing the woman, I formed a plan of attack in my head. If Jackson moved his men quickly, and Colonel Curtis Jackson always made his men hustle, it would take them forty minutes to break camp, cross the spaceport, and board the transports. They might get bogged down cutting across the grand arcade, but I doubted it. The locals had quieted quickly when they saw blood the day before, and I did not think they would make another show of defiance.

Twenty minutes to board the transports and five minutes to fly from the spaceport to the base. Flight Control on the *Churchill* would override the base computers and take control of the landing bays.

Riley outnumbered us three to one, but the *Churchill* would send more troops once we established a need. Riley would still outnumber us, but our transports had protective shields; he'd have no way to hurt us until reinforcements arrived, and we lowered those shields. By that time, he'd know he had no place to hide.

I passed through a mess hall. A base this size would have a large mess for enlisted men and a smaller one for officers. I spotted a group of natural-borns sitting around tables chatting and eating. I did not see clones; nor did I see banners with slogans about

Legion. If anything, the mess hall looked regulation.

The people paid no attention to me as I walked by and I pretended to ignore them as well. I listened to their conversation as I passed, but they did not say anything important.

After leaving the mess hall, I entered the next set of doors and found myself in a large auditorium/ briefing hall. The place was empty, huge, and dark as the inside of a coffin. I left, moved on down the hall, and entered the base's nerve center.

This area of the building bristled with life. Computers whirred. People gathered in clusters and spoke in whispered tones. Diagrams and maps hung on the walls. Holographic images wavered in the air. All of the people I saw were civilians, natural-born, some of them women.

I stepped into an empty cubicle. A woman followed me. She said, "We've been watching you since you entered the train station."

I turned, and met her gaze.

She said, "You're a tall one. You must be Wayson Harris."

"Who are you?" I asked.

She smiled and said, "We were going to come to you, but you were kind enough to save us the trouble."

There was a scent in the air, a sharp chemical scent that was unpleasant and familiar. I knew I had smelled it recently, but I couldn't remember when or where. I caught a whiff of it, then everything stopped. I did not become dizzy. I did not spin and fall to the ground. I did not have time to do any of these things. The universe had already ended.

12

"You can't lose a specking regiment of Marines. You might as well say you misplaced gawddamned Mars. What's the matter with you?" I asked. No, "asked" is too subdued. I snarled. I growled. I cannot remember ever in my life feeling such intense anger. "They're here. They're in the Air Force base right now. I ordered them to come, and they came."

"How did they get there?" Cutter asked.

"What the speck do you mean, 'How did they get here'?" Everything about the man irritated me. I hated the way he stared back at me through the screen. I hated the confused look on his face.

"I mean, Harris, how did that regiment of Marines travel from the spaceport to the base? They didn't fly to the base. We've been watching the spaceport. None of the transports have launched. They couldn't have taken the train; you told us to shoot out the rails."

"Either your crew is asleep at the wheel, or your ship is broken, Admiral," I said. I kept my voice even, hoping to hide just how much I hated the bastard. "They flew here. They boarded fifteen transports, and they flew here. How the speck do you miss fifteen transports? They're big. They're slow. They probably radioed in for clearance before they left the spaceport. Check your damn records.

"You know what? Don't check your records. The transports are here, my men are here, I don't give a shit what your specking records say, Cutter. I watched Jackson walk down the ramp. If your records say something else, then you've got bigger problems than a few missed transports."

"Maybe," said Cutter. He outranked me, but I was the one who gave him his stars. I was starting to wonder if he deserved them, the incompetent bastard.

Everything about him irritated me. I didn't like his idiot expression or the way his face looked like the face of every other sailor in the Enlisted Man's Navy. If he'd been here in the flesh, I might have hurt him. When I got a shot at him, I might even allow myself to kill the son of a bitch just for the fun of it.

I took a deep breath and held it. *Stand down,* I told myself. *He's just another clone in a Navy of clones, it's not his fault.*

"Listen, Cutter, we've infiltrated Martian Legion headquarters. Okay? I'm closing in on the objective. I've almost finished what I came here to do. You got that? Am I getting through to you?"

"Yes, you are," he said. He was losing his temper, which meant nothing to me. *Freeloading son of a bitch*, I thought. *Let's see you climb off your specking ship and face the enemy.*

"We've almost got this operation complete, and the last thing we need is for you to get in the way, so pack up your specking space patrol and get the hell out of here. Do you understand? Do you read me?"

He looked so angry that I thought he might lose control. That would have made two of us. For a moment I thought he might try to pull rank on me; and then we would have a real problem.

"We'll clear out," he said.

"Good move," I said.

"Do you want me to leave Watson?"

"Why the speck would I want him around?" I asked. And then I said something that made no sense. I did not know how the words had entered my mind or what they meant. I said, "Give him a message for me, would you. Tell that bastard anything that's programmed can be reprogrammed. You tell him that. You tell him that for me."

My head felt like someone was pounding an inch-thick spike through my skull, as though someone had stabbed a dagger into my brain, and the bastard was using it to pry the lobes apart.

"What was that?" Cutter asked. "What was your message?"

"Not my message, asshole. Tell him Ray Freeman said that."

I said those words, and the world went dark.

13

I remembered the conversation I had with Don Cutter, but the memory seemed far away, like a dream; and, like a remembered dream, it felt surreal and unlikely. I could not recall how the conversation began or how it ended. What mostly came back was the emotion I felt, the anger and the frustration. Try as I might, I could not remember what he might have said to make me so furious.

As I tried to work that out, it occurred to me that I did not know where I was. Well, I was in a bed. Not a bed, a cot, a thin mattress stretched over a metal rack.

The moment I woke up, I knew I was alone in a cell. I knew prison cells when I saw them. I'd spent time in a few. I recognized the featureless metal walls and the bright light that shone down from the ceiling.

Wondering if I had been beaten or drugged, I sat up. My body responded, and I felt no pain. Pain. Pain? I remembered pain so sharp it felt like my head would split open as I spoke with Cutter. Was it a dream?

I never experienced pain in my dreams. If I'd felt that much pain in a dream, it would have woken me.

I knew who I was—Wayson Harris. I knew what I was—a Liberator, a Marine.

I stood and walked the eight feet from my rack to the door.

This was a civilian prison, which meant it was a lot more comfortable than a brig. I had a modicum of privacy. The cell had a door and walls instead of bars or an electrical-containment field, but there must have been cameras in the cell. I could not see the people watching me, but they could see me as clearly as if the walls were made of glass.

The cell was designed for isolation and had no windows. Isolation was the universal solvent of torture techniques. A slow process of mental erosion that leaves the physical intact, isolation will wear anybody down given sufficient time to do its work.

The room had a cot, a toilet, a sink, and bright light shining from the ceiling. I stared into that light until spots danced in my vision, then I looked away and rubbed my eyes. Several minutes passed before the spots went away.

Half-expecting an electric charge, I touched the door. There was no current, but the door was locked. I knew it would be, but I had to try it.

I wondered who had captured me, and just as quickly I knew. I was on Mars. I had taken the train from the spaceport to the Air Force base. And then what? My memory ended when the train reached the platform.

How much did these people know about me? Did they know I was a Liberator? Did they care?

Frustration welled in my brain. Trying to distract myself, I searched the walls for cameras, knowing that I might as well search for microscopic germs. The walls were completely smooth and cool to the touch, and dark gray in color. I ran my hands over the walls, feeling for bumps and seams, possibly pin-sized holes for cameras and microphones. I found nothing.

The door had some sort of rubberized airtight seal, but it was not an air lock—at least it wasn't any kind of air lock I had seen before. I thought I might be able to rip the rubber from the doorway, but that would not buy me freedom.

Kneeling on the ground, I located discreet vents running along the walls. The air in the cell must have flowed through those vents. A fine, sturdy microfiber mesh lined those air ducts. I tried to push it in with my finger, but it did not give, and I would have needed a blade as fine as a scalpel to cut through it.

I looked at the toilet and knew I could break it. If I had shoes, I could mule-kick it until the chrome pipes gave way. *Chrome pipes on the fixtures and a ceramic sink… definitely not a brig*, I thought. I did not have shoes. My feet were bare and cold.

The sink looked breakable, but I saw no point in destroying it. Even if I shattered it, all I would get for my trouble would be an armed guard and possibly handcuffs. I might even get myself drugged.

Drugged?

This was a civilian holding cell, which meant I was no longer on the Air Force base. When had they returned me to the spaceport, and how? They couldn't have used the train unless… What if Cutter didn't destroy the tracks between the spaceport and the base? As his name crossed my mind, I remembered thinking he was "incompetent," but I did not know why. It seemed like that was part of that dream.

Okay, I had searched for panels and cameras. I had checked the plumbing. There was one more way out of here, the most obvious way of all. I pounded my fist on the door and shouted. Nothing happened. I knew no one would come, but I had to try.

I ran a hand across my chin and found about one day's worth of stubble. Had I been in the cell for a day? Maybe I had been in there longer and someone had shaved my beard.

I slammed the heel of my fist against the door and shouted again. Nothing.

I asked myself if I was hungry and decided that I was not especially hungry or thirsty. I felt claustrophobic. I wasn't going stir-crazy, but I did not like the feeling of confinement.

Sometime later—I had no sense of time—the door opened. The

airtight seal gave way with a hiss, and an acrid chemical odor filled the air. My body stopped working, and I fell, helpless, to the cold floor.

The paralysis was nearly complete. I still had feeling in my fingers and my toes; but I could not move anything, not even my eyes.

A woman walked through the door. Lying on my side, I could only see her calves and knees and nothing more. She knelt in front of me. Her voice sounded so specking cheerful. I realized that she could hurt me or help me or do whatever she pleased, and there was nothing I could do to stop her. She said, "Will you look at that! Wayson, you managed to stay awake. What a remarkable man you are."

The woman gently rolled me onto my back.

She had silky brown hair and liquid blue eyes. I did not recognize her; but on some level I must have known her because I felt the stirring of a combat reflex.

I tried to speak, but the muscles in my jaw would not work.

"Can you hear me?" she asked as she touched two fingers to my throat to take my pulse. I wanted to recoil even though the warmth from her fingers felt good against my cold skin. She checked my pulse, then she stroked a finger along my cheek. Her touch was soothing.

Despite my paralysis, blood still flowed freely through my veins. Some of my blood had gathered in my lower regions, inconveniently revealing my attraction to this bitch.

A man entered the room. In a casual voice, he noted, "Look at that, Sunny, he remembers you."

The girl blushed. She looked at my crotch and gave it a dismissive pat.

Anger, humiliation, and rage surged through me. I wished I could break free of my paralysis, but my arms and legs ignored me, and I remained perfectly still as the man hoisted my useless body onto a gurney.

I studied both of their faces. The girl was pretty and young, with chocolate brown hair that hung past her shoulders and ivory skin.

She looked pampered, the kind of girl you expect to find lounging beside the pool of a yacht club. She wore a white lab coat, which she left unbuttoned over a low-cut dress. I got a clear view of the tops of her breasts when she fastened me onto the gurney.

"He's looking at your tits," said the man.

"Franklin, he can't move his head, and he can't move his eyes," said the girl. This time her exasperation showed.

"So you moved your tits where he could see them?" the man asked.

"You're such an ass," the girl answered.

"At least I'm not giving peep shows," the man said. He was short and muscular, with a face like a movie star. He had green eyes and blond hair that he kept patting into place. I swear, he was like a specking woman, touching his hair, brushing it with his fingers. I'd only seen the man for a moment, and already I knew that the bastard obsessed about his appearance.

He might have been thirty years old; and despite his fascination with himself, he gave off a menacing air. There was something unstable about him. He was calm and joking with the girl, but under the surface, I sensed he was ready to explode.

"Leave him alone," said the girl. She sensed what I had about the guy. He scared her.

The man stuck a finger in one of my nostrils and turned my head so I was facing him. He said, "They don't want me to hurt you, asshole. If they find a bruise on you, I'll be in deep shit."

Then he placed his hand so that his palm covered my mouth as he pinched my nose. I could not breathe or struggle.

"Franklin, stop it," the girl said. "Stop it!"

He pulled his hand from my mouth, then he leaned so low that our faces almost touched, and he said, "See that, asshole. I can kill you with one hand behind my back."

He stood, laughed, and fixed his hair. He said, "Look, Sunny, he's drooling. Think he's drooling for you?"

I could not see her reaction; she had stepped out of my field of vision. I heard her say, "Go away."

"Tell you what, Sunny, you and me… why don't we do a little dance on that gurney once he's through with it."

"Get specked," she said.

He laughed, and said, "Exactly."

Of all the people I had met up to this point in my life, this "Franklin" was the one I wanted to kill the most. I lay on that cold gurney, on my back, my face pulled to one side. I could not control so much as a muscle in my body. I could not swallow. Drool leaked from my mouth.

Trying to sound professional and in control, the girl, Sunny, said, "He's on the table. I can take it from here."

"Oh, but he's so much fun. I want to stay."

"Do I need to report you? What do you think Silas will say if I tell him you're endangering the program? What do you think he'll say when I tell him that it's your fault that Wayson is starting to remember?"

"Maybe he'll let me kill him," Franklin said. He tried to sound confident, but I heard worry in his voice.

So did the girl. She said, "Do you think he'll have you transferred or shot? Maybe he'll flush you through the moon pool with the rest of the garbage."

"Just when do you think you are going to talk to Silas?" the bastard asked.

"Tonight," Sunny said, sounding confident.

"What makes you think you'll live that long? Who's going to protect you? All you have is the dummy, and he can't even protect himself. I could kill you in front of him, and he wouldn't remember. I could kill you and say he did it."

"Are you threatening me?"

"Take it any way you like," he said. "You want rough, I can give you rough. You want sweet, baby, I can be sweet. I'll give it to you any way you like."

Having shown he was not afraid, the bastard turned and strutted out of the cell. I was able to see him leave only because he had turned my head in the right direction.

The girl said, "Don't worry about Franklin. He won't hurt you. He can't touch you. You are the most important man down here, Wayson."

The girl... Sunny, wheeled the gurney down a brightly lit hall and into a long, large room. The tables and furniture reminded me of an operating room, but the place was huge.

There was a row of occupied incapacitation cages along the wall. Incapacitation cages weren't really cages, they were gurneys with electric diodes. The men on those gurneys, all of them clones, lay motionless, rendered helpless by electricity channeled from the gurney into the napes of their necks. The electricity made their muscles contract.

I looked at the men as she wheeled me past. They were dressed in surgical gowns, their legs stretched out, their feet a shoulder's width apart. If they'd been standing instead of lying down, I would have described them as being at "parade rest."

Someone had implanted metal filaments into the necks of the men on the incapacitation cages. The filaments channeled the electricity into their spines so that even a small electrical charge left them helpless. They were aware of everything around them and paralyzed from the neck down. As the girl rolled me past them, a couple of the clones even muttered something.

"It would be so much easier on everyone if you were more like them, Wayson," Sunny said. "But don't worry, we won't treat you like that. We want to keep you perfect. No holes. No burns. No wires. You see, Wayson, you get VIP treatment. You're very important to us."

We passed rows and rows of men on gurneys. There might have been a thousand of them. There might have been fifteen hundred. *Fifteen hundred less two*, I thought. *We lost two men in the grand arcade.*

She rolled me into a private room, and whispered, "We don't want anyone to interrupt us, dear." She stroked my arm, then she reached her hand into my pants.

Under other circumstances I might have enjoyed her attentions.

Her hands were smooth and warm and soft, and she knew all the right spots. But I did not like her taking advantage of my paralysis. The term "rape" came to mind. So did the term "violated," but those were not terms Marines used to describe their situation.

If I had not been paralyzed, I might have willingly joined in… and yet… and yet… there was something in the back of my mind, something subconscious, maybe even deeper seated than the subconscious. I hated this woman. She repulsed me. And I feared her, too.

She was beautiful and her touch was warm and she had protected me from Franklin, but I hated her; and it wasn't just that she had captured me.

"Don't worry about Franklin. He won't hurt you. I won't ever let him hurt you."

I felt her warm hands around my genitals. If it weren't for the feeling of nausea and helplessness, it might have been erotic. She squeezed a couple of times until my body began to react, and then I felt a sharp, stabbing pain that did not go away. She had clamped something cold and sharp to my scrotum.

She leaned over me so that her face was an inch from mine, and she smiled. "There now, that wasn't so bad." She moved her mouth to my ear, and whispered, "You know, I don't have to massage you like that."

She kissed me, not on the lips but on the forehead.

I was raised in an orphanage for clones. Before I learned that I was a clone, I believed that I had once had a mother and a father, and I used to dream about my mother kissing me on the forehead, right between my eyes, in the very spot that this woman had just kissed me.

Next she strung a long, thin breathing tube beside the gurney. She clipped the tube to the bottom of my nose.

She said, "This isn't going to be pleasant, Wayson. But lucky you, you won't remember a thing."

The pain was so searing, that I thought my eyes might roll out of their sockets. The world seemed to turn to the color of lightning, but I managed to hold on to one thought... one thought... *Anything that can be programmed can be reprogrammed.*

During my last instant of awareness, I realized that I was what had been programmed. I was a clone.

14

I woke up in a cell. Even before I opened my eyes, I knew it would be a civilian facility instead of a brig. I kept my eyes shut and eked out the details from the fused clay of my brain. The room would be small with no windows and a rubberized airtight seal around the door. The air would come through a ridge of discreet vents at the base of the wall. There would be a toilet with chrome pipes and a ceramic sink. There would be a beautiful blue-eyed woman with a soft smile who would be kind to me, but her kindness came with pain. Her touch was warm and filled with venom. There would be a man who wanted to torture me.

I opened my eyes and sat on my rack.

The room was precisely as I had imagined... not remembered, imagined. To the best of my knowledge, I had never entered this cell; but here I was. I must have been in here before, or I would not have known the details. Maybe I woke up as the pretty woman and the sociopath dragged me in.

What other details could I think of? The man's name was Franklin. He looked like a movie star and fussed with his hair. If I could, I would hurt him; but I knew I could not hurt him. I could not understand why, but I knew I was no threat to him.

I imagined a room filled with clones, too. At first I dismissed it as a stray memory from my childhood—an orphanage dormitory with hundreds of clones sleeping on rows of racks. As I tried to grab hold of the image in my mind, I saw that the clones were grown men.

"Anything that can be programmed can be reprogrammed," I whispered. Then I added something else. I said, "Even me."

Something had happened to me. Somebody had done something to me, and they had tried to erase it from my memory; but I had held on to these images.

In my head, people and emotions ran together. The girl with the liquid blue eyes represented torment, and I wanted to kill her. I wanted to kill her every bit as much as I wanted to kill Franklin. I had a strange pseudosexual fantasy about strangling her and kissing her on the forehead as she gasped for breath. The thought was repulsive and seductive at the same time.

What was happening to my mind? Was this reprogramming?

I felt weak. When I stood, the world seemed to spin. My throat did not feel dry, and I was not especially hungry. I tried to remember the last time I had eaten. I'd had a meal on the *Churchill*. Was that a day ago? Was it a month ago? Was Cutter searching for me, or had he written me off as dead?

Don Cutter had been at the meal. The bastard questioned me. He undermined my authority. I wanted to kill him. Did I hate him as much as I hated Franklin and the girl? Sunny. Her name was Sunny. I wanted to kill Sunny. I wanted to choke her. I wanted to kiss her as she gasped her last breath.

Warmth ran through my body. I was having a combat reflex. With the warmth came clarity of thought. I realized that I was supposed to hate Don Cutter. Somebody wanted me to hate him.

I was not supposed to hate Sunny. I think I was supposed to love her and fear Franklin, but I was not supposed to remember them. I was not supposed to remember this cell.

"Legion," I said to myself. "I am not Legion, I am not possessed by Legion. I am not one of the swine that ran into the sea." I whispered so softly, Sunny could not have heard me if she'd pressed her ear to my lips.

"Sunny," I said. I would kill her. I would kill Franklin. I would not kill Cutter. They were programming me to hate him, but I would not give in.

The seal around the air lock broke, and a faint chemical scent trickled in. I did not expect my body to turn limp, but a familiar feeling of helplessness entered my brain as I tumbled to the ground. I lay there, staring straight ahead, unable to do so much as blink my eyes.

The girl walked in, and so did the man. I could only see their feet, but I knew who they were. She said, "He's awake again. That's so odd. It's supposed to put him to sleep."

"Maybe he's fighting it," said Franklin. He knelt in front of me and turned my head so that my eyes stared directly into his. He was a young man, maybe in his late twenties, maybe in his thirties. He asked, "Are you putting up a fight? Are you in there?"

I remembered his face. I remembered his face vividly. He looked exactly as I expected, green eyes, jutting jaw, smooth skin. I would hold on to that face. No matter what happened, I would hold on to the image. Nothing short of death would make me forget this man's face.

"Leave him alone, Franklin. I told Silas you were bullying him," said the girl. She had tried to be friendly, and now she turned angry. They did not like each other.

Franklin stood. He reached under my arms and hoisted me onto the gurney. He was short and trim and young and strong. I weighed two hundred pounds, but he lifted me as easily as he might have lifted a child.

I was helpless. If he'd wanted to, he could have snapped my neck. Instead, he played with me. He curled his forefinger under his thumb, and then he flicked it into my open right eye. His fingernail tapped against my eyeball.

He laughed, turned to the girl... Sunny, and asked, "Do you think he knows that I did that?"

"If you scratched his eye..."

"I didn't."

"Even a bruise or a chipped tooth..."

"I did not hurt him."

"I'll wheel him to the O.R. I can take it from here," she said in a pouty voice.

"I'll be specked, you really do have a thing for him. You're hot for the breathing cadaver."

She did not say anything.

As he left, Franklin said, "Maybe I should tell Silas about the two of you."

Silas, I thought. *Remember the name Silas.* He was another person I needed to kill.

From the moment I smelled the chemicals, my combat reflex had not stopped. Now it increased to battlefield proportions.

I could feel the heat in my veins. I needed violence. Violence became more vital than breathing.

The girl walked around the table to examine me. I imagined myself strangling her. I imagined her lips forming a circle, her face turning purple, her mouth and tongue turning blue. I saw her eyes changing to glass, and I imagined myself kissing her as the death rattle escaped from her lungs. The thought was both sadistic and sexual. Cruelty and sexuality had never gone hand in hand in my thinking. I generally hated and occasionally loved but never had both feelings for anyone.

Sunny's smile was sweet, and her eyes were as liquid as I had imagined. I could lose myself in those eyes, and I saw her concern for my safety. What could she possibly have done to me? Why did I want to kill her?

She brushed the hair from my forehead, and said, "He can't hurt you, Wayson."

Her voice was soft and soothing. I caught a hint of peppermint spice in her breath. My muscles might not have worked, but my blood flowed, and my body betrayed my feelings. She reached down and stroked my crotch, and she whispered, "You're at attention."

Sunny wheeled the gurney through the halls and into a large medical facility, the one I had known we would enter, the one with rows of men. This was not like the barracks in the orphanage, it was a torture chamber. The men did not lie on military racks, they were stretched out on incapacitation cages. Fine metal filaments had been drilled into their skulls. The filaments conducted electricity into their spines. These men were alive and alert and as helpless as me.

My combat reflex increased as images lined up in my head. I remembered the operating room and some of what would happen when we entered. She would arouse me, then there would be pain. I tried to struggle, but the only struggle was in my brain. My body ignored me.

We entered a room in which we were alone. She whispered to me, then she caressed me. She rubbed me and reached into my pants. Her touch was soft and she stared into my eyes... and I fought. I could not wiggle a finger or flutter an eye, but I put up a fight in my head.

She closed her hand around me. She tugged. She rubbed.

I thought about battles. I thought about men dying on bloody fields, Marines, clones, synthetic people like me. I once had a sergeant named Tabor Shannon. He was a Liberator. He was my mentor. He died in a cave on a planet called Hubble.

Her hand was warm. She stroked. She grasped. She pulled.

My first friend in the Marines was a clone named Vince Lee. We went on leave together to Hawaii. I saved his life during the battle of Little Man. Vince and I were two of the Little Man Seven—seven survivors from a force of two thousand.

Vince always suspected that he was a clone. He took a drug called Fallzoud that enabled him to live with the knowledge that he was synthetic, but the drug made him crazy. He died on a ship called the *Grant*. I helped kill him.

"Come now, sweetheart. Relax. Relax," Sunny purred.

I once loved a girl named Ava. She was a clone of an old movie actress. When the natural-borns exiled the clones from Earth, Ava came with me to a planet called Terraneau, and she loved me; but I did not love her the way she wanted to be loved. I was restless, and I wanted revenge.

She died alone in an apartment on an evacuated planet. I left her there to die. She wanted me to leave.

Sunny pressed herself against me. I could feel her body on top of mine. Her hair fell across my neck. Her lips brushed across mine, and I inhaled her breath. It smelled of peppermint and spice.

I had a friend named Ray Freeman. I went to Seattle to find him the night I killed those three men. I did not find him. I did find him. He told me that anything that can be programmed can be reprogrammed. He said there was a back door in my neural programming. He said my conscious mind could be switched off.

CRACK. Sunny's hand slapped across my face. Because my neck was relaxed, the force of the blow spun my head to the side.

"Bastard," she said.

She grabbed my chin and turned my face so I could look at her. A tear leaked from the corner of her eye. "I protected you," she said. "Do you have any idea what Franklin would have done to you if I hadn't been there? Do you?" In her anger, she became less pretty. Her chin and forehead wrinkled, and her lips went tight. She stared at me with cold eyes.

She held up a probe. It looked like a metallic model of an infant's hand curled into a fist. "I wanted to make things good for you," she said in a silky voice that was sensuous and hateful. She brandished that probe. I did not know what it was meant to read, but I knew where she planned to clamp it.

"I shared myself."

Instead of stroking me, she gave my genitals a nasty slap. Bright pain shot into my head, but my muscles did not respond, not even when my brain told my body to curl into a ball. Sharp pain followed as she clamped the probe into place.

She said, "You won't remember any of this." Then she smiled, and added, "Next time... maybe next time I'll let Franklin do what he wants with you."

She pulled a tube into my view so I could see it before she clipped it under my nose. Chemical fumes entered my head. Pain followed.

The hormone from the combat reflex raged in my brain. Between the hormone and the chemicals, I felt like my brain would shred to pieces. A pulse of electricity tore at my groin. The electricity tied my muscles into knots. When the current stopped, my body went numb and limp. The electricity surged and ebbed, surged and ebbed, like waves on a beach, like the pain in my head, like my thoughts.

Anything that can be programmed...

The electricity seemed to jump between my testicles and my teeth, making my muscles contract in spite of my paralysis. I curled up into the fetal position. I had no control over myself.

When the electricity stopped, my body went limp. I lay on that specking table as limp as a freshly killed corpse.

The gas I had inhaled contained ammonia, that much I recognized. It burned my nose and filled my sinuses with flames. Just as every trace of thought left my brain, the combat reflex took over.

Anything that can be programmed can be reprogrammed.

Another trickle of gas floated inside my nostrils, followed by a new wave of electricity. My thoughts turned to the color of lightning; my body curled into a ball. When the jolt stopped, I went limp. A wave of nausea rolled over me, and I vomited on myself. I could not move, so I lay there, in my bile, my body trembling as a third cloud of gas entered my nostrils, and a new surge of electrical current tightened my muscles.

I passed out after ten minutes. The pain and the drug finally got me, but this time I remembered everything.

15

"You're awake already? That's probably not good for you, darling. You're fighting me, and that means we're going to need to speed things up." Sunny sounded so damn cheerful, as if she had forgotten her failings (or mine) from the night before. "I don't suppose you remember what we do here, but it's quick and painless... and I will make it worth your while once we're done."

I was weak, too weak to even sit, and my mind was fuzzy. It wasn't that I had just woken up, it was as if my brain had somehow been removed from my body. Maybe this was what near death, as opposed to death itself, felt like—as if I were a ghost hovering over my body on an operating table.

I had been scrubbed clean and was lying on a clean bed. A crisp white sheet stretched over me from my feet to my chest. There were no straps holding me down, not that restraints were needed.

As I became more aware, I realized that there was a tube running from a computer beside the bed to a clip fastened beneath my nose. Parts of my scalp felt numb. I wanted to reach up and feel them, but my arms would not have responded.

Faint odors entered my nostrils. The scent kept changing. At first I smelled organic scents like fruits and grass and oranges, things I recognized. Sunny stood by the computer and smiled down at me. Her brown hair was soft, her eyes were luminous. I felt revulsion at the sight of her, but I desired her, too.

As I breathed the chemicals, a rapid succession of images appeared in my head. I saw Don Cutter, actually saw him as if he'd appeared in the room. I saw the *Kamehameha*, the first ship on which I served. I saw planets—Earth, Terraneau, New Copenhagen, Providence Kri, Mars, Little Man, and Hubble. I saw a satellite from the old Broadcast Network, the pangalactic highway that once connected the arms of the Milky Way. The parade of images stopped on a picture of Ray Freeman.

Ray was seven feet tall, bald, and powerfully built. He was a black man. The Unified Authority had tried to do away with races, but a Japanese colony still existed. And Freeman was an outcast from a recently exterminated colony of African-American Baptists.

"What do you see?" asked Sunny.

Her computer must not have been able to read the images the scents evoked in my head, only my reactions to them. I cannot explain what made me do it, but I decided to lie. I said, "My civilian advisor."

"That's Watson, right? Isn't that Travis Watson? You've told me about him."

"No, someone else," I said.

I could see it in her eyes—she did not believe me. I felt a chill, and I wondered if I had just condemned Travis Watson to death.

The images began to flash again. They came and went in such quick succession that I did not have time to identify most of them. By the time Sunny pulled the clip from my nose, I could not hold on to a single thought.

She gently removed the clip from my nostrils, then she kissed me and pulled a series of telemetry patches from around my scalp. Her breath smelled like peppermint. Her hair felt like silk as it brushed against me.

She took a step from the bed so I could see all of her, and she removed her smock, then her red dress. She was naked beneath the dress. Then she climbed into the bed beside me, and she whispered things I did not understand into my ear, and I discovered that I had more strength and ambition than I previously imagined.

Somewhere in my mind, I imagined myself killing her.

Sunny took me to a cafeteria and told me to sit at a table. I had no trouble walking. I felt weak and lethargic, but when she told me to walk or stand or make love, I found strength and obeyed.

The cafeteria was filled with clones. They sat at tables with trays of food in front of them, but they paid no attention to their meals. Mostly, they stared straight ahead.

I sat at a table. The men around me were mostly young though a few appeared to be in their thirties. I did not check to see if I knew any of them. They were clones, just clones, just nameless, faceless, synthetic, military men, much like me.

The man sitting beside me picked up his knife. He turned it around in his hand, staring at the flat of the blade as if it were a mirror.

"Hey, he's doing it! We better stop him."

Two men in white uniforms approached the table, then they paused. One said, "No... no. Let him do it. I wanna see what it looks like. You ever seen it happen?"

The other stood mute.

The clone stared into the blade. He moved it around so that it reflected different parts of his face—an eye, his hair, his mouth.

"Yeah, that's you... just another clone," one of the orderlies said. He turned to the other and explained, "This is what happens when they fight it."

Still holding the knife, the clone rose to his feet. His body convulsed for just a moment, and the knife fell from his hand, then he crashed back to his chair and fell face-first into his food. Blood pooled in his ear.

"That's it? That's the death reflex?" The man sounded disappointed.

"That's it."

"Should we haul him out?"

"We can get him later."

They left the clone lying in his food, a thin stream of blood now leaking from his ear down to his chin.

Sunny came and placed a tray on the table in front of me. She looked at the dead clone, then called the orderlies over. In an angry voice, she asked, "When did this happen."

"Just a moment ago."

"Did you see it happen?"

"He picked up a knife and looked at his reflection."

"Are you saying you could have prevented it?"

"He did have a knife."

"Clear him away," she said in a voice that could have been either angry or sad.

She came back to me and placed a warm hand on my shoulder, and she whispered, "Eat," in my ear. "And be sure you drink the water and the juice. I don't want you getting dehydrated, Wayson. I want you healthy and strong."

After I ate, she took me to a bathroom. Then she took me to my cell and helped me into bed. She kissed me on the mouth, and said, "I'll see you soon. Now sleep."

I shut my eyes and did as I was told.

16

I knew where I was and what was happening to me. I was in a cell in Mars Spaceport. In a few minutes, my captors would pipe gas into the cell to disable me. It was supposed to knock me unconscious, but it would only paralyze me. My Liberator combat reflex was fighting the gas, pouring testosterone and adrenaline into my bloodstream, giving me more control over my thoughts than they wanted me to have. They could amputate the gland, but an operation would leave a scar, and they needed me whole.

They planned to brainwash me without using anything that might puncture my skin, not even a hypodermic needle.

Maybe if I broke a bone, I thought. They could fuse the bones together again, but an examination would uncover recently fused bones. If I broke my forearm on the sink, what would they do?

I could...

I smelled the gas and sank back on my rack. The airtight door hissed and opened. In walked Franklin. He stood over me.

The combat reflex started immediately. It was strong. My head was even with his knees, but I found I could move my eyes enough to see his face.

He glared down at me, laughed, and said, "I came early today, Harris; hope you don't mind. I thought we might have some fun together."

I looked up at Franklin. I was paralyzed and helpless, but I thought, *One day I will kill you.* Then the thought of Sunny and her sexual-sadistic obsession entered my brain, and I amended my objectives. *One day I will kill you both.* The thought gave me peace.

I knew that without Sunny protecting me, Franklin could kill me when he chose to. No one would stop him. I couldn't even speak, let alone protect myself.

He picked me up and slung me over his shoulder in a fireman's carry. I suppose it took a little exertion on his part to lift me since he groaned slightly as I flopped over his shoulder. Then he carried me to the toilet and dropped me ass first into a sitting position.

I was his work in progress. He bent over and studied me from several angles, then he took a moment to fiddle with his hair before pulling my pants down to my ankles. He smiled, said, "Don't get any funny ideas," then pulled my underwear down as well.

He studied me as if he were a sculptor. I was like a doll or a mannequin that he could pose as he wished. He spread my legs so that my groin was exposed. Then he sat me up straight, and said, "You know, if I wanted to cut your balls off, I could do it. If I wanted to kill you and make it look like you committed suicide, I could do it. Without that dumb bitch to protect you, you're just a toy, Mr. Liberator."

I could not speak so I said nothing, but my thoughts centered on murder.

"One of your buddies died this morning. He had a death reflex. I hear he was sitting right next to you, and I bet you didn't even notice. Some killer you turned out to be, Harris. The way I hear it, you sat there and watched your buddy die."

I did not believe what he said about a clone's dying. I could remember almost everything that happened. I now had a clear understanding about what Sunny did to me when she wheeled me into the operating room. I knew about the electricity and the gas.

Franklin said, "Sunny says you're fighting the treatment. I think she's making it up. She just wants more time with you... psychotic bitch."

He thought for a moment, then he said, "You know what... Let's see if you remember this." He lowered his pants and urinated into my face, then he laughed. He was sitting on my rack, pointing at me and laughing, when Sunny arrived.

Franklin had posed me so that I faced the door. He probably wanted me to see Sunny's reaction when she entered the cell. So there I sat with my pants and my underwear down around my ankles, urine dripping down my face.

Franklin had the cruel laugh of a teenage thug. "Look at that, Sunny, I made a living sculpture."

Without saying a word, Sunny turned and started to march out of the cell. Franklin grabbed her arm, and she slapped him hard across the face. He said, "You're not going to tell anybody."

"Like hell I'm not," she said, and she pounded her fists into his chest. He was short but strong. Her fists bounced off him as if they were balloons.

"What do you think Silas is going to say when I tell him how you've been servicing the clone?" Franklin asked. "I watched you last night. It looks like you're losing your touch."

She started to slap him across the face, but Franklin caught her hand. He asked, "Do you do that with all the clones, or are you giving the Liberator special treatment?" He was still gripping Sunny's wrist when she slammed her knee into his groin.

She said, "I have work to do."

Franklin might have been strong, but he wasn't ready for that shot to the balls. He slumped to the floor. He was still on the floor, when Sunny said, "I spoke to Silas this morning. I told him about the way you have been bullying my patients. He says I can do what I want with you.

"If you ever touch this man again, Franklin, I will have you flushed out of the moon pool. You might want to think about that."

125

Then she rolled the gurney over to the toilet. She lowered the bed so it was below my knees and tilted me onto it. Sparing one last glance at the man sprawled on the floor, she raised the gurney and pushed me out of the cell.

17

Sunny pulled my shirt and pants off my body. "I hope you're not shy," she joked as she took out a hose and ran warm water over me. "I'm not sure how much you remember, darling, but I've seen every bit of you quite a few times."

I lay helpless on the gurney as she toweled me dry, and said, "Look at this. Look at what that jackass did to you." She paused for a moment, then she added, "I'll make sure Franklin never comes near you again." She rubbed my shoulders and hugged me.

I had that image in my head, Sunny's face as I strangled her. I could see her lips darkening and her swollen tongue leaving her mouth as her eyes bulged. I saw myself kissing her forehead.

She was my protector, my sexual sadistic protector. Franklin was a wolf waiting to snap me up, and Sunny was my shepherd. She led my kind to still waters, and shaved us, and butchered us for meat. If sheep had any brains at all, they would fear wolves and hate shepherds.

As she rolled me to the operating room, I tried to work my muscles. I could not sit or stand or run. I could not make a fist; but I had the ability to move my eyes and tense my shoulders. I could harden my biceps and forearms. I tightened the muscles in my neck and turned my head. I wasn't able to hold my head up, but I turned my chin. It wasn't much, but it was everything.

She wheeled me past the other clones and into the room where we were alone, then she began the process the same way she had before. *How many times have I done this?* I wondered.

This time I allowed my body to react. I hated this woman, but she was my protector. I needed to keep her on my side.

She played with me until she was happy. There was very little difference between her and Franklin. He bullied me while I was paralyzed and helpless, and she seduced me. As far as I was concerned, I would gladly have killed either one of them... and yet my reaction to this woman went beyond that to somewhere disturbing. I fantasized about her gasping and dying as I strangled her at the same time I fantasized about holding her, caressing her, kissing her.

Maybe her psychosis was contagious.

"You are more cooperative this evening, Wayson," she said. She kissed me on the cheek. I wanted more.

She stroked me, lazily running her fingers along the contours of my body. Then she brought out the clamp. She said, "You've been a good boy so I'll be gentle." She laughed, and said, "Gentle... genitals, there's got to be a pun in there."

She was more gentle than she had been the last time.

"It's sad. You and I have tonight and tomorrow, then we set you free." She sounded sad. She frowned as she strapped the hose to the bottom of my nose. The moment we had entered this infirmary my combat reflex had begun. Now that reflex went wild. I felt like I could handspring from the gurney, do a backflip, and run a three-minute mile, killing every person who crossed my path.

"I wish we could have met some other way, dear," she said. "I think I would have made you happy."

The gas came first, clawing at my sinuses, then my brain. It started with a whiff of ammonia, as I remembered it would. The shit flowing up my nose flew from one scent to the next. It was a series of chemical odors, some strong, some hidden behind others. I reacted to each scent differently. Some calmed me, most made me sick... and then came the first surge of electricity, weakening me, causing my muscles to contract and pull me into the fetal position.

Something in the gas made me so sick that I vomited onto my arms and legs. I could taste the bile in my throat, but the clip across my nostrils blocked the acrid fumes from my nose.

One of the gases was worse than the others. It seemed to bore into my skull like a laser drill, like a slow-moving bullet. I wanted to scream, but I could not work my jaws. My mouth hung open.

The scent ended, then electricity jolted me again, bending me and twisting me, making me roll on that gurney. I rolled back and forth in my warm puddle of vomit.

I cannot be reprogrammed...

I cannot be reprogrammed...

I cannot be reprogrammed...

I cannot be reprogrammed...

I focused on that phrase, telling it to myself again and again even though I had no idea where I heard it.

Man, not machine, I told myself. *I am a man, not a machine. They cannot program me, I am a man.*

In my head, I saw people and places from my past. Places that meant something to me caused me pain, caused me to convulse, came with chemical stabs and jolts of electricity. I remembered Orphanage #553, the place where I grew up, and the electricity turned my thoughts to the color of lightning. The electricity made my thoughts vanish into a silver-white sheath.

Anything that can be programmed, I told myself. The chemicals and the electricity and the pain combined until I passed out.

18

I woke up knowing that the end of this adventure approached. If I did not escape before the chemicals wafted into my cell, I would not escape, not ever.

The mornings were always the same. I might have ten minutes or I might have an hour. Sooner or later, the gas would spill out of the vents along the floor of my cell, and I would lie helpless as Sunny came to collect me. She would kiss me and soothe me, and then she would torture me. Well, in the past she had tortured me. This time she would come as my executioner. She and some orderly would load me onto the gurney. It would not be Franklin; she'd fired the bastard. Sunny would talk sweetly and smile as she took me to my final reprogramming, and then only Legion would exist in my head.

I went to the toilet, rolled small wads of paper tight, and shoved them into my nose. Each of the plugs was wide enough to fill a nostril, but I crammed two plugs in each side. Maybe if I jammed enough paper up my nostrils, I would not smell the gas and would become immune to it.

I kicked the chrome fixture behind the toilet, smashing the ball of my foot against the pipe until it broke free. A foot-tall geyser of water spouted from the top of the pipe as I tore it from its base.

I expected guards to rush into the cell, but nobody came, so I sat on my rack and watched the water form a pool, then a two-inch layer on the floor of my cell. Maybe an hour had passed. I could not tell. I spent the entire time digging the jagged edge of the pipe into the side of my thigh, twisting and cutting, creating a three-inch-long gash that I hoped would need stitches. They could remove the scar with a cosmetic laser, but I doubted Mars Spaceport had that kind of equipment. If Cutter heard I had stitches in my leg, he'd ask questions.

The pain from the slicing was physical pain. It didn't go straight to my brain like the chemicals from the tubes Sunny attached to my nose. That hurt my head. This pain remained in my leg, sharp and constant, and the combat reflex it set off remained constant as well. The pain and the reflex filled my head with the need for violence. I saw myself as if I were a snake, coiled, ready to strike, ready to kill. Blood ran down my thigh, but I didn't care. As the jagged edge of the pipe cut deeper and deeper into my leg, the pain increased. So did the hormone in my blood.

This was my last chance. Whatever they had planned for me tonight, I doubted my original programming would survive it, so I twisted the pipe and I concentrated on controlling my muscles. When I went limp the night before, I still managed to flex and relax; this time, I would need to use them.

I had no idea how much time had passed when it began.

The nose plugs had been a bad idea. It didn't matter whether I inhaled the gas through my mouth or nose; so long as I breathed, the gas incapacitated me. With the plugs in my nose, I did not catch that warning whiff before my body went limp.

I slumped onto my rack, and one of my feet dropped down into the layer of cold water covering my floor. The pipe, though, I managed to keep my fingers closed around it even as the strength vanished from my sagging arms.

The door hissed and opened. I envisioned myself rising from

the bed, swinging the pipe, and striking Sunny. She would see the water on the floor. It would distract her, then she would see me struggling off the bed. She would be angry, then she would see the pipe; but it would be too late.

It wasn't Sunny who walked through the hatch. It was Franklin. He looked at me and smiled. "I bet you were expecting your plaything," he said. "Sorry to disappoint you. She won't be returning."

His eyes were so intent on mine that he didn't even notice the water on the floor. A moment passed before he spotted my bloody leg, and his expression went serious. If they couldn't risk a hypodermic needle penetrating my skin, the inch-wide hole I had carved in my thigh might be a deal-breaker.

Franklin looked around the cell. The bastard stared at the geyser coming from the toilet. He grinned, and said, "You've been busy."

This is it. This is the moment, I thought. I focused my thoughts on the hormone flooding my veins and the pain in my thigh, and I launched myself at him. I wanted to leap from the cot, crack him across his skull, and drown him; but the most I could manage was to step into the water and stand on my sagging legs with the pipe hidden behind my back.

The dumb speck still had not pieced it all together. He looked at me, brushed back his hair, and said, "Able to stand up, are you?" He wore the same movie-star smile he'd had when he'd posed me on the toilet.

Franklin's smile vanished a moment before I stabbed the bloody end of the pipe into his forehead.

He shrieked and fell into the water, as I stumbled out of the cell.

Had I been more sure of my strength, I would have drowned the bastard or bashed his head with the pipe. There was nothing I wanted more than to kill him; but weakened as I was, I wasn't sure I could win a fight with a three-year-old. Lifting the pipe wore me out. I didn't have strength enough to keep swinging, so I ran, not knowing whom I could turn to if I managed to escape.

I had no allies in Mars Spaceport. Colonel Riley was a

traitor, possibly brainwashed the same way they'd been trying to brainwash me. Gordon Hughes might help me; but I thought he would be too weak an ally. Like me, he was just another inmate on death row.

In her own way, Sunny was worse than Franklin.

I found a control panel with buttons and levers and cameras outside my cell. Its workings were labeled, but in an unreadable language. I recognized the letters but not the words.

Inside the cell, Franklin lay on his back on the wet floor. If I went in... If I turned him on his stomach... if I forced his face into the water... I could place my hands on the back of his head and press all of my weight down on them.

The bastard stirred and moaned. One of his legs rolled.

I needed to make a choice. If that bastard caught me, he would kill me. I could try to drown him. I could try to hide. He lifted an arm and rubbed a hand against his damaged face.

I stumbled away as fast as I could.

As I headed down the hall, I heard sloshing behind me. It did not sound like he had made it to his feet yet. He yelled, "Come back here, you specking son of a bitch!"

There was a silent pause. A moment later he screamed, "Speck! You speck! You cut me! You specking bastard, you cut me!"

The hall was dim... damn near dark. I ran a few steps, walked a few steps, and staggered on. My brain felt like it was twisting inside my head. Needing to rest, I promised myself I would sleep for two days straight when I made it out of here. *If I made it out.*

I would not need to run far. If I was right, and this was the spaceport, there would be people. There were people everywhere. I did not have the strength to run very far, but I would not need to. If I made it out of this holding area, I would find crowded halls and hide among the picnickers and rest. What other choice did I have?

I held on to the pipe as I stumbled past the row of dark, empty cells that neighbored mine. All the while, Franklin continued screaming, yelling for me to come back, swearing that he would murder me. I should have stayed at the control panel and tried to seal him in. Maybe I should have rolled the dice and tried to drown him. It was too late to go back.

The cell doors all hung open, the rooms inside as dark as night until I reached the final door. Light shone from that final cell. As I approached it, I raised the pipe above my head in case someone waited inside for me. Then I saw her body.

Sunny lay on the floor exactly as I had imagined her so many times. Her face had turned purple. Her lips had turned blue and formed a circle around her swollen tongue. Her vacant eyes stared up at me.

"Where are you?" Franklin screamed from the cell.

Franklin had ripped Sunny's clothes, torn her dress and lab coat to shreds that hung from her shoulders.

I wanted to kill him. I wanted to return to the cell and beat the son of a bitch's head in.

Sunny was psychotic, and she would have destroyed me, but she had saved me as well. I felt something for her, maybe even sympathy; and I realized that I would have saved her if I could have. Had there been time, I might have kissed her dead forehead just as I had fantasized so many times.

In the fantasies, I had crushed her throat and killed her. Now that I actually saw her dead, I felt sorry for her.

I heard splashing and knew Franklin had finally climbed to his feet. He was hurt, though, hopefully badly hurt. The way I had stabbed that pipe into his forehead should have messed up his balance. He would be stronger than me but not much faster. I had probably bought myself time. After one last glance at the girl who had helped me and tortured me, I shuffled into the darkness.

"Where are you, you specking son of a bitch!"

If Franklin caught me, gurneys and gases would be the least of my worries; and that was fine with me. I'd fought enough wars. I was going to die sometime; that was something I accepted. Having my brain gutted and becoming a puppet, that was far worse.

"Harrisssss!" He began shrieking like a wild animal, like an injured animal. There was not a shred of control in the voice that came from the cell.

I rounded a familiar corner and saw the sick bay that Sunny had wheeled me through those many times. It was almost empty and dark, lit only by the soft green glow from an instrument panel. Looking through the window, I saw a pile of corpses, maybe twenty of them, stacked roughly one on top of the other.

I moved like the walking wounded, leaning on walls, hunched over, my right hand still clutching that foot-long pipe, my left arm supporting my weight when I passed walls or rails. I took short steps and fought for balance. My breathing was fine, nothing wrong with my lungs. There was nothing wrong with my heart, either, except that the adrenaline in my blood had it pumping so damn fast.

The air was cold. My breath turned to steam. The bottoms of my bare feet began to stick to the iron floor as I padded on. I could not afford to stay in one place.

I kept expecting to run into other people. I expected to turn a corner and find halls packed with picnickers.

But I continued to move through one dark hall that emptied into another, then another. The place was abandoned. As I stuttered forward, I wondered where they had found so much space in the spaceport. The only explanation I had was that I was wrong about the jail itself. Maybe this was a brig, and I was still on Mars Air Force Base.

Even as I considered the possibility, I knew this had to be the spaceport. This was a civilian facility. The curved doorways, the windows along the hall, the chrome pipes in the cells... this place was built for natural-borns.

"Harris, where are you? Where are you?" Franklin's voice still had that insane tone. *KLANK! KLANK! KLANK!* Metal hitting metal. He struck the metal walls with a pipe or a hammer to get my attention.

The world started to spin as I pushed forward. I was tired and cold and dizzy from fighting against chemicals meant to paralyze me. I had no idea how they impacted my sensory perceptions. The floor seemed to rise and lower every time I lifted my feet. The walls seemed to bend and close in around me. My breath turned to steam.

I limped ahead.

"I'm coming for you, Harris. Better run. Better run!" Franklin sounded farther away, not closer. Maybe he had taken a wrong turn.

I tried to orient myself.

This had to be an area of the spaceport that was not open to the public. *There have to be people. There are people here... seventeen million. Where are they?* I thought.

I found a hall that was wide and dark, and I followed it. Here and there I saw signs on the walls; but the dark lighting and the drugs played tricks on my perception. I recognized the letters, but the words made no sense.

I had a trace of a memory, something I had dreamed or possibly something I heard while drugged. I remembered a conversation with Don Cutter. His name entered my head, and a wave of hate rolled over me. I tried to resist the feeling. It was all part of the brainwashing. They had trained me to hate my friend.

Have to keep moving, I told myself. If I could buy myself more time, my strength would return.

The sign over the door said: PISCINE LUNE. Was it a hallucination?

I stopped for just a moment and I stared at it. The drugs had addled my brain. I'd never been dyslexic, not until that moment; but the letters I knew, the words I did not.

My head throbbed. The walls around me seemed to bulge and shrink as if inhaling and exhaling. The floor seemed to roll under my feet. I could hear Franklin behind me, far behind me.

I pushed through the door.

There was something in the air; I breathed it in, and it made me dizzy. The room I had entered could not exist, not on a spaceship and certainly not on Mars. It was a chamber as large as any auditorium I had ever seen, bigger than the ones back in the orphanage.

The metal walls formed a dome, and in the center of that dome sat a pool the size of a football field.

The pool was nearly as flat and smooth as a mirror. The only light in the room was the yellow glow rising out of the pool. Powerful lights shone under that water.

I closed the door behind me and stole over for a closer look. The water was brutally cold but not frozen. A metal catwalk spanned the width of the surface. Placed a mere five feet above the water, it was slick and the iron was cold and some kind of gritty white canker had formed on it.

The moon pool, I reminded myself. Sunny had said "moon pool" and I had not put two and two together. I had heard the term in school and filed it away as trivial. Boats and submarines and underwater buildings had moon pools, open areas that faced down into the water. The water didn't come in because the air pressure balanced it out.

As I stepped onto that catwalk, I looked up and saw a series of cranes hanging above my head.

If I hid in this chamber I would slowly freeze to death. With my body still weak, I could not swim. If Franklin threw me in the water, I would drown. The entire room, with its watery floor and mystic lighting, made me nervous. I peered down into the pool and saw that beneath its lit mouth, it was as dark and mysterious as death, as vast and heartless as outer space.

I backed away from the pool and out the door. If I ran into Franklin at that moment, I might have welcomed a swift end. He did not scare me as much as the chilly and dark depths of that pool. Franklin was in a rage and had lost control. If he caught me, he would kill me, and everything would end, but that was something I could understand. Those dark waters represented the unknown. Somewhere in my subconscious, the moon pool and reprogramming were almost equivalent, unfathomable depths, unknowable mysteries, the end of existence.

"Harrissss!" the voice was far off, but moving closer. It had a frantic quality.

Some of my strength had returned, and I found I could walk better. I could support my own weight.

I followed the corridor that circled the outside of the enormous domed chamber. The way would have been completely dark except for little lights built into the wall at knee level. I traveled from one light to the next, keeping my steps as silent as possible.

I came to a door, eased it open, and stopped breathing.

There in front of me, spread wide and dark and endless, was an entire abandoned city complete with streets and buildings. This wasn't Mars Spaceport. This place was large enough to hold a dozen Mars Spaceports.

I knew where I was now. I was no longer on Mars, or even in space at all. I was in one of the abandoned Cousteau deep-sea colonies.

19

Four hundred years ago, when the Unified Authority had just started exploring the galaxy, a nation called France began an undersea colonization initiative called the Cousteau Oceanic Exploration Program. The ocean, according to the French, was closer than outer space, more safely traveled than outer space, and brimming with life. To prove their point, they constructed three underwater domes in which they nested enormous cities, each of them large enough to house a population of three million people.

Four hundred years had passed, and this fossil still stood. The French abandoned the Cousteau program in 2115. Over the last few centuries, mankind established and lost colonies in the six galactic arms. Man had conquered space and been chased back to Earth, where France's underwater cities still stood.

Somewhere along the line, I had dismissed them as no more real than Cibola or Mount Olympus. Now mythology had caught up with me.

The top of the dome might have been four hundred feet above me. A halo of pale light shone down from its curvature, artificial light; sunlight could not possibly penetrate this deep in the ocean.

That much I knew. The French built their underwater cities near thermal vents, in waters several miles deep.

I looked for anything I could use to seal the door behind me, but I was in an empty street in a vacant city that had never been populated. This place had streets but no cars, apartment buildings without beds, offices without desks or workers. It was the opposite of Mars Spaceport. One hosted millions of people with nowhere to house them; the other had housing for millions and no occupants.

I walked to the nearest building, a four-story framework that had never seen walls. Looking for hiding places on its naked concrete floor, I passed through its unfinished frame. The building was all girders and framework with no place for concealment.

Advancing as slowly as a scared dog, I entered the city. Hearing nothing to suggest that Franklin had followed me out of the cell area, I realized that I now had an entire city in which to hide.

I walked into a tall building, stumbled to a stairwell around which no walls had been built, and climbed until I was so tired that I would have had to crawl to continue. My strength was spent. All of the hormones from my combat reflex had worn off. My muscles ached, and my brain burned.

Somewhere behind me, a door slammed. In the surreal stillness of the abandoned city, it sounded like a gunshot.

Distant shouts. "Harris. Harris! HARRRRISSSSS!"

Sitting four floors up and far away, I leaned against a wall and fell asleep.

Nothing woke me. No sounds. No movements. No lights. My sleep had been deep, and when it ended, it ended on its own terms. When I finally woke up, I felt stronger. How long had I been down here? How long had it been since that half-remembered conversation when I sent Cutter away?

First things first: *Where the hell could I find shoes?* The floors in this place were so specking cold that the skin on the bottoms of my feet seemed to fuse to the ground.

I sat up and reoriented myself. The building was a latticework of beams and frames with concrete floors and open stairs. The atmosphere was dark, with a faint haze of phosphorous lumens coming from the dome above.

The dome could have been made of glass, or it might have been made of steel or even cement. It didn't matter. The French built their cities in the deepest oceanic troughs and trenches. Down this far, the ocean was as devoid of light as any underground cavern.

I went down the stairs and toured the unfinished city. Now that I had rested, I saw my surroundings more clearly.

The silence was absolute. The air was cold and dry. There was not so much as a breeze to disturb the peace. I was hungry, trapped in a world that was vast and sterile, relatively safe but absolutely empty. I could stay here and starve or return to the cells for food, warmth, and destruction. Franklin waited there. Given rest and nourishment, I could kill the bastard; but waiting out here, I would only grow weaker.

I was not starving, but I was hungry. I had no idea how many days had passed since my last meal. Though I could not remember eating, I had never been hungry as a prisoner. Maybe Sunny fed me, or maybe the chemicals deadened my internal sensors.

I needed shoes, food, and water.

The French would not have started a project like this without first installing a desalinization plant, maybe several; but I had no idea how I would find it.

My thoughts ran wild. *What if Franklin left me here?* He might do just that. Instead of chasing me into the unfinished city, he could abandon me deep beneath the sea. The bastard could report my death—assuming he reported to anyone. To Silas, I reminded myself. Sunny had threatened him with a man named Silas. She said Silas might flush Franklin out a moon pool. Now I knew what she meant.

I knew something else. I knew that I was more valuable to Silas than Franklin. I was the lynchpin in Silas's plan. Franklin was just a cog on a gear, useful but expendable.

Unless he wanted to answer to Silas, Franklin would not abandon me, and he would not kill me. We were stuck with each other; but there was one difference between us: I didn't worry about angering the mysterious Silas. Let Silas come after me. Once I finished with Franklin, maybe I'd go for a swim in the moon pool. That sounded better than starving to death.

The thought of killing Franklin made me happy, but I was cold and though my strength was returning, it had not returned. As I thought about this, my head started to hurt, and I went back to sleep.

Once again, I woke with no way of knowing how long I had been out.

The terms "day" and "night" had no application in a man-made bubble two miles beneath the sea. To people living in this trap, the sun and moon would sound as mythological as this city had to me.

I woke quickly but rose slowly, wondering why I should even bother rising from my bed. I probably would not find food or water; and even if I did, how would I protect myself from Franklin? Even if I found food and killed Franklin, I'd still be stuck on the bottom of the ocean.

I remembered fantasizing about going for a fatal swim in the moon pool; but I could not do that. I could not kill myself, not with my neural programming. Liberators had more autonomy than other clones, but it did not include suicide.

I played a game to cheer myself up. I imagined the ways I could kill Franklin. *Strangle him*, I thought, just like he had strangled Sunny. *Beat him to death. Drown him in the moon pool.* As he sank, I would tell him, "Give my regards to Sunny."

Then I came up with the winner. *Throw him from a building.* Throw him from a third- or fourth-floor landing, just high enough so he'd break an arm or a leg or maybe both. Then I could haul his whining carcass back up the stairs and throw him again. If I dropped him carefully, he might last three or four tossings before his neck finally broke.

When I stood, I found that my legs were strong, but the blood rushed to my head. I waited through a moment of dizziness in which I nearly stumbled, then my head cleared, and I walked to the ledge and tried to make sense of the city below. The streets formed a dark maze of lines and boxes. I had hoped that the designers had laid their project out as logically as a checkerboard with rounded edges. They hadn't. Instead of spokes and rings, the streets formed cul-de-sacs and spirals. The men who designed this dome had created a community, not a military base, the bastards.

Under normal circumstances, I might have admired that decision—at a time when I was not trapped and hungry.

I looked for lights in the city. If Franklin was looking for me, he'd use a flashlight, or he might illuminate a section of the city… or he might use the night-for-day lenses in the combat armor of a dead Marine. Just because he had the armor did not mean he could use the complicated optical interface, but I suspected he knew how to use it. Franklin was part of something bigger and more organized than a gathering of fanatics. Behind the rage was a regimented logic. He could have killed me anytime he wanted, but he'd waited. He was undoubtedly a criminal, but a war criminal. He might have been a spy, an assassin, an interrogator, or a mercenary, someone with intelligence training.

If Franklin did come after me in combat armor, I'd have another reason to kill him… for the temperature-controlled bodysuit and the armored boots. I was so specking cold, and that left me weak.

And then I saw it. The key to understanding this city was not in the streets, it was in the sky. What I had mistaken for random lights were actually markers. The city was an octagon with eight triangular sectors, each marked by a phosphorous pillar in the sky.

As I figured out how to read the sky, the streets made sense. I shuffled down the stairs to the street level and exited through the rear of the building. In recon training, I had learned to stay in the shadows when possible. Now, it was impossible to leave them. This entire world was shadow.

I cut through unfinished buildings and moved along the narrowest streets. After an hour, I found what I was looking for, a doorway leading into the circular, dark hallway that led around the moon pool.

I was returning to the wing that I had escaped. I had no choice. Franklin and Sunny and fifteen hundred reprogrammed clones ate food there. They drank water.

The air was cold, colder than I remembered.

I followed the hall to its end and entered the port with its glowing moon pool. I approached the bridge that ran across the top of the pool. I could not help myself. The moon pool fascinated me because it opened into the ocean with its bottomless depths. Held back by an invisible cushion of air were Earth's final secrets, creatures that glowed and fish and squid more strange than anything man had encountered in space.

I stepped on that metal catwalk, trying to ignore the way its cold metal bit my feet. I was halfway across when I stopped and stared down into the illuminated depths.

Had those lights burned for the last four hundred years?

Indistinct shapes moved in the water below me. I understood the cycle. The light attracted swarms of small creatures. The availability of small creatures attracted minor predators that hovered just outside the light. Larger predators lurked lower still.

As a teenager, I studied biology in the orphanage, but that class had more to do with venereal disease than fish. The instructor mentioned something about sharks and giant squid. I imagined a squid staring up at me through the darkness, a big one, something sixty feet long with tentacles the size of fire hoses. I imagined it blending into the shadows, staring up at me from the darkness, ready to pull me into the inky depths. Ready to hold my body with two tentacles while tearing off each of my limbs with others.

Was I scaring myself? Hell yes.

Whatever Franklin and his friends had planned, I could ruin

it for them with a short leap from this bridge. I would land in the water. Maybe a shark or a squid would kill me, maybe I would freeze or drown or both. The creatures that lived in those blackened depths represented the unknown to me; they gave shape to my fears.

I had vague memories of the tortures Sunny had inflicted upon me. What she had done to me was worse than drowning. If Franklin caught me, it would start all over again. Given a choice, I would take a few moments of water filling my lungs over hours of torture, then betraying my friends.

But I could not kill myself, my programming would not allow it. Liberators had been designed to fight an unknown enemy in the unexplored center of the galaxy. We had been designed for dark duty. The people who made my kind needed an army of soldiers that would continue fighting no matter what happened, no matter what they ran into.

My knees buckled, then they gave. As I fell down on that cold, metal catwalk, I tried to catch myself on the rail; but my arms did not respond. I fell flat on my face.

Franklin stood at the edge of my vision. "I'm not done with you," he said.

I could not turn my head to follow him, so he vanished from my view as he stepped onto the catwalk. I heard his footsteps, the soft soles of his shoes padding on the cold metal until he stood over me. He said, "You should have jumped, Harris; but then you couldn't. I'll fix that."

He did not kick me as I expected he would. He did not urinate on me. He just stared down at me as I lay on that bridge, then everything went dark.

PART II

THE LOST SHEEP RETURN

20

Travis Watson entered Admiral Don Cutter's office with a casual air that the admiral interpreted as a swagger. As a civilian, Watson seemed to see himself as exempt from military protocol. Cutter did not share that view. He asked, "When was the last time you heard anything from Harris?"

Harris must have taught the boy something. He knew enough military culture to remain standing until invited to sit.

"Have a seat," Cutter grunted.

Watson sat.

Cutter didn't have anything he specifically needed to discuss with Watson; but he wanted to vent his anger on somebody close to Wayson Harris. Watson was the closest target. Had Harris been around, Cutter would have gone after him instead; but Harris's communications went dark two days ago.

Sometimes Harris did not bother checking in. He was like a cat. He prowled and fought his battles, then returned to base when he felt like it.

Cutter wanted to box somebody's ear. Watson might have been an innocent bystander/civilian, but he was Harris's adjutant. In the admiral's mind, Watson's connection to Harris made him fair game.

"What do you hear from Harris?" he asked, knowing full well Watson had not heard anything.

"I haven't heard from him," said Watson. "Have you heard anything?"

Have you heard anything… sir, Cutter thought. He said, "The reason we left Mars was because the general ordered us out of the space lanes."

"He ordered us out?" asked Watson. He looked confused.

Cutter took some satisfaction in the perplexed expression on Watson's face. *At least the boy knows who is in charge*, he thought. "Ordered us out," he repeated.

"Admiral, maybe I don't understand the chain of command. Harris told me you gave the orders."

Cutter heard this, and his tension eased again. He said, "I thought maybe things were getting hot for him. When things heat up, Harris acts like a rabid dog. It's a Liberator thing."

"Did he say why he wanted us to leave orbit?"

"When Harris goes rabid, he doesn't make a lot of sense. He called my crew incompetent and told me to pack up and leave."

"He hasn't contacted me," said Watson, "not since he left for Mars."

Cutter leaned back in his chair. He stared at Watson but said nothing. He bounced the chair back gently, let it rock forward, then settle back. Finally, he said, "Maybe you can help me interpret something. Harris gave me a message he wanted me to relay to you. He said, 'Anything that can be programmed can be reprogrammed.'"

Watson shook his head, and said, "I'm not familiar with the phrase. Did he say what it's supposed to mean?"

"If he had told me what it meant, I wouldn't ask you to help me interpret it," said Cutter, smiling with a new sense of smug satisfaction. "He said that anything that can be programmed can be reprogrammed, and he said to tell you that Ray Freeman wanted you to know that."

"Ray Freeman again," said Watson. "Is Freeman on Mars?"

Cutter shrugged his shoulders. "I don't know. I don't know how he could have gotten there, but no one ever knows how Freeman does anything. The man is more mysterious than God himself."

"Admiral, I still don't know anything about Freeman—just that I wouldn't want to be trapped on a transport with him."

"I've met him," said Cutter. "He's a merc."

"A what?"

"He's a mercenary. No. Stow that. That's a euphemism. Freeman isn't a mercenary, mercenaries fight wars. Freeman's a damn sight worse than a merc. He's the scariest man alive. The bastard's eight feet tall with skin as dark as night and fists the size of rucksacks."

"You're joking, right?" asked Watson. "He sounds like a troll in a fairy tale."

"I may be exaggerating a bit," Cutter admitted.

Watson said, "He can't be any worse than Harris."

Cutter laughed. "Harris looks like a missionary next to Freeman; no, a Boy Scout. We're all babes in the woods compared to that man. He's a grenade without a pin."

"How do I find him?" asked Watson.

"Didn't you hear what I said?" asked Admiral Cutter.

"I heard you."

"And you still want to find him."

"It sounds like the only way I'm going to decode Harris's message is to find Freeman and ask him what it means."

Even warned that Freeman is dangerous, the kid wants to find him, Cutter thought. He found new respect for Watson, maybe even for Harris. Harris was the one who'd hired him. Cutter tapped a few keys on his computer, and said, "Here's the video feed of my conversation with Harris. You tell me what you think of it."

* * *

The officers aboard the *Churchill* referred to the spaces in which they rested as their "quarters" or their "billet." Watson referred to his as his "cabin." Military men spoke military jargon. Travis Watson took pride in his ignorance of military terminology.

"Anything programmed," he said to himself as he entered the room. "Computers," he whispered. *Too obvious*, Watson decided. If Harris had wanted to communicate the obvious, he would have come right out and said it.

He went to the workstation, sat, and thought, *Anything with a computer... bombs, missiles, ships, tanks, cars, clocks, the entire mediaLink*. A hijacker could use the mediaLink to send subversive messages.

You know what, he thought, *Cutter was right. Harris was irrational. He was acting like a lunatic. Maybe it was a Liberator thing. What he said, the way he was acting... and Freeman. What could Freeman have to do with any of it? When did Harris hear from Freeman? Unless he was on Mars, how would Harris have talked to him?*

But something about what Harris had said resonated with him. Something about *reprogramming things that are programmed*. Watson had watched the video feed closely. He had seen the way Harris had fought to say those words. Irrational or not, they meant something. Even if they only had meaning for Harris, he must have seen something significant in them.

It must have had something to do with weapons. The only thing Harris ever worries about is guns and weapons, Watson thought. *Weapons... If it was important to Harris, they were reprogramming weapons.*

And so he went through a litany of weapons in his head.

Guns and knives—unprogrammable. Not a problem.

Tanks and jets had computers. What would you achieve by reprogramming them? You could make them crash or blow up. You could stop them from working. Maybe you could program them to attack each other.

But why go to the trouble of reprogramming them. There would be simpler ways to sabotage a tank or a jet.

There are computers in a fighter carrier. There are lots of computers in a fighter carrier, navigation, life support, weapons systems. There had to be more computer systems. Watson knew that there had to be more computers on board this giant ship, but he could not enumerate them.

The same question occurred to him again and again: "Why bother?" If you could get close enough to the computers on a fighter carrier to reprogram them, what would prevent you from destroying the ship?

Whatever they were reprogramming, it had to be big, big enough to justify the risks... big enough to cause damage to more than just itself and the clones inside it. Big enough...

And then he lit on an idea—*Clones are programmed.* The neural programming in clones was hardly a secret; but if there was a way to reprogram them... Watson explored the idea of reprogramming clones. It seemed unlikely, but then he asked himself, *Isn't that the point? Anything, ANYTHING that could be programmed, could be reprogrammed, even the programming you'd think was sealed.*

How would you do it? he asked himself. Would you need to catch them one at a time and cut into their brains? Would you lobotomize them? That hardly seemed like a reprogramming.

He imagined an army of clones, all of them with long incisions across their skulls and bald spots where the hair would never grow. He imagined an army of zombies and laughed it off.

Then Watson considered the ramifications and the ugly possibilities—a shadow government controlling the synthetic government that appointed Earth's puppet government. The clones had been benevolent conquerors, more interested in maintaining order than avenging past wrongs. No one wants their nation conquered, but the Enlisted Man's Empire had been benign.

Watson, whose father had fought as a SEAL, recognized that the clones had plenty of reasons for wanting revenge. Though he feigned a casual air around them, he admired Harris and Cutter for the measured way they ran their empire.

Cutter had said he would send the video feed of Harris to Watson's computer.

Watson pressed an icon on his monitor and brought up his mail. The message from Cutter sat at the top. Watson ran the feed. The screen split in half, the right side tight on Wayson Harris's face, the left side not quite as tight on Cutter. At first glance, they looked like mirror images of each other.

Harris stared into the camera, waiting for Cutter to respond. He looked irritated. When the admiral answered a few seconds later, Harris looked angry enough to kill. Harris asked, "When's the last time you visited the spaceport?"

Cutter, clearly not realizing that Harris's anger was directed at him, asked, "How bad?"

"Bad. I saw a couple swapping speck on a blanket. There were people all around them, but they didn't care. Rabbits have more inhibitions than these people."

"They didn't mind the audience?" asked Cutter.

"What options did they have? You either get used to it or go eunuch. It's not like the spaceport has speck-swapping rooms you can rent by the hour."

Cutter said, "I hope you didn't stare."

Cutter and Harris were friends. Watson had seen them joking freely with each other. On this call, Harris lashed out. *"I didn't come here for fun."*

"Are you okay?" asked Cutter. He looked concerned.

"What the speck is that supposed to mean?"

"You seem tense."

"Yeah, well, you come here and see how you like it. It's not like lounging around on a spaceship."

"Spaceship?" Watson muttered. When Harris spoke about Navy ships, he generally referred to them by name or by class. Harris always referred to the *Churchill* by name or by class, a Perseus-class fighter carrier.

"Real or not real?" he asked himself aloud. It was a game he'd begun playing with himself shortly after taking the job as Harris's adjutant. It was his way of controlling the paranoia that came with the job.

On the feed, *Harris said, "These people can't even take a shit without a hundred people waiting in line behind them. They plan a day in advance just to take a shit."*

Both men remained silent, traces of anger evident in both their expressions.

"Harris, something's happening back in the spaceport. We can't reach Jackson."

"What do you mean, you can't reach him?"

"There's no Link connection. They're lost. I'm going to send down a team to look for them."

"You can't lose a specking regiment of Marines. That's like saying you misplaced a gawddamned planet. What's the matter with you?

"They're here, in the Air Force base with me. I ordered them to come, and they came."

"How did they get there?"

"What the speck do you mean, 'How did they get here?'"

"I mean, Harris, how did that regiment of Marines travel from the spaceport to the base? They didn't fly to the base. We've been watching the spaceport. None of the transports have launched. They couldn't have taken the train, you told us to shoot out the rails."

"Either you have someone asleep at the wheel, or your ship is broken, Admiral.

"They flew here. They boarded fifteen transports, and they flew here. How the speck do you miss fifteen transports? They're big. They're slow. They probably radioed in for clearance before they left the spaceport. Check your damn records.

"You know what? Don't check your records. The transports are here, my men are here, I don't give a shit what your specking records say, Cutter. I watched Jackson walk down the ramp. If

155

your records say something else, then you've got bigger problems to fix than a few missed transports."

"Maybe," said Cutter.

Damn, Watson thought as he watched the blistering. *No wonder Cutter was fuming.* Watson had seen Harris get angry; but he had never lost control like this. Harris was like a child having a temper tantrum… a homicidal child. From what Watson knew about Liberators, they killed entire populations when they lost their temper.

On the screen, *Harris said, "Listen, Cutter, I've already lost two Marines on this op. We've infiltrated Martian Legion headquarters. Okay? I'm closing in on the objective. I've almost finished what I specking well came here to do. You got that? Am I getting through to you?"*

"Yes, you are," said Cutter. His face turned red, and his expression became steely.

Harris said, "We've almost got this operation complete, and the last thing we need is for you to get in the way, so pack up your specking space patrol and get the hell out of here. Do you understand? Do you read me?"

Watson could not understand what was preventing Cutter from threatening Harris or maybe relieving him of command.

Cutter was the superior officer. He had every right to slap back.

Cutter said, "We'll clear out."

"Good move," said Harris.

He's acting like a schoolyard bully, thought Watson. It wasn't enough that he got his way; he had to have the last word and humiliate the other guy.

"Do you want me to leave Watson?"

Oh God, no! thought Watson.

"Why the speck would I want him around?" asked Harris. Then he said something so random Watson suspected that someone had edited the video feed. His face tightened as if he were fighting back pain, and he said, "Give him a message for me, would you. Tell that bastard that anything programmed can

156

be reprogrammed. You tell him that. You tell him that for me."

Watson reversed the feed and watched it again.

"Why the speck would I want him around?

"Give him a message for me, would you. Tell that bastard that anything programmed can be reprogrammed. You tell him that. You tell him that for me."

He reversed and replayed, studying Harris's face carefully, watching for any break in the transmission, anything that might suggest that Cutter or someone else had edited the feed.

There was a clock in the corner designed as a security to prove the transmission had not been altered. It ran smoothly.

"Why the speck would I want him around?

"Give him a message for me, would you. Tell that bastard that anything programmed can be reprogrammed. You tell him that. You tell him that for me."

"What the hell?" said Watson. He noted the crazed look in Wayson Harris's eyes and the way he drew back his lips. The man was either insane with anger, in pain, or both.

Watson played the remaining seconds of video feed.

"What was that?" Cutter asked. "What was your message?"

"Not my message, asshole. Tell him Ray Freeman said that."

21

The people who ran the Unified Authority had seen themselves as creating a glorious history, a history they wanted preserved for future generations. They preserved the public side of that history in an archive that could be accessed from anyplace in the galaxy using a standard mediaLink connection. More private documents were stored on government computers. Highly classified files could only be accessed inside the Unified Authority archive building, in Washington, D.C.

Information involving Ray Freeman was kept in the archive building.

The Unifieds had listed him alternately as a contractor, a fugitive, an envoy, and an enemy. The files included several video records as well as documents.

Watson found and examined several photographs of Ray Freeman.

The man was a giant. He was not eight feet tall with "skin as dark as night" and "hands the size of rucksacks," as Admiral Cutter had described him; but still, a dark-skinned giant.

In one photograph, Freeman stood beside a row of clones as they waited to enter a transport. Freeman wore combat armor, but no helmet. To Watson, who had grown up in a world devoid of ethnicities and races, the color of Freeman's skin looked like an optical illusion. He thought that perhaps Freeman was standing in a shadow. He also thought Freeman might be standing on a curb or a platform. The next photo proved both theories wrong.

In this one, Freeman, Harris, and an unknown clone stood talking. Harris was nine inches shorter than Freeman; the top of his head was even with the big man's chin. The unnamed clone was five inches shorter than Harris. His head was level with Harris's nose and Freeman's chest.

A third photograph was taken with Freeman looking away. The back of his head was covered with scars. From the back, he looked like a burn victim.

The archive collection included a list of video feeds labeled with names and dates and marked EXPEDITED. The first one was marked, JOHN TURNBOW—EXPEDITED, 03/06/03. Watson ran the feed and immediately recognized it as a view seen through the computerized scope of a sniper rifle. Readouts along the edge of the scope tracked wind velocity—fifteen miles per hour—and distance—2.3 miles. As the time stamp along the bottom of the screen ticked off seconds, lines closed in around the target, a man walking toward a car.

A voice so low that it reminded him of a kettledrum asked, "Do you confirm identity as John Turnbow?"

"Identity confirmed. Expedite."

Without responding, Freeman fired.

The rifle made a sound no louder than a muffled cough. Having never witnessed a murder or an execution, Watson felt his breath catch in his throat. For a moment, Watson thought the bullet had missed. One second passed and nearly another, then a bright red halo appeared around the target's head, and he fell.

That was it. From this distance, it looked like Freeman might have shot him with red paint.

Watson found one file marked, EXPEDITED—MORGAN ATKINS, 11/08/09. "Morgan Atkins?" he whispered.

Until that moment, Watson had believed that Atkins, whose fanatical followers had nearly overthrown the Unified Authority, had merely disappeared. His prurient interest overpowering him, Watson booted the feed.

The video was captured using night-for-day lenses to compensate for the lack of ambient light. Up ahead, a shuttle sat on a runway surrounded by a small army of guards.

Watson wondered if he was looking through the lenses of a combat visor.

"Are we on?" the now-familiar voice asked.

"Yes."

"Yes," just "yes." That simple word had signed the death warrant of one of the most famous figures in human history. Watson sat transfixed.

There he was, the legendary Morgan Atkins, looking old but very much alive. Atkins, with a stooped back and a flowing white beard that reached below his chest, walked at the head of an entourage looking for all the world like a modern-day messiah out for a walk with his apostles.

Still looking distinguished, despite the beard and degradations of age, Atkins stopped to speak to the soldiers guarding the runway. As he stood there, Freeman held out a handheld scope and captured his image. He asked, "Identity confirmed?"

A voice said, "Confirmed. Expedite."

Atkins spoke for several seconds with one of the guards. They shook hands. The guard said something, and Atkins laughed and responded.

A device in Freeman's helmet measured the distance. Atkins was 323 feet away.

Freeman climbed out from behind the boxes he'd been using for cover. Nobody noticed him until he started running toward the shuttle; by that time, it was too late.

A series of small explosions went off around the landing strip. These were not large detonations, just small geysers of flame that shot ten feet up. Hoping to protect their leader, some of the members of Atkins's entourage pushed him into the shuttle as bombs exploded and guards fell dead. The explosions continued for over a minute, a chaos of fire and smoke that sent bodies flying into the air.

The shuttle could not drive across the runway, not in all of the chaos caused by the bombs. Freeman darted into the smoke and flame without hesitation, paused long enough to fire shots at the last of the guards, and leaped into the shuttle as the hatch began to close.

Three men with guns stood just inside the door of the shuttle. Freeman shot them before they could even aim their weapons. He gave no pause to mercy. He simply stepped through the doorway and shot them.

A man ran at Freeman with a knife. Freeman shot him in the head. Atkins sat unarmed. He looked terrified. Freeman shot him without saying a word. Then he went to the cockpit. He grabbed the pilot by his head and snapped his neck, then threw his dead body out of the chair.

The feed ended.

When it came to murder, Freeman seemed utterly indifferent. He did not speak to his victims; nor did he offer them the chance to surrender. From what Watson could tell, Freeman's sense of morality belonged only to the people who had contracted his services.

Watson scrolled through the EXPEDITED files. The last one was marked, WAYSON HARRIS, 12/18/16. He stared at the monitor in disbelief, realizing that until that moment, he had considered Harris indestructible. Now Watson decided that if it came to a war between Freeman and Harris, he would bet on Freeman.

Seeing a file with Harris's name on it, Watson wondered how Harris had survived. Maybe Freeman had killed him and the Harris leading the Enlisted Man's Empire was a clone of a clone. Not knowing much about cloning technology, he had no idea if clones could be created with experiences and knowledge imprinted in their brains.

That thought brought him back to where he began. *If clones are programmed, maybe their intelligence can be replicated*, he thought as he booted the video feed.

The feed showed a Johnston R-27, a civilian craft capable of both space and atmospheric travel, landing on a small runway at night. The R-27 rolled past a row of military transports and stopped near a fence. The door of the R-27 opened and a man carrying a rucksack climbed out.

The scene was recorded through the computerized scope of a sniper rifle, possibly the same one Freeman had used when he shot John Turnbow. The lines closed in around the target.

"Do you confirm identity as Wayson Harris?"

"Identity confirmed. Expedite."

Freeman fired the shot, hitting the man square in the chest. A woman screamed. The file ended.

As Wayson Harris's aide, Watson had the authority to launch an "all-points alert" search, commandeering every camera on every satellite orbiting Earth. The cameras and satellites performed their normal functions, but Freeman's image had been added into their instructions set. Security cameras in police departments, military bases, government buildings, and transportation hubs now searched for Ray Freeman. Communications networks analyzed all transmissions, searching for his voice.

If Freeman walked down a street, spoke on a telephone, or entered a grocery store, the networks would spot him.

22

The fight took place in the train station.

I had no idea how the speck the bastards got from the spaceport to the Air Force base, but there they were.

Whoever they were, they entered the base through the train station, caught the Marines guarding the platforms napping, and blew their fool heads off. Then they crossed the tunnel and sent a team up the escalator that led into the base. That was when the shooting began.

The bastards were not well trained or well armed, but they had one thing going for them—they considered martyrdom a privilege.

I was on the far side of the lobby talking with Curtis Jackson and a lieutenant when the first grenade rolled across the floor. Someone yelled, "Grenade!" and everybody jumped.

The grenade skittered across the granite, bouncing along an erratic path. In the spaceport, with its glass walls and civilian-friendly construction, a full-yield grenade would have caused a cave-in. This was not a full-yield grenade, and we were on a military base. The grenade exploded, but the walls remained in place.

The percussion of the grenade sent a few men tumbling through the air. It knocked me over. Feeling like my head might explode, I reached down and found my M27.

I tried to stand, but my head was in a funk. I was dizzy. I was tired. I was confused. Maybe I had a concussion. Six men ran from the tunnel. I shot them at the same time as thirty other Marines did. The miserable bastards stood and shredded as hundreds of bullets perforated their front sides and sprayed their backsides all over the walls in reds and purples.

Six more men charged up the stairs. So many Marines blasted those poor bastards that I didn't waste my bullets on the slaughter. Instead, I fished in my belt and found a grenade, which I primed and tossed into the train tunnel.

A grenade, I thought. It almost felt like I shouldn't have had one.

My grenade arced over the bursting bodies at the front of the tunnel and vanished behind them. A moment passed, and the blast from my grenade spat body parts all over the platforms below.

The invaders caught us unaware; but we were combat-hardened Marine killing machines. Our instincts took over. As the smoke and dust cleared from the tunnel, I crouched low and rushed into the chaos. Not knowing if any of my men had already entered the quagmire ahead of me, I held my fire, which turned out to be the correct decision. As the smoke cleared, I saw men in combat armor lined up along the rail overlooking the train platforms.

The tunnel was long and dark with a squared ceiling and three sets of tracks. A train sat dormant below me.

The bastards took the train? I wondered. *I told Cutter to destroy the tracks.*

Using night-for-day vision, I saw thousands of men crammed on the platform below me. They were not dressed in uniforms. They looked more like a mob than an army.

Three of my men sprinted down the escalator toward the platforms below, the muzzles of their M27s flashing so steadily they looked like welding torches. Buckshot nicked the metal rails along the escalator, sending dandelion sparks in the air. My Marines ran fast, presenting difficult targets; but with thousands of shotguns, even the Martian Legionnaires were dangerous. The first men down the stairs were atomized. The third guy down died as well, but he left a corpse.

I fished a second grenade out of my belt and tossed it into the sea of men blow.

"Fire in the hole!" I yelled over the interLink. Those were the first words I actually remembered speaking since I had left Mars Spaceport. I'd been thrown around by explosions in other battles, but never dazed like this.

The Legion had placed itself in an unwinnable situation. There were only two ways out of the train station, back into the desert or up the escalator. They couldn't go back out into the desert without breathing gear, and they'd be sitting ducks trying to file up the escalator. They had one train, and many of them started to board it.

"I need men and guns now, now, now!" I yelled into the interLink even though I already had more than enough men to finish this skirmish.

My men responded like Marines. A wave of men ran into the tunnel, guns raised. They stormed the rails overlooking the platform and shot the enemy like fish in a barrel.

The Legionnaires carried shotguns. They hit several of my men, killing some and merely injuring others. A Marine in combat armor slid down the side of the escalator, fired, and was hit in the face. The spray from the shotgun didn't just penetrate his armor, it tore it to pieces. Buckshot and shredded plastic slit his skin. He slumped down, a gush of blood washing through his shattered exoskeleton.

A Legionnaire pulled a grenade. Only the ones in the very front could reach us with a grenade, and it would have required a good arm to hurl that pill up to the mezzanine and laser precision to arc it over the rail. Several people shot the bastard as he stepped forward to throw. He dropped the grenade and fell on his ass.

"Live one!" I yelled into the Link.

The force from the explosion shook the tunnel. I stood, peered over the rail, and saw the swamp below. The blood looked black through my visor. It covered the floor, the walls, and the tracks. Limbs and shredded bodies stuck out of the gore like rocks in a low tide.

My men and I wore combat armor that protected our ears. Most of the surviving Legionnaires either knelt or rolled on the ground. I could hear them moaning. Amazingly, a few continued the fight. A handful of Legionnaires ran along the platform, firing their shotguns and trying to reach the bottom of the escalator. They made easy targets that my Marines picked off with their M27s.

Throughout the five-minute battle, more and more of the attackers slipped onto the train. As the fighting slowed, the lights in the cars flicked on and the train started to move. A few last Legionnaires dived into the doors as it rolled toward the air locks. My Marines fired at the train, splintering its windows and punching holes into its sides until it looked like a sieve.

With the windows gone and walls shot to shit, the men on the train would suffocate once their ride entered the Martian badlands.

"Hold your fire. Hold your fire," I told my men.

"You're just going to let them ride out of here?" Jackson yelled.

"Let them go?" I asked. "They're already dead."

I watched the ghost train as it slowly rolled into the locks. The windows had shattered and fallen from their casings, the walls were riddled with holes. No one could have survived that fusillade, it would be like running through a hurricane and dodging the raindrops.

I was curious to see if the train would run all the way back to the spaceport. If it did, it would deliver a message. We'd lost round one in the grand arcade. They'd killed two of my men and gotten away with it. I wanted them to know that further attacks would not be tolerated.

I placed a new clip in my M27 as I walked down to the platform. A couple of dead Legionnaires lay partway up the escalator. I stepped around one and nudged the other out of my way with my boot. Then I came to the knot of bodies at the base of the escalator. Instead of pushing them out of my way, I vaulted over the rail and walked around them.

Body parts. Men killed by the grenade had been thrown against the walls and onto the railroad tracks. Not even their own mothers would have recognized these blood-soaked cadavers. Some had lost arms. One guy had both his arms still attached to his shoulders. He lay in a pool of blood with what looked like a third arm sprouting out of his gut. There was no determining which limbs were which without significant DNA tests.

A shotgun lay on the ground under the train track with a hand hanging from it, the finger still trapped in the trigger guard.

A group of New Olympians ran toward me along the platform, slipping in the blood and stumbling over body parts; but they did not have the opportunity to shoot. My men spotted them and shot them from the balcony.

The wounded did not give up. Men with multiple bullet holes tried to aim their shotguns at me. I killed some, my men killed the rest. The only Martian Legionnaires who would survive this battle were the ones who lost so much blood that they were no longer conscious, and they'd die soon enough.

23

Watson entered the Blue Duck, wearing a charcoal gray suit and a red tie. He knew where to sit and what to order. He knew how to discourage the women he did not find attractive and how to welcome the ones he did.

He kept his coat unbuttoned because he wanted to look casual. The cut of his jacket emphasized his broad shoulders and his narrow waist. As he crossed the bar, he scanned for girls of interest and past playmates. He had come for new blood; revisiting old acquaintances did not interest him.

Watson had cruised the Blue Duck before. It was one of his favorite east-side bars, but he only visited it twice a year to avoid developing a reputation. Players who went to the same establishments too often exposed themselves as players.

Travis Watson did not want to be known as a player; he wanted to play.

There were thirty-two people in the bar, eighteen of them women, one of whom mildly interested Watson. She had long blond hair with curls and twists, blue eyes, and a black dress that showed off two-thirds of her cleavage. Watson liked her face. Her breasts were small, far too small for the panoramic showcase in which she had placed them. He didn't mind girls with small breasts, but small-breasted girls with pretensions did not interest him.

If she was around for another hour and nothing better came in, Watson might introduce himself.

In the meantime, Watson found a secluded table. He sat and watched patrons as they entered and left. Three girls walked into the bar together. One had short black hair and a red dress. Another had dark brown hair that hung past her shoulders. Both appealed. The third had red hair. Watson could not see her face. In Watson's mind, they were not a package deal. Even when women came in with dates, Watson did not necessarily consider them unavailable.

There had been occasions when Watson had gone home with a couple of girls. In recent times, that had become fashionable, two or three women taking one man home with them. Watson had fallen into that trap a couple of times, and did not enjoy it.

When a waitress came by to take his order, Watson asked for Scotch. She returned a moment later with his drink. By this time, the dark-haired girls and their redheaded friend had chosen a table no more than ten feet from where he sat. The redhead stole a glance at him. So did the girl with the pixieish black hair. The redhead was pretty and voluptuous, but he liked the look of the girl with the short hair.

This was a moment Watson enjoyed. As they inspected him, he neither looked away nor stared in their direction. He did not pretend not to notice them. He smiled. The girl with the short hair smiled back. So did the redhead. The one with the long, dark hair turned to have a look.

Watson settled back in his seat, in his own world. Any one of these girls would have interested him. All three did not. He pushed the girls out of his mind.

He thought about his visit to the U.A. Archives and Freeman

while trying not to think about video feeds marked EXPEDITED. He tried not to think about the red vapor that surrounded Turnbow's head and the look of terror on old Morgan Atkins's face... and Wayson Harris flying backward as his chest exploded.

How could Harris have survived that? Watson asked himself. He knew the answer. He could not have survived it. In his mind, bullets were more lethal when they came from Ray Freeman's rifle.

"Should I feel insulted?"

Watson looked up. It was the girl with the short black hair. She had a lithe, slender figure. Her breasts were smaller than the ones the blonde had on display, but this girl did not misrepresent them. She had a short, sunset red dress that showed off her hips and her legs and her tiny waist, and clung to the curve of her ass. She looked athletic.

Glad to wash Freeman from his thoughts, Watson said, "I wouldn't want to hurt your feelings."

She smiled and sat in the chair across from him.

Watson's patter did not include rehearsed lines. He knew how to flirt and how to make small talk. Mostly, though, he knew how to listen. He liked listening to women, though he had no interest in listening to the same woman for the rest of his life.

In Watson's mind, men and women did not so much chat in bars as hold negotiations. He liked the sound of women's voices and the cat-and-mouse games of intergender conversation. They knew what he wanted, but they pretended not to know. He, being an experienced negotiator, recognized smart women pretending to be ditsy and dumb girls who needed to be praised for their intellect.

He gave them what they wanted. If a girl with insipid thoughts wanted to be told she was profound, he did it. Those deals were easy. He enjoyed both the challenge of women who were comfortable with themselves and the ease of girls who wanted compliments for what they weren't.

Watson said, "I saw you and your friends come in." He left it at that, leaving it to her to make the next move.

"Don't you like parties?" she asked.

"It's my traditional upbringing," he said. "Two is company, four's a crowd."

She considered her options, made her decision, smiled. "You could buy me a drink."

After years of flirting and playing the field, Watson had developed a reliable ability to profile and categorize. He already knew the woman better than she would have guessed. She would be a secretary or a receptionist with ambitions of office management. She was bright but not college educated. Judging by the way she talked, the way she dressed, the style of her hair, and her walk, Watson guessed that she liked to dance, and she liked the outdoors.

"What would you like to drink?" he asked.

She was not the beer type, not in this setting. If he went home with her, he thought he might find beer in her fridge, but he thought she would order something with vodka or whiskey.

She said, "How about a whiskey sour? Was that what you expected?"

He smiled. "Not far off," he said.

"How often do you troll these parts?" she asked.

"Is that what I'm doing? Trolling?"

A smile crept along the left side of her mouth and spread to the right. Her eyes sparkled in the bar light. She said, "I bet you can name every bar in the east end."

He said, "You'd lose that bet," then signaled the waitress as she walked past and asked for the whiskey sour.

"With whiskey, not bourbon," the girl said. As the waitress walked away, she told Watson, "Sometimes they use bourbon instead. It's supposed to be more upper-crust."

"Good to know."

"Do you have a name?" she asked.

He let her control the conversation because she wanted to lead. He didn't mind. He said, "Travis."

"Travis?" she asked in a voice that suggested she did not

believe him. "Not Bob? Not Frank or Ted?" She laughed, and added, "That's a good name; how long have you had it?"

"All of my life. What is your name?"

"I'm not sure I'm ready to answer that," she said.

"It's Tina," said the girl with the red hair.

"Bitch," said Tina.

"Slut," said the redhead.

"You're just jealous," said Tina. She smiled at Watson, and said, "She's just jealous. Anna and Kim wanted in."

The drink arrived in a four-inch glass, a wedge of lemon balanced over the rim, a bright cherry drowned near the bottom. Tina let the waitress place the drink on the table, waited for her to leave, then lifted her drink. Watson could tell that she saw the waitress as competition. He saw it in the way she turned quiet and watchful as the waitress approached.

"What kind of work do you do?" she asked.

"Government work."

"Are you a holdover from the U.A. government? I hear things are tough."

"I work in the Pentagon."

"You work with the clones?" She was interested. "Shit, that must be scary."

"Not really," he said. "Usually, it's pretty boring."

"You don't plan attacks or anything?"

He laughed, and said, "Purely civilian work. I'm natural-born... but then every clone thinks he's natural-born. Maybe I'm fooling myself." As he said this, he thought about Harris, who knew he was synthetic. *Does he know he's a duplicate?* Watson wondered. *He could not possibly have survived Freeman's bullet.*

The video files had polluted his mind, and he was having a flashback.

"What are they like? Are they polite to you? Do they really not know they are clones?"

"They're just people. There are nice ones and real bastards. I mean, well, they're soldiers, but they're just like everyone else."

"Do you really believe that?" she asked. "They're not... I don't know, violent and scary? Don't they scare you?"

Watson noticed that she had used the term "scared" twice now. He wondered why she feared them. "They have never given me any reason to be scared."

"You must be brave," she said.

"Not particularly," he said. He was telling the truth.

They talked for an hour. He bought her three drinks, but she barely touched the third. By that time, her friends had left the bar. Watson paid the tab and left the waitress a large tip.

Tina took Watson home to her apartment. She was not drunk, and neither was he. He let her control the conversation and he let her decide when to stop talking. After that, he took control.

24

The ringtone woke Watson. He sat up in bed, found his pants, and fished his phone from the pocket.

Tina asked, "Do you always get calls at three in the morning?"

He looked at the phone and saw the call was from Admiral Cutter. He said, "Comes with the job. The guy on the phone is an admiral."

She moaned, and asked, "Why is he calling at three in the morning?"

"He's in space. He probably doesn't care about Earth time zones."

Tina rolled so that her back faced him as he climbed out of bed. Speaking in a whisper, he said, "Watson."

Cutter asked, "Have you heard from Harris yet?"

"Not a word, Admiral." Watson drifted across the apartment as he spoke, leaving the bedroom, crossing the hall, and hovering in the kitchen near the sink. It was a small apartment. The bedroom and the bathroom had doors. The kitchen, living room, and entry blended into each other.

Watson glanced back at Tina lying on her bed with her sheets pulled up to her chin, and asked, "Are you sure the man who went to Mars was really Harris?"

"Who else could he have been?"

"The Unifieds may have assassinated Harris. While I was at the archive, I saw a video feed…"

Cutter interrupted to say, "I know what you're talking about, but he didn't die. The Unifieds shot him when they attacked Terraneau."

"What if he did die? What if they killed him? Could the Unifieds have killed him and recloned him?"

Cutter said, "No, that's our Harris all right. There's only one Wayson Harris, thank God."

"But what if he did die on Terraneau?" asked Watson.

"That would make the one we have now a very good imposter."

"He's a clone. Clones should be the best kind of imposter."

"What are you getting at?" asked Cutter.

"Freeman killed Harris on Terraneau. I saw it. I saw the video feed," said Watson. "His whole chest was blown out. Ray Freeman shot him."

"Freeman?" asked Cutter. "That doesn't make sense. Freeman and Harris are friends. Harris may be the only man in the universe Ray Freeman wouldn't kill."

"I found the feed in the U.A. Archives. It was dated December 18, 2516. Harris landed a civilian aircraft on an airstrip outside Norristown. He stepped off the plane, and Freeman shot him in the chest."

"And you're sure he died?" asked Cutter.

"The bullet blew out his chest."

Cutter whistled. "If anyone could kill Harris, it would be Freeman," he said. "But they couldn't have killed him and replaced him. Not Harris. It's just not possible. Liberator DNA is in short supply."

Watson listened quietly, but he was not convinced.

They spoke for a few more minutes, then Cutter hung up. Watson stole into the bedroom as silently as he could, but Tina was already awake. She said, "Is everything okay?"

"My boss is on Mars," Watson said.

"Oh, God, I hear Mars is a mess," said Tina.

Watson climbed under the sheets with her. She kept her apartment cold, but her body was warm, and she pressed herself against him. She was young and athletic, with long legs and a flat stomach. She had that girl-next-door kind of beauty, friendly, not glamorous. He liked her more than most, but he had no intentions of seeing her again.

"He's a Marine. He's used to bad places," Watson said as he silently asked himself, *Could Harris have died on Terraneau?* He was the last of the Liberators, but that did not make him bulletproof. Watson decided he would not know the answer until he found Freeman, and he wondered how Freeman would react when he was found.

His thoughts did not remain on Freeman for long, however. Tina distracted him.

Leaving Tina's apartment building, Travis Watson knew without looking behind him that the only moving car on her street was following him. He decided someone other than Ray Freeman must be driving. People did not see Freeman until it was too late.

It was a particularly cold day for April in Washington, D.C. Puddles gleamed like mirrors along the curb. Dressed in his suit and tie, now wrinkled from spending a night folded on a desk, Watson pretended not to notice the car.

He was not a fighter or a soldier by nature. He was tall—six-foot-five, and naturally strong, but he had a peaceful disposition. *What would Harris do?* he asked himself. *He'd have a gun. He'd turn around and shoot.*

He asked himself another question, *What would Freeman do?* First he answered, *He probably carries a nuclear missile in his pocket.* Then he came to another conclusion, *This wouldn't happen to Freeman; you can't find him unless he wants to be found.*

Watson continued along the street. Hoping to catch a glimpse of the car, he stopped and stared into a store window; but the car was too far back. After a few seconds, Watson moved on.

When he reached an intersection, he stopped to consider his options. If he crossed the street, he would catch a glimpse of the car, but he might catch that glimpse as the car ran him down.

He walked to the corner and stopped. Pretending to read the street sign, he watched the car out of the corner of his eye. It was a silver-colored sedan—four doors, dark windows, absolutely nondescript. The car pulled beside the curb and waited.

Instead of crossing the street, Watson turned right and headed around a corner. A moment of silence passed, then he heard the hum of a car engine.

In his imagination, Watson saw Freeman behind the wheel of the car. In his mind's eye, Freeman held a rifle that was equipped with a microphone and a scope, and asked, "Identity confirmed?"

He reminded himself that he'd already decided that Freeman wasn't driving the car. Hoping to reassure himself with the sound of his voice, Watson whispered, "Not even close."

He wished he were still in bed with Tina.

Maybe it's the clone pretending to be Harris, he thought. No, real or an imposter, Harris was on Mars.

Not Freeman. Not Harris. Watson was still scared, but not as scared.

He started to reach for his cell, but then he stopped. The phone might act like a catalyst. Suspecting he would call for help, the people in the car might react.

A row of storefronts opened onto the sidewalk. The first was a pawnshop with a window full of jewelry. Watson passed it.

The next store was an old shoe shop that must have gone out of business years ago. He stopped and pretended to look at the dusty display in the window. Mice had gnawed holes in the shoes and left pellets along the shelves; spiders had built a network of webs. The display would have fitted better in a haunted house than a store window.

Watson entered the third shop—a small convenience store. He

walked up to the checkout stand, and asked, "Got a back door?"

Violent or not, Travis Watson stood six-five. His size made him intimidating. Even when he smiled, and he was not smiling at that moment, he intimidated other men.

The clerk, a man in his fifties, nodded, and said, "It's got an alarm."

"Can you let me out without setting it off?" asked Watson.

"I've got a key."

"There are men waiting out there on the street, I need to get away from them," said Watson.

Starting to warm up to Watson, the clerk asked, "Do you want me to call the police?"

The men in the car had driven slowly down an otherwise-empty street. They had not broken any laws.

"Better not," said Watson. "Just let me out the back and say I went to the bathroom if anybody asks."

"We don't have a bathroom."

Watson glanced back at the street and saw the car hovering. "Just let me out the back."

The man pulled the key from under his register, pointed it at the back of the store, and clicked the single button. He said, "You're good to go."

"Thanks." Thinking the men in the car might be watching, Watson forced himself to walk calmly. He stepped around some shelves and entered a small employee area with a table, some cases, and a janitorial closet. The metal door at the very back did not have a knob. Watson pushed and the door swung open to an empty alleyway. He looked to the right, then to the left, and stepped out.

He made a call, and whispered, "Pentagon Security." When an officer answered, he said, "This is Travis Watson with General Harris's office."

A moment passed, and the officer said, "You're the general's civilian assistant."

"Yes," said Watson.

"What can I do for you?"

"A car is following me."

The officer said, "Okay, I have your location on satellite. Is it the silver sedan?"

"Yes. That's the one."

"Listen, Mr. Watson, I've run a thermal scan on the car. There's a driver and two men sitting in the back. Their engine is running. My guess is that they are waiting for you."

"Yeah?" said Watson, his fears now confirmed.

"Head west."

"What?"

"Take a right and walk to the end of the block, then turn left and head to the next intersection. It's going to take me five minutes to get a car out there, so we need to put some space between you and that car."

"What if they come after me?" asked Watson.

"I'll keep an eye on them."

25

"Interesting friends you got there, Watson," said Major Alan Cardston, the head of the Pentagon's security unit. "Want to take a wild guess where they came from?"

Watson and Cardston sat beside a conference table in the Pentagon Security office. Cutter was there in image only. His holographic image was visible through a windowpane called a confabulator. Looking through that device, it appeared that he was actually in the room.

Having arrested the men who had followed Watson, Cardston had called this meeting to learn what he should do with them.

"Are they stowaways from Mars?" asked Cutter.

"That was my first guess, sir," said Cardston. "They are Earth residents with clean records."

"That doesn't make sense," said Cutter. "Are you sure they were following you?" he asked Watson.

"They could be holdovers from U.A. military intelligence."

"War criminals?" asked Cutter.

"Not criminals, just rank-and-file soldiers. We know they all served in the U.A. military," said Cardston. "The driver was a staff sergeant. The two in the back were corporals. We only prosecuted captains and up."

"You're sure they were following you?" asked Cutter a second time.

"It's a safe bet, sir," said Cardston. "I don't suspect three U.A. enlisted men hopped into a rented sedan to go for a 6:00 A.M. joyride."

"I don't like the implications," Cutter said. "Do we know what they planned to do with Watson?"

"They say they don't know who he is," said Cardston.

"Maybe it had something to do with my trip to the U.A. Archives," said Watson.

"That's a safe bet," said Cardston.

"And you are holding them now?" asked Cutter. "Does anyone know you arrested them?"

"No, sir," Cardston said with obvious cheer.

"Not even their lawyers."

"We haven't asked them about lawyers."

"That's good," said Cutter. "That buys us time."

"What do you want me to do with them?" asked Cardston.

Cutter thought about that for several seconds before finally responding, "I'm open to suggestions." He added, "Maybe we should throw them in a dark hole and forget about them."

"Or we could let them go, sir," said Cardston.

"Let them go?" Cutter asked.

"They were enlisted men, sir. Even if they are working for some faction of the Unified Authority, they'll just be worker bees. If we let them go, maybe they will lead us to the brains of their operation," said Cardston. "They may just be a dead end, in which case we can pick them up again and ship them someplace far away; but they could be the tip of a conspiratorial iceberg.

"If we follow them, who knows where they might lead us."

Cardston asked Watson, "What were you researching in the Unified Authority Archives?"

"I sent him. He's trying to find Ray Freeman," said Cutter.

"Freeman?" asked Cardston. He sat up straight and pretended to shiver, then he said, "That specker gives me the creeps."

"Me, too," said Cutter. "Watson says he watched a feed that showed Freeman shooting General Harris."

"That's got to be a fake," said Cardston.

"Unless they recloned him," said Cutter. "The Unifieds kept the feed in their most secure archive."

"Interesting," said Cardston.

"There's something else," said Watson. "The last time we heard from Harris, he sent us a message." He looked at Cutter's holographic image to make sure he had permission to continue.

The admiral said, "Maybe you can help us with it, Major. Harris said, 'Anything that can be programmed can be reprogrammed.' He said it was a message from Freeman."

Cardston thought but did not speak. Finally, he asked, "What is that supposed to mean?"

"Sounds like gibberish to me," said Cutter.

"What about you?" Cardston asked Watson. "Did you find anything in the archives?"

Watson looked to Cutter for permission a second time.

The admiral nodded.

Both men being clones, Watson worried how they might react. He said, "I think he means clones can be reprogrammed."

"Reprogramming clones?" Cardston asked. He whistled.

"That's neural programming, it's different," said Cutter.

"He did say *anything*, sir. *Anything* that was programmed can be reprogrammed," Watson reminded the admiral.

"Why is neural programming different?" asked Cardston.

"Major, clones have brains, not circuits. I grew up in an orphanage, and I can tell you that I never saw anyone with a data port."

"I grew up in an orphanage, too, sir," said Cardston.

"What's your point?"

"They do have data ports, but we don't think of them as data ports."

"What are you talking about?" asked Cutter.

"Sight, smell, touch. Every sense provides data."

"So what, then, hypnosis? Brainwashing? Clones aren't the only ones who can be brainwashed. You can brainwash natural-borns as well."

"Brainwashed people act strangely."

Watson asked, "Do they have temper problems?"

"Brainwashing leaves evidence behind. There are ways of telling when people are brainwashed. They don't act natural. Brainwashing creates internal conflicts, the people are always fighting battles in their heads."

"Reprogramming... Sir, if someone erased a clone's neural programs and rewrote them, there'd be no way of knowing. There wouldn't be any internal conflicts. We can spot brainwashing with psychological profiling. That would not work on reprogrammed clones; they'd be as natural as the day they left the tube. And the things you could do with a reprogrammed clone, sir. The possibilities are endless."

"Like what?" asked Cutter.

"Admiral, we are talking about clones with brown hair and brown eyes who have been so thoroughly programmed that they don't even recognize their own reflection when they see it in a mirror," said Cardston. "If you can program someone not to see himself in a mirror, you can program him to do just about anything."

Only seeing the smaller picture, Cutter did not grasp the ramifications. "What are they going to do, reprogram them one by one to see that they have brown hair? Wouldn't it be easier to shoot them instead?" he asked, hoping his sarcasm would not be wasted on Cardston.

"They're also programmed to accept anything they are told by a superior officer. What if they caught an officer, say... a three-star general in the Marines, and they programmed him to tell all of his subordinates that they were clones?"

Watson answered, "You could demolish the entire Enlisted Man's Marines in a day."

"Watson, I think it's time you quit the Marines," said Cutter.

"Why would I do that?" asked Watson.

"Job security for openers," said Cutter. "It sounds like your boss has been reprogrammed, and there is no job security working for reprogrammed officers."

"I see what you mean," said Watson.

"And then there is the question of your personal safety. If Harris is working for the same people that sent these men after you, you'll be a lot safer working for me. It seems like they have already picked you as a priority target.

"From here on out, you're a Navy man. You work for me. Think of it as a promotion; you just went from working for a man with three stars to working for a man with four." Cutter laughed, and muttered, "If this doesn't piss Harris off, nothing will."

26

At Admiral Cutter's insistence, Watson moved to Bolling Air Force Base.

Watson did not want to move onto a military base, even if it meant living in nicer accommodations; but Cutter paid no attention to Watson's objections. The military could not ensure Watson's safety while he slept on civilian soil, so Cutter gave him a choice of billets on the base. He could either move into officer's housing or the brig.

The house was built for visiting dignitaries. Watson saw the brick façade, the elm-tree-lined driveway, and the cut-pile carpets, and he absolutely despised the place. It was like moving back into the quiet home he had fled when he entered college.

Watson dropped his suitcase on the jade-colored leather couch and examined the kitchen. It was big and spacious with a full pantry and sparkling appliances. Watson did not cook. He bought sandwiches from delicatessens and sometimes lived on candy bars.

He went to the bedroom, stabbed his fingers into the queen-size bed, and sneered at the wooden headboard. Next came the bathroom, with its booth-sized shower, a token effort, and its hundred-gallon tub. Watson was too tall for the shower. He loathed taking baths.

A team of military policemen came with the house. They were his bodyguards. *You can leave the gardens, the kitchen, and the tub behind every morning*, Watson told himself. But the bodyguards stayed with him wherever he went.

When two bodyguards followed him into the bedroom, he spun, and yelled, "Out."

The two MPs ignored him. They searched the room, then settled by the door, standing as attentively as guard dogs. Watson sneered at them and hung his clothes.

One of the bodyguards said, "We need to get moving, sir."

Watson nodded and followed the bodyguards out of the house.

Some promotion, Watson thought. *Living quarters and a company car, wouldn't Mom be proud?* The car had armor plating and bulletproof glass. It came with a chauffeur—standard equipment. The chauffeur was a Marine commando; even the MPs were nervous around him. Watson wasn't impressed.

He did not feel any safer with these men than he had on the street. Now that he'd seen Ray Freeman in action, the military police no longer impressed him. He knew it was an irrational fear, but Freeman lurked in Watson's brain like a malignant tumor.

Watson gave the house one last, disapproving glance, and said, "We wouldn't want to be late."

Bolling Field was eight miles from the Pentagon. Watson liked the ride because it took him along the Potomac.

It was a cold day, with nickel-plated clouds. The buildings of the capital mall peeked over the skyline, and the buildings of uptown D.C. loomed like a mountain range in the hazy distance. Watson welcomed these urban decorations; they made him feel at home.

The driver pulled into the Pentagon's underground parking lot. The two bodyguards followed Watson into the building while the driver stayed with the car. Watson had a new office on the fifth floor, two doors away from Admiral Cutter's office.

When he opened his door, Watson found Major Cardston waiting for him. As Watson stepped in, Cardston asked, "How are you at poker?"

"I know that two kings beats an ace," said Watson.

"A pair of deuces beats an ace," said Cardston.

"So lone aces don't count for much in poker," said Watson.

Cardston asked, "How are you at lying?"

"Above average," Watson said, thinking about the compliments he gave girls in bars. "Mostly pickup lines."

Watson's new office was large and nearly empty. His enormous metal desk faced four hundred square feet of open floor. Chairs and file cabinets lined the walls.

"They usually reserve offices like this for generals and admirals," said Cardston. "Admiral Cutter is taking good care of you."

"You should see my housing," said Watson.

Cardston said, "This time you will be lying to a man."

"Who am I lying to?"

"Your old boss."

"Harris? Do you know where he is?"

"He's on Mars."

"Was he there all along?" asked Watson.

"Who the speck knows," said Cardston. "I can't come up with any reasons for his ordering everyone out of the space lanes unless he planned to use them."

"Wouldn't you be able to track that from Earth?" asked Watson.

"Not if the ships had stealth technology."

They stood in the doorway. The hall outside was empty— wooden doors surrounded by windows, brass nameplates, and light fixtures. The air was musty.

Watson asked, "Do you think Harris left Mars?"

"If he did, I want to know where he went," said Cardston. "Theories don't count; the only thing that matters is what actually happened. He wants to talk to you."

A communications console poked out of the wall beside the big empty desk. Cardston nodded toward it, and said, "Get what you can. I'll be listening in on you."

Watson walked to the desk. He looked at the console. Harris stared back at him. He smiled at Watson, and said, "Cutter tells me that you're a swabbie now."

Watson sat down in the seat behind the desk, well aware of the way his heart thumped inside his chest. He could feel his pulse quickening. He liked Harris, had enjoyed working for him; but in his mind, Wayson Harris was dead and had been for a couple of years. This was an imposter.

Hoping he looked calm, he said, "Admiral Cutter gave me a raise and a housing bonus."

"Did he?" asked Harris.

This was the Harris Watson had known. Other than the physical similarities, he bore no resemblance to the rabid dog in the video feed with Cutter. Harris laughed, and said, "If that's all it takes, I'll match your pay and throw in your own personal LG with an endless fuel supply."

"What's an LG?" asked Watson.

"It's a low-gravity tank," said Harris.

"What would I want with a tank?" asked Watson.

"I'm making a counteroffer, Watson. You tell me what you want."

"What's the situation on Mars?"

"Copacetic," said Harris. "We ran into the Martian Legion yesterday; now the New Olympians have two Nights of the Martyrs."

"A second Night of the Martyrs?"

"They tried to attack us."

"With what? There aren't supposed to be any guns in Mars Spaceport."

"They had shotguns. I lost fifty-two men."

"But you took care of it?"

"Like I said, it's the second Night of the Martyrs," said Harris. "They thought they were God's Army; we sent them to meet their commander in chief," Harris joked. "That was where all that Legion shit came from, they found shotguns in the Air Force base and thought God wanted to liberate them. They attacked us, we wiped them out, and the Legion banners disappeared from the spaceport the very next day.

"Now, about your joining the Navy, Watson, I could really use your help up here."

Watson stared into the face on the screen. He listened for fluctuations in Harris's voice and watched his eyes. He checked other details, too—the narrow scar across his left eyebrow, the nicks on his face. Watson said, "I think I'm stuck here on Earth. Admiral Cutter has me running errands for him."

"I see," said Harris.

"What did you want me for?" asked Watson.

"I need a liaison," said Harris. "My normal staff can work out the logistics, but I'm going to need a natural-born for the public-relations side of this."

"Side of what?"

"The big transfer. Now that we have taken care of that Martian Legion business, it's high time we transferred the New Olympians down to Earth, don't you think?"

When Harris finally signed off, Watson slumped in his chair and stared across his enormous, empty office. *Ah God*, he thought, knowing that Cutter was going to want him to depart for the *Churchill* within the hour.

27

In preparation for Harris's return, Cutter placed the crew of the *Churchill* on alert and informed the naval office that the ship was under quarantine. He ordered them to treat her as a threat if she tried to return to Earth without his personal clearance.

He watched the fleet of transports approach on the tactical display and felt the stirrings of mistrust. *Could they have caught you, Harris?* he asked a phantom Harris in his head.

Harris was a clone, just a clone, nothing more than a clone. In the old days, the term "clone" was a euphemism for a disposable man. Major Alan Cardston, the head of Pentagon Security, was a clone as well; though, of course, he did not know it. He instructed Cutter not to trust Harris. His exact words were, "If he has been reprogrammed, he won't know it. He'll think the people who reprogrammed him are the good guys and we are the bad guys, and he'll be just as nasty with us as he was with the Unifieds."

Believing that Harris had been compromised, Cardston wanted

to leave him on Mars. "You could call him into your office and shoot him," Cardston suggested. "That is what Harris would do if he thought you'd been reprogrammed."

Cardston was right, but he was also full of shit in Admiral Cutter's opinion. Harris was a hero. He had saved the *Churchill* and earned Cutter's loyalty. While other generals hid behind the lines, Harris led his men into battle after battle. The rest of the clones were loyal to the Enlisted Man's Empire, but the Marines were loyal to Harris.

Reevaluating his own loyalties, Cutter lighted upon an irony— the first time he had spoken to Wayson Harris was during the evacuation of Olympus Kri. Now Harris was talking about relocating the New Olympians a second time. The first relocation had ended in an ambush. How would the second relocation end?

On the display, the transports did not fly so much in a formation as in a swarm. One of the transports flew at the front. Cutter knew from experience that Harris would be on that ship.

His eyes still on the display, he spoke into the communications panel. He said, "Watson, Harris's ETA is fifteen minutes. I want you to come with me to the landing bay."

"On my way," said Watson.

Cutter winced. Unlike Harris, the admiral cared about military protocol. Civilian or not, Watson's familiarity bothered him. He said, "On my way... *sir*," even though Watson had already signed off.

Cutter had flown Watson out to the *Churchill* to observe Harris. Having worked with him for a year, Watson might bring extra insight into the man. Cutter sincerely hoped that Harris and his Marines had not been compromised, but he wasn't hopeful.

Cutter contacted Lieutenant Nelson, head of ship security. "Do you have everything in order?"

"Yes, sir."

Sensing hesitation in the voice, he asked, "Are you certain everything is in order, Lieutenant?"

"Yes, sir."

Again, hesitation. "Is there something you are not telling me?"

"No, sir. My men are on silent alert. I have armed men stationed in every landing bay, just as you directed."

"But?" asked Cutter.

Nelson waited several seconds, then said, "Sir, the general has a regiment of armed Marines. If it comes to a fight between my MPs and fifteen hundred Marines..."

"I'm not expecting trouble," said Cutter.

"Aye, sir," said the lieutenant, who still sounded nervous. "My men are in place. I have armed guards posted in the bridge and the engine room."

"That will be all," said Cutter. Cutter took a deep breath and headed for the landing bay.

28

The Marine compound was on the bottom deck of the *Churchill*, well away from Engineering and the sailors' living quarters. The Navy separated us "Sea Soldiers" from its sailors.

The compound was a typical Marine base in miniature, with a barracks, a firing range, an obstacle course, a mess, an officers' club, and a canteen for enlisted men. The Navy provided the food, space, and transportation, everything but hospitality.

Marines who did not remain in the compound faced a nasty reception on the upper decks. The animosity between Marines and sailors was as old as war. We considered sailors to be glorified cargo handlers because they delivered us to battles and sped away. Sailors considered us live cargo.

Having just come from battle, my men would be emboldened. They had endured the spaceport with its overcrowded conditions and angry mobs. Any sailors getting in my men's way were in for a surprise.

My boys were coiled and ready to strike. I needed to keep them in the compound, where I could work them hard. I would burn down their nervous energy and their bravado before easing them back into society.

We touched down, and the transport's rear door slowly opened. I contacted Curtis Jackson, and said, "It's like we drilled. I want the men, gear, and K.I.A.s off-loaded. I want the men shaved, showered, and deloused. I want the gear sanitized. I want the bodies in the creamer. You have two hours."

The creamer, by the way, was the crematorium. Men killed in action were taken to the crematorium, where they were incinerated, bag and all.

"Aye, aye, sir."

"Nobody leaves the compound," I said.

"Just like we discussed, sir," said Jackson.

When the officer of the deck came up the ramp looking for the Marine in charge, I sent Jackson to meet him. They traded salutes, then Jackson asked for permission to come aboard the *Churchill*. The OOD granted his request.

This was all standard, and I had no reason to feel nervous, but I felt this awkward sensation as I walked down the ramp, as if I had been away for months or years instead of a week. As I stepped around the back of the transport, I spotted Cutter and Watson waiting for me. I spotted something else, too. Cutter had stationed armed MPs all around the landing bay, not just men with sidearms, but guards with M27s. Some stood by the doors, others watched us from second-floor railings.

"You expecting us to put up a fight?" I asked Cutter as I approached.

"I run a secure ship," said Cutter. "You know that."

Something had changed, and I knew why. I'd bounced him hard the last time we spoke. I owed the man an apology.

Over the last few days, I had run that conversation through my head several times. I remembered swearing at Cutter and threatening him. I remembered the conversation clearly; but thinking back, I felt like I was watching the conversation rather than participating in it. I was out of control, and I regretted everything I said.

Friendly, but distant, Cutter said, "We need to debrief."

I said, "Do us both a favor, let me shower and delouse."

"Delouse?" asked Watson.

"Yes," I said. "I've become acquainted with Mars's only indigenous species." He looked confused, but he did not respond. He must not have known about Martian head lice.

I said, "So, Mister Navy Liaison, do you think you can talk your natural-born friends into making room for a few million guests?"

Cutter spoke first. He said, "You're serious about moving the New Olympians to Earth."

"Yes, I am."

"And you think they are loyal to the empire?" asked Cutter.

"I do."

"What about the Martian Legion? What about the Night of the Martyrs?" asked Cutter, starting to sound belligerent.

"They canceled each other out," I said. They had a Martian Legion, then they had a second Night of the Martyrs, now they don't have a Martian Legion anymore. Personally, I was happy with the way things turned out.

I said, "I'll tell you all about it after I've had a shower," and I followed my men out of the landing bay. I got to the compound and went to the delousing station, an all-purpose sanitation facility. I stripped out of my armor and passed through the red line—a booth in which a laser light was used to kill vermin and germs alike. Any lice on my body were neutralized and fried, as were the eggs they might have laid.

I left my bodysuit and armor for sanitation and put on a pair of freshly minted boxers, then I found the CO's billet and took a hot shower.

It had been a week since I'd stepped into a shower. As the hot water splashed over my head and rolled down my spine, I felt the stress evaporate out of me.

I stood there, under that stream of nearly boiling water, feeling it dissolve the dirty crust from my skin; and I forgot about time. A few seconds, or a minute, or an hour, it didn't matter to me. The water washed away my resolve until I felt dizzy and tired.

I soaped and I washed and I shaved, and I stayed under the water as the struggle to stay awake became unbeatable. My head bobbed up and down, my eyes kept closing, and I started to fall asleep on my feet. Without even bothering to dry myself, I stepped out of the shower and stumbled over to my rack. Using everything I had left, I sent Cutter a message, I said, "I'm going to be another hour."

29

In the short time that Travis Watson worked as Harris's assistant, Harris had never given in to fatigue. Now the Liberator needed a nap?

Watson took advantage of the unexpected break. His bodyguards in tow, he went to the crematorium and asked to speak to the officer in charge.

The clone who came out was an overweight, overage senior chief petty officer with whiskers and a lit cigar. He ignored Watson and spoke to the bodyguards, both of whom were also chief petty officers. The senior chief asked the CPOs, "What do you want?"

Watson answered. He said, "The Marines just dropped some bodies off for disposal..."

One of the bodyguards nudged him, and whispered, "Honors. The term is 'honors.' Disposal sounds like he's burning trash."

"The Marines just brought some bodies here for honors," Watson said. "I need to have a look at them."

"Yeah? And who are you?" snarled the senior chief.

Harris had warned Watson about this kind of officer, junior-grade men who treated their departments like their own personal fiefdoms. This particular kingdom was cramped and smelled of death and machine oil.

Watson said, "Admiral Cutter sent me."

The clone stared at Watson while the words sank in. His expression softened, and he asked, "He sent a civilian to inspect the stiffs? What do you plan to do with 'em?"

"Orders," said Watson. He gave no further information.

The man stared at Watson for several seconds. His blank expression lingered until he finally said, "Come on back. We haven't started the honors yet; just don't do nothing disrespectful."

"What state are they in?" Watson asked. Having never worked with dead bodies or been in battle, he did not know what to expect. He hoped they would be neatly wrapped and not too badly disfigured. He got half of what he wanted.

"They're bagged and tagged," said the senior chief.

He led Watson into the crematorium, where dozens of body bags lay in a heap. He pointed to the bin filled with bodies and the conveyer belt that would drag the bodies to the incinerator, then he asked, "Doesn't Admiral Cutter want them flittered?"

"What does that mean?" asked Watson.

"Incinerated and flushed into space," whispered one of the bodyguards.

"That would not be a good idea," said Watson. "Like I said, he's ordered me to examine them."

"Examine them for what?"

Watson generally liked people, both clone and natural-born; but he did not like this man. He asked, "Do you have anyplace you can store them?"

"We can keep 'em right here if you want."

"Thanks, but if we don't get them refrigerated, they're going to start to decay," said Watson.

"The bags do that," said the senior chief petty officer. "The body bags keep 'em on ice."

Watson took in the information with pretended nonchalance. He nodded, and said, "Send three of the bodies to sick bay. Once the medics are through with them, we'll send the bodies back for honors." In the battle of semantics, Watson preferred the term "honors" to "flittering."

"Yes, sir," said the senior chief petty officer.

"One last thing," Watson said as he prepared to leave. "Do we have any way of identifying the individuals in those bags?"

"I told you, they been bagged and tagged. They died with their armor and their tags on, the bags ID 'em."

"The bags?" asked Watson.

"Hell, yeah. These bags read their IDs and categorize their DNA. You could pull these dead boys out and shuffle them like playing cards, and the bags would still be able to tell you which is which."

Watson was impressed.

Three hours later, while Harris still slept, Watson went to sick bay. The ship's surgeon met him and led him to the back, where the bodies lay in their bags. He said, "I can show you the bodies if you want a look, or we can just talk about the results."

"Is there anything I need to see?" asked Watson.

The doctor shook his head. "There are fifty-two bodies. Two of the men had broken necks and fractured skulls. I found fragments of shattered armor embedded in their backs. They were reported as having been crushed to death; my findings are consistent with the report."

"They were crushed?" Watson repeated, making sure he understood.

The surgeon nodded. "That is correct."

"What about the others?" asked Watson.

"Almost all of them were shot with shotguns at close range. The damage is extensive," said the doctor. "Something strange, though, the uniformity of the damage. All of these men were shot from the same distance and from the same angle. It's almost like somebody lined them up and shot them in the face."

Watson realized that he wasn't grasping the significance of what the doctor was telling him. *All the same?* he thought. *Same distance… same angle… so what?* He tried to imagine Mars Spaceport, Harris and his men racing through a crowded hall as men with shotguns fired at them. In his mind's eye, they ran through a narrow spaceport hall, unable to put more distance between themselves and the shotguns because of the wall behind them.

Another scenario came to mind, a firing squad with men tied up and shot from close range. He asked, "Are you saying they were executed?"

The surgeon said, "Most of these men were already dead when they were shot."

"What?" Watson was appalled.

"These men were already dead. I found traces of propafenone in their blood. Are you familiar with the term, 'propafenone'?"

Watson shook his head.

"It's a neurotoxin."

"You're saying they were poisoned to death, then shot?" asked Watson. It didn't make sense.

"They weren't poisoned, the propafenone was already in their bodies," said the surgeon. "'Propafenone poisoning' is the medical term for the death reflex. Clones die of propafenone poisoning when they find out they are clones. Propafenone is the death hormone."

30

Before I did anything else, I needed to settle the score with Don Cutter. I'd ridden him like the enemy during that confab, and he'd never been anything but square with me.

The unnatural act of apologizing had never come easily to me. I lied to myself about the inability to apologize having been programmed into my Liberator DNA.

I dressed in a crisp Charlie service uniform—blue pants, khaki shirt—and left for the bridge. I did not have ribbons and medals decorating my chest, but I had my stars on my collar. Swabbies may be territorial by nature, but they clear out of the way when they see a man with stars.

I spotted armed MPs stationed along the hall as I left the Marine compound, at least two dozen of them, most carrying sidearms and a few with M27s. The MPs eyed me as I left the compound, taking in my every step but making no effort to intercept me. I walked past the MPs and rode a lift to the top deck, where I spotted another team of armed guards.

Cutter had a row of M27-wielding MPs on the bridge as well. As I approached, he glanced at them before turning to greet me. He forced a smile, and said, "Back from the dead? How are you feeling?"

I said, "The day I found out I was a clone, I drank so much Crash that I should have died. My head hurt so much the next morning that I almost shot myself. That was the worst morning of my life... this comes in a close second."

"What happened on Mars, Harris?"

"Where do I start?" I said. In truth, the mission was mostly a blur. I remembered landing, marching through the spaceport, and stowing away on the train to the Air Force base. I knew everything that happened after that, but I didn't actually remember much of it. I knew my men flew to the Air Force base on transports and that I met them as they came down the ramps. Sometime after that, I had that argument with Cutter. I knew that each event took place, but I remembered none of the details. Nothing stood out in my mind until the fight with the Martian Legion. I remembered every detail of that one-sided battle.

I said, "Mars is the worst place I've ever been."

I meant it as an exaggeration, but the words rang true in my head. I once ran a mission on a planet called Hubble. The planet was saturated with a heavy gas that could eat through combat armor. The gas seeped into the armor of any Marine unfortunate enough to step in a hole or trip in a ditch, and it dissolved their flesh. The sergeant who mentored me, a Liberator, died on that planet. He climbed into a crevice and never came out again.

Hubble should have scared me more than Mars, but it didn't. Some deep-seated fear of Mars Spaceport now clouded my subconscious, carrying with it evil connotations.

"I owe you an apology. I was way out of line when I..."

Cutter brushed my apology aside, and said, "That's water under the bridge. You found yourself surrounded by a hostile enemy, and you lost men."

I lost men, I repeated to myself. It took me a moment to remember how many I had lost. At the time I contacted Cutter, only two men had died. Fifty more were about to die, but I would not have known that during my conversation with Cutter.

Everything that had happened on Mars blurred together.

Cutter's tone became very serious as he asked, "What happened down there, Harris? I know about the riot and the shoot-out; you already reported those events. I want details."

"What kind of details?" I asked.

Maybe he could tell I hadn't fully regained my strength. He prompted me, saying, "You met with Hughes on Thursday."

"Yeah. Right. We landed in the spaceport and marched across one of the outer wings. There were people everywhere."

My thoughts came out sounding disjointed. Images seemed to form out of mist in my head.

I said, "We entered the grand arcade, and the people started yelling and throwing things at us. That's where we lost two men. They were tossing shit at us from the upper floors."

"You reported in right after that," said Cutter.

"Did I?" I asked. Now that he mentioned it, I remembered calling in. We had just set up shop in the food court.

To an admiral like Cutter, two men killed in action wasn't much of a loss. He had 63 fighter carriers, each manned by thousands of clones. He had 193 battleships, each manned by two thousand sailors. Losing one of those ships would count as a loss.

"What happened with Hughes?" Cutter asked.

"I told you about it. We talked right after I saw him," I said.

Cutter was not himself. Generally, he was an opinionated man, a big talker, the kind of man who likes the sound of his own voice. Not this time. He said, "What do you think now that you've had time?"

"I think Hughes would have been better off if we'd left him on Olympus Kri."

"He'd be ash," said Cutter.

"He'd have been remembered as a hero."

"Do you think he feels the same way?" asked Cutter. "You've never cared what people thought about you."

There was a barb buried in that statement.

I said, "Hughes is useless. I heard the locals laughing at him. He's worse than useless. He's a joke."

Cutter looked confused. He said, "I thought you said you wanted him involved in the relocation efforts."

"I do."

"But he's a joke?"

"He's also a skilled administrator. We can appoint him as an interim governor over the New Olympians."

"Maybe so. What happened after you left Hughes's office?"

We were still on the bridge of the *Churchill*, which looked a lot like I imagined the executive offices of an insurance company would look. There were computer workstations, cubicles, and desks. There was nothing that even remotely looked like a flight yoke or a steering wheel. The pilots and navigators typed commands on keyboards. The weapons area had a large, glowing table with holographic displays that looked like architectural designs.

Sailors in uniforms walked the area, speaking in hushed library tones. Messages appeared on Cutter's communications console. He ignored them. An aide came with orders for him to sign.

"We set up a bivouac in a food court."

"Was it empty?"

"No, we had to flush the locals. They tried to attack a few hours later." I thought about what I had said and amended it. "They pumped chlorine gas into the air vents. It wasn't much of a problem. I mean, chlorine gas doesn't penetrate combat armor.

"I had civilian clothing under my armor, so I stripped down and followed a couple of their men to the base."

"The Air Force base?"

"Yes."

"And that was when you radioed me," said Cutter.

"Yeah, I told you to destroy the tracks… which you did not do."

"We destroyed them."

"There were three sets of tracks. Your pilots got two of them. The Martian Legion used the third. I guess that was a good thing. They came after us in the Air Force base. Thanks to that track, we didn't need to go hunting in the spaceport. It worked out."

Cutter's tone turned icy as he said, "We destroyed the tracks."

"Then somebody must have fixed them," I said. "The Martian Legion came to the base by train."

"I would have spotted their repair crew if you didn't tell me to clear out," Cutter said. "Why did you want us out of the area?"

I shook my head, and confessed, "Don, I have no idea what came over me. I think I was out of my specking mind."

Cutter calmed himself as he heard my apology. He said, "So you entered the spaceport and visited Gordon Hughes on Thursday. On Friday you broke into Mars Air Force Base. What happened next?"

"I did old-fashioned recon until my men arrived. I counted heads, broke into computers, and hid in the rafters," I said. I remembered everything I did, but I did not really remember doing any of it. The details would not come to mind. It was almost like I was reading an itinerary.

I said, "I didn't get much sleep before the mission. By the time my men arrived at the base, I'd gone forty hours without sleep." Were the excuses for my benefit or for his? I didn't know who I was trying to convince. I said, "It was a specking miracle the bastards running the base didn't catch me."

Cutter listened carefully. He seemed to consider every syllable.

"You said the Martian Legion was in the spaceport. Who was on the base?"

"Legionnaires, I suppose," I said. "There weren't very many of them."

"I see," said Cutter. "And you killed them?"

"They fought to the last man," I said.

"What did you find once you had control of the base?"

"I found out about the religious movement," I said. "And I found out how they smuggled five thousand men to Earth for the Night of the Martyrs. They caught rides on freighters. Some of their boys stowed away in empty containers, some bribed their way on, some caught rides as sailors."

"Five thousand of them?" Cutter asked. "We would have heard something."

"We should have," I agreed. "We also found out where the Martian Legion got its shotguns. 'Nickel' Hill forgot some crates when he abandoned the base." General George Nicholas "Nickel" Hill was the last commander of the Unified Authority Air Force.

"And the New Olympians found them," Cutter guessed.

"All part of their religious revival," I said. "Some guy found five thousand shotguns and decided to build an Army of God around them. They thought they were on a divine errand and that God would protect them."

"Seems a little optimistic," Cutter observed.

"Like I said, having one of the rails intact worked out for the best," I said.

"We destroyed them."

"Either way," I said, not wanting to argue with Cutter. I said, "They came after us. Hunting them down in the spaceport would have been a problem.

"We've recovered 4,993 shotguns. I think it's safe to assume that the Martian Legion is no more."

As Cutter thought about this, he must have seen the same thing I saw, that Mars and the New Olympians did not pose much of a threat. A small, fanatical portion of the population led an unpopular revolt and was massacred. They smuggled a few helpless slobs to Earth, and we made short work of them as well.

This ship had missiles and particle-beam cannons and torpedoes and fighters and thousands of trained fighting men. On this one ship, we had more firepower than the New Olympians and the conquered people of Earth combined; and the *Churchill* was only one of the sixty-three fighter carriers in our fleet. Cutter had more than five hundred ships under his command.

I had no doubt that Cutter saw the same thing I saw, that the New Olympians posed no threat to the Enlisted Man's Empire.

31

NAME	**CALL, MATTHEW C**
RANK	**FIRST LIEUTENANT**
SERIAL NUMBER	**CM768-74-951**
AGE	**27 RAISED IN ORPHANAGE #351**
CLASSIFICATION	**CLONE (STANDARD MAKE)**
STATUS	~~**KILLED IN ACTION**~~
	DEATH BY PROPAFENONE POISONING

Call's personnel file had hundreds of bits of information, but those first six fields said it all. He was a clone, he'd risen to lieutenant, and he died from a death reflex. Watson ignored the photos, the metals, the requisite blood type, hair color, skin color, and eye color. Once you classified Call as a clone, the physical description became irrelevant.

Watson skipped the findings from the autopsy and read ahead in the file.

Like every sailor, soldier, and Marine in the Enlisted Man's Military, Call had seen action. He'd fought aliens on St. Augustine. He'd participated in the evacuations of St. Augustine and Gobi. When the Enlisted Man's Empire invaded Earth, Call had taken part in the first wave of the invasion.

Like most clone servicemen, Call had a clean record. He'd never been arrested.

"Looks like you were a model citizen," Watson observed.

Before joining Tarawa, the recently reinstated Second Regiment of the Second Division, Call had been stationed at the Mountain Warfare Training Facility, a base located on the West Coast of the former United States. His Military Occupational Specialty was infantry.

On January 9, 2519, Lt. Call was attacked by three civilian men while on leave in Los Angeles. He killed one of the men, the other two escaped. The bodies of men fitting their descriptions were later found dead in an apartment. They had committed suicide.

Both the local and military police investigated the crime. Both determined that Call's actions were in self-defense.

"You were a target on the Night of the Martyrs," said Watson. He laughed, and said, "You and Harris, two homicidal peas in a psychopathic pod."

Don Cutter's voice came from the console. "Watson, you there?"

"Speaking," said Watson.

"Speaking... sir," said Cutter. He continued, "Your old boss is back from the dead. We just had a long chat about Mars."

"What did he say?" asked Watson.

"I'm not going to answer that."

"Classified information?"

"No. Not at all. If what he told me is true, there's nothing worth classifying," Cutter said, sounding neither irritated nor sarcastic.

He said, "I have a job for you, Watson. Have you ever met Colonel Curtis Jackson?"

"The commanding officer?" asked Watson.

"The commanding officer of Second Regiment," Cutter said.

Watson frowned as he realized that he liked working for the

brainwashed Marine more than the admiral with the stick up his ass.

"I want you to debrief Jackson," said Cutter.

"How do I debrief him?" Watson asked. He was not familiar with the term.

"By asking him what happened," Cutter answered, irritation obvious in his voice. "*Debrief*, interview, interrogate, ask… Look, just get me a feed of him telling you what happened on Mars. I want to compare his story to the one Harris told me. I want to see how they match up."

Watson went to the Marine compound and asked for Jackson. He was taken to an office near the barracks, where he sat and waited. Outside the window, the compound bustled with life. Marines jogged past in packs. Lines of men exercised.

A clone walked into the office. Watson knew him by his name tag and by the eagle on his collar. He reached out an arm to shake the clone's hand as he said, "Colonel Jackson, I'm Travis Watson. Admiral Cutter sent me to debrief you about Mars."

Jackson shook his hand. Still gripping Watson's hand, he said, "I thought you worked for General Harris."

"The admiral transferred me to his staff while you were on Mars," Watson said as he returned to his seat.

Jackson's normally intense expression split into a smile, and he laughed long and loud. He said, "Isn't that rich? I always hear about wives running off while their husbands are on missions. This is the first time I heard about an unfaithful staff member doing it." He sat down in the seat next to Watson's. "How did Harris take the news?"

"He keeps calling me 'Mr. Navy Man.'"

"'Mr. Navy Man,'" Jackson repeated. "You know, there's a lot of bad blood between the Marines and the Navy."

"To hear Harris tell the story, there's bad blood between everyone and the Navy," said Watson.

Jackson grinned and nodded. He liked that. He said, "I guess that's true. The Army and the Air Force don't have much use for swabbies." He thought it over for a moment, and added, "As Navy brass go, Cutter's better than most."

Watson placed his computing tablet on the desk, angling it so the pinhole-sized camera pointed toward Jackson. It was a wasted effort. The camera had a 360-degree fish-eye view of the room, and it turned everything it saw into blurry distorted data that the tablet's processor interpolated and set right.

Watson had never used the video-feed function on this particular tablet, but the application and equipment were nearly ubiquitous in twenty-sixth-century technology. He said, "Tell me what happened on Mars."

"What happened on Mars? That's a tall order, isn't it? A lot of things happened."

Watson leaned back in his chair, and said, "Start at the beginning."

Jackson drew a deep breath through his nose, held it in his lungs for several seconds, then exhaled. His eyes opened wide for a moment, then narrowed as he considered what to say. A man in his late forties, he had scattered white strands in his bristly regulation-cut brown hair. He sat with his back perfectly erect and placed his hands on his knees.

"We landed. We marched around a bit, and then we went to visit the speck who was supposed to be in charge."

"You mean Governor Hughes?"

"Yeah, Hughes. He was supposed to be in charge, but he wasn't. The bastard was just another grasshopper hopping around the anthill."

"What does that mean?" asked Watson.

"What do you think it means? Grasshoppers are bigger than ants, aren't they? If an ant and a grasshopper scuffle, the grasshopper wins because it's a hundred times bigger than the ant. The grasshopper can crush it, bite it in half, or stomp the little bastard into the dirt, no problem. But, see, there's no such thing as one solitary ant in nature, am I right?"

"I've seen scouts," said Watson.

"Me, too; and there's always another one a few inches away. Maybe that grasshopper sees the second scout and stamps the little bastard out as well; but that doesn't make him king of the anthill because there's another scout after that and another one after that until you get all the way to the anthill, and there's a whole sea of ants waiting inside that hill. There's a flood of ants, just waiting there, under the surface... ready to erupt from that hill."

"And Hughes is the grasshopper?"

"He knows he's not in control."

"What about the Martian Legion?" Watson asked.

"History. Gone. We butchered the bastards."

Watson watched the colonel speak, fascinated by his individuality. Jackson had the same face as a million other clones, but his expressions, his posture, and the way he spoke made him unique. He spoke slowly in clipped sentences, as if he had just woken up.

As far as Watson knew, no clone had ever attended college, but the ones in the Pentagon seemed educated. Harris was well-read. He talked about philosophy and history. Cutter's interests were not as wide, but he had good diction. Jackson did not. He didn't swear much, less than Harris, but his vocabulary was limited, and he did not strike Watson as particularly bright.

Jackson launched into how the Legion had tried to attack the regiment that first night. He said, "They should'a come straight at us then. There were five thousand of them against a lone regiment. We were fish in a barrel. No place to run. No place to hide. Shot beats bullets at close range.

"You heard what they did instead?"

"The chlorine gas?" asked Watson.

"Yeah. Chlorine, right. We neutralized it while it was still in the vents, then Harris went out after them."

"What happened after he left? I heard he lost contact with you."

"For a minute or two. They blocked our signal."

"How did they do that?"

"Speck, easiest thing in the world. They call it 'sludging.' You jam the airwaves with a strong signal that drowns everything else out. The interLink isn't an easy signal to block, but I've seen it happen. They sludge the airways and they off their own transmissions, too. I guess they didn't have anyone they needed to contact."

Watson said, "They could have warned their partners in the Air Force base."

"If they knew Harris was coming."

"How did you get your signal back?"

That seemed to confuse Jackson. He shrugged, and said, "We got it back."

"That was when Harris ordered you to go to the Air Force base?"

"Yeah, right."

"How did you get there?"

"We flew in transports."

Watson nodded, and said, "Let me make sure I have the details in the correct order. You landed on Thursday."

"Late Thursday," Jackson corrected.

"You marched to Governor Hughes's office."

"Yeah, what a waste of time that was."

"Then you stopped for the night."

"Something like that. We bivouacked in an abandoned food court... Course we had to convince the locals to abandon it."

"Later that night, the New Olympians attacked..."

"And Harris followed them out. He contacted us from the Air Force base, and we followed him out."

"And all of that took place on Friday?"

"I suppose so, I lost track of time. The whole mission flew by. We spent some time searching the base, then we had a firefight with the Martian Legion, next thing I knew, we'd landed on the *Churchill*, and we'd been gone for a week."

Watson asked, "Did you sleep while you were exploring the Air Force base?"

"Damn well right we slept. We hot bunked—eight hours of

duty, eight hours R&R, not that there was much recreation to be had, eight hours sleep."

"How many rest periods did you have?"

"I don't remember. They all blur together, don't they?"

"I suppose," said Watson, though Jackson's spotty memory had raised some suspicions. "Do you think we should move the New Olympians to Earth?"

Jackson said, "That's Harris's story."

"But you don't agree?"

"We took their shotguns. They don't have guns as far as I can tell. I suppose that makes them peaceful."

"But...?" Watson prompted.

"We took away their shotguns; that doesn't mean we took away their fight. That's not the same thing."

"So you don't believe we should relocate the New Olympians to Earth?" Watson asked, genuinely interested in Jackson's response.

"I don't get paid to think. I'm a Marine. I get paid to kill people and break things. My opinion doesn't matter."

"Do you have an opinion?"

"About bringing the New Olympians to Earth?"

Watson nodded.

"I don't trust them."

"I see," said Watson. They talked for fifteen minutes longer with no substantive results. Realizing that he was spinning his wheels, Watson turned off the camera in his tablet. Now that the interview had ended, he asked as an aside, "Did you ever know a Lieutenant Matthew Call?"

"The name sounds familiar. How do I know him?"

"He was one of the men that died during the fighting at the Air Force base."

"One of the lucky fifty," said Jackson.

"Not so lucky," said Watson. "It wasn't just Mars. The poor guy was attacked on the Night of the Martyrs."

"Another member of the club," said Jackson.

"What do you mean?" Watson asked, though he thought he

knew. He thought Jackson was referring to Harris.

"I didn't know Call, but I guess he's number six," said Jackson. "I got three majors in this regiment. All three of them were attacked. I contributed a few martyrs myself that night. Then there's Harris. I guess you already knew the bastards attacked him in Seattle."

32

Watson returned to his quarters and the personnel files. Instead of sitting at the desk, he kicked back on his bed, tipped off his shoes, and rested his head on a pillow. He looked at personnel files.

NAME	**JACKSON, CURTIS C**
RANK	**COLONEL (COMMANDER SECOND DIVISION, SECOND REGIMENT)**
SERIAL NUMBER	**FM721-65-039**
AGE	**42 RAISED IN ORPHANAGE #018**
CLASSIFICATION	**CLONE (STANDARD MAKE)**
STATUS	**ACTIVE DUTY**

The man had seen action. Back when the clones were still part of the Unified Authority, Jackson fought against Mogats on Hubble and aliens on New Copenhagen. When the Unified Authority sent clones to recapture lost planets, he'd been one of the Marines who'd gone to liberate Providence Kri. After the rise of the Enlisted Man's Empire, Jackson saw action on Bangalore and Earth.

Of the Night of the Martyrs his file said:

On January 9, 2519, Colonel Jackson was attacked by three civilian men in Los Angeles. He killed two of the men, the other escaped. A man fitting Jackson's description of his attacker was found dead by hanging two days later. After an investigation, the Los Angeles coroner office pronounced the hanging a suicide.

Local and military police determined Jackson's actions were in self-defense.

He looked through Second Regiment's line of command and found the three majors. As Jackson had said, all three had been attacked on the night of January 9. Picking the names of Second Regiment Marines at random, Watson worked his way down to the privates. Every man had been attacked on the Night of the Martyrs.

Watson tried to call Cutter, but an aide took the call. Watson said, "I need to speak to the admiral."

"He's busy," said the aide. "Can I take a message?"

"It's urgent," said Watson.

"Then you'd better leave your message quickly," said the aide. Watson hung up on him.

Since boarding the *Churchill*, Watson had sensed discrimination at every turn. The sailors saw the ship as their domain and made no attempt to hide the disrespect they felt for their natural-born passenger.

Not deterred by an officer he considered little more than a receptionist, Watson walked to Cutter's office. The same aide met him at the door. Watson recognized the name and the attitude.

He said, "I told you, the admiral is busy."

Watson said, "Fair enough. Please tell the admiral that there is a bomb on the ship." He turned around and walked out.

The aide, a lieutenant, followed him out the door saying, "Excuse me. Excuse me! Excuse me!"

Watson stopped but did not say anything.

"Did you say a bomb?"

Bureaucratic prick, Watson thought as he kept walking past the man.

The lieutenant ran ahead and stepped in Watson's path. He repeated, "You said there is a bomb?"

"Yes. You might inform the admiral when his schedule is clear?"

"Where is it?" demanded the aide. "I'll send security."

Watson did not break stride, and the aide, a much shorter man, had to run to keep pace with him. *Funny little man,* thought Watson. *Like a yelping lapdog.* He wondered if other naval officers were cut from the same cloth.

"Wait."

Watson walked to the elevator and stopped.

"Is it armed?" asked the aide.

Watson said, "Armed, primed, and ready to explode."

"Come with me," said the lieutenant.

"Admiral Cutter can contact me when he has time to speak... assuming it's not too late."

The aide spoke into his communicator. He said, "Admiral, that civilian wants to see you. He said something about..."

Cutter said, "Lieutenant, I hope you haven't kept Watson waiting."

A look of desperation spreading across his face, the aide looked at Watson, and said, "Sir, you... You said you did not want to be disturbed."

"Lieutenant, please show Mr. Watson in." That was all he said, but the chill in his voice presented other implications.

The lieutenant led Watson to Admiral Cutter's door and left without a word. Watson knocked on the door.

"That you, Watson? Come on in."

Admiral Cutter sat at his desk holding a heavily creamed cup of coffee. He said, "You find something good?" and drank half the cup.

Watson asked, "Do you know how they selected the men in the Second Regiment?" He sat in one of the chairs beside the admiral's desk.

Cutter laughed, and said, "How the hell would I know that? That's Marine business. Ask Harris."

"Do you know anything about the regiment?"

"I work with fleets, not regiments." He sat back in his seat, laced his fingers, sat deep in thought. After a few seconds, he leaned forward and typed something on the keyboard built into his desk. He looked at the screen, and said, "It's a newly formed regiment."

"How new?" asked Watson.

"Formed last month."

"Was Harris the one who formed it? Did he select the men?"

"Not that regiment. All of the men in that regiment asked for the transfer," said Cutter. He finished his coffee and crumpled the paper cup. "What is this about?"

"Every man in the Second Regiment was attacked on the Night of the Martyrs," Watson said.

"Might be a coincidence," said Cutter.

"Admiral, of the one thousand six hundred men who were attacked, fifteen hundred joined the same regiment. That's one hell of a coincidence."

"It's Tarawa," said Cutter. "The Second Regiment of the Second Division is a prestigious unit. It's got history. It's got tradition. Marines respect tradition," said Cutter. He thought a little longer, and asked, "What do you think it means?"

Watson said, "Something must have happened on the Night of the Martyrs."

"Yes, something did happen; sixteen hundred Marines were attacked by a suicidal army of imbeciles. You don't see that every day."

"More than that," said Watson. "I think they were brainwashed during the attacks."

"That's ridiculous," said Cutter. "It's not possible. Have you seen the profiles of the New Olympians who died that night? They weren't scientists. They were religious fanatics. The ones who survived went home and killed themselves."

"Maybe they were the bait," said Watson. "It's like a magician's trick. You get the audience to watch your right hand closely, then you pull the sleight of hand with your left. Harris and the other victims were so busy beating off the meaningless dopes that they didn't notice something bigger."

"Can't be," said Cutter. He left his desk and poured himself another cup of coffee. As he poured, he mumbled, "Son of a bitch. Son of a bitch."

"The Night of the Martyrs was probably just the down payment," said Watson, "something quick, not a complete reprogramming, just a seed to get things rolling. Then they get to Mars, and it happens all over again. There's a meaningless attack. Two men are killed in a riot. A few fanatics try to shower them with chlorine gas. Jackson remembered every detail about the attack, but he went vague when I asked him what happened next."

"Just like Harris," said Cutter. Then he repeated himself. He said, "Son of a bitch. Son of a bitch."

33

Cutter tightened security on the ship. There were so many MPs guarding the landing bays, the lifts, and the engine room that I expected to find a skeleton crew on the bridge. Wrong again. He had a full crew on deck and another fifty MPs patrolling the area.

That meant he was raiding his rotation. Instead of giving his men eight hours to eat and recreate between shifts and lights-out, he had them playing policeman.

I asked him, "You expecting an invasion?"

Cutter said, "You can never be too careful."

I said, "Yes you can."

He said, "Maybe so."

So I came right out with it. I said, "Unless the EME declared a new war while I was on Mars, those MPs must be for me and my men."

Cutter looked me in the eyes when he responded, and he did not make excuses. The man was honest, I'll give him that. He said, "Harris, I'm confiscating your weapons."

"Just mine?" I asked.

"Your regiment's. We're going to stow them in a secure hold

for safekeeping."

"Safekeeping from whom?" I asked.

He did not answer the question, so I asked, "What the speck is going on here?"

Cutter said, "Let's go to my office."

It seemed like a good idea.

We entered his office, and he left the MPs outside the door. They weren't far away; but if I'd wanted to kill him, those men outside the door would not have been able to stop me. Cutter was older than me, and his form of combat involved fighters, torpedoes, and ships as big as shopping malls.

I said, "Okay, we make you nervous. I can see that. What's going on?"

For this showdown, Cutter did not hide behind his desk. He stood in front of it. We stood and faced each other. He crossed his arms, and said, "You and your men may have been compromised on Mars."

"What do you mean by compromised?"

In the last days of the Unified Authority, the U.A. military came up with infiltrator clones—specialized clones that murdered EME clones and assumed their identities. They were assassins and saboteurs, and they broke through our security by the thousands. I said, "I'm not a Double Y."

The infiltrators differed from regular clones in that they had two Y chromosomes. It made them stronger. It also made the bastards mentally unstable, which made them all the more dangerous.

"No. I don't suppose you are," said Cutter.

"Do you think they infiltrated my men?"

"No."

"So what do you think happened?"

Cutter responded with a question. "What did you mean when you said that anything that can be programmed can be reprogrammed?"

"You're not still on about that. I told you, I was sorry. I don't know what was wrong with me."

"Neither do I," said Cutter.

"Let me get this straight, you're lining your decks with military police because I was rude?" I had a sardonic smile on my face. In truth, I was pissed, and I wanted to share my irritation with Cutter.

It didn't work. A few seconds of silence passed during which he watched me with the impassive expression of a chess master. This was a man who had always given me the benefit of the doubt in the past. Those days were gone.

He watched me with eyes that never blinked, at least not in that five-second block. Finally, he asked, "Anything that can be programmed can be reprogrammed. What do you think that means?"

The words sounded familiar, but I did not remember speaking them. I said as much. "Did I actually say that?"

Good old Cutter, the son of a bitch was ready for that question. He tapped a few keys on his desk, and there I was, staring out of the screen looking frenzied and angry.

"Do you want me to leave Watson?" Cutter's voice asked off camera.

"Why the speck would I want him here?" I asked. "Give him a message for me, would you. Tell that bastard that anything that can be programmed can be reprogrammed. You tell him that. You tell him that for me."

Something was happening to me on the screen. I winced... well, the me in the video feed winced. It was a slight action. I was in pain and trying to hide it.

The Cutter in the video feed clearly had no idea what that gibberish meant. He asked, "What was that? What was your message?"

Sounding like a paranoid lunatic, I said, "Not my message, asshole. Tell him Ray Freeman said that."

Cutter switched off the screen and stared at me.

I said, "I don't think you have enough MPs." It was a joke. I hoped to ease the tension, a wasted effort.

Cutter asked, "So what did you mean?"

"I have no idea. You saw how I looked in the feed. I hadn't slept in days. I don't think I was clinically sane."

Cutter's eyes betrayed no emotion, not anger, not pity. He kept his unblinking gaze as steady as a rifle on a firing line. I wanted to shrink away from his gaze.

I said, "There's no meaning in those words. What if I said, 'Tuna fish eat isotopes'? Meaningless. I was a raving lunatic." Until that moment, I hadn't realized how much of a lunatic I'd become. "There is no meaning to what I said, it's the product of fatigue."

"What does Ray Freeman have to do with it?"

That shut me up. "I haven't seen Freeman in over a year," I said.

"Watson says you went looking for him on the Night of the Martyrs."

"I didn't find him."

"Do you know how to find him?"

I shook my head, and said, "He finds me when he wants to chat."

Cutter said, "You were in Seattle on the Night of the Martyrs?" Watson must have told him; either that, or he looked it up in my files. "What made you think he'd be in Seattle?"

"The last time I heard from him, he was in Seattle," I said.

"You went looking for him, but you didn't find him?"

"I was preoccupied," I said.

I did not know how to interpret Cutter's expression. It wasn't anger. His eyes hardened, and his mouth froze in an unconvincing smile. Behind the mask, I thought I saw disappointment. He said, "General, you are relieved of command."

His words stunned me. At first I wanted to laugh. I was the one who had promoted him to admiral in the first place. Okay, yes, I gave him an extra star; but in my mind, I had as much of a right to relieve him as he did to relieve me.

I wanted to threaten him. I wanted to laugh at him. I wanted to take away his command. Instead, I said, "I am relieved."

34

"What the hell do you mean you were relieved of command!"
Jackson demanded. "Cutter is a damned cargo hauler. Who the
speck placed him in charge?"

"I did."

"General, we could take this ship."

"That's why Cutter has so many MPs guarding the decks."

Jackson laughed. "We could take care of them rapid, quick,
and pronto, couldn't we? Swabbies with pistols... Hell, we might
not lose a single Marine."

"He wants us to hand over our guns."

"Speck that!"

"I said we would."

We walked around the compound as we spoke.

"You've been relieved of command, sir. That makes it my
decision." We walked in silence for two minutes, before he finally
said, "Shit. I'll deliver the weapons."

Then he asked, "Who's taking your post?"

"There's only one general in this man's corps," I said.

"Ritz?" Jackson asked. "'Run-and-Gun Ritz'? Outstanding.

Once Cutter gets a whiff of Ritz, he'll beg you to come back."

I wasn't so sure. Brigadier General Hunter Ritz had all the reckless bravado of a young Marine; but following orders and observing the chain of command had been hardwired into his brain. He was brash, and he and Cutter would clash, but Ritz always produced in the end. He was irreverent, but he was also inventive, hard-hitting, and ruthless. Cutter would appreciate those qualities.

"Did Cutter say why he wanted you out?"

"He thinks I was compromised. He thinks I'm working for the New Olympians."

"Bullshit," said Jackson.

"I'm not going to do myself any favors when we get back. I am going to push to bring the New Olympians to Earth. We need to get those bastards off Mars."

"No, we don't," said Jackson.

"We owe them that much," I said. "They're humans living in inhuman conditions."

"We don't owe them anything," said Jackson. He sounded angry. He said, "We saved their specking hides on Olympus Kri, didn't we? We pulled them off the specking planet before it burned... and then we got ambushed for helping them!"

"That was a U.A. attack," I said. "The New Olympians didn't have anything to do with it."

"We lost ships. We lost men. We lost our specking chain of command, all for helping those bastards," said Jackson. "The way I see it, we've done too much for them already. And don't get me started on that specking Night of the Martyrs shit.

"Look, General, maybe I'm bigoted against my own kind, but that's the way it is. I'm natural-born, but I still specking hate the bastards. Give me the company of synths any day.

"The New Olympians might be loyal, but that doesn't explain why they formed a Martian Legion."

"We killed the Martian Legion," I said. "We destroyed their army."

"We took away their weapons, but they may still have an army."

"They need to be repatriated. We can't leave them on Mars."

We had made our way to the firing range. Ahead of us, a company of men fired at targets, some moving and some stationary. Most of the men used special M27s designed for use aboard ships, guns that fired holographic bullets. A few of the men used real M27s that fired live ammo. Cutter would confiscate the real ones in another hour. The holographic guns posed no danger.

We had seen so much war over the last fifteen years that Darwin's survival of the fittest had occurred in a nation of clones. Our weak men had died over the last decade. The clones who remained did not miss many shots, nor did they waste bullets. Training hardens men, combat forges them, attrition turns the weak ones into statistics.

Jackson was right. If we wanted to take the ship, Cutter and his MPs would not pose a problem.

35

The message from the office of Gordon Hughes, Governor of Mars Spaceport, came with the governor's virtual security seal. It said, "I have Howard Tasman. Do not send clones."

Cutter read the message and verified the seal. The name, Howard Tasman, meant nothing to him.

He tried calling Hughes. No one answered. He sent a short message of his own—"Who is Howard Tasman?" An hour passed, then a day, then a week. He received no reply.

In the meantime, Cutter tried to solve the mystery on his own. Having started his career as an enlisted man, Cutter did not mind doing a little legwork. He started with a quick search of the mediaLink, a mostly entertainment-based network that included magazines, encyclopedias, and reference books.

There were no references to Howard Tasman, not even a record of his birth. Apparently, he had not been an actor, writer, politician, or professional athlete.

227

Cutter accessed military records, using his office computer. Tasman did not appear to have had a military career.

He called Watson. Instead of saying "hello," he asked, "Have you found Freeman yet?"

"Not yet," said Watson.

Cutter thought, *Not yet, sir*. He said, "For God's sake, Watson, the man is seven feet tall. He eats bullets and shits out dead people. What's taking so long?"

Cutter wasn't really bothered by Watson's not having found Freeman. It was the boy's inability to say "sir" that bothered him.

"I've got every satellite and traffic camera on the planet looking for him. It's like he never steps into the sunlight," said Watson.

Or he's off planet, thought Cutter. When the Enlisted Man's Empire attacked Earth, its Navy had a self-broadcasting spy ship. That ship disappeared after the war. In the admiral's view, that ship's disappearance was a security nightmare. She was a modified cruiser, with three decks and three landing bays, that was capable of carrying nine transports. She had a stealth generator that rendered her invisible until she broadcasted. Like any other self-broadcasting ship, the spy ship created an anomaly that could be detected from millions of miles away whenever she broadcasted; but that was the only time she could be detected.

"I have another job for you," he told Watson. "Maybe you'll be able to get this one done."

"What do you want me to do?" asked Watson.

What do you want me to do, sir? Cutter thought. He asked, "Ever heard the name Howard Tasman?"

"Can't say I've heard the name; is he important?"

"Apparently Gordon Hughes thinks he's important."

"Hughes?"

"Hughes sent me a message saying he has Howard Tasman."

"Did he say anything else?"

"Yeah, he said not to send clones."

"Are you sending me to Mars?" asked Watson.

"Not yet, not until we know something about Tasman first. I

want you to go to the U.A. Archives to see what you can dig up."

"Not a problem," said Watson. "Anything else?"

"Yeah. When you leave Bolling Air Force Base, make sure to take your guard. I know about you sneaking out at night."

36

So Cutter knew he went out at night. Watson could not escape the feeling that the admiral was using the bodyguards to look over his shoulder. He felt both angry and embarrassed.

He did not like living on a military base. The irony was that now that he lived among clones, he identified more with them than before. They grew up in the orphanages believing they were natural-born children living in facilities for synthetics. He now believed the same thing about himself. He was a natural-born citizen living on a base for military clones.

He knew he was natural-born, of course; but weren't they as certain of their origins as he was of his?

Watson was a man who could not sleep unless he'd had an orgasm. He had slept well every night since returning from Mars. Since leaving the *Churchill*, he had slept in nearly every part of town except Bolling Air Force Base.

His bodyguards, on the other hand, always looked tired. When he spent the night in a woman's apartment, they spent the night in the car.

Watson opened the door of his office. His guards waited on

the other side. Two were sitting, the third was asleep on the floor. Their clothes were wrinkled, and their faces were puffy and blotchy from the lack of sleep.

"We gotta go," said Watson.

The bodyguards did not argue. One asked where. Watson told him. The driver went ahead to check the car. One bodyguard walked ten feet ahead of Watson; the other remained a few paces behind him.

They rode into Washington, D.C., and drove down a ramp into the underground parking lot of the archive building. No one spoke until after they parked, then one of the bodyguards told Watson to stay in the car while he searched the building. The driver and the remaining bodyguard sat in tired silence.

Once the bodyguard returned, the driver stayed with the car while Watson entered the archive, his bodyguards in tow. The Enlisted Man's Army guarded the archive. Six clone officers sat behind a bulletproof barricade, all holding M27s.

Watson went to the security station and showed his identification.

The officer in charge typed some information into a computer. Watson's security clearance wasn't enough, he needed authorization from Admiral Cutter's office before he could enter.

Apparently, the authorization came through quickly. The officer glared at Watson, scrutinized him, then told him to pass through the posts.

"The posts," a security device that identified people right down to their DNA, looked like a postmodern attempt at re-creating an ancient Grecian archway—two ten-foot pillars, spaced six feet apart, topped by a ten-foot rectangle, all made of polymerized metal.

The pillar on the left side of the posts was known as the "sprayer" because it shot a fine mist made of oil and water vapor. The sprayer dislodged flecks of skin, dandruff, and hair, which the column on the right, the "receiver," vacuumed and analyzed.

Watson stepped between the pillars, felt the gust, and was admitted through. The process took under a second. The bodyguards passed through the posts also, the security team checking their identities as well.

After his last visit, Watson knew his way around the archive. He found a computer station and made himself at home. His bodyguards remained on their feet, standing a few feet behind him, their arms by their sides, their hands near their guns.

The inside of the archive was a three-story vault with a domed ceiling and a circular balcony. The walls were square, but the computer stations were arranged in concentric rings.

Watson sat down. He typed a security access code, the last gate between the archives and a break-in. The leaders of the Enlisted Man's Empire considered the archive to be a temple of forbidden knowledge and admitted only its highest of high priests to enter. In this library could be found information for assembling a broadcast network, creating clone farms, and undermining nations.

The clones needed to retain this information if they hoped to extend their empire beyond the current generation.

Tactile sensors in the keyboard of the computer verified Watson's DNA and fingerprints every time he tapped a key. A discreet retinal scanner in the screen confirmed his identity 120 times per minute. Watson did not notice the additional security precautions as he trolled for information about Howard Tasman.

A menu appeared.

Tasman, H—Biographical Information
Tasman, H—Liberator Project, Linear Committee
               Briefing—June 24, 2453
Tasman, H—Neural Programming Code—March 8, 2454
Tasman, H—Need for a Death Reflex—August 17, 2461
Tasman, H—SECURITY PROFILE, Updated 2506

Watson started with the security profile and discovered that if Howard Tasman was still alive, he was an exceptionally old man. He'd been born on a planet called Volga in December, 2428. That made him eighty-nine years old.

Watson read the name of his home planet and stopped. He'd

heard of Volga, but he was not sure where or how, maybe in school. It was not one of the big planets, not one of the capitals of the six galactic arms.

The file included a birth picture, fingerprints, a footprint, photographs of Tasman's parents, and a DNA sample. Watson skipped all of that. He scrolled through the file, stopping at a picture of Tasman as a young adult, just finishing college. He'd studied gene replication and neural enhancement before being hired by the Unified Authority to work in the military cloning program in 2448.

Pictures of Tasman showed a man who could blend into any crowd. He was average height—five feet nine inches. He was slightly on the thin side and weighed 162 pounds. He had short brown hair, brown eyes, no tattoos, no scars, no identifiable markings. Watson examined a photograph of Tasman at the age of twenty-one. He had a soft, doughy face. He had narrow shoulders and long, skinny arms.

In 2452, after a fleet of ships had been lost in the Galactic Eye region of the Milky Way, the Linear Committee drafted Tasman to work on a top secret cloning project.

Top secret, Watson thought. It was possibly the worst-kept military secret since the atomic bomb. Thinking that aliens had arrived in the galaxy, the Linear Committee—the executive arm of Unified Authority government—commissioned a team of scientists to create an army of superclones that would be known as "Liberators."

As he began work on the Liberator program, Tasman proposed a method for making the clones more effective in battle. He suggested creating a gland that would release a combination of testosterone and adrenaline into their blood. He called this a "combat reflex." He also proposed a rudimentary version of neural programming that would include two sets of active instructions:

1) Inability to commit suicide.

"These clones will be inserted in a bleak, hostile environment and forced to battle an enemy with superior technology

and weapons. There will be a high rate of suicide among them unless we render them incapable of suicide through programming."

2) A diminished sense of conscience.
"Since we will not have time to properly train these clones for battle, we will need to make them especially aggressive to make up for their lack of combat skills."

He's talking about creating sociopaths, thought Watson. The next picture showed the naval officer in charge of the Liberator Project—a skinny beanpole of a man named Captain Bryce Klyber who later rose all the way to the rank of five-star admiral. Klyber held an iconic place in the history of the Unified Authority. He had created a supership called the *Doctrinaire*, which would supposedly protect Earth from invasion.

Watson was still in school when the Morgan Atkins Fanatics attacked Earth, but he remembered the destruction of the *Doctrinaire*. The Mogats destroyed Klyber's ship with a single shot. By that time, though, Klyber had already been assassinated.

If Klyber created the Liberators, he had been behind two disasters. The *Doctrinaire* did not survive her first great battle, and Congress outlawed Liberator clones after they massacred the civilian populations of several planets.

The last remaining Liberators were sent to the farthest ends of the galaxy and banned from the Orion Arm of the galaxy. In other words, they were banned from Earth... eliminated by attrition. Watson did not know the particulars about how Wayson Harris came into existence, but he had been created decades after the massacres.

According to the profile, Tasman proposed using neural programming to build safeguards into future generations of military clones after the Liberator-clone disasters.

Watson watched a video feed of a young Howard Tasman speaking to the Linear Committee. Looking out of place in a suit and tie, he spoke before the committee in a high, monotone voice. He said, "Theoretically, there is no limit to the amount of instructions we can program into their brains, but if we input too many sets of active instruction, we run the risk of creating fundamental conflicts in their programming. Even if there are no conflicts in their programming, overprogrammed clones may lack the initiative to act on their own."

Watson went on reading Howard Tasman's theory of programming. He said, "It does not matter how many sets of dormant instructions you place in a clone's brain because dormant instructions do not impact behavior. Only active instructions matter."

According to the "Tasman Theory," clones could hold an infinite amount of dormant instructions that could later be activated should new situations arise. Technology that had not been available during the creation of the Liberators, he believed, would play an important role in designing later models.

Watson read this and thought about Harris. He'd known about some of the programming. He'd said he could not commit suicide because of his programming. *What would it be like to know that someone had programmed your brain?* Watson wondered. *You would never know which of your thoughts were really yours.*

He thought about the Night of the Martyrs. Harris had killed three men. He'd butchered them. His diminished sense of conscience had been in fine form on that evening.

In 2451, the Liberator Clone Program was discontinued.

According to his psychological profile, Tasman blamed himself for the program's shortcomings. After winning the war in the Galactic Eye, the Liberators were sent out as peacekeepers; but the programming that ensured their success in the Galactic Eye made their term as galactic policemen a disaster.

When Liberators were sent to stop a riot at Albatross Island, a galactic penal colony, they became addicted to the hormone from the combat reflex and killed all the convicts, including convicts that had turned themselves in. After they finished with the convicts, the Liberators butchered guards and hostages.

In 2457, at the age of twenty-nine, Tasman returned to his home planet of Volga, where he received a hero's welcome.

Volga had been one of those planets that never caught a break. It had no undiscovered minerals, no famous actors, no remarkable athletes. Its economy limped along, and it produced enough food for its inhabitants, but nearly 15 percent of the population emigrated once the Unified Authority relaxed its ban on planetary migration.

Tasman married a local girl in 2458 and moved to the capital city of Niva, where he continued his neural programming research. He and his wife had their first child, a girl, in 2459. They had a boy in 2460.

Somewhere in the back of Watson's mind, a memory stirred. He tried to ignore that memory, but he could not ignore the chill running down his spine. It wasn't the name, Volga, that dislodged the memory. Twenty-four sixty was a year students memorized in school.

The Volgan economy finally failed in 2460. Toxic storms spread around the planet, killing crops and destroying property.

Populations never starved during the golden age of the Unified Authority. The government sent food and terraforming specialists who claimed they could fix the environment. By the time they arrived, 80 percent of the population had submitted emigration forms. The kind of mass migration that the U.A. Congress had always feared was about to begin.

The U.A.'s first response was to bribe the people to stay. Along with food and tractors, the Unifieds sent the latest line of mediaLink glasses, built sports facilities, replaced automobiles, and sent enormous stores of luxury foods.

It was too little and too late. When the U.A. Congress began rejecting all emigration requests, the people protested, and then they rioted.

None of this information was in the files. Watson had learned it in grade school. He learned about the outcome of the riots in grade school as well. The watered-down stories had caused him nightmares when he was a boy.

The Unified Authority responded by sending a battalion of Liberators and the Volga Massacre began. Seven hundred thousand people died.

Watson expected to read that Tasman's wife and children were killed, but he was wrong. He and his family survived the siege. The government relocated them to another planet.

Probably a good idea, Watson thought. When things go wrong, people need a villain. On Volga, the people probably blamed Tasman, their former hometown hero.

The Unified Authority moved Tasman and his family to Olympus Kri.

In 2461, after three more Liberator massacres, Tasman appeared before Congress with designs for a new class of clones that would not know they were clones. His design included a gland that secreted propafenone—a neural toxin. The programming and the gland would ensure that no clone would discover his origins and survive.

Tasman proposed programming the new clones to believe they were natural-born and raising them in orphanages. Liberators and earlier models started life in adult bodies.

Watson watched a video feed in which Tasman told Congress, "Clones must never realize that they are separate and, therefore, different. If they do, they may rebel. Cloned soldiers who realize they are not human may decide that they owe no debt for their creation."

Tasman's wife died in 2484. He did not remarry. His children and grandchildren were killed during the first wave of the alien invasion. The date listed was 2514.

According to the file, nobody knew Tasman's identity on Olympus Kri. About that they had been wrong.

Somebody must have known.

37

Without realizing it, Watson had spent four hours in the archives. He sat at the computer thinking about Tasman, realizing how much he disliked the man. Thinking that clones were no different than computers, Tasman had created a generation of clones to be sent into the nether regions of the galaxy for a brutal war, then taken away their only means of escape: the God-given right to suicide.

No matter what they ran into in the Galactic Eye, the Liberators would have fought to the final man and suffered every last privation because it was written in their "instruction set."

Watson looked back at the two clones who had entered the archive as his bodyguards. Tired or not, they stood alert, their hands near their weapons, ready to die in the line of duty. Synthetic or not, they were honorable men.

Until that moment, Watson had thought of his bodyguards simply as "BG1" and "BG2." He didn't even know their names. He wondered if he was just as antisynthetic as Tasman.

Watson asked BG1, "Are you ready to leave?"

The bodyguard did not speak, he nodded.

Watson thought about thanking these men for protecting him,

but he knew better. His gratitude meant nothing to them.

The hall that led back to the security station was long and curved, with marble walls and a black granite floor that sparkled in the bright light. There was an odd, biting scent in the air, something sharp that reminded Watson of the smell of ammonia. He wondered if a cleaning crew had arrived, and tried to imagine the security protocol for admitting janitors to clean the archive bathrooms.

Up ahead, he could see the soldiers manning the security station. One of the guards drew his M27. He started to raise the gun.

Because of the bend in the hall, the bodyguard to Watson's right had the clearest view of the station. The clone Watson had always thought of as "BG2" stopped walking, drew his pistol, fired two shots, hitting the security guard both times—once in the chest, once in the head. The back of the guard's head seemed to explode, splattering a yard-wide burst of blood and tissue onto the bulletproof glass behind him. His hands still holding the M27, the guard fell to the ground as the rest of his team opened fire. Because of the curve in the wall, Watson only saw two of the soldiers, but he had counted six guards when they first arrived.

BG2 kept firing. He took a shot in the left shoulder, a shot in the stomach, a shot in the chest before he slumped to the ground, gun still out, finger still working the trigger. He opened his mouth to say something, and blood poured over his lips.

BG1 pulled Watson backward as another bullet tore into BG2's chest. Blood seeped from his wounds forming a puddle around him. Bullets scraped the wall above him, carving gouges in the smooth marble.

BG1, a combat-tested MP, understood what was happening, but Watson had never experienced a gunfight. Frantic thoughts flashed in his brain while primal fear paralyzed him. He heard the gunshots, saw the blood and the body of the clone he'd called BG2, but he did not comprehend what was happening. He tried to run to the dying clone and help him. BG1 closed a hand around his arm and wrestled him back.

"Move!" the clone snarled.

Still staring at the body, Watson stumbled backward as his remaining bodyguard dragged him into the vault. Bullets ricocheted off the wall. A bullet hit a curve in the wall and looped around it like a train going through a tunnel. A bullet hit a light fixture in the ceiling, sending an electric arc into the air. Tiny shards of glass spread through the air like confetti.

One of the guards ran around the bend in the hall. Aiming his pistol over Watson's shoulder, BG1 shot him twice, once in the chest and once in the head. The sound of the shots echoed in Travis Watson's ear.

The archive guards fired a long stream of bullets down the hall. By this time, Watson and his bodyguard had retreated into the research area. Pointing at a door across the floor, the bodyguard said, "Once I hit two of theirs, run for that door."

A soldier sprinted out of the hall. Not seeing where Watson and the bodyguard were hiding, he stopped and waved his gun. As he turned to the left, BG1 shot him. The bullet passed through the man's throat. He dropped his M27 and managed to get a hand to his throat as blood sprayed from the wound splashing everything around him. Still holding his throat, the man crumpled to the floor.

Having seen what happened, the next guards knew where the fatal shot had come from. Two of them dived into the room with their M27s already firing, hitting the wall, hitting the doorway, hitting BG1's left arm and chest as he pushed Watson out of the line of fire. His eyes wild with pain, the bodyguard shoved his gun into Watson's hands and died.

Watson crouched behind a computer, holding the bloody gun in trembling hands. When he heard the last three shots, he did not know what happened. He continued to cower and stare at his pistol.

His driver, BG3, stepped into view. He held a pistol in one hand and an M27 in the other. He said, "It's me," and placed his pistol back in its holster. He eased the gun out of Watson's trembling hands and said, "Wilder sent me a distress signal."

Slowly standing, Watson looked down at the dead bodyguard. He looked at the dead soldiers, their blood forming a pool of red syrup that stretched into the hallway.

Two days later, after the drugs had finally calmed his nerves, Watson asked the driver, "How did you know to come get me?"

The clone's name was Simpson. He said, "I told you, Wilder sent me a distress signal."

"Who is Wilder?"

"Tim Wilder… your bodyguard… he was killed in the hallway," Simpson said.

Watson thought about that. He had considered the man who had died saving his life so unimportant that he had never bothered to learn his name.

38

"Have you met Glen Healer?" asked Cutter.

"He's an admiral, right? Isn't he the head of Naval Intelligence?" asked Watson. Watson cursed himself again. He didn't know Curtis Jackson from Martin Riley from Glen Healer from Joshua Simpson. They were all clones. All men who stood five feet ten inches tall, had brown hair, brown eyes, and the same face. He couldn't tell them apart.

"Close," said Cutter. "He's a captain, not an admiral. He's over interrogations. He keeps offering to go to Mars to collect Tasman from Hughes.

"Hughes said no clones, right? Healer's a clone, but he thinks he's a natural-born. They all do, it's in their programming; so he keeps volunteering to go."

"You can't send him," said Watson.

Cutter said, "I walk a fine line. If Healer figures out that I turned him down because he's a clone, he's going to have a death reflex."

"You have to lie to him," said Watson.

"I can't. He's a trained and experienced interrogator. He can

242

hear it in your voice. He can see it in your eyes. The clone is a walking, talking lie detector."

"Send him a memo," said Watson.

"He'll call to follow up."

"Don't take the call," said Watson.

Cutter smiled, and said, "Yeah, that's pretty much what I plan to do."

Then he became more serious. He said, "Look, Watson, I need a natural-born with a security clearance. That doesn't leave a lot of options."

"You're sending me to Mars?" Watson asked, his spirits plunging.

"I'd go myself, but I'm too old for this," said Cutter. "At least you're young."

Even the clone at the top doesn't know he's a clone, Watson thought. He said, "You can't go, they'd recognize you." *Whoever they are,* he thought.

"They might," Cutter agreed. "Listen, Watson, I watched the video feed of your bodyguard's debriefing. I heard how you panicked in the archive. Panic like that on Mars, and you will get yourself killed."

"I hear most people lose their head their first time in combat," said Watson. "Maybe I'm used to it now."

Cutter said nothing.

39

LOCATION: MARS
DATE: APRIL 30, 2519

Watson did not think money would help him on Mars, but he thought it might help him get off the planet if things went bad, so he brought a wad of it. He brought three tubes of nutrient paste, something he'd hoped never to eat. He also took a tiny pistol, which he hid in the pocket of his jacket.

He stood among the crates in the back of a freighter wearing dirty clothes he hoped would help him blend in with the New Olympians. Compared to the civilian dockworkers off-loading the crates, he looked like a vagrant. By Earth standards their uniforms were scuffed, but Watson would have had to have washed, patched, mended, and tailored his clothes before they could be described as merely scuffed.

The freighter was huge, almost too large a ship to fly in atmosphere. She would not fit inside a landing bay. Instead, she touched down on a freight platform. Once the ship was settled, a mechanical gangway closed around her entrance, forming a seal, then the cargo hatch opened, and the work began. Men used forklifts and lifters to transfer crates onto trailers. The work was loud. Engines growled. Men shouted at one another.

The cold dry air in the freighter turned to steam and vanished when it mixed with the humid spaceport air. Condensation dripped down the gangway walls and formed an inch-deep stream that ran down the ramp. When carts ran through the water, their tires squealed.

Nobody paid attention to Watson as he entered the spaceport. Carts with ten-foot stacks of crates sped by him. Bright lights shone down on him. Men with robotic lifters stomped nearby, some carrying crates, some stacking them.

So this is how they came to Earth, Watson thought. The escape hatch cut both ways. He strolled unmolested through a warehouse that seemed to stretch forever. He followed an aisle between rows of shelves. Maybe it was an optical illusion, but the aisle seemed to stretch into its own horizon.

He'd been cold on the freighter. His breath formed clouds of steam as he'd waited to make this walk. Now sweat formed on his hands and feet and back. Drops of perspiration raced down his sides.

"Hey you. Yeah, you," a man yelled at Watson. The man was large and fat and dirty. Whiskers lined his cheeks and jowls. "Th'speck you think you're going?"

"I'm on break," said Watson.

"Yeah? Well, we got a shipment to clear."

Watson heard something in the man's voice, menace, but not anger. The man wasn't threatening him. He seemed to think that Watson would happily spin around and jog right back up the dock.

Watson did not know how to work any of the equipment, and he did not understand the procedures. He needed to leave the docks as quickly as possible, or his ignorance would attract attention. He said, "I've been here since last night. I should have gone home three hours ago."

"I don't care when you got here, hole. It's another load, you got to stick it out."

"Give me a specking break."

"Yeah? You got a name, kid?"

Not wanting to give his own name, Watson almost said Wayson Harris. That was the first name that came into his mind; but the man might have recognized it. Instead, he said, "The name's Freeman."

Having identified himself as Freeman, Watson decided to behave in a Freeman-esque style. He said, "Pleased to meet you. Now are you going to get out of my way, or are we going to have a problem?"

Even as he said this, Watson realized he sounded nothing like Freeman. Freeman didn't try to intimidate people, it came naturally as breathing for him.

The other man was older than Watson, shorter than him, and fatter; but he was probably not afraid to fight. Watson had not been in a fight since grade school. The thought of being hit in the face scared him.

The man sneered, and said, "You watch your mouth, kid. I'll kick your specking teeth in."

Watson thought about the things he knew about Ray Freeman. He was not a big talker. Harris said he seldom spoke, so Watson did not answer.

The old guy was tough, but he was no taller than five-ten, the same size as a clone. He was fat and fifty and Watson was six-five, dressed like a bum, and fit. He towered over the dockworker; and now that he was silent, the dockworker took note of it. He said, "The guys in charge see you walking out, they'll can your ass. You really want to spend the rest of your life sitting around out there?" He pointed over his shoulder with his thumb.

Watson said nothing and stepped around the man.

He had bluffed and gotten away with it. Once again he had relied on his size, and the other man backed down. Watson knew that someday someone would call his bluff. He hoped it didn't happen on Mars.

He walked out a door at the back of the warehouse and passed through a break room in which a handful of men lounged and chatted as they drank coffee. These men ignored Watson, but he could not ignore them. They smelled like year-old laundry.

The next door he took led him out to halls.

You knew what it's like, he reminded himself. He'd seen video feeds on the mediaLink. He'd seen some of the feeds Harris sent back, and he was still unprepared. The sights and sounds overwhelmed him. The smell of sweat and garbage filled his nostrils, and made his head swim.

Within three minutes of stepping off the freighter, he started scratching his scalp and remembered about the lice.

The pungent air was so thick that Watson felt smothered. The crowds seemed to close in around him. He closed his eyes, and when he opened them again, he saw that no one had moved.

No one seemed to notice the tall stranger standing outside the warehouse door. A dozen preteen boys ran down the hall, snapping and yelling like a pack of wild dogs. Men and women drove by in slow-moving carts hauling food and supplies. Watson folded his arms across his chest, not because he was cold or tired but because he wanted to reassure himself that his pistol was still hidden in his jacket. Pinching his fingers over the barrel, he traced the shape of the gun until he reached the butt.

The gun was an S9 stealth pistol, a fléchette-firing weapon good for close-range combat but useless past twenty yards. Watson would have preferred a more powerful weapon, but the ammunition for the S9 came in the form of playing-card-sized metal wafers, each one of which held three hundred needle-sized fléchettes. Three hundred bullets would be heavy and hard to hide. But with one wafer in his pistol and three more wafers in his pockets, Watson carried enough ammunition for twelve hundred shots.

Feeling nervous, he looked down the hall.

Watson had never visited the spaceport before. As a boy, he'd never traveled outside the solar system. By the time he graduated college, the Morgan Atkins Fanatics had already destroyed the

Broadcast Network, and civilians no longer traveled across the galaxy.

He and Cutter had spent hours discussing the mission. His objectives were simple: first, find Gordon Hughes and determine if he was trustworthy. If he could not be trusted, Cutter wanted Watson to kill him. "Kill him, or he will kill you," Cutter had said.

When Watson pointed out that Hughes was now a tired old man, the admiral answered, "He could kill you from his deathbed, Watson. A single word would do it. All he'd need to do is expose you while you are behind enemy lines."

Watson hoped he could trust Hughes. He'd never killed anybody. He hoped he never would.

Before leaving Washington, Watson memorized the layout of the spaceport. He knew the spot in which he stood and where he had to go. After taking a deep breath, he started walking. When people spoke to him, he ignored them.

He did not blend in. His dirty, tattered clothes were too clean. He was tall and skinny, but he looked fat compared to the people around him. These people were not starving, but they were not far from it.

He thought about the fat old guy who had stopped him as he left the loading dock. The guy had said something about not wanting to end up sitting in the halls. It wasn't a threat so much as a warning. Maybe workers were paid with food.

In preparation for Mars, Watson had shaved his head. On the video feeds, shaved heads seemed to be the fashion on Mars. Now that he walked the halls, he saw it was not a fashion statement. The reality of taking five-minute showers twice per month manifested itself in head lice. Men who did not want to become overly acquainted with Mars's first indigenous species shaved their heads.

The warehouse was connected to a major trunk in the spaceport floor plan that would lead to the grand arcade. The corridor had low ceilings, maybe twelve feet high. It was packed with people and lined with openings that led into what had once been the loading docks for stores and restaurants.

Watson entered the two-mile-long grand arcade. One hundred feet above him, condensation dripped from the dirty, steam-stained glass. He tried to find the Martian sky through the atrium roof, but the roof's dusty patina blocked out the light.

Watson thought the air in the service hall had smelled bad, but he could barely breathe once he entered the grand arcade. Sewage, garbage, mass flatulence. He nearly gagged, realized that the sharp smell of his vomit would be drowned by the other odors, and the thought of the other odors made him all the more nauseous.

Looking at the balconies above him, he realized that millions of people had shoehorned their lives into this long narrow corridor. What must once have been a miracle mile was now a nightmare alley. This was where the trouble had begun for Harris. This was where the two clones died.

Watson looked at the stores around him. He took in the darkened signs, many with familiar names. The jewelry store to his right was part of a chain with locations in Washington, D.C. An enormous department store, now a sea of people, belonged to a chain that only operated in pangalactic spaceports. With all of humanity returned to Earth and Mars, there were no more pangalactic spaceports. Space travel had disappeared, taking the department stores with it.

Watson had heard Harris use the term "picnicker," but until he saw how the people were living for himself, it had never made sense. These people lived on blankets. Blankets had become their floors, their beds, their homes.

His thoughts returned to the fat old man in the loading dock. He had asked Watson, "You really want to spend the rest of your life sitting around out there?" Now Watson knew what he meant. The dockworkers were the lottery winners, the men and women who could leave their blankets because they had jobs.

Doing the math in his head, Watson estimated the number of people needed to run the spaceport might be less than one hundred thousand, maybe only fifty thousand. That left more than 16.9 million people with nothing to do.

The Martian Legion suddenly made sense, as did the religious revival. Men living on blankets with nothing would grasp at fool's gold promises of self-respect and redemption. *Fanaticism comes naturally when you have nothing to lose*, he thought.

As Watson cut across the grand arcade, he passed empty fountains now used as platforms for handing out food. Workers arranged boxes on tables. People milled around below them like stray cats in an alley. They created a fuzzy sort of line, but Watson thought any hint of organization would disintegrate into entropy once the food appeared.

Harris is right about this place, he thought. *We need to get these people out of here.*

When he reached the hall that led from the arcade to the administrative area, Watson took one last look at the stores. People noticed him. He was tall and heavy by Martian standards, and he stood erect. These people slept on blankets and concrete, they had little to eat, and they had little opportunity to exercise. Their bodies had degraded.

He entered the hall—ten-foot ceilings, offices instead of stores. This had been a public-access area of the spaceport, one used by travelers who had lost their luggage or needed assistance. He passed generic office spaces from which the doors had been removed. People seemed to occupy every inch of available floor space.

As he neared the administrative complex, Watson smelled a sharp odor of burned plastic in the air, something he had not smelled in other parts of the spaceport. He turned the last corner and saw the buildings... what was left of them.

The area was a cul-de-sac, a rounded dead end with a raised ceiling. In the briefings, the buildings of the administrative complex looked like they were three buildings on a street. They had façades like office buildings with doorways and windows.

Two of those buildings had burned to the ground. Their walls had melted, and glass from the shattered windows sparkled among the debris. The buildings had been made of plastic, but now only their twisted and shriveled skeletons remained.

Unlike the grand arcade and the halls, the cul-de-sac was abandoned. This was the first empty stretch Watson had seen since the warehouse. He had not liked the crowding. Now he liked the emptiness even less.

His arms crossed over his chest, he reached a hand into his jacket and gripped the S9 pistol as he looked right, then left, and walked to the third building, the one that had not been burned.

As he took a step, he felt pressure on the spot between his eyebrows. It was not hot or hard. As he reached a finger to touch the spot, he saw the scarlet light play on his fingertips. It was a laser, an old-fashioned aiming device. Someone wanted him to know there was a gun trained on his head.

Watson stopped. He left the pistol in his jacket and held his hands out so that anyone watching would know they were empty.

He waited. No one spoke. The person aiming the laser did not ask for his name or tell him to go away, and the laser continued to shine on him.

Keeping his hands up and out, Watson traced the beam to an open window four floors up. He saw the pixel-sized glowing red dot and the barrel of the rifle below it.

A young woman came out of the building. Moving with graceful self-assurance, she picked her way toward Watson. She stopped twenty feet away from him, and asked, "What are you doing here?"

The girl was pretty, but Watson did not care. He could still feel the laser on his forehead. He could feel his heart pounding. He said, "Governor Hughes sent for me."

She said, "I doubt that," and turned to leave.

Beginning to panic, Watson said, "It's the truth. He sent the message to Admiral Cutter."

She stopped and stared at him quizzically. "What message?"

"He said that he had Howard Tasman. He told the admiral not to send a clone."

"You're not a clone," the girl agreed.

"I work for Admiral Cutter."

Her long blond hair hid the discreet earpiece that she wore. Watson didn't notice it until she pressed a finger against her ear. She stood listening for a moment, then she said, "He says you can come to the building, but he'll kill you if you're lying."

"Who will kill me?" asked Watson.

"Mr. Ray Freeman, that's who. He's the one who sent the message."

40

Freeman was not one of the three armed men who met Watson as the woman led him to the door of the building. Those men were just over six feet, athletic, and so uniform in appearance that Watson nearly mistook them for some new class of clone. He thought they might be brothers.

The men moved in quick, precise motions. One held the door, another stood to the side, pointing a military-grade M27, the third dodged behind Watson and shoved him into the building.

Watson didn't know about the other two, but the one who shoved him had powerful arms.

"Ease up, Liston," said the one at the door.

The girl gave Watson an apologetic glance. She said, "This is only the welcoming committee, just wait until you meet Freeman."

Watching the three men, Watson saw what they were hiding. They were scared. Their eyes darted back and forth. They spoke in fast bursts. They were irritable, men on edge.

Watson watched the girl and realized that she, too, was scared. She hid it better than the three men; but for all of her talk about the terrors of Freeman, she was petrified of something else.

One of the men—Watson thought it might have been Liston, he seemed to be the man in charge—shoved Watson into the wall, then searched him for weapons. Without saying a word, he reached into Watson's jacket and pulled out the S9 pistol. He said, "You'll be safer without this."

They stood in a spacious lobby with marble floors and leather furniture. Elevator doors opened at the back wall, and out walked Ray Freeman, tall and massive and dressed in combat armor.

Watson, who stood six-foot-five, was used to being the tallest man wherever he went. With Freeman in the room, he felt a disorienting shudder to his psyche. At a glance, Watson could tell that Freeman was taller, stronger, older, more dangerous.

He had dark skin and nearly black eyes. The icy indifference in his expression revealed nothing. He had a rifle and an oversized particle-beam cannon strapped to his back. Bandoliers packed with ammunition and weapons crisscrossed his chest.

To Watson, Freeman personified death.

A tiny man with white hair stood beside Freeman. At first, Watson thought the white-haired man might have been a dwarf, because the top of his head was even with the big man's chest; then he remembered Freeman's height and realized that the white-haired man might have been five-eight or even five-nine. It was Gordon Hughes, the governor of Mars.

Freeman asked, "Do you still work for Harris?"

Watson shook his head. He said, "I think he was reprogrammed."

Freeman nodded, and asked, "If you're not with Harris, who are you with?"

"Admiral Cutter."

"Does he know what's happening in the spaceport?" asked Hughes.

Watson said, "Nobody knows what is happening. You sent us a message about having Howard Tasman; that's the only thing that anybody knows."

Hughes looked up at Freeman in astonishment, and asked, "You got a message through?"

Freeman ignored him. He asked, "Where is Harris now?"

"He's retired. Cutter relieved him of command."

"Gone to the islands?" Freeman asked.

"I don't know where he went," Watson admitted. "Admiral Cutter relieved him of command, and that was the last I heard."

"He relieved Harris of command?" asked Hughes. "He relieved Harris, and he's still alive? That's a good sign. Maybe there's hope."

Freeman did not answer. He listened and considered the news.

Watson said, "If that's Harris."

"What do you mean, 'If that's Harris'?" asked Hughes.

"I saw a video feed of you assassinating Harris." Watson spoke to Freeman, not Hughes.

"You shot Harris?" asked Hughes.

Freeman did not answer, though the slightest of smiles formed on his lips.

"What about Tasman?" asked Watson. "You said you had him."

"He's upstairs resting," said Hughes.

"He's the one who got us in this cockspeck," said one of the bodyguards. "Him and Harris."

"Things never went back to normal after Harris arrived," said Hughes. "They've been blocking all communications."

"Who?" asked Watson. "Is it the Martian Legion?"

Freeman said nothing.

Hughes said, "The Martian Legion? Gawd, you're not still talking about the Martian Legion; Harris massacred those misguided bastards."

41

LOCATION: HAWAII
DATE: MAY 1, 2519

I wasn't under arrest, or Cutter would have locked me in a brig. I wasn't under house arrest, either. I lived in officer housing on Kaneohe Marine Base, and I could come and go as I pleased.

I was under surveillance. They—"they" probably meaning Naval Intelligence—had people watching my house. When I borrowed a jeep from the motor pool, it came complete with a tracking device in the steering column—a small sender about the size of a ladybug. It included a microphone, a camera, a stress sensor that read my pulse and heart rate, and a locator—a marvel of eavesdropping engineering.

The incompetent speck who installed the device did a shitty job. I didn't even need to break anything to find it. Running my hand along the bottom of the steering column, I felt a tiny pimple, and there it was. I could have yanked the device, but I didn't think they'd let me off base without some kind of tracking device. Had I not found it, I would have still assumed it was there, just like I assumed there was a backup monitor hidden somewhere else in the jeep.

I drove the jeep to the front gate, and the guard let me out.

Oahu had bases for all of the branches, an Air Force base and a Naval yard along its south shore, an Army base in its central region, and a Marine base in the northeast.

In my borrowed jeep, I set out to exercise. I drove a few miles and parked near a long stretch of sandy beach.

It was a beautiful day, bright sun, turquoise water, powder blue sky. The Hawaiian summer had already dried out the brush growing on the nearby hills, turning it gray.

The sun-warmed sand felt good under my bare feet, and the temperature of the water was comfortable as I entered the shallows. Two feet deep, the ocean was clear as glass. I could see the sand beneath me and could watch for rocks as I started my run.

The sun beat down on my head and shoulders, and the water fought against my stride. Fifty yards out, surfers caught waves on boards and kayaks. Kids built sand castles on the beach. Dogs played. A little mongrel kept up with me for a few yards, running sideways along the beach so it could bark and snarl in my direction.

The heat, the air, and the exercise worked in concert to clear my thoughts. My thoughts. I kept wrestling the same questions. I remembered everything that happened on Mars, a full week's worth of events; but the details remained hazy. I remembered landing in the spaceport and fighting the Martian Legion, but very little in between.

How had I lost those days?

I usually preferred swimming to jogging. I liked diving, my lungs burning as I struggled to wring energy out of every oxygen molecule. I liked pushing myself to see how deep I could go without wearing breathing equipment. I liked the feel of gliding through water.

In the past, I preferred swimming to running; but ever since returning from Mars, the thought of swimming made me nervous.

I wasn't sure why. I used to ignore my fears, but now I was giving in to them.

I stopped running and turned away from the shore. The water was only up to my knees at this point. I waded into thigh-deep water and paused. A swell rolled past. That first cold splash across my crotch was always the most bracing.

The water around me was the color of clean glass. It turned darker as I looked farther out. The bluing started a few yards away. Then there was the drop, where the ocean turned royal blue.

Before going to Mars, I could not have resisted the urge to dive into those depths. They called to me even now. Little islands rose out of the water not far from me. I wondered if I could reach them, dared myself to try.

I took another step out. The sky was bright, and the horizon was a perfect division of pale sky and blue sea; but in my mind, I saw water so cold that the world seemed to freeze around it. I saw strange shapes gliding in water as dark as ink.

Looking for fins cutting cross the surface of the depths, I took another step out. The water came up to my waist. Cool water on a warm day, it felt refreshing.

I started to dive, but that was as far as I got. I stood there another minute, staring out to sea, hating the invisible barrier that stood in my way; and then I turned and walked back to my jeep.

42

Someone was tailing me.

They drove the most nondescript car they could find, a boxy white sedan that I might have mistaken for a tourist rental had it not had darkened windows.

These guys were not from Naval Intelligence. The swabbie spooks didn't need to follow me; they had doped my jeep and programmed their satellites to track me. I couldn't pick my nose without those clones watching, so why send a car to follow? Even military redundancy has its limits.

The car traveled a hundred yards back as I drove toward the base, then turned into a neighborhood as I reached the gate. *Well-trained monkeys*, I thought. *They're smart enough to watch the gate instead of the subject.* Built on a small peninsula, Kaneohe Marine Base had only one entrance. Watch that gate, and they would spot me when I left again.

The sergeant at the gate saluted me as I entered.

I drove to my billet. Having been relieved of command, I should not have had access to weapons, such as grenades and S9 stealth pistols; but I was on a Marine base. Relieved of command or not,

I was among friends. My first day on base, a captain had dropped by to look in on me and told me about the box of weapons he'd hidden in my closet.

I pulled out the small box and removed the grenade. It was the size of a golf ball, all black, with a little screen for setting detonation parameters. Not wanting to take any innocent bystanders with me, I selected the lowest possible setting. On high yield, the blast from this grenade would conflagrate half a city block. On low yield, it wouldn't do much more than spray my guts and ceiling into the neighbor's yard.

I held the grenade in my left hand, studied it carefully, and pulled the pin. The countdown would not begin until I released the lever that my thumb now pressed. I released it. I had known I would be able to release the lever even as I had pulled the grenade out of the box. Now I sat and watched as the seconds ticked down on the screen. When the screen reached two, I casually covered the lever with my thumb and replaced the pin. I had no doubt in my mind that I could have waited those last two seconds. Had I wanted to, I could have detonated that grenade.

Fear had entered into my psyche. I felt afraid of swimming in the ocean even though I knew I was in good shape and would not drown. Fear.

I remembered everything that happened on Mars as if it was written on a list, not as if I had experienced it. There was that breakdown in which I had ranted like a madman at Don Cutter, an ally and a friend. And now I could commit suicide. I had simply pulled the pin of the grenade and watched as its timer wound down, something that had been made impossible by my neural programming. I added it all up and came to an obvious conclusion. Somebody had tinkered with my neural programming. Somebody had reprogrammed me.

Before Mars, I had not had the ability to commit suicide. It was not in my programming. I could not have pulled that pin without a target other than myself in mind. Now I could pull the pin as easily as I could unzip my pants.

I considered pulling the pin a second time and letting the timer finish its countdown, not because I wanted to test my theory but because I hated myself. I had allowed myself to be reprogrammed. I had allowed someone else to control the gears inside my head.

But there was something I wanted more than an easy way out. I wanted to know who had specked with my head, and I wanted to give that person a very different piece of my mind.

After that, maybe I would pull the pin on my life, too.

I stashed the grenade back in the box and took a shower. I shaved, I ran the blue light over my teeth, then I dressed like a civilian. My clothes included slacks and a loose shirt that hid the form of the S9 pistol I had tucked inside my waistband.

Then I went to my jeep and drove away. It was now early afternoon, with a bright, high sun and a few crawling clouds. As I coasted to the front gate, the sergeant saluted. I returned his salute, and he let me through.

Instead of heading over the mountains and into Honolulu, I headed east, back toward the beach I had just visited. A minute later, when I checked my rearview mirror, I saw the white sedan.

They kept far away, which was fine, though I would have preferred for them to close the gap. I slowed, they slowed, cars came between us. Apparently the bastards did not worry about keeping me in their sights. I turned left into a small neighborhood of beachfront homes. They followed.

I parked beside a public access way that led between two houses. Off ahead of me, the ocean sparkled in the sunlight. Walking casually, I traveled from the road to the beach, glanced back to make sure no one was watching, and sprinted along the sand. I ran past three houses, then hopped a fence and cut across somebody's yard.

I ran along the side of the house and out along the driveway, staying low, keeping an eye on the street. And there it was, the white sedan, parked along the side of the road with three men standing beside it. They must have wondered where I had gone, and they'd climbed out of their car for a better look.

All three stood with their backs to me, facing the access way I had used to enter the beach. They might or might not have been civilians, but they were not clones. They came in different heights and builds. One had brown hair, two had blond. They chatted quietly among themselves. Their voices sounded like a low rumble. Staying low and quiet, darting between parked cars and hedges, I stole within twenty feet of the bastards.

As I said before, I only needed one of them to get the information I wanted, so I shot the blonds in the back with my S9. The third guy watched his buddies fall and still needed a moment to process what happened. He spun to face me. I showed him my gun, and he raised his hands. He had some kind of metal box in his left hand.

My combat reflex took over. I fired the first fléchette through his thigh, causing the bastard to topple to his knees. He fell to the ground as silent as a leaf. My second fléchette passed through the bastard's left bicep. It was like cutting the strings from a puppet's limbs. His hand flopped to the ground, but he managed to hold on to that box.

It must be some kind of weapon, I thought.

His hands twitching as he struggled to maintain his grip on the metal cylinder, he fell on his ass and tried to sit up. My third shot drilled through his wrist. His fingers fell open, and the box rolled out of his hand. That was when he started screaming.

I picked up the cylinder. It was about three inches tall and an inch wide. It weighed next to nothing. It was not a grenade, not a bomb. The more I looked at it, the less it looked like a weapon.

The bastard's screaming had attracted an audience. People came running along the street. They saw me and my pistol and the cylinder. They saw him, squirming on the ground, little fountains of blood shooting out of his leg, arm, and wrist. He cried and screamed, sort of an "Owweee Gawd! Owe. Owe," sort of noise.

I said, "We'd better get you to the hospital."

He tried to stand, maybe he thought he could run, so I shot him in the other leg and he fell flat on his face, screaming until his mouth filled with dirt. Then he started sobbing, his whole body twitching and blood spurting out of his arm and legs. I grabbed him by the shoulders and tossed him into his own car. Then I threw his buddies in on top of him.

By this time, a crowd of people stood a long way off, some dressed in bathing suits and some dressed in house clothes. No one came closer than fifty feet. Someone yelled something about calling the police. I didn't care.

Slipping into the driver's seat of the sedan, I remembered my jeep. Once I had my new friend checked into the base hospital, I would send someone to retrieve it.

I had something else on my mind. I thought about Seattle and how I had inadvertently killed the man I wanted to question. This time, I would make sure the victim survived.

43

The sergeant at the gate generally waved me through, but this time he stopped me. He came to my door, saluted, and said, "Sir, I have orders…"

"Sergeant, you better let me through or the sorry son of a bitch in the backseat is going to bleed to death," I said.

The sergeant looked behind me, and said, "Sir, my orders…"

"That man back there is dying," I said.

"There are three of them, sir, and they look pretty dead," said the sergeant.

"Not the one on the bottom," I said. In truth, I only hoped he hadn't. I wasn't sure.

The sergeant tapped his earpiece and spoke. He leaned into the window, and said, "They're sending MPs to meet you at the infirmary."

The gate opened, and I sped through. The sound of sirens filled the air. A trio of jeeps with flashing lights caught up to me and stayed snug on my ass. I didn't mind.

I sped around barracks, past a baseball field, and into the infirmary parking lot. I skidded to a stop near the door, then hopped out of the car. Three sets of MPs parked a few feet away and watched as I dumped the stiffs.

The man I had shot babbled incoherently as I hefted him off the car floor. The blood had drained out of his face, leaving his skin chalk white. The holes the fléchette had left behind were not much bigger than a pinprick. They went all the way through the bastard. In the heat of the fight, I had shot him several times, including the one through the wrist; now I wondered if perhaps that had been a bit excessive.

The guy was in shock. I slung him over my shoulder and dashed into the infirmary. He hung as limp as a wet towel, still mumbling shit I could not understand.

Two medics, both clones, waited with a gurney outside the door. I flipped the bleeding, babbling victim onto his back and laid him down for them.

The medics hauled my victim away and a half dozen MPs came to join me. They did not draw their guns or make any move to arrest me. The urgency had gone out of the situation now that they had me.

Along with the base cops came a man from Intelligence, a lieutenant who looked scared to death as he approached me. He said, "General, um... sir, I noticed that there were two dead men on the ground beside the car."

"Yeah."

"Did you kill them, sir?"

Somebody had to, I thought. I said, "Affirmative."

The poor bastard had no idea what was going on. He was just the highest-ranking Intelligence officer on a far-flung base. Someone from Washington probably told him he had a three-star problem without going into details.

I walked to a row of chairs and sat down. He followed me; so did the MPs.

"What are you doing?" asked the lieutenant.

"I want to have a word with that fellow when he comes out of E.R.," I said, trying to sound civil.

265

He stood a few feet from me nodding and trying to figure out what to do next. Finally, he ordered the MPs to bring in the bodies.

He sat down in the chair next to mine, and asked, "Why did you shoot them?"

"They were following me," I said.

"How do you know they were following you?" he asked.

I smiled, and said, "Just a hunch."

Along with my S9, I had that strange cylinder in my pocket. I pulled it out and showed it to the lieutenant.

"What is that?"

"I took it off the guy with the holes," I said, nodding toward the emergency room. Normally, I spoke more respectfully to junior officers, but I was still coming down off a combat reflex.

I twisted the metal cylinder around and looked at it from every angle. "I think it is a weapon of some kind," I said. "Whatever it is, the bastard did everything he could to hold on to it. I had to shoot him through the wrist to get it out of his hand."

I gave the cylinder to the lieutenant and told him to get it analyzed.

"I hear you're piling up bodies again," Cutter said, when I picked up the infirmary phone.

"Maybe today is the third Day of the Martyrs," I said. "Were there other attacks?"

"Just you," said Cutter. "I've seen the video feed. It doesn't look like they actually attacked you."

"Bad camera angle," I said.

"There are twelve witnesses who claim they saw you shoot three unarmed men."

"Ridiculous," I said. "One of the men was armed with a flask."

"So I hear. We'll open it in Langley. In the meantime, what do you intend to do with your victim?"

"I've got some questions I want to ask him."

"Do you plan on arresting him?"

"That depends on what is in that flask," I said. While waiting

266

for my victim to come out of the emergency room, I reviewed the fight in my head over and over again, looking for ways of justifying my attacking those men. I decided the term "flask" conveyed a note of scientific menace. It would need a lot of scientific menace to justify shooting two men in the back and drilling the third guy multiple times.

Cutter said, "You can't detain him, Harris. You either need to arrest the guy or let him go."

"Or I can keep him here in the hospital until I'm sure that he's healthy enough to leave," I said.

"You are creating a diplomatic nightmare."

"Look, Admiral, he's not going anywhere. He took fléchettes in both knees," I said. "If I need to arrest someone to make this official, I can arrest his two pals."

"The ones you killed?"

"The ones who were down when I loaded them into the car. The witnesses don't know that I killed them."

"All twelve witnesses reported them as dead," Cutter pointed out.

"What do they know?" I asked. "This is a state-of-the-art medical facility." It wasn't, but I didn't care. "We might have resuscitated them."

"One of the witnesses saw you shoot a man in the throat. He said there was blood spurting out of both sides of the man's neck," said Cutter.

I decided to change the subject. I said, "I need Intel to ID the bastards."

"Intel has already IDed them," said Cutter.

"New Olympians?" I asked, thinking they might be members of the Martian Legion looking for a little revenge.

"No," said Cutter.

"No?" I asked, beginning to think that maybe I had just killed a couple of innocents.

"Unifieds," said Cutter. "They worked for the Central Intelligence Agency. I don't suppose you can tell me what two former spies and a retired assassin were doing in Hawaii?"

I gave the first answer that came into my head, I said, "Bleeding." Then I said, "Unifieds. Admiral, if the Unifieds are involved, this is going to get ugly."

44

When Mr. Arthur Hooper woke up, he found me and three armed MPs waiting in his room. He looked at us, sighed, and said, "Specking hell."

I said, "Hello, Art. Glad you could join us. Did you have a good rest?"

He glared at me, and said, "Get specked."

By this time I had seen Arthur's personnel files. His buddies had been the brains of the operation. One specialized in surveillance and interrogation. The other was an interrogator with a medical degree—a particularly nasty sort of parasite.

Unfortunately for Arthur and company, they'd learned their trades back in the day when the Unified Authority owned and operated all of the satellites and the security cameras. Running surveillance was easy for them back then. Now we owned the cameras. Surveillance was easy for us.

Arthur, never the subtle surveillance type, had specialized in captures and assassinations, the bastard. He'd occupied a world of murky ethics, the world of black operations.

I said, "The big wheel of Karma seems to have spun a full circle,

Art. I was just reading your personnel file. You were a scary guy."

He was big and strong. Before he ran into me and my S9, he'd been tough, and he was not backing down now. Even with two holes in his right arm and a hole through each of his legs, he stood his ground... metaphorically speaking.

Our war-tested MedTechs were more than qualified to suture veins and staunch bleeding; but the only way they knew to deal with pain involved copious amounts of drugs. At the moment, Arthur Hooper's bravado was chemically enhanced. I wondered just how resolute he would remain if I shut off his pharmaceutical courage.

At least he was lucid.

I asked, "What were three former Unified Authority spooks doing outside a Marine base?"

"We went to the beach," Hooper said in a sullen voice.

"So you were sightseeing," I said. "Hoping to go for a swim, maybe take in some sun."

"Something like that, yeah," he said. "Then you came along."

Lying bastard, I thought to myself. Using satellite transmissions meant to track me, Cutter's Intelligence operatives found the house Hooper and his friends had rented.

I said, "I want to tell you an interesting story. I found a cylindrical metal flask on the ground beside your car after I saw you collapse."

Hooper only grunted.

"Thinking maybe you used it to hold medicine, I sent it to a lab in Washington to have it analyzed. You know, the laboratories in Washington, D.C.... the ones that used to belong to the Unified Authority but now belong to the Enlisted Man's Empire.

"We had three scientists analyze the contents, two were civilians..."

Hooper shifted in his bed. He snickered, and said, "Collaborators."

"Two were civilians... natural-borns, of course. The third was from Naval Intelligence, a clone. They scanned the flask to make sure it was not explosive. Can you imagine, they thought maybe you had parked beside a landmine." I knew he had dropped it, and he knew that I knew he had dropped it; but we still played the charade.

"It turns out that it wasn't a mine after all. It was just a vial, just a hollow metal flask.

"Do you know what they found in that flask?" I asked. "They found chemicals. Maybe hollow isn't the right word. It was filled with tiny chambers."

Hooper remained silent.

"Each of those chambers had its own little lid, and all the lids were designed for a synchronous release. One opened and then the next and then the one after that. Each chamber held a gaseous substance that they released in quick succession.

"The mix included ozone and neutralized chlorine. I understand that both chemicals are highly corrosive, downright dangerous in big doses," I said.

"Here's the interesting part. There were still traces of that gas in the air when the scientists removed their breathing gear. It didn't affect the two civilian scientists; but the third one, the clone, caught a whiff of it and fainted... passed right out.

"You know what else? When he woke up again he had no idea he had fainted. He sat up and stared around the room. Then he stood up and acted like nothing ever happened."

As I told my story, I approached Hooper's bed so that I now stood over him. The MPs remained near the door. Hooper did not look at any of us. He stared straight ahead, his eyes fixed and mechanical, and he said, "I wouldn't know anything about that."

45

Howard Tasman was a little old man. If he could stand, he probably would have stood a shriveled five-foot-eleven. He might have weighed 160 pounds after a big meal. His head balanced on his neck like a bucket on a broomstick, and his twiglike arms looked like they belonged on an insect. He stared up at Watson from his bed, and asked, "Who the hell is this?"

Freeman said, "The Navy sent him."

"Can he get us out of here?" asked Tasman.

"No," said Freeman.

"Than what good is he?" growled Tasman. "I am not saying anything, not until you get me to Earth." His voice was as desiccated as a desert wind.

Without responding, Freeman left the room. Watson followed. He asked, "That's Howard Tasman?"

"What's left of him."

"And he wants to help us? He's on our side?"

Freeman said, "He's not on anybody's side. He's out for himself."

"Admiral Cutter said the same thing about you," said Watson.

Freeman did not answer.

They walked into a large office. Watson assumed it was Gordon Hughes's gubernatorial office, but he did not ask. The office had a huge window with a panoramic view of the hallway and the burned buildings on either side.

Buildings within buildings, Watson thought as he gazed through the window at the charred ruins.

He asked, "What happened out there?"

"Spaceport Security came for Tasman a few days ago," Freeman said.

Watson stood staring out the window, taking in the avenue that led back to the grand arcade. He asked, "It wasn't the Mars Legion?"

"The Mars Legion was a ruse," said Freeman. "Cutter should have figured that out by now. The shotguns and the religious fanatics were just a distraction."

Watson asked, "A distraction from what? Who's distracting us?" He turned from the window and studied Freeman. The man was massive. He was like an ocean with a volcano hidden in its depths, placid on the surface, violent down below.

Freeman said, "The man who designed the neural programming in the clones is lying in the next room."

Watson said, "We arrested some men back on Earth. They all worked for Unified Authority Intelligence back before..."

"Who do you think is calling the shots in Spaceport Security?" asked Freeman.

"The Unified Authority?" asked Watson.

"What's left of it," said Freeman. "They got to Harris, too. You know that, right?"

"Is that really even Harris?" Watson asked. "I saw a video feed in the U.A. Archives..."

Freeman put up a hand to stop him. He said, "I wasn't

273

supposed to kill him. I was supposed to deliver a message. I hit him with a 'simi.'"

"He was bleeding. You blew his chest out."

"I hit him with a soft round. The blood came from inside the bullet. Andropov wanted him to know he wasn't too far away to touch. He wanted Harris to know that he was still an easy target."

Andropov, Tobias Andropov, had been the ranking member of the Linear Committee right up to the fall of the Unified Authority. An Enlisted Man's Empire military tribunal had found him guilty of war crimes.

"The Unifieds have declared war on him again."

Watson said, "Andropov is in jail and he's never getting out."

Freeman said, "Robards and St. John got away." Jay Robards and Al St. John were also members of the Linear Committee at the time of the invasion.

"They don't have weapons? The clones have a Navy and jets and gunships," Watson said. He was invested in the Enlisted Man's Empire, and he knew it. The natural-born world saw him as a collaborator. "What are they going to use? What weapon do they have?"

In a soft, low voice, Freeman said, "They have Harris."

Watson struggled to understand Freeman, to piece together his thoughts and reasoning. One thing he realized already was that Freeman viewed conversation as a means of transferring information, not as entertainment or as a tool for establishing relationships. He did not chat, did not care how people felt or what made them happy.

Watson said, "I need to get a message to Admiral Cutter."

"We can't get through."

"You got a message through," said Watson.

"Part of a message. Mars security shut us down. Now we can't even use walkie-talkies," said Freeman. "We're stuck until Riley reopens communications."

"Riley has five thousand men. If he wants Tasman, he can do a lot more than burning down neighboring buildings and sludging airwaves," said Watson. "If he's working for the Unifieds, why doesn't he march right in? You don't have enough men to stop him?"

"The Unifieds want Tasman alive. They need him as much as we do."

"He hasn't told them anything?"

"He hasn't told them everything," said Freeman. Then he said something that caused Watson to question information he had accepted as a given. He said, "Harris doesn't remember seeing me on the Night of the Martyrs." Though Freeman said this as a statement, Watson had the feeling he was looking for verification.

"He didn't see you," said Watson. "I was there, in Seattle. He went looking for you, but he never found you; and then he was attacked."

Freeman did not answer.

"You saw him… and they attacked him and they reprogrammed him after you saw him," said Watson.

"Not reprogrammed. They didn't have what they needed to reprogram him. You might say they rebooted him. They rebooted fifteen hundred Marines that night," said Freeman. "They only reprogrammed one man on the Night of the Martyrs."

"But it wasn't Harris?" asked Watson.

"Colonel Curtis Jackson."

"Jackson?"

"Jackson volunteered Second Regiment for the tour of Mars. Jackson led his men into the trap; Harris just came along for the ride. They knew he would. Anyone who ever met him knew he would. Harris always takes point when there's hazardous duty."

Not saying a word, Watson walked behind a desk and dropped into the seat. His mind raced as he considered the ramifications. *Wayson Harris, a puppet, one that every Marine in the EME would happily follow. A puppet leading puppets*, he thought. *Like the lemming at the front of the herd.*

"Has Cutter disbanded Second Regiment?" asked Freeman.

"No," said Watson.

Freeman nodded. He said, "Tasman has run out the various

strategies for what you could do with reprogrammed clones. The biggest threat is that they spread the reprogramming through the entire empire like a virus. Cutter disbands the Second Regiment and reassigns the infected Marines around the Corps, then they spread the virus into their new units. If some of them are assigned to ships, then the virus spreads to the Navy as well."

Watson listened carefully, but he did not understand. "You're saying reprogramming is contagious? That doesn't make sense."

"You're thinking of natural viruses, but this one is synthetic. If you wanted to build an army, what would be the first order you'd give a reprogrammed Marine?" asked Freeman. He showed no emotion. His voice was flat, his eyes unblinking.

Watson worked the scenario in his head. *A single Marine could be a saboteur or an assassin. You could kill Cutter and Harris, maybe blow up a ship or the Pentagon and kill many.* As he gamed the possibilities, he realized that the single Marine was as vulnerable to security precautions as a natural-born. Maybe they were paranoid, but the clones at the top took security seriously.

If a lone Marine is vulnerable, Watson reasoned, *his best bet would be to recruit. If he did not break any rules, that one Marine could turn an entire base. When those Marines were transferred to ships, they could infect crews as well. How long would it take to turn every ship and fort?*

"We have to warn Cutter," said Watson.

Freeman said nothing.

There was no need to ask the obvious question, but Watson asked it anyway. "How?" And then he answered the question as well. He said, "Maybe we can get Riley to contact Cutter for us. Why would they still need Tasman if they had complete control of their clones?"

46

Much of the time, Mars ran on solar energy. Acres of solar cells glittered around the plains outside the spaceport, panels the size of Ping Pong tables mounted on rods that lowered into the ground when windstorms overran the mountains. Even in the best of times, though, the solar panels were efficient but not sufficient, which was why the spaceport housed a nuclear reactor in its bowels.

Along with the reactor, the spaceport had a massive automated electrolysis plant for generating breathable oxygen; a robotic mining operation that harvested veins of underground ice; a chemical synthesis plant for converting carbon dioxide to oxygen; and an overworked tertiary processing plant that filtered and reissued water while disposing of waste materials.

These were the guts of the spaceport, the hidden organs that travelers never saw and New Olympians were not allowed to visit. The various plants were housed in an underground level of the spaceport, a clean, large, well-lit area with concrete walls and floors, and pipes running along the ceiling.

The steel doors barring entrance into the nuclear plant

reminded Watson of the rear hatch of a military transport. He paused to stare at the doors and think about the times he and Harris had traveled together in transports. He tried to inherit courage from his memories of Harris, but he was just another hungry man dreaming of food and finding no nourishment.

The halls were long, and straight, wide enough for carts and pedestrians to move in tandem. Watson heard the hum of machinery. *There should be workers*, he thought. If there were workers, and they were not clones, maybe they would help if he found himself in trouble. The question was who? Who would run the nuclear power plant? Then he remembered Cutter mentioning that the plant was now run by computers and monitored from Earth. He wondered if the signal was still getting through, but he thought it unlikely.

During the golden days, the Port of Mars employed an army of civilian technicians. Now they were gone, replaced by robots and computers. Watson wondered what would happen to the plant once the New Olympians transferred out.

He passed the entrance of the oxygen-generation facility. There were no doors, just halls as wide as a basketball court that led down into brightly lit chambers filled with pipes and wires and cables and giant machines working in silence.

The sewage-filtration system was loud. The smell wafting out of its cave made Watson's eyes water. He frowned and held his breath, not yet having escaped the stench when he reached the door marked, SPACEPORT SECURITY BARRACKS.

Forgetting the bad air, Watson looked around the hall for people. He saw no natural-borns. He saw no clones. He was alone and nervous.

In his mind, crowds and potential witnesses offered a margin of safety. If something happened to him down here, no one would see it, no one would help him… no one would know. There would be no one to report the attack except the attackers themselves.

The walls of the barracks had no windows or ornamentation. The sign beside the door said, BARRACKS. Watson took in the meaning more than the word. The word denoted a building meant to house soldiers; but for him, the connotation was simply, soldiers. He waited, told himself he would be safe, then took a final breath of the foul air and opened the door.

The barracks were filled with men. Some sat around in their underwear, some wore uniforms, some wore armor; but none wore helmets. The men were awake and alive, but they did not speak, and they did not interact with each other.

Watson approached the closest clone, and said, "I'm looking for Colonel Riley."

The Marine ignored him. All of the Marines ignored him. He tried to speak to several of them, but they all stared straight ahead and did not respond.

A row of dead men lay stretched out side by side along the wall. Watson drifted toward the bodies; he could not help himself.

He asked, "What happened to these men?"

No one answered. No one looked in his direction.

Watson knelt beside one of the bodies. The clone had been in his thirties. He still had a regulation haircut though fuzz had started to grow around his ears, an area most Marines shaved. When he spotted dried blood on the man's ear, Watson stood and stepped away.

Some of the bodies had bloated, stretching their pants and shirts, their skin having turned a greenish gray. It was hot and humid in the barracks, and the sickeningly sweet smell of their decay filled the air.

Another scent hung in the air as well, something faint and sharp and acrid. It cut through the odor of the decay like a pinch of pepper in a spoon of sugar. It was a chemical scent.

A Marine approached Watson, then walked right past him without a second glance. The clone had seen Watson and stepped around him, but he didn't seem to care that a civilian had entered his barracks.

Six men sat at a table no more than twenty feet from the row of fetid bodies. The men did not chat among themselves.

They weren't playing cards, though they sat erect and facing each other like men in a game.

When Watson approached the table, the men did not gaze up at him. He tapped one of the Marines on the shoulder. No response. He wondered if Harris had been like this? *Could Harris have ever been catatonic?*

Some of the men had thick stubble on their chins, as if they had not shaved for days.

They did not soil themselves, though. As Watson hovered around the table, one of the men stood and walked away. Watson followed him to the bathroom and watched as the man entered a stall. When he unhitched his trousers, Watson decided he had seen enough and left.

The barracks had a recreation area with card tables, computer games, and video screens. Nothing showed on the screens. The games sat unused. The men at the card tables sat staring straight ahead.

Watson left the recreation area and entered the sleeping quarters, a room as long as a bowling alley with three-tiered rows of bunks, most filled with men. The walls and doors that separated the room from the recreation and eating areas had been designed to filter out light, but overhead lights burned brightly above the beds.

The men who lay in the cots lay with their eyes open and their faces blank. They were clones. All five-ten. All brown-haired. All brown-eyed. Every man in every cot looked like a repeat of the men around him. Some were older or thinner. Not a one of them showed any interest in Watson.

"Hey, you! You son of a bitch, what are you doing here?"

Watson heard the loud voice and jumped involuntarily. He turned to see a natural-born rushing toward him. The man was no more than five-eight, a short man with a face so startlingly handsome that it was almost pretty. He had a thick chest and broad shoulders, and barely controlled rage seemed to exude from him. As the man rushed toward him, Watson noticed the circular scar in the center of his forehead, a jagged saw blade of circle that rose out of the space between his eyebrows as if it had been embossed.

Not intimidated by Watson's height, the man came in so close that their chests nearly bumped. He said, "I asked you a question," and stared at Watson for a moment. Recognition worked into his expression. He said, "You."

Watson said, "I'm looking for Colonel Riley."

"Freeman should have known better than to let you come... unless he doesn't care," said the little man, and he shoved Watson hard enough to make him stumble. Then he said, "Save your bullshit for Harris."

His mind reeling, Watson remembered that he had nowhere to turn for help. Now, when someone was finally calling his bluff, he was alone.

The man poked Watson's chest, and asked, "How long have you been here?"

"I just came down," Watson stammered, not sure if the man meant the barracks or the planet.

"Yeah? You find anything interesting?" the man asked. Seemingly out of nowhere, his right fist flew up and hit Watson on the mouth. "Did you find what you were looking for?"

Watson stumbled back. He felt liquid rolling down his chin. It might have been blood. It might have been drool. He tasted the faintly tinny flavor of blood in the back of his throat. His head spinning, Watson did not rub the wound. He did not want to give away his helplessness.

"I asked you a question, asshole," the man said. "Did you see what you came for?"

Watson did not answer. He did not know what to say. Thinking the man meant to kill him, he asked in a soft voice, "What did you do to them?"

"To these clones? You think I did something to them?" the man asked. His fist flew up again. This time Watson saw the blow coming. He stepped back, dodging it. The man lunged forward throwing another punch, which Watson slipped, and then the man's knee found its mark, ramming into Watson's crotch.

Watson felt the world spin. All the muscles in his body seemed to tie themselves into a knot around his stomach. He felt helplessness spread through his body as his legs slowly gave way, and he sank to the ground. Bile formed a geyser in his throat. When he opened his mouth for air, vomit spewed.

He was still conscious when the man kicked him in the face. "If you still have a brain when you wake up, tell your boss that Franklin Nailor sends his regards," the man said.

The toe of the shoe caught the side of Watson's head. He heard the words and knew he'd been struck, but he blacked out before the pain or its meaning registered.

47

"Are you General Harris?" the woman asked.

Surprising question. I was in the Pentagon building, in an office with my name on the door, sitting behind a desk with my name plaque. The master sergeant at the front desk had obviously told her, "The general will see you now," before letting her in.

Okay, granted, I did not have any stars on my uniform; they remained in Don Cutter's vault, but still.

The woman walked up to my desk as if we'd been friends for years. She held out her hand for mc to shake.

Okay, yes, she was pretty, maybe even beautiful. She had dark brown hair and watery blue eyes, a startling combination that went well together. Curtis Jackson was in my office as well. She certainly caught his attention. He could not take his eyes off of her.

I pretended to be nonchalant, but I felt a connection to this woman that I could not explain. When she smiled, I saw something vulnerable in her eyes, and I felt the need to protect her.

I wondered if this was a schoolboy infatuation or something deeper. *What, suddenly you're Pavlov's dog?* I asked myself. Ring the bell, and the dog salivates. Show the pretty girl, and the clone... Let's just say I wasn't coming out from behind my desk for a while.

It wasn't all bells and saliva, though. Along with the lust and the protective feeling, I felt a stab of revulsion. Maybe it was envy? Here was this incredibly beautiful woman, and I knew she was out of my league.

As I mentioned before, Curtis Jackson was in my office. When the woman reached across my desk to shake hands, I noticed he was staring at her ass as if it had a thousand-dollar bill taped to it.

Instead of shaking her hand I pretended not to notice it. I looked at my calendar. The woman's name was Sunny Ferris. She was Arthur Hooper's lawyer.

I said, "You're Miss Hooper."

I caught the mistake as soon as I said it, but by then it was too late.

She said, "Ferris. I'm Arthur Hooper's lawyer."

"My mistake," I said.

She smiled. She had a wide, toothy smile that invited all kinds of mischievous thoughts.

I said, "Please, sit down."

She brushed her hands along her skirt to smooth it, then sat, her blue wool suit doing little to hide her curves.

She might have been thirty, making her just about my age. She had a professional look about her. At least the suit was very professional. An image flashed in my brain. I imagined her dead. *What the speck is wrong with you?* I asked myself.

I asked, "Are all of your clients former U.A. interrogators?"

Her smile wavered almost imperceptibly. She said, "You'll need to forgive me, General, I'm just getting started on this case. I don't know anything about my client's employment history."

"In that case, allow me to educate you, ma'am," Jackson said, looking like he couldn't wait to join the conversation. "He was a

Unified Authority Intelligence officer. He interrogated prisoners. That's a polite way of saying he tortured clones."

She had to turn around to see Jackson, so I could only imagine her expression. I imagined it as a pasted-on smile under a thinly disguised glare. She said, "I would prefer to avoid conversations about Mr. Hooper's employment history before discussing it with Mr. Hooper himself," which I interpreted as a *polite* way of telling Jackson to speck off.

"I'm sorry, I should have introduced you," I said. "This is Colonel Jackson."

She did not offer to shake his hand. She nodded, said, "Hello, Colonel," and focused her attention on me.

I said, "The colonel brings up a fair point. What do you know about your client?"

"Technically speaking, he's not my client," she said, making herself comfortable, leaning on one side of the chair, her legs crossed. "I don't work for Mr. Hooper, General. My firm, Alexander Cross Associates, represents the entire Olympus Kri encampment."

"So you got seventeen million clients?" Jackson asked.

"Mr. Hooper was never a resident of Mars," I said. "I can show you his records; he's not from Olympus Kri."

"No?" she asked.

"Born on Earth, raised on Earth, served in the Unified Authority Navy," I said. "Maybe the New Olympians hired him to follow me."

I did not believe that story on several levels. I still believed that the majority of New Olympians were loyal to the Enlisted Man's Empire... desperate to relocate to Earth, but loyal. I had not believed they were loyal before going to Mars, but I came back convinced of it. Was that part of my reprogramming?

Trusting New Olympians, fearing the ocean, and now weird fantasies about a woman I had never seen before... Was this the by-product of reprogramming? I tried to sort out my feelings and realized that I did not trust this woman... Sunny Ferris. She might have come to my office representing Arthur Hooper, or she might have been working for the New Olympians; but I found it hard to believe that the New Olympians had hired her to defend Hooper.

Hooper was a mercenary. If there was one hard-and-fast rule about mercenaries, it was that the people who hired them abandoned them when things went wrong. That was one of the benefits of hiring mercenaries—they were disposable. You owed them nothing but the price of their hire.

I wondered if Sunny's visit was less about helping Hooper and more about implicating the New Olympians. The question was, who was setting them up? Was Sunny a pawn or a player?

I asked, "Have you met Arthur Hooper?"

"No. I was told I needed authorization from your office."

Damn straight you do, I thought as I smiled, and said, "He's currently in intensive care. Perhaps his doctors will say that he is strong enough to receive visitors."

Jackson, who clearly wanted a role in this conversation, asked, "Really, I thought they had him in solitary confinement?"

"Solitary confinement?" Sunny asked. "How can he be in solitary confinement? Are you saying he's under arrest?"

Thanks, Jackson... asshole, I thought. "He was taken into custody while following one of our Marines."

Sunny said, "As I understand it, he was on a beach."

She really was pretty. Her irises had this watery blue tint. *She might also be dangerous*, I reminded myself. She came representing a former U.A. interrogator.

Jackson answered. He said, "Ma'am, the area was under surveillance. We have a video feed tracking Mr. Hooper from the time he left his house to the moment of the confrontation."

Sunny allowed Jackson to speak, but she kept her eyes on me. She leaned over my desk, and said, "Innocent until proven guilty, General, or have the rules changed now that the Enlisted Man's Empire has seized control?"

"We believe in due process," I said.

"I'm glad to hear that."

"I would like to know why Hooper and his friends were

following me." She locked her eyes on mine, and, I swear, it was as if Jackson had left the room.

"Have you read the police report? The witnesses say you attacked Hooper and his friends."

Feeling attacked myself, I said, "I apprehended them." Feeble.

"You shot Arthur Hooper four times!" Those watery eyes were so expressive. What they said at the moment was bordering on hate and loathing.

We sat in silence for several seconds, a silence that Curtis Jackson broke. He brought up an excellent point. "You said your law firm works for the New Olympians. If Hooper was vacationing in Hawaii, and he is not from Olympus Kri, why are you representing him?"

"My boss gave me the case. I guess I just assumed it had something to do with Olympus Kri," Sunny admitted.

"Maybe it does," said Jackson. "Is there anyone on Mars looking to hire retired Unified Authority thugs?"

The look on Sunny's face went from hateful to disgusted. You would have thought Jackson was talking to her with a finger up his nose. She glared at me, then at him, and she said, "Please explain what you mean by 'thug.'"

"He worked in U.A. counterintelligence," I said. "Mostly he captured and tortured suspected enemies, but his records show that he may have been involved in assassinations as well."

Her expression shifted from anger to something resembling shock. She said, "I had no idea. I… I did not know anything about that."

I said, "Mostly he captured and executed clones."

"Really?" she asked.

"He is a low-priority war criminal," I said. "If I'd known who he was, I might not have shot him. Now we need to wait until he heals before we can hang him."

What was it about this woman that hit me so hard? In another minute, she would leave my office, and I would feel a void. I did not think the emptiness would last long, maybe a week or two;

but why had I fallen so hard for her in the first place? She was beautiful, but I had seen many beautiful women. I had lived with an actress that people described as "one of the most beautiful women of all time." Surely this girl, this lawyer, was not nearly as beautiful as Ava had been; and yet Ava never stunned me like this.

You will never see her again, I reminded myself. Washington, D.C. was a big city made even bigger because lawyers and generals did not travel in the same circles. As her parting gift, I said, "I'll clear you to see your client, Miss Farris."

She thanked me and left.

I watched her walk away, knowing that I would think about her.

48

Watson, who had always hidden behind his size, no longer saw Freeman and Harris as heroic figures. Having now experienced violence, Watson saw them as demigods. They operated comfortably in a world that now terrified him.

Until entering the barracks, the worst pain Watson had endured in his adult life was a headache brought on by an overchilled vodka tonic. He'd begun to think he had a high pain threshold.

His jaw throbbed. When he moved it, he heard a clicking noise. It was a soft noise, almost drowned out by the silvery flash of pain that filled his brain.

Sharp pain stabbed at him under his ribs when he took a deep breath or moved. He thought the ribs were probably broken. He touched a finger to an area that had turned a florid purple just below his chest—pain. He gasped, and his jaw clicked. The sharp pain from his jaw smothered the ache from his chest. For the first time in his life, Travis Watson understood the difference between an ache and a pain. Aches hung around; pains shot through him and disappeared.

His eyelids were swollen, squeezing his eyes in their sockets. It felt like somebody was pressing the heel of their hands against each eye. When he tried to look from side to side, dull ache filled his head.

His nose was broken as well. Because he couldn't breathe through his nose, he gulped air through his mouth, which meant he had to keep his mouth open so that his jaw would not move.

Those aches and pains and injuries had come from a beating. The cramps and bruises and charley horses below his neck had come afterward. His spine and pelvis hurt from lying on a cold, hard floor. It was a morning-after kind of ache, the kind of persistent throb that came with a hangover.

In other situations, that soreness would have consumed him; but Watson had no idea where he was. He did not know if he was a patient or a prisoner.

He sat up and tried to massage the knots out of his shoulders. He rolled his head to the left and felt a sharp stab of pain. He rolled his shoulder to the right and felt a similar stab. He moaned, but he did not give in. Flexing and swiveling his shoulders, he got the blood to return to his arms, bringing with it the feeling of a million microscopic needles pricking his skin. The sensation burned in the beginning, but that burn soon felt pleasant.

Watson's eyes had already adjusted to the dim environment. His vision was poor, but he understood the shapes around him. He had been placed in a bathroom. A toilet poked out of the wall beside his head. Not far from the toilet, a paper dispenser hung on the wall.

It was a small bathroom, not the communal latrines Watson had seen in the moments before he was attacked. He did not know where he was, but he suspected he was no longer in the barracks.

When he moved his mouth to yell for help, pain filled his head and silenced him. It barreled around his skull like a train through a tunnel. Bright spots appeared before his eyes, distorting his vision. He kicked in a spasm and banged his shin hard against the toilet, but he barely noticed. The pain in his skull overshadowed the sting in his shin.

Blinded by the synapses in his head, Watson reached his right arm out and groped the wall for balance. His eyes closed against the pain, he stuck his hand into the toilet without hearing the water splash or feeling the wet. His hand slipped on the slick surface, and he slid.

Trying to balance himself, he kicked a stall door, which slammed into a wall, creating a thunderlike racket reverberating through the empty bathroom.

A door opened on the far side of the bathroom.

First a female voice. "He must be awake."

A cheerful male voice followed. "Lazarus come forth." Then the man saw Watson lying face-first on the ground with his hand stuck in the toilet. He said, "Shit, that's embarrassing."

"Shut up, Dempsey," said the female voice.

The man reached a hand under one of Watson's arms and helped him to his feet, then steadied him as he started to lose his balance.

"I'll tell you what, son, I don't know whether you're the luckiest man I ever met or the unluckiest." The man seemed to find humor in Watson's suffering, but he did not sound unkind.

Watson recognized the name. Dempsey was one of Gordon Hughes's bodyguards. He also recognized the girl's voice. She was Hughes's granddaughter, Emily.

He started to ask Emily where he was, but the movement pinched a nerve in his broken jaw. The pain shot through him, and his legs gave way.

Dempsey caught him by the arm. He said, "We don't have many of these, and you're going to need them for the trip, but now might be a good time to use one." He opened an envelope and pulled out a paper patch about the size of a postage stamp. One side of the patch was smooth, the other covered with millimeter-long needles.

Dempsey pressed the side with the needles into Watson's

neck. The effect was nearly instantaneous, a mind-clearing, pain-reducing burst of energy.

Emily said, "Your jaw is broken."

"He's probably figured that out by now," said Dempsey.

Emily touched his shoulder gently, and added, "Your nose is broken. So are some of your ribs."

"If they hit your right nut any harder, it might have shot out of your nose," Dempsey joked. "That patch is going to hide the pain, but it won't fix things. We won't be able to fix you till we get to the base."

Emily shushed Dempsey, but she need not have bothered. Watson sank to his knees as his strength disappeared. Dempsey caught his left arm and eased him down, then leaned his back against a wall.

Watson heard him speak a few words, then he faded.

"His name is Franklin Nailor," Gordon Hughes was saying. "You might say he's the new Unified Authority's chief recruiting officer on Mars. If a more satanic man has ever lived, I've never met him."

"The new Unified Authority?" Watson asked. He should not have spoken, the pain punished him for forgetting about his jaw, but hearing the term "new Unified Authority" had caught him off guard.

"That's what we call it around here. I'm not sure if anyone is using that name.

"The fact is that we don't really know who he works for, just who he used to work for," said Hughes. "He was an Intelligence officer with the Unifieds. I assume he still is, only now that makes him a criminal."

Someone had moved a mattress into the bathroom while Watson lay comatose.

Now Hughes, sitting on a nearby toilet, explained the situation.

"You know why he let you live, don't you? He thinks you're working for Harris." He paused and thought. "You know, I'd give everything I own to see what happens when Harris gets his hands on Nailor. That will be... artistic."

Along with the mattress, Watson found a new pain patch. As Hughes spoke, Watson applied the patch to his neck. The warmth bloomed in his neck and spread across his body.

Knowing that the pain would return, Watson took stock of his injuries. He rolled his tongue along the inside of his jawbone and found three breaks along the contour. Each time he felt a break, an electric jolt ran the length of his spine, but the patch reduced the sting from those jolts.

Along with the mattress and pain patch, Hughes produced a third gift that morning: an interactive notepad that he gave to Watson as a replacement for speaking. Dragging his finger like a pen over the glass surface, Watson wrote, "Where is Freeman?" He showed the question to Hughes.

"Freeman? Ah, Freeman? To use his terminology, he is *clearing the path*." Hughes, the veteran politician, knew how to work a crowd. He gave Watson three seconds to ponder the term, then explained, "Our defenses are woefully depleted. We're down to three M27s, Freeman's sniper rifle, and some butter knives.

"The window of opportunity is closing around us. We are running out of bullets and food, Watson. If we don't exit Mars Spaceport soon, we'll never make it out.

"Well, that is not entirely true. Nailor has offered to allow us to leave if we hand over Tasman. I bet he'd even let us hop on the next freighter to Earth. He doesn't care about you or me or even Freeman. All he wants is Tasman... and another shot at Harris."

Watson wrote something on his comms pad and showed it to Hughes.

"What does Nailor have against Harris?"

The governor's wispy white hair was messed and clumped, oily because he had not been able to shower for over a week. Red splotches had formed on his face and neck, but there was a charisma about him. He had a rugged chin for an old man, and the wrinkled face gave him character. Watson had to remind himself that Hughes was in his seventies.

"Everything, I suppose. Wayson Harris brought about the downfall of the Unified Authority.

"I don't know when Nailor entered the spaceport. I don't even know if he was on Mars when Harris arrived last month. He might have been here. For all we know, he could have been hiding on Mars since the Unifieds first built the spaceport.

"All we really know is that after Harris left, Nailor showed up, then Freeman showed up; and the trouble began."

49

Emily stole into the bathroom quietly. She carried a bowl filled with warm water and a clean, soft sponge. When Watson squirmed on his mattress to see who had entered, she said, "I'm supposed to clean you."

Since his arms were not broken, Watson was entirely capable of cleaning himself. His mind was not broken, either. He knew that Freeman, who did not bother with other people's hygiene, had not sent the girl. He also doubted that Gordon Hughes, who seemed to have a puritanical side, had sent her.

Watson lay silently on the bare mattress and watched her silhouette as she moved through the near darkness. She placed the bowl on the floor and sat beside him.

He could tell that she was a player in the same way that he had always been a player. She was pretty, but in his current state, Watson had no interest in playing.

He heard her dipping the sponge, but she had moved into one of his blind spots. He could not see what she was doing. He heard the splash of excess water as she wrung it out. She moved in front of him, and he watched her silhouette. He saw her lean over him, felt the gentle touch, the warm sponge on his cheek.

He started to say something. She said, "Shhhh," and touched her finger to his lips so gently that it soothed him. She stroked the sponge along the length of his forehead, then dabbed it so softly along his jaw that he only felt the warmth.

She held a new pain patch, which she gently applied just below his ear. The medicine spread across his body quickly. She washed him more, and the warm water helped him relax.

She unbuttoned his shirt and cleaned his chest. Even though she tried to be careful, he drew in a sharp breath when she touched the bruises just below his heart. She cleaned his chest and worked her way down to his stomach; but he stopped her hand before she could go lower. Even with the new patch, intimacy was an impossibility.

He pulled her down and she lay on the mattress beside him, and that was how they fell asleep.

They were still asleep when Gordon Hughes walked into the bathroom the next morning, and shouted, "Oh good Lord. Get your hands off my granddaughter."

50

They were not only leaving the administrative complex; they were leaving the spaceport. Freeman said that the safest place on Mars would be the Air Force base. Once there, they might even be able to signal Cutter for help.

Hughes thought that meant they would have open radio contact with Cutter and his ships. Though Freeman privately told Watson the entire planet was sludged, he allowed Hughes and the others to believe differently.

To get to the base, they would need to cross the spaceport and enter the train station.

Under normal circumstances, a party of thirty people would not be easy to follow in the overcrowded environment of the spaceport, but Freeman said that Nailor had sent clones and allies to watch in case they tried to escape. Here, though, the sludging worked against Nailor and Riley. The sludging left their men cut off.

Freeman "neutralized the threat," then returned and said it was time to leave.

Freeman separated the people into smaller groups. He was the first to go. Dressed in combat armor that did nothing to hide his size, he left the administration building and vanished into the shadows, where he waited for the next group—Liston, Dempsey, and Sharkey, carrying Howard Tasman on a stretcher, draped in a blanket, as if he were a corpse headed for disposal. With seventeen million people living in squalor, death was common enough in the spaceport that no one would ask questions. Freeman, tracking them from the shadows, would eliminate anyone who did.

After warning Watson not to touch his granddaughter, Gordon Hughes left with his three sons. He wore a hat that covered much of his face.

The Hughes wives and grandchildren left as a group. The women looked grave, the kids excited. They blended into the sea of people and disappeared.

Watson and Emily Hughes were the last to leave. Like Gordon Hughes, Watson wore a large hat that covered his face in shadow. Hughes wore the hat because he was easily recognized. Watson wore it to hide the bruises and cuts on his face.

The various groups took different routes. Watson and Emily would travel through the heart of the grand arcade.

Following Freeman's instructions, Watson kept an arm around Emily to make sure they were not separated. If they lost each other in the overcrowded spaceport hub, it might take them an hour to find each other again.

Instead of skirting around the crowds, they pushed upstream. Watson normally avoided crowded areas, but Freeman had told them they would be safer surrounded by people. Freeman instructed them to enter the grand arcade, climb the stairs, and cross on the second floor, claiming they would be harder to follow if they left the main floor.

Hunched over Emily the way that he was, Watson did not look especially tall. Standing together in their dirty clothes, passing through the crowd, they blended in just as Freeman had predicted.

People pushed and shoved against Watson. An elbow struck one of his broken ribs, sending a wave of pain through his body, but he had two epidural patches stuck to his neck, and the medicine kept him going.

Emily seldom spoke as they walked. Acting as Watson's crutch, she carried some of his weight.

Emily whispered, "I'm scared," but Watson did not hear her. Realizing that her voice had been drowned out, she repeated herself, nearly yelling to be heard above the din. "I'm scared."

Watson responded by tightening the arm he had around her waist, pulling her into him. He did not speak.

People whirled past them like leaves in a strong wind.

Watson stood straighter so he could see up ahead. In the dim of the simulated evening and with his battered eyes, he had trouble recognizing the arcade's features. He knew they would soon turn down a hall, but he could not see the hallway. He searched for clones. He searched for Nailor.

Families on blankets lined walls. Watson saw the hall they needed to enter. He saw the stairs that would take them back to the main floor. People camped on the stairs. Kids sat along the walls. A steady stream of people walked up and down the stairs. Watson patted Emily's shoulder as he led her down a set of stairs. They turned and entered the hall that led away from the arcade.

After the hundred-foot ceiling of the grand arcade, the hall looked small and tight and dark. Its twenty-foot ceiling seemed dangerously low to Watson, as if it might crush them. He knew it was a trick of the shadows, but he could not shake the claustrophobic feeling.

"Shit!" said Emily.

"What?" Watson mumbled through clenched teeth.

"Three clones."

"Clones? Are they wearing white armor?" he asked, though he knew they had to be dressed in the white armor of Spaceport Security. Harris was a hundred million miles away. The only clones left on Mars were Spaceport Security.

They continued walking forward, pushing through the crowd.

Watson tightened his arm around the girl, not wanting to lose her as he accelerated his pace.

Emily needed to jog to keep up with him.

He said, "Don't run."

She said, "It's the only way I can keep up with you."

Knowing that the door to the train station could not be more than forty or fifty yards away, Watson slowed, and asked her, "Where are they?" He did not want to fight. If it came to a fight, he would be helpless.

"We just walked past them."

"Did they see us?"

"I don't know."

Watson slowed to a stop.

"What are you doing?" she asked.

"I need to see if they're following us." Still hunched over, hoping he was camouflaged by the horde around him, Watson peered over the top of the crowd. Men and women pushed past him. Now that they had slowed, people tried to shove them out of the way.

"We need to move. We can't stay here. We need to get to the train," Emily said.

"We'll never make it... if... they..." He saw them, three clones wading into the crowd, walking toward him and Emily. After seeing the catatonic state of the clones in the barracks, Watson expected them to move like robots. These men were fast and alert.

"Damn, they saw us," he said. He tightened his arm around Emily, and said, "Just stay with me."

Emily would not have been able to keep up with him if he ran, but Watson kept a protective arm around her. He walked quickly, ignoring the pain that his patches could only partially hide. He held his left arm out like a battering ram and shoved people out of the way. People complained, a few tried to push back, but mostly they cleared out of his path.

Ignoring the urge to look back, Watson moved on. Soon they would start down the stairs that led to the train station, and he told himself that he would rest once they arrived.

His heart pounded. He struggled for breath. His ear was close enough to Emily's mouth to hear her wheezing, drawing in short shallow breaths.

"We're almost there... almost there," he told her.

She did not answer.

Behind them, one of the clones fired three shots. The bullets ricocheted off the walls. People screamed, but the clones did not seem to care.

People dived to the ground and covered their heads with their hands.

"You, stop!" yelled one of the clones.

Still surrounded by a throng, Watson continued to force his way toward the train station. He could hear Emily beside him, sobbing and gasping, terrified, but still staying with him.

The clones fired more shots. Screams of panic. Screams of pain. Somebody yelled, "He's been shot!"

Some of the people remained on the ground, whimpering in fear. Some jumped to their feet and ran for safety. Some stampeded in the same direction as Watson and Emily, toward the forbidden train station.

The clones fired into the crowd. Watson heard the thud of bullets striking flesh. Five feet from Emily, a man yelped and collapsed. A woman screamed, grabbed her injured arm. She kept running as blood squirted from between her fingers.

Still holding Emily, Watson veered to his right, causing her to lose her footing. He pinned her body to his. Carrying her as she struggled to balance herself, he winced at the pain in his ribs. Still cradling Emily, he dived into a line of picnickers.

A woman tried to help Emily to her feet. A man punched Watson, hitting him in the thigh, then the back.

Watson rose to his full height. His reactions were automatic. He pulled Emily to him and mule-kicked the man in the head at the same time. Emily tucked herself under his shoulder. The man grunted and fell on his back.

The clones continued shouting and firing their weapons, but they hadn't seen Watson dive into the picnickers. They fired at the herd. Watson pressed Emily against the wall, concealing her behind his mass. He wrapped his arms around her and hung his head over her as he listened to the sounds of the terrorized people.

He heard the people run by. Moments later he heard the clatter of armored boots as they passed. When he looked for the door that led down to the trains, he saw that it was only ten yards away.

Watson turned toward the door and started running. Ten yards away. Eight yards away. Three bullets struck the wall in front of him. Full of terror, he dug his fingers into Emily's waist, then spun like a dancer performing a pirouette. He lifted her off her feet, then heaved her through the opening marked SERVICE PERSONNEL ONLY. She ran, spun, and flew all at once, crashing to the tiles away from the gunfire.

A bullet cut across Watson's back, tearing his clothes and creasing his skin. A bullet skimmed the top of his arm, singeing his shoulder, cutting a shallow groove.

Watson could feel the blood and the burn on his ear and shoulder, but the epidural patches prevented the pain from becoming an issue. He dived for the doorway, saw that Emily had already started down the long narrow set of stairs, and sprinted to join her.

Below them was the train station, as bright and empty as the promise of living happily ever after. Fifty feet of stairs stood between them and the white-tiled platforms. Watson ran as fast as he could, his calves burning, his thighs numb, his lungs trying to wring breathable oxygen out of stale air, his jaw clenched because the pain from every bounce of his jaw brought tears to his eyes.

He knew that there would be no place to hide if the clones caught him on the stairs. They would shoot him in the back.

He heard a jangle of noise and kept running. He heard shouts. A shot was fired. Out of the corner of his eye, Watson saw two white enamel suits fall through the air. The third followed a moment later.

He reached the bottom of the stairs and saw clones lying dead on the ground, little beads of blood rolling down the slick surface of their combat armor. Their armor shattered by the three-story fall, they lay in a quickly spreading puddle of blood.

Afraid of what he might see, Watson turned to look up the stairs and saw Freeman, dressed in green armor, sprinting toward the platforms. He held the three dead clones' M27s as if they were toys, and he yelled in a low, rumbling voice that was both fierce and calm, "Get on the train."

51

The entire caravan squeezed into the first train car, the people taking up less than one-third of the space while the gear Freeman had packed filled the rest. The people sat in groups, their stifling silence nearly palpable.

Freeman, wearing his armor but not his helmet, sat with Gordon Hughes. The old man's face had gone a pale, nearly bloodless white. He kept an eye on his three sons, who sat with their wives and children. Tasman sat with his bodyguards around him. Emily, the oldest of the Hughes grandchildren, sat with Watson in a distant corner of the car.

As the train pulled away from the platform, Watson examined Freeman's gear. He saw a motorized wheelchair with low-slung wheels that almost looked like tank treads, which Freeman had obviously brought for the bedridden Tasman.

Freeman had stacked his rifle and particle-beam cannon with the guns. Including the weapons Freeman had taken from the clones he'd killed in the train station, they had six M27s. They'd only had three when they left the administration building.

Watson craned his neck for a view of Hughes. The old man's

skin was pale, and his eyes were dark and hooded. He met Watson's gaze and glared back at him. Watson leaned over to Emily, and whispered, "You should go sit with your family."

"I want to stay with you," she said.

Watson could not read Emily's mood, but he was not interested in *playing* anymore. His entire life, he had never been in need; and now that he was nearly helpless, she cared for him. He did not know if what he felt for her was dependence or love. He thought it might be both.

She stayed with him and took care of him, and he hoped she had attached herself to him. He did not know if he would want his freedom once he no longer needed her, but he suspected he wouldn't. He said, "We'll have lots of time together."

She smiled, kissed him on the cheek, and went to sit with her parents.

Watching Emily walk away, Watson felt more lonely than he had ever felt in his life. He would have liked to have gone with her, but he knew he would not be welcomed. He noticed that everyone, even Freeman and Tasman, had someone sitting with them, everybody but him.

Back on Earth, Watson preferred to be on his own during daylight hours. Now though, with the pain and the danger, he felt vulnerable. He felt hollow. Just as the realization that he was utterly alone began to weigh on Watson, Freeman came to join him.

Watson said, "Thank you for saving us."

Freeman did not answer.

Hughes walked over, bent down to speak to Freeman, and whispered a question so that Watson would not hear him.

As Freeman turned to answer, Watson stared at the massive nest of scars on the back of Freeman's shaved head. He could not pull his attention away from it. It looked like Freeman's skin was laced with flesh-colored centipedes. Ray Freeman, the mercenary giant, the man who had killed Morgan Atkins and shot Wayson Harris... even he could be injured.

The train slid through the tunnels under Mars Spaceport, traveling silently along a single raised rail.

Staring out the windows, Watson saw doors and arches and platforms. He asked, "We're not out of danger yet, are we? They're going to come after us."

Freeman shook his head. He said, "Not by train."

"Admiral Cutter destroyed the other tracks," said Watson. "You'll disable this car when we reach the base."

"Not the car, the train station," said Freeman.

"The station in the Air Force base?" asked Watson, not sure why that would stop the clones from following them.

Freeman did not answer.

Watson thought about it and realized he meant the station in the spaceport, not the base.

They reached the far end of the spaceport and entered the atmospheric locks. Heavy doors slid open to admit the train, then slid closed behind it. One set of doors, then another, then a third, and they launched into the desert. The world outside the train was sandy and strewn with rocks and rock shelves. Rust-covered plains stretched as far as the eye could see. It blended into a mauve-colored sky.

Watson looked back and saw the dome of the spaceport shrinking into the horizon. He was no astronomer, but even grade school kids knew that you did not need to travel far on Mars before objects vanished into the horizon, not nearly as far as you would have traveled on Earth because Mars was a smaller planet. Seeing the spaceport disappear, Watson breathed a sigh of relief. He wanted to put as much distance as he could between himself and Franklin Nailor.

He asked, "If you destroy the station, won't that stop the train?"

Freeman did not answer.

Watson pieced the puzzle together. The train was a convenience, but Freeman had found armor. They could travel on the surface. By destroying the train station, Freeman might kill the security clones. He might even get Nailor.

It made sense. Freeman had to rig the train station because the computers that could retrieve the train back from the Air Force base could also be used to stop the train as it sped away.

Watson had noticed that the gear Freeman had loaded included rubberized armor—engineering suits with oxygen for breathing. He turned to Freeman, and said, "It looks like we have a walk ahead of us."

Freeman did not answer. It was answer enough.

Five minutes later, when the lights went out, and the train came to an abrupt stop, Watson knew that Spaceport Security had entered the train station. He did not know how big a bomb Freeman would use, but he hoped it was big enough to kill Nailor.

Along with lights and motion, the electricity powered the train's enhanced-gravity field. Martian gravity being about one-third of the gravity on Earth, objects did not float in the air on Mars, but they weighed less than Watson expected.

"You better dress quickly, there isn't much air in this car," Watson told Emily as he stepped into the lower half of the armor, squeezing his shoes into the foot compartments. He reminded himself that this was not the same kind of armor that Harris wore when he went to battle; this was the equipment of engineers and window washers. Instead of hardened plates and a bodysuit, this was a unitard with a faceplate and a sealed hood. A ring of small lights circled the transparent faceplate.

Watson pulled the suit up to his waist and cinched the ties that held it in place, then he turned to Emily to help her into her suit. He pulled it from her hands and held the back open as she stepped into the pants.

"Don't be scared," he said. "They'll never catch up to us."

She paused, stared at him, and said, "Aren't you scared?"

"Specking terrified," he admitted. He smiled at her as he pulled the armor up so that she could thrust her arms into the sleeves.

Once she had finished dressing, he finished as well. It was not an easy fit; he had to bend his legs and hunch his back to get the unitard over his shoulders. His ribs still hurt from the beating. The pain from his jaw, which still hung broken, now cut through the haze from his patches.

Before sealing himself in, Watson peeled the old patches from his neck and placed a single new one in their place. He'd have liked to use two or maybe three, for the long walk to the Air Force base; but this was his last.

The one-size-fits-all armor was a tight fit for Watson. It would not have fitted Freeman, but he had his combat armor. He strapped a rifle on one shoulder and the oversized particle-beam cannon over the other. Crisscrossing bandoliers hung across his chest plate.

On the other side of the car, two of the bodyguards helped Howard Tasman dress. Once he was ready, one of them rolled the old man and his wheelchair out of the train while the other two stood outside and received him.

On a heart monitor on the back of Tasman's wheelchair, bars of light flashed, showing the rhythm and strength of his heart. Watson did not know if the old man had a weak heart, but Freeman clearly wanted to keep an eye on it.

Once Tasman and his guards were out of the way, Hughes came next, followed by his progeny.

The microphones inside their helmets might or might not have worked; but with Spaceport Security sludging, there would be no communications. Freeman pointed along the side of the tracks that led to the Air Force base, and the convoy started to move. First Tasman and his bodyguards began walking, following by the Hugheses.

With everyone wearing armor, Watson could not tell the Hugheses apart. He could not tell Emily from Gordon from the three sons. He wondered if that was how the clones felt, unable to tell one from another without memorizing fine details.

The bodyguards performed their job well. As long as Tasman's motorized wheelchair scooted him at a quick enough pace, they seemed to ignore him. When the wheels became bogged in sand or rubble, they picked him up and carried him like pallbearers hauling a casket.

Tasman, a cantankerous old fossil under the best of circumstances, waved his arms in the air every time the bodyguards touched his chair. At first Watson thought he was thanking them, then he realized the old bastard was pitching a fit.

Freeman grabbed Watson by the shoulder. As the others walked away, he handed Watson one of the M27s.

Watson took the gun and started to sling it over his shoulder, but Freeman stopped him. He held his own M27 by the forestock and trigger. Watson nodded and held his gun the same way.

Watson looked down the rails toward the Air Force base.

He saw the people walking far ahead, shrinking into the distance. He looked back toward the spaceport, which had long ago vanished below the horizon.

How far have we gone? he asked himself. *How far do we have to go?*

During his briefing, he'd been told that the two facilities were ten miles apart. *Maybe three miles left*, he told himself. *Maybe three miles*. Three miles in low gravity on rough terrain in the wrong-sized space suit was a long walk.

How will they travel if they don't have the train? Watson asked himself. He hoped they had to travel by foot. Maybe those were the only choices on Mars, by train or by foot.

Holding his gun the way Freeman showed him, Watson started to leave, but Freeman stopped him again. He signaled for Watson to follow as he returned to the train. Without climbing back into the car, he reached into a doorway and pried open a crate that lay on the floor.

There was a control panel in the crate. Freeman flipped a switch on the panel, and a circle of red diodes blinked once in response. They blinked, then a second passed, and they blinked again.

Freeman closed the crate; and then he closed the train doors.

A bomb, Watson thought. *Not a bomb... a trap*. If they opened the train, they would set off the bomb; and, of course, they would open the train, they had no choice but to examine the train. Watson wondered how many of them the bomb would kill. He hoped Nailor was among them.

52

About a half mile from the train, the bodyguards stopped while Tasman puttered on. They stood in a group, and others soon joined them. When Freeman and Watson reached the spot, they stopped as well.

This was the area where Cutter's fighter pilots had destroyed the rails. The ground where the tracks had been was burned black with yard-deep holes. Two of the three rails, sturdy metal pipe about two feet in diameter, had become an ambiguous wad that looked like melted candle wax.

As Watson walked along the third rail, he saw where it, too, had been destroyed, its melted remains lying in blackened soil. A new rail had been grafted over the expanse. Watson knelt and touched his gloved fingers into the soil. He reached forward and patted his hand against the ground. He stood and ran the same hand across one of the newly restored rails. *So Cutter did destroy all of them*, he thought.

Freeman stood over Watson, no doubt spotting the same things that he saw. He stuck his forefinger in the air and twirled it to catch people's attention, then he pointed ahead, signaling the convoy to move on.

Tasman was the first to move. The bodyguards followed, having to jog a few steps to catch the old man. The Hugheses followed. Watson and Freeman brought up the rear.

Soon after they passed the break in the rails, Mars Air Force base appeared in the distance. It stood out like a mountain range against the flat plains around it. The building was close enough that Watson could see details in its architecture.

The "soft-shelled" armor Watson wore weighed about thirty pounds on Earth. On Mars, with its weak gravity, the armor weighed less than ten pounds. Heavy enough. In the beginning, the walk felt like an adventure; but fighting the weight and stiffness of the armor, the convoy crossed less than three miles in the first hour.

Tasman's wheelchair, with its tiny wheels, moved easily across the terrain; but it teetered in slag and sank in sand. Some of the teens had held broad-jumping competitions in the beginning; but an hour into the hike, their energy had drained.

As long as the people kept ahead of him and did not stray from the tracks, Freeman ignored them. When a boy meandered away from the rails, Freeman picked the kid up and carried him back to the fold by his arm.

Since their radios did not work, the people found other forms of communication. As Freeman walked away, the kid spun around and flipped the bird.

Tasman and his bodyguards continued to lead the way.

Watson looked back along the track. Seeing a cloud of dust rising to the sky in the distance, he tapped Freeman on the shoulder and pointed back along the rail.

Freeman looked and nodded.

53

They were less than a mile from the base when an explosion shook the ground and hurled bits of train in every direction. It was the flash that caught Watson's attention. He looked up in time to see a silvery shape tumbling through the air. He yelled, "Heads-up," but no one could hear him, so he ran ahead and tackled people to the ground.

Debris started to fall from the sky. Some people saw the bits of metal and plastic and just stood there. Tasman slithered out of his seat and curled into a ball on the ground. Age and disappointment had not dimmed the old man's will to survive.

A metal sheet fluttered like a butterfly with a ten-foot wingspan over their heads. Watson heard its warbling song through his hood. Shards of glass whistled past. Most of the dangers flew high overhead. Because of the limited Martian gravity and atmospheric resistance, they flew much farther than they would have on Earth.

Just as Watson determined that the "metal butterfly" must have been part of the roof of the train, a twenty-foot section bench dropped from the sky and stabbed upright into the dirt ahead.

Thank God for slow learners, Watson thought. Maybe it was

Nailor, maybe it was Riley, or maybe it was just some of the foot soldiers; but Freeman had been able to trick one or more of them twice, once with a bomb in the train station and once with a bomb on the train. *Natural selection*, he thought. When they reached the base, he would congratulate Freeman for being an agent of Darwinism. Then he thought about Freeman and his cold glare and his humorless ways and changed his mind.

A minute passed, and nothing more fell out of the sky. The bodyguards stood, looked around to be sure they were safe, and loaded Tasman back into his wheelchair. The other people stood. Freeman walked to the front of the pack and directed them on.

Watson spotted something the others had missed. A person remained on the ground, a body lying facedown in the sandy soil. Watson could not tell if the person was breathing, not through the armor.

Praying that it was not Emily, he sprinted to the spot. He knelt beside the body and rolled it onto its back. Gordon Hughes stared up at him, his face the color of a ripe plum, his eyes bulging as if he'd been holding his breath. A layer of bile coated the inside of his glass faceplate.

Watson looked into the governor's visor and nearly vomited himself. He did not know what to do. He had no medical training. Even if he had, he could not open the sealed engineering armor without exposing Hughes to Mars's carbon-dioxide air.

He looked over his shoulder and saw that the others had not noticed, all but Freeman. In his dark green armor, he stood like a shadow. *The angel of death*, thought Watson. *The harbinger.*

Freeman approached slowly. Showing no interest in the body, he tapped a finger on Watson's visor then pointed back in the direction of the spaceport... of the nearing dust cloud.

Let the dead bury the dead, thought Watson.

The cloud of dust was much closer now. He guessed it was only half a mile behind them. The dust looked like a curtain skirting the desert floor.

Watson understood Freeman's message. The Spaceport

Security clones had some kind of vehicle, and they were gaining ground. Freeman had reduced their numbers with his bomb, but the survivors were closing in.

Freeman unslung his sniper rifle.

Watson followed the angle of the rifle and looked back along the track. At first he saw nothing but tracks and desert, with a backdrop of dust and smoke and matte sky. Then some tiny black shapes along the bottom of the dust cloud came into view. At a distance, they looked like insects, but they were men on buggies—two-man, four-wheel carts formerly used by spaceport maintenance for servicing the train tracks and working around the landing zones.

Watson knew he could not run from this fight. He tightened his grip on his M27 and raised it; but Freeman laid his hand across the barrel and forced it down. He raised his rifle and aimed.

Heard through the hood of the armor, the rifle sounded distant, like Freeman had fired from a hundred feet away. Five hundred yards away, a six-wheeled buggy veered and swerved, then rolled upside down.

Freeman fired again. This time a buggy flipped onto its front end like a racehorse that has lost its front leg. As two Marines climbed out of the wreckage, Freeman shot them.

He fired again. A second passed, and he fired another shot. The first shot had hit the Marine driving the buggy. When the man beside him grabbed the wheel and righted the vehicle, Freeman shot him, too.

Watson wondered how many bullets the big man could carry. Did he have a hundred? Did he have a thousand? Spaceport Security had five thousand Marines.

But Freeman did not intend to kill every clone in Spaceport Security, just the ones on the buggies, the scouts. There were twelve vehicles. They were the advance guard, so to speak, the first ones on the scene.

They were only a couple of hundred yards out now. Freeman reloaded and fired.

Two of the drivers pulled their buggies nose to nose, forming a barricade. Four Marines in combat armor milled around the makeshift barricade. Watching them, Watson had the feeling that they thought they were safe behind their waist-high barrier.

Two of the Marines shot their M27s at Freeman and Watson. The guns were set to automatic fire. Bursts of gunfire echoed across the grounds. Watson had no idea where the bullets went. Except for the muzzle flashes and distant sounds, the gunfire could have been imaginary.

Freeman aimed at one of the Marines and fired. One of the men flew backward, tossing his M27 into the air.

Freeman picked off two of the three remaining Marines. The fourth cowered behind the buggies. He fired one quick burst from his M27, then he stood, tossed the weapon away, and raised his hands in the air.

Freeman pointed at the man with his rifle, then signaled Watson to go after him. He tapped Watson with the muzzle of his rifle, then swung the rifle in a long arc that ended in the direction of the buggies and the dead Marines.

"You have got to be kidding me," Watson shouted though he knew Freeman would not hear him. He shook his head in an exaggerated motion, making sure to turn the entire hood from one side to the other as he shouted, "No."

Freeman wrapped a hand the size of a small frying pan around the front of Watson's faceplate, and shoved him backward. Watson's feet came up from under him, and he landed on his ass.

As he stood, he saw Freeman walking toward that last Marine. He walked slowly and steadily, like a man fighting against a strong wind. Watson knew that Freeman did not intend to take the man to the base; he did not want prisoners.

He intended to kill the man, maybe with his hands to save a precious rifle round.

Watching Freeman walk toward that last Marine, Watson had to fight back the panic and revulsion. Freeman had wanted him to kill the man when he could have picked him off as easily as he shot the others. They might as well have been stationary targets on a shooting range.

Why did he want me to bother killing this one, when there are more on the way? Watson asked himself. *There will be plenty to kill.*

"Plenty to kill," he repeated the words out loud. "Batting practice."

Like a father teaching his son how to swing a bat before a real game, Watson thought. *I have to learn to kill.* Freeman wasn't trying to teach him how to fire a gun, he was trying to acclimate him to the feel of murder. *Eliminate the moral dilemmas now, then I can shoot without worrying about my conscience later.*

Thirty feet ahead of him, Freeman approached that final Marine. Watson followed, walking at first, then sprinting. Freeman glanced back and waited for him.

They stood together in silence, almost as if Freeman could read the resolve in Watson's posture. Watson stalked past Freeman.

You wanted to kill me. You came here to kill me. If I surrendered, you would have killed me. You would kill me. You would kill Emily. Harris would have killed you, Watson told himself.

He tried to ignore a louder voice in his head screaming, *I don't want to do this. He's alive. He's a man, a human.*

The Marine stood with his hands in the air.

He's not a man; he's an insect, Watson told himself. The combat armor was hard and dark, like the shell of a beetle. It had no face, just a shiny glass plate.

Not a man, a bug. He would kill me. He came to kill me. More are coming.

The man was nameless and faceless.

I don't want to do this. I don't want to do this!

Eight yards away. Watson imagined it was Franklin Nailor hidden inside the armor and fired his M27.

54

Naval Intelligence had no information about Sunny Ferris. The clone military services did not maintain records about private citizens unless they posed a threat. Ferris, apparently, did not pose a threat.

Alexander Cross Associates, the law firm that employed her, was another story. The founder, Norman Alexander, had been a successful lobbyist during the days of the Unified Authority. He'd represented a consortium of military contractors. His clients manufactured the latest-generation tanks, guns, and armor. Those were the weapons the Unifieds kept hidden until after they evicted their clones.

Cross himself had served as a captain in the Navy. He'd served under Admiral Che Huang, an antisynthetic prick of an officer. Huang was long dead, may his natural-born soul rest in natural-born Hell. I had nothing to do with his death, not that I would have hesitated, given an opportunity to kill the bastard.

Intelligence found Sunny Ferris's birth and school records, some tax files, all useless. She was twenty-eight years old. She lived outside of Washington, D.C., in a ritzy suburb. She was not married. I found myself pondering that factoid time and again.

I wanted to call her. I had no reason and every reason to call.

Something was wrong with me. The phobia of swimming and the ability to pull the pin on that grenade proved it. Somebody had screwed with my programming. Somehow, somewhere, someone had gone into my head and rearranged the furniture. I had a pretty good idea about where it happened—Mars. Who and how were coming into focus as well.

I thought about downing a case of beers and visiting a Pentagon psychiatrist, but why bother? Cutter had people shadowing my car and listening to my calls, he probably had mikes and cameras in my billet and my office. And what would he do with the data he gathered—he'd send it to a shrink. Why bother visiting a psychiatrist when my commanding officer was already having me psychoanalyzed?

Anything that can be programmed can be reprogrammed. Freeman's words repeated in my head again and again, though it never seemed to be his voice that said them. I had been reprogrammed. Never in my life had I wanted anything more than I now wanted to get my hands on the people who performed that little piece of magic.

I wanted to talk to somebody… anybody. Okay, I wanted to talk to Sunny, but that wasn't going to happen. I wanted to speak to someone who knew me well, somebody who could tell me if and how I had changed. The list of candidates was short—Don Cutter and Travis Watson were the only names that came to mind.

I hadn't known Cutter all that long, but I respected him. Calling him was out of the question. He was a four-star and I was technically retired. He'd take my call and let me talk, but he wouldn't be interested unless I could give him something of strategic value.

Then there was Watson. The boy had jumped ship on me. He'd

joined Cutter's staff while I was on Mars. I felt jilted, which meant I really liked the kid. He was smart; but he was wise, too. Wise was better than smart.

I punched up Watson's line on my communications console and let it ring as I glanced over Sunny's data once more. She had grown up on the West Coast of North America and never traveled off Earth. She went to school at Harvard, the Unified Authority's oldest college. Twenty-eight years old. Not married.

I dialed up the Navy office.

Not married.

"Office of the Navy," the man said. He was probably a petty officer.

"I'm looking for Travis Watson," I said.

"I can put you through to his office, General," said the receptionist.

"Do you know if he's in?" I asked.

"He isn't. It's been a few days."

A few days. Watson was out. He was traveling. He liked visiting cities, seeing the nightlife, trying new brands of scrub. "Is he on vacation?" I asked.

"No, sir. Admiral Cutter called him up to the *Churchill*."

"The *Churchill*," I said.

"Yes, sir."

I found this news funny because Watson did not like space travel, and now, as a Navy man, he was off to space. Then a thought finally struck me. Cutter was on the *Churchill*, and the *Churchill* was orbiting Mars. *Something must be happening on Mars.*

I thought about Arthur Hooper, the bastard I shot up in Hawaii. I thought about the scientists who had tried to analyze the chemicals in his flask. The civilians could breathe it but the clone passed out. No, he didn't just pass out. He winked out and he didn't know that he had winked out when he woke up. *It was like restarting a computer.*

"He passed out, but he didn't know he'd passed out," I said to myself. *Woke up in a haze but it never occurred to him he'd been*

320

out, I thought; only this time I wasn't thinking about the scientist. *Programmed... reprogrammed.*

Hooper wasn't a New Olympian, I reminded myself. He was a former officer of the Unified Authority with no connection to Mars or Olympus Kri. Which begged an interesting question: Why had Sunny come to defend him?

Mars and the Unifieds. My thoughts channeled to Mars. Everything seemed to point back to Mars. I remembered the shoot-out. I remembered the riot. I knew what else had happened, but I did not remember it. I knew the time and date that Jackson and the rest of my regiment flew from the spaceport to the base, but I had no mental image of meeting them in the landing bay. I had no image of them marching off their transports.

Hoping to find out if the other members of the regiment remembered Mars the way I did, I turned to my communications console and dialed Curtis Jackson's office. Nobody answered. I called the regimental headquarters in Camp Lejeune; no one answered the telephone. I called Second Division headquarters. Nothing.

I tried calling Jackson directly on his personal communications device. He did not answer. My next telephone call was to the Swansboro police.

When I reached Cutter, he began by saying, "Harris, I'm very busy..."

I interrupted him. I said, "What is the *Churchill*'s location?"

"We're orbiting Mars."

I asked, "Where is Travis Watson?"

"That is classified information, General," he said, suddenly sounding bureaucratic.

"Is he on Mars?" I asked.

"That is none of your business."

I doubted that. Any mission that would take Watson to Mars would have had a lot to do with me. I asked, "How many ships do you have with you?"

"What are you getting at?" Cutter started to sound concerned. We had worked together during the invasion of Earth, and he knew my triggers. He asked, "What do you have?"

I said, "Tarawa is missing." I did not worry about using the nickname with Don Cutter. He may have been a Navy man, but he knew his Marine Corps lore.

"Second Division? What do you mean Second Division is *missing*?"

"They are supposed to be in Lejeune," I said.

In a placating voice, he said, "Harris, they don't report to you anymore. You might want to remember that you've been relieved of command."

I said, "Did you close Camp Lejeune?"

"Why would I close Lejeune?" he asked. Lejeune was the second largest Marine base in the empire.

"You tell me, Admiral," I said. "Lejeune is empty. There aren't even any sentries guarding the gates."

"No one?" he asked.

"Not a living soul on base," I said. "I had the Swansboro police send a car. They said the base was empty and the gates were open."

Cutter went silent for a moment, then he said, "Harris, that's not just Tarawa, that's the entire Second Division. You're talking about twenty thousand men."

"They left in a hurry," I said. "Would you like to know where I think they are going? I think Second Division is headed to Mars."

Cutter said, "General, you are back on active duty. Get your ass out here. Bring whatever you need."

If I was right, and Second Division had been compromised, twenty thousand Marines were headed to Mars. They'd need a ship, of course. I called the Office of the Navy and discovered that the EMN *de Gaulle*, a fighter carrier, had left for Mars two hours earlier.

If a fighter carrier with twenty thousand combat-hardened

Marines was headed to Mars, Cutter would need a lot more asses than mine.

There were two questions I always asked myself at the start of operations. The first question was obvious, every officer asked it: "What men and material will I need to succeed?" The second question sounded similar, but there was a world of difference. That question was: "What men and material do I have available?"

The first was a question of tactics. The second, logistics.

I had dozens of ships and millions of fighting men to send to Mars, but they would arrive too late to save Cutter and Watson. If I was right, they would arrive too late to save the New Olympians as well.

I called Navy headquarters and ordered the *Lancet* and the *Christy* to Mars, knowing that they would not arrive until long after their mission had already failed. They faced a four-hour flight to Mars, and the *de Gaulle* had a two-hour head start on them.

Then I had a grand idea. The only problem was, it would only work if a junior officer had ignored my orders.

55

"This is Major Dunkirk." Good thing he announced his name and rank, I hadn't bothered committing either to memory. The only thing I remembered about him was that he was the officer over Smithsonian Field, and that he had argued with me when I ordered him to dismantle the self-broadcasting fleet.

I said, "Dunkirk, this is General Wayson Harris."

"Yes, sir," he said.

"I came out to inspect the airfield a few weeks ago."

"Yes, sir. I remember, sir."

"And I gave you orders to destroy the explorer fleet. Have you carried out my orders?"

Bracing himself for the explosion that would surely follow, he took a deep breath, and said, "No, sir."

"No?" I asked.

He must have misinterpreted my excitement as anger. He said, "No, sir. It is my understanding, sir, that you have been relieved of command. I cannot carry out those orders until they are confirmed by an officer on active duty."

I said, "Major, I have been reinstated."

Silence.

I said, "Listen to me, and listen to me carefully. I want those birds gassed up and ready to fly. I want their broadcast generators charged and their broadcast engines humming. They're going wheels up as soon as I get my men together."

At first he did not respond. Then he said, "Sir, I will need authorization from Admiral…"

"Believe me, Dunkirk, Naval HQ will be on the horn with you rapid, quick, and pronto. In the meantime, I want those birds juiced."

"Sir, even if I receive the authorization… Sir, those ships are over one hundred years old. They might not fly."

"They better fly," I said. "The future of the Enlisted Man's Empire will be riding on those wings."

56

Don Cutter thought he had worked out the conspiracy. In his mind, the same people who organized the Martian Legion had hired Arthur Hooper to kidnap and brainwash high-ranking clones. He had thought maybe they had started with Harris.

The disappearance of Second Division threw a wrench in the works. It was too big to fit the matrix he'd created.

After getting off the horn with Harris, Cutter sent a team of Intelligence officers to investigate. They found Camp Lejeune evacuated. They reported finding no signs of a struggle. The Marines had simply walked off, but not all twenty thousand of them.

Some had died. Cutter's investigators found 132 newly turned graves behind a parade ground.

Could someone have reprogrammed an entire division? he asked himself. He didn't believe it was possible. But if Tasman really was part of this, maybe "reprogramming" a division wasn't out of the question.

And then there was Harris. He'd acted strangely on Mars; but now that he had returned to Earth, he seemed to have reverted to his old reliably homicidal self. *Harris wouldn't be Harris if he didn't leave a trail of corpses*, Cutter mused, though he did still wonder about the video feed Watson had seen in which Freeman shot Harris.

He sat in his billet trying to make sense of the situation, considering each piece of the puzzle as he named it softly out loud. "Harris." "Reprogramming clones." "Tasman." "Lejeune… abandoned." "Mars." "Freeman." "Legion." "Night of the Martyrs." "Olympus Kri."

He said the words, and they appeared on virtual cards displayed on the audio-and tactile-sensitive screen of his computer. Dragging the cards with his pointer finger, he arranged them into various combinations, trying to imagine an order in which they might fit together. Harris fitted with Mars. Harris fitted with the Night of the Martyrs. Harris fitted with Reprogramming. He did not fit with Camp Lejeune.

Freeman fitted with Reprogramming and Harris, but he did not fit with anything else. Tasman fitted with Reprogramming and Mars but nothing else.

A message appeared on his communications console: Captain Thomas Hauser requested permission to speak with him.

"Cutter."

"Admiral, a train left Mars Spaceport several minutes ago, sir."

"A train? I thought we destroyed the tracks?"

Hauser, a nervous clone under normal circumstances, said, "Oh! Speck! Sir, there's been an explosion in the spaceport."

"Send me the feed," said Cutter.

Hauser transferred the video feed and stood by. Mentally shelving his virtual note cards, Cutter started the feed. The first twenty seconds showed nothing but Mars Spaceport, sitting silent and still. Then a train snaked out of the building and down the track.

Cutter thought the train leaving the spaceport looked like a worm squirming out of an apple. He zoomed in and followed the train, all the while whispering the question, "Are you on that train?" as if trying to reach Watson telepathically.

There was an explosion in the spaceport. It was not a large explosion. Neither the roof nor the walls caved in. Fire belched from vents along the roof. Sensors reported vibrations in the outer walls of the spaceport.

A few miles down the track, the train stopped halfway between the spaceport and the Air Force base. Three minutes passed, and then two men in engineer armor pulled a man in a wheelchair from the front car of the train. They were deep in the middle of nowhere. As far as Cutter was concerned, Mars was a shit hole to begin with; but out in the middle of nowhere, it was worse.

As he watched the feed, a convoy of people in soft-shell armor climbed off the train and started walking toward Mars Air Force Base. They could have been clones, they could have been natural-borns; Cutter had no way of knowing. One man wore combat armor. Zooming in for a closer look, Cutter saw how the man towered over everyone else. *Freeman.*

"Hauser, can we contact them?" he asked.

"No, sir. Somebody must be sludging the airwaves. We've tried reaching Colonel Martin and Governor Hughes."

The people from the train moved at an impossibly slow pace as they followed the track toward the base. In the meantime, a small army of clones in combat armor poured out of the spaceport. Most of them marched, but a few scouts rolled ahead on civilian carts of some kind.

"Are you sure we cannot get through?" asked Cutter.

"Yes, sir."

"Keep trying, Captain."

"Aye, aye, sir."

The carts scooted over the barren surface. In another fifteen minutes, the carts would overtake the people on foot.

That has got to be Freeman in the combat armor, thought Cutter. *The one in the wheelchair is probably Tasman.* He decided that Watson was likely with Freeman as well... if he was still alive.

The clones on the carts would have been Martin Riley's men. As he considered the scenario, he decided Harris had been right: Martin Riley and his men were reprogrammed clones. There were thirty carts. The men in the carts wore white combat armor and held M27s. The men from the train had a few M27s... and Freeman's sniper rifle. Harris had told Cutter stories about Freeman's sniper skills.

If that was Freeman and Watson was with him, the boy still had a chance.

The clones on the carts reached the stalled train. Most of them stopped to investigate, but a dozen darted on. Their tactics seemed so uncoordinated. *If Riley is sludging, they're as cut off from each other as we are*, Cutter reminded himself.

Cutter knew what would happen, but he still jumped when the train exploded. It was that kind of explosion, powerful, resonant, a brilliant flash, a wide brim of fire, so much shrapnel and debris that the carts and clones around the train were obliterated. Harris had also told Cutter about Freeman's skill with explosives.

The admiral watched debris fly in every direction. He watched Freeman send the other people on while he and another man stayed back to greet the remaining clones. Freeman did all the shooting while his useless partner watched.

That has got to be Watson, Cutter thought, then he changed his mind. When the shooting ended, one of the security clones had survived. He threw down his M27 and tried to surrender, but the man with Freeman killed him. He murdered an unarmed clone.

Freeman would kill an unarmed man. So would Harris. Not Watson.

When he saw that Freeman and the rest of the refugees would reach Mars Air Force Base before the security clones caught them, he said, "Hauser, scramble a transport down to the air base. We need to get Watson out of there."

"Aye, aye, sir."

"Send a fighter escort. Better safe than sorry."

Hauser started to answer, but the Klaxons drowned him out. The scream of the Klaxons erupted through the *Churchill*.

"Admiral, two battleships just broadcasted into Mars space," Hauser said. "We're taking evasive action."

Broadcasted? Unified Authority ships? The Enlisted Man's Navy did not have self-broadcasting ships or a broadcast station. If ships had just broadcasted in, they had to belong to the Unified Authority. Cutter sprang from his desk. As he ran to the door, he called, "Launch that transport, Captain. Launch those fighters."

57

The three bodyguards, Dempsey, Liston, and Sharkey, stood beside the outermost door of the air lock. This twenty-foot-high steel door was the portal through which the train would have entered the base. Though they could not communicate, all three bodyguards had roughly the same thought: *That damn door probably weighs a hundred tons.* In truth, it weighed three in Martian gravity. On Earth, it would have weighed closer to ten.

The entire convoy slowly clustered in front of the massive door. Unable to speak to one another, people pointed and gestured. They could not enter the building, and panic slowly set in.

Liston, one of the bodyguards, knelt and used his finger to write a question in the dry soil. He tapped Dempsey, the lead bodyguard, and pointed to the words he had written: "Do you know any other way in?"

During his term in the Air Force, Dempsey had been stationed on the base. He shook his head and stamped the words with his boot.

Tasman rode back and forth along the door in his wheelchair. Everyone else in the convoy ignored him.

Three hours had passed since the train left the spaceport. The day had ended, but the night had not yet begun, and the sky had turned to a shade of gray that most closely resembled pewter.

Their armor, which was designed for the absolute cold of space, kept them warm. The lights etched along their faceplates provided light. They were not blind or cold, but they were still desperate.

Watson, the pain patches on his neck now expended, studied the convoy as he searched for Emily. Every little movement hurt. Anything that shook his body shook his jaw, sending electric spasms through his skull. His labored breathing hurt his ribs. Every movement hurt his ribs.

While the Hugheses stared out into the desert and the bodyguards examined the doors, Ray Freeman found a small panel built into one of the train rails. He pulled a laser welder from his bag. This he used to slice the panel, revealing the inner workings of the train track. He used other tools to test and probe at the wires and relays inside the rail.

In another minute, he located the relay he wanted. A moment later, the outer door of the air lock slid open. Tasman immediately steered his wheelchair through the opening. His bodyguards followed. The beleaguered Hugheses, who seemed to have overlooked their patriarch's absence, were slow to file in.

The convoy traipsed onto the base, marching along the train track, with Freeman and Watson bringing up the rear. Once they were in, Freeman tripped a lever on the inside of the air lock, and the outer door slid closed. A vent drew out the native environment while an oxygen generator pumped in breathable air. Once that process finished, the inner door opened automatically and the convoy entered the train station.

The station was entirely dark. In the light from his headlamps, Watson saw the rust-colored stains that covered the platforms. Harris and company had disposed of the bodies, but they had not bothered steam hosing the blood.

Inside the base, the train tracks were five feet above the ground. When trains rode those rails, their floors would be exactly even with the platforms.

Freeman walked to a metal ladder fastened against the wall to the platform. He stood by the ladder, his rifle strapped over his shoulder, his M27 in his right hand.

The rest of the herd watched him, the light from their lamps shining on his back like searchlights, bathing him and the area around him in circles of bleaching white light. If a sniper waited in the Air Force base, the convoy had just illuminated his prime target.

Freeman waved at the people and tapped on his helmet, indicating to the others to power down the lights on their helmets. Watson understood and cut off his lights immediately. The bodyguards had learned military signals and went dark as well. The others watched him curiously, the beams from their visors lighting Freeman like stage lights shining on an actor.

Dempsey, Liston, and Sharkey stepped into the crowd. They grabbed helmets and tapped on visors. People responded by dowsing their visor lights, leaving the train station as dark as a cave.

The soles of Freeman's hardened boots made a metallic *clank* as he climbed the ladder. He sprang up the final rungs and rolled over the top, landing in a crouch, with his M27 pointing into the darkness. His movements were quick and fluid, designed to provide enemies a minimal target, but there was nothing he could do about the clatter his armor made as he moved across the platform.

Freeman used the night-for-day lenses to disarm the darkness. He searched the platform and the escalator that led into the base, then he switched to heat vision so he could search the stairs and the entry to the base for any phantoms hiding behind walls.

The platform was clear, but that did not mean the place was empty.

The escalator rose at a forty-five-degree angle from the train station to the base. With a high-ground advantage like that, a lone gunman at the top of the escalator could stop a small army. If anyone in the party questioned the value of the high-ground position, the bloodstained platform offered proof.

Looking up the escalator through heat-vision lenses, Freeman saw a trace of orange glow off to the side. He aimed his rifle and waited. As it moved away from the walls, the orange specter resolved from a smudge into a man-shaped form.

With the patience of an alligator waiting to snap, Freeman knelt on the platform, his rifle trained on the top of the escalator. The standoff lasted two minutes, but Freeman was a patient man. He would outwait the assassin.

After two minutes of motionless silence, the assassin swung out from his hiding place, and Freeman fired a single, fatal shot. The sequence occurred in a fraction of a second. Freeman discarded his rifle, the long-range weapon of an assassin, and pulled his M27. He waited another minute before running up the escalator. He'd killed that assassin, but he did not know if another lurked nearby.

The interior of the Air Force base had an enhanced-gravity field. Weighing in at over three hundred pounds, wearing armor and carrying forty pounds of weapons and ammunition, Freeman was winded by the time he reached the top of the escalator. His heart pounding, his lungs drawing in huge pulls of oxygen, he held his M27 ready as he knelt and searched the dark lobby.

While Freeman climbed the ladder and surveyed the train station, Watson rested his body against the tracks. So much time had passed since his epidural patches had worn off.

The patches had caused his body to generate adrenaline, which made him stronger and more tolerant of pain. When the medicine in the patches ran out, so did his strength. Aware that he might not have the strength to stand up again, Watson dropped to his knees and lowered himself onto his back.

He remained in his isolated corner as his strength gave out, and he fell into a dreamless sleep.

Time passed. He had no idea how long he'd been asleep when Emily woke him up. She shook him once and waited a moment. He'd started to wake when she shook him again.

She had removed her helmet and her armor. "Travis, we need to go," she said.

Leaning his weight against the wall, Watson worked his way to his feet. His legs wobbled and buckled, and his internal gyroscope whirled as he searched for balance. He did not speak.

Emily said, "Go slow, Travis. There's no rush." She put a hand on his shoulder to prevent him from rising too quickly. When he straightened, she slipped a steadying arm around his back and said, "I'm going to take you to the infirmary. I'll fix you up."

His mind fogged, Watson did not comprehend the meaning of her words. All he knew was the comfort of her voice.

Leading him like a sleepy child, Emily guided Watson to the ladder. She placed his hands on the rungs and waited patiently while he pulled himself up. He climbed a few, then stopped to clear his head before climbing the rest of the way.

He looked back, and asked, "Do you know about your grandfather?"

Emily did not answer.

She led him across the platform, then bade him rest before riding the escalator up to the base. Sitting at the end of the platform, he saw men moving back and forth. Watson looked for Freeman but did not see him. A minute passed, then he stepped onto the escalator. As the stairs lifted him, he held on to the rail the way a drowning victim holds on to a life preserver.

They crossed the lobby and entered the base, passing offices and a cafeteria before Emily helped him into an elevator. He slumped against a wall for the two-second ride. When they finally reached the infirmary, Emily had him lie on an unmade bed. She applied a patch to his neck, and he fell asleep.

When he woke, his jaws were aligned but he could not move them.

58

The call to stations threw the crew of the *Churchill* into an organized frenzy. Sailors sprinted through the halls. Red and amber lights flashed. Officers had to shout to be heard.

As Cutter ran to the chart table, the Klaxons faded.

"Is the transport away?" he asked Captain Hauser.

"Aye, sir."

"Fighter escort?"

"Launched, sir."

"Did you warn them about the battleships?"

Hauser deferred that question to his second in command—Lieutenant Frank Nolan, his communications officer.

"Aye, sir. They're going to land behind the base," said Nolan.

"Good," said Cutter. Only after hearing this did he allow himself to breathe. He looked at the holographic image of the space around Mars, noting the *Churchill*'s position before looking for intruders. "Good God, are those Nike-class ships?" he asked.

"Yes, sir. Nike-class battleships, sir," responded Hauser.

Nike was the last generation of warships built by the Unified Authority. They were smaller than the Perseus-class ships used by the Enlisted Man's Navy—ships that the Unifieds had abandoned along with their clones. Nike-class ships had nearly impenetrable shields. Some of them carried shield-buster torpedoes that could render EMN ships defenseless with a single hit.

It had been more than a year since the Unified Authority Fleet broadcasted to the Scutum-Crux Arm and vanished into history. No Nike-class ships had been seen since that time.

"Where the hell did those bitches come from?" Hauser muttered.

Cutter watched the ships on the holographic map. One of the ships was less than five hundred thousand miles out and approaching slowly. The other was still a full million miles away. She appeared only as a dot on the display.

According to telemetry tracking, both ships were traveling at no better than ten thousand miles per hour with a low acceleration factor.

"What are they doing here?" asked Cutter.

"What is their weapon status?" asked Hauser, who was the commanding officer of the *Churchill*. Cutter ran the Navy, but the *Churchill* was Hauser's ship.

"The first ship's shields are hot, sir," an officer called. "We're picking up erratic energy fluctuations. There's something wrong with her."

"What about the second?" asked Cutter.

"Too far to read, sir," answered one of the weapons officers.

"Have you made contact?" asked Cutter.

"They're not responding," said Lieutenant Nolan.

"That bitch has been through the blender," said Hauser.

"I don't care if she's pissing blood," said Cutter. He started to say, "We can't go one-on-one with a Nike..." Then he saw the extent of the damage. Burns covered her hull. Entire sections of the battleship were dark. *She's half dead*, he thought.

Looking at the holographic representation of the ship, Cutter saw the miscolored areas where her hull had been broken and hastily patched. He said, "God, she shouldn't be moving."

"Admiral, we have help on the way, sir," said Lieutenant Nolan. "I just got a message from the *de Gaulle*. She's twelve million miles out."

"Oh shit," said Cutter. He did not explain himself.

"Sir, do we stand our ground?" asked Hauser.

Staring at the display, Cutter muttered "How the hell did those battleships get here?" Then he switched his attention to Hauser, and said, "Those are Nike-class battleships, Captain. Keep one hundred thousand miles between us and those ships at all times."

"Aye, sir," said Hauser, and he relayed the orders.

Once he received confirmation, he asked Cutter, "Admiral, do you think they came from Terraneau?"

"I don't know anyplace else they could have come from," said Cutter.

"Aye, sir," said Hauser. Then he added, "They're as slow as glaciers, sir."

One of the weapons officers approached the table and waited for permission to speak. He said, "Captain, the first ship is leaking radiation."

Hauser smiled, and said, "We might be able to sink that bitch with a spit wad!"

"Give me an updated position on the *de Gaulle*," said Cutter.

"She's eleven million miles out, sir," said Lieutenant Nolan. "Should I send her a distress signal?"

Eleven million miles, about twenty minutes away, Cutter reasoned. *We might be able to play cat and mouse with those limping Nikes; but once the* de Gaulle *arrives, they'll surround us.*

59

Watson watched the scope that tracked the twelve Tomcats and the transport as they entered the atmosphere. The fighters could have annihilated the security clones if they caught them on open ground; but the pilots headed straight for the Air Force base, a choice that seemed to make no sense.

Moving as quickly as he could, Watson shuffled up the stairs to the observation deck, a loft with chairs and a bar fronting a twenty-foot circular window. Staring into the darkened sky, Watson located the fighters by their vapor plumes, brushstrokes that evaporated quickly.

Why would the fighters come here? he asked himself.

Cutter must have been monitoring them from the *Churchill*; otherwise, he would not have known to send the transport. Specking sludging, he thought. *If only we could reach them.*

"Hey, there's a battleship. Two battleships! Two battleships just entered the area," said one of the bodyguards, Sharkey or

Liston or Dempsey. Watson could no more tell them apart than he could tell clones apart. In his mind, the bodyguards were interchangeable cogs, three burly guys, not particularly bright or brave or motivated. Without being aware of it, he was comparing them to Freeman and Harris.

The fighters and the transport slowed as they flew over the top of the Air Force base. For just a moment, Watson glimpsed the tails of the Tomcats. The transport, her shields glowing a ghostly blue, glided past the building last. They were low to the ground and coming in for a landing.

Two battleships. The words echoed back and forth in Watson's head. *Battleships. Why would Cutter call in more ships, a single fighter carrier could… unless the battleships aren't his.*

He could not make sense of it. As far as Watson knew, the enemy was reprogrammed clones and whatever remained from the Martian Legion.

The fighters and the transport parked on the massive airstrip behind the base. Dempsey went to open the rear air lock for them, but the pilots remained in their ships. With a hostile force advancing on the base, they could not leave their ships. With enemy battleships looming outside the atmosphere, they could not stay in the air.

60

My driver slowed to a stop as we approached the last gate.

The guards at the gate wore combat armor. If we'd come yesterday, we'd have found them in service uniforms breathing fresh air; but the rules had changed over the last twenty-four hours. Thanks to reprogramming, reality no longer meant what it used to mean.

Three armed guards accompanied Major Dunkirk as he walked out to my jeep and saluted. I had no doubt that the missiles in the battery beyond the fence were trained on me at that moment.

I said, "We're in a hurry, Major," and I nodded toward the line of thirty-five trucks on parade behind my vehicle.

"May I see your orders, sir?" he asked. He did indeed need to see my orders. Until Cutter returned to Earth and officially acknowledged my commission, I would hold no more authority than any other retiree. As far as Dunkirk was concerned, the stars on my collar were only for show.

I handed him my papers.

He took them and scanned them, not reading the words but checking the authorizations. What I was about to do was bending the rules to say the least. If I was a traitor, my actions might put the entire empire at risk.

In this case, the authorization did not come in the form of a signature. The paper contained "notary dots," microscopic computer chips sealed in the paper, which had been activated by Don Cutter's staff. I could write my own orders, and I could forge Cutter's signature, but only the admiral could activate the dots.

The dots were invisible to the naked eye. Dunkirk scanned them using the equipment in the visor of his Marine combat armor. The spots were filled with codes, notes, and an activation date. Hell, each dot held enough data storage for the complete works of Shakespeare.

Once I was fully reinstated, my office would be able to use notary dots as well. That was one of the useful technologies we inherited from the Unifieds when we took Washington, D.C., away from them.

So were the antiques I had come to commandeer.

Apparently Major Dunkirk liked what he saw when he scanned my orders. The gate opened. He saluted and stepped out of the way.

The explorers were already out of their hangar—207 spacecraft, each unarmed and unshielded. These birds had been built for scientific research and serenity. They were slow, they were delicate, they were ancient; but they had working broadcast engines. That made them indispensable.

"No disrespect, General, but are you sure this is a good idea?" Colonel Hunter Ritz asked me over the interLink. Ritz, my new second in command, was a "loose cannon" in whom I had complete confidence. Had I not returned to active duty, he stood to inherit the entire Corps, but commanding the Marines was not one of his ambitions.

"I'm sure that it is a bad idea," I said. "I don't see any other options."

Ritz said, "Let the speckers have Mars, then blow their asses off their legs when they try to come home... sir. That gives us a home-field advantage."

The afternoon had ended, and the first signs of evening showed on the horizon. I said, "Stow it, Colonel. You have your orders."

"Yes, sir. Aye, sir," he said.

Ritz was the devil I knew. He liked to argue. He liked goading men who outranked him, even generals. He pushed "asking for instruction" to the brink of insubordination, and he was so lazy between missions that he'd been written up for dereliction of duty; but he was energetic, inventive, and fearless in battle. His commanding officers loathed him, and his men swore he was the fourth member of the Trinity.

"Permission to ask one final question, sir?" Ritz asked.

"What is it, Colonel?"

"Are we doing this for one man, General?"

Am I placing three thousand fighting Marines in harm's way just to rescue one man? I asked myself. The answer was probably, "Yes." Ritz had asked the wrong question. He should have asked me if we were doing this for Howard Tasman, the father of neural programming, or Ray Freeman, the mercenary who had pulled my ass out of the fire on more than one occasion, or Travis Watson. Even I would not have known the answer to that question.

I said, "No, Colonel, this isn't about saving one man. This is about saving the Enlisted Man's Empire."

He answered by saying, "Aye, sir. Yes, sir. Once more into the breach. Hoorah."

Orange light shone on some of the clouds in the distance, but the true harvest night was still several hours away.

The scientific explorers were too small to be practical from a military standpoint. Designed to ferry scientists and soil samples, the hatches on these birds weren't wide enough for jeeps, let alone tanks, not that it mattered. Their jump-jets were not powerful enough to lift heavy artillery in Earth's gravity.

We could fit one hundred men and a modicum of artillery in

a transport. These little birds had room for fifteen men so long as they did not carry anything larger than M27s or grenades. With 207 explorers, we could shuttle approximately thirty-one hundred men.

We were in for a fight.

We loaded up quickly and launched, a measly fifteen men per ship, and my sergeants had to wedge them in like a foot in a boot.

Explorers had very delicate-looking retractable wings—the thrusters were in the base of the ship. The thrusters fired, and we lifted into the air smoothly enough. Apparently, the weight of the men did not impact our liftoff.

One nice thing about explorers, they had portals and viewports along the walls and the ceiling. I caught a brief glimpse of trees and clouds as we flew.

It took a few minutes for the old birds to leave the atmosphere. Broadcasting, a process involving ridiculous amounts of electrical energy, was restricted to the vacuum of space.

When a ship broadcasted, it was coated with enough joules of electricity to disintegrate everyone on board. The electrical field was so intense that seeing its glare through closed eyes could leave a man blind. Metal shutters closed over the insides of the windows to protect our eyes.

"General, do you have any idea how old these ships might be?" Ritz asked me, as the windows vanished.

"No idea," I admitted. "They're old."

"Are they sixty years old?" Ritz asked.

"Older," I said. "You sound nervous."

"Nervous?" Ritz asked. "Me, nervous? I had a look at Corps regulations. Did you know we swap out toasters after seven years of service. Doesn't matter if they've shorted out or not; after seven years, we melt them into scrap metal."

"I did not know that, Colonel," I said. That was the difference between me and Ritz, he wanted to live. Me, I'd seen enough. Death did not bother me, phobias did.

"Corps regulations say we retire portable latrines after twelve years. It doesn't matter how well scrubbed they are, after twelve years, the Corps no longer considers them sanitary."

"Fascinating," I said.

"We retire fighter jets after five years of service," he said. "Tanks after twenty."

It was all bullshit. Those regulations were written by Unified Authority hacks who didn't give a flying speck about cloned Marines squatting in unsanitary shitters.

As Ritz continued to complain, the ships broadcasted. Colonel Hunter Ritz, who could indeed be a genially insubordinate asshole, took his coffee straight and entered battles head-on. I let him rant until he took his first breath; and then I told him, "We've already broadcasted, Colonel. Congratulations, you survived the safest part of this mission."

61

"There are incoming ships," one of the bodyguards called from the nerve center. A moment later, he added, "Holy hell! There's a shitload of them."

Freeman stood behind him and watched the screen. Watson, his body still stiff, stumbled and came for a look.

Modeled after the manner of a spaceport control tower, the nerve center was entirely dark except for the glow from the screens and displays. Liston and Dempsey stood beside a flat table over which shimmered a holographic map.

"They just broadcasted outside the atmosphere." Watson wasn't sure, but he thought the bodyguard who'd spoken might have been Liston. It was Dempsey. He added, "There are 207 of 'em."

Watson looked from the whited-out area above the virtual atmosphere on the holographic display to a two-dimensional readout that showed data instead of images.

Self-broadcasting ships? He thought, *There cannot possibly*

346

be that many self-broadcasting ships in the entire galaxy. Two hundred seven ships. Then he remembered. Those had to be the explorers from Smithsonian Field, and only Wayson Harris would have thought to send them.

"It's Harris," Watson said. His jaws had been set with a device that kept the bones aligned, but he was able to growl the words. "We have to warn him."

"Communications are still down," said Liston.

"If it's Harris, he'll figure it out," said Freeman.

Watson did not answer.

62

"One of the battleships is changing course," said Lieutenant Nolan. "It looks like she's headed toward the spaceport."

"Is she shooting the explorers?" asked Hauser.

"Not yet, sir."

Cutter smiled. They had just made the tactical error he had hoped they would make. He told Captain Hauser, "Good news, Captain. We take this play one-on-one." In his mind, he added, *until the* de Gaulle *arrives*.

Hauser asked. "Should we attack her now or wait for *de Gaulle*?"

Cutter gave him the bad news. He said, "The *de Gaulle* is on their side."

Cutter turned to his communications console. He dialed in a code, and said, "Harris, do you read me? Did those antiques come with working radios?"

Harris said, "Fully equipped... everything but shields and guns."

Cutter said, "We don't have much time, General. Riley is

sludging the airwaves down there. We're going to lose contact when you enter the atmosphere."

"Understood."

"It's getting crowded around here; there are two U.A. ships patrolling the area, and the *de Gaulle* is closing in."

"I see the Nikes," said Harris. "Do you have any idea where they came from?"

Harris recognized them by their shields. Nike-class ships had glowing orange shields that wrapped around their hulls like skin. They were the only ships that had those advanced shields.

"They're Nike class; they broadcasted in. How the hell would I know where they came from…? Probably Terraneau. You better get to safe harbor before they arrive," said Cutter.

Harris did not respond.

Cutter watched the holographic display. He studied the U.A. battleships. *Rookie mistake*, he thought to himself.

He said, "I'm pretty sure Watson is in the air base. Now listen up. Their reinforcements are going to arrive before ours do. We'll do what we can to help, but you're on your own until the cavalry arrives."

Cutter tried to imagine what course the battle might follow. Several seconds passed in silence. Harris signed off, but Cutter didn't notice.

Drawing with his finger on a touch tablet, he sketched a plan, which he sent to navigation along with a single-word notation, "Possible?"

A moment later, a two-word response appeared on his tablet. The words were, "Aye, sir."

Cutter showed Captain Hauser his plan. The *Churchill* was Hauser's ship. He gave the orders.

Hauser looked at the tablet and smiled. He told his navigators, "Come around hard. Let's poke that bitch in the ass and see how she squeals."

Both of the Unified Authority ships appeared to be damaged, with inadequate repairs, especially the second ship. As the ships chased the *Churchill* out of Mars orbit, Cutter analyzed their energy signatures.

Just as Captain Hauser had said, "They'd been through the blender." They might have survived the battle at Terraneau, but they'd limped away.

The *Churchill* veered starboard, then spun hard to port, amassing intense acceleration as she followed a path that led above and around the enemy ships. Traveling in a vacuum, devoid of gravity, fighter carriers turned wide along imprecise arcs that spanned thousands of miles. The U.A. battleship did not respond quickly.

The Unified Authority ships continued to travel in a straight line as the EMN carrier dashed around them. Dragged by their inertia, the battleships flew straight ahead as the *Churchill* completed a thirty-thousand-mile loop in less than two seconds. Cutter watched the whole thing in holographic miniature.

He'd seen Nike-class ships in battle. Broken or not, they posed a threat. The glowing orange shields did not buckle. In a fair fight, those shields presented a nearly impervious barrier to torpedoes, particle beams, and EMN lasers.

But these battleships were different. They'd been injured. Cutter hoped their shields would fail.

"We're coming up behind the lead ship," said Hauser.

Cutter didn't need the update. He'd watched every instant of the maneuver on the holographic display, taken in every nuance of it. "Violate her," he whispered. "Particle beams, torpedoes, missiles, everything but our fighters."

"Aye, sir," said Hauser. He relayed the order.

The U.A. ship was long and narrow, shaped like a knife, like a badly dented dagger. Looking at the holographic display, Cutter saw two of her main engines sputter. The readouts suggested problems with her guidance systems. She handled like a barge, almost like a bullet. Her turns would be wide, slow, and shallow, if she could turn at all. Her engines showed no ability for sudden acceleration.

In pristine condition, the U.A. ship would have had faster

acceleration and more maneuverability than the *Churchill*; but this ship was far from pristine. In an act of desperation, her captain launched his fighters. They showed on the display as tiny white dots, like sparks rising from a burning log.

The *Churchill* opened fire.

The particle-beam cannon fired first, thick webs of sparkling green light. The torpedoes and missiles launched from tubes above and below the cannon, flying along a line that would not intersect with the disruptive beams until the moment of impact.

The *Churchill* launched torpedoes, then missiles. The missiles homed in on the disrupted area of the quickly recycling shields. The particle beams stopped, and in that same moment, the missiles struck. A split second later, the torpedoes slammed home, lighting the stern of the U.A. ship.

"She's hitting back!" Nolan shouted. "Lasers and torpedoes!"

"Get us out of here!" Hauser shouted. "Fire decoys! Defensive bursts! Defensive bursts!"

Cutter felt the yaw and pull from the rapid changes in acceleration and direction. He watched the holographic display, saw the icon representing the *Churchill* turn and speed in one direction as the model of the U.A. battleship became blurred by particle beams. A moment later, the torpedoes struck. The ship was undamaged, her shields remained.

"Damn," Cutter muttered to himself.

Hauser yelled, "I need a report!"

"We're out of danger, sir," said Nolan. Some of the officers on the bridge applauded, some merely sighed. Cutter, who had paid no attention to the counterattack, said, "We didn't even nick her." During the entire time, he had never taken his eyes off the 3-D tactical display.

Lieutenant Nolan pressed a forefinger to his earpiece, then said, "Yes, sir. You're right, sir, but I bet her crew is puking."

"What do you mean?" asked Hauser.

"Look at her course. She's flying sideways."

"Gawddamn," said Hauser. "No wonder she's so damned slow.

She's doesn't have any thrusters. They might as well be flying a specking zeppelin."

"A zeppelin with shield-busters," Cutter reminded him.

Hauser did not need a second reminder. He said, "Good point, Admiral." Then he told navigation to put some distance between them and the battleships.

63

"Cutter, are you there?" I asked. He did not answer. We'd entered the atmosphere and lost communications with the *Churchill*.

"Pilots, call out," I said over a communications panel.

One pilot answered, my pilot. Since we were in the same ship, our panels were wired together. He said, "Here, sir." Cutter had called it right—someone had sludged the airwaves; but that blade cut both ways. I could not contact my men, and he could not reach his.

A window on my comms panel identified my pilot as Major Anthony Hines, EMAF. I said, "Major, the enemy is sludging our communications."

"Yes, sir," he said.

I looked out one of the windows, hoping to count other ships, but was distracted by what I saw on the ground. The planet looked like a museum display in miniatures. I saw little models of the Air Force base and Mars Spaceport, tiny toy train tracks

353

spanning the gap between them, and an army of figurines about three-quarters of the way to the base.

I generally entered battles riding in the kettle of a transport, the windowless, comfortless cast-iron belly of the most spartan bird that ever flew. Riding in a kettle, I never saw the field until the ramp opened at the rear of the ship. The explorer had observation ports and portholes everywhere. She was designed for scientific exploration, viewing nebulas and counting stars.

As I studied the scene, I decided to play a hunch. Instead of landing by the air base to defend allies, we would set down by the spaceport to draw the enemy away.

I told the pilot, "Put us down on the spaceport runway."

"What about our other explorers?" he asked.

"They'll follow your lead."

"Yes, sir."

"Once we're clear, fly to the Mars base and start charging your broadcast engines. I want you to broadcast out as soon as your engines are charged."

"How do we tell the other ships?" asked Hines.

"I don't think that is going to be a problem," I said. "Unless I miss my guess, they will clear the airwaves the moment we touch down."

"Yes, sir."

"Once communications go up, I need you to keep your ear to your box. If you hear anything, anything, you send this antiques society back to Earth. You got that? You tell them to rendezvous at Smithsonian Field."

"Yes, sir."

"Everyone but you. You evacuate that air base. You find out who is in that base and deliver them to Smithsonian Field."

"Yes, sir," the pilot said. He tried to mask his nervousness, but I heard it in his voice. Piloting this relic over a battlefield would be like flying a paper kite in a hailstorm, and he knew it. If he moved quickly enough, he might survive it.

"And Hines, broadcast in the atmosphere if the space lanes

look clogged. Just make sure you deliver those people back to Earth," I said.

In theory, the atmosphere would absorb the electricity from a small broadcast the same way it absorbed the energy from a lightning storm. The shared anomaly of two hundred ships broadcasting in a relatively tight area, however, could create all kinds of damage. Who knew what kind of a chain reaction that much energy could set off?

My pilot said, "Yes, sir." He was an Air Force cargo pilot. He accepted his orders with the stoicism of a man who flies supplies over battlefields.

The area around the spaceport was flat and rocky with rust-colored soil, a flat plain ringed by distant mountains. From the ground, it would look like a nearly endless plain; but from the explorer, I could see the mountain range. I could see the three sets of raised rails that ran from the spaceport to the Air Force base and the remains of a train, but we were dropping quickly, and I soon lost that bird's-eye perspective.

We touched down.

The explorer landed delicately, like it was made of tissue paper and glass.

As I had suspected, the enemy had tracked our descent. When I opened my commandLink, and yelled, "Hit the tar! Now! Now! Now!" I reached all three thousand of my Marines.

They had expected us to fly to the Air Force base, which was the logical move, to retrieve Tasman and Watson. But we had chosen a more aggressive route, and the people in charge now needed to call their forces back or face us alone.

As I said before, sludging was a blade that cut both ways. They could not call their men back without opening the airwaves for me as well.

The company commanders on the other explorers heard my orders and off-loaded their Marines in record fashion.

Had guards been waiting at the spaceport doors, they could have picked us off as we disembarked; but the people running the show had not counted on my having a fleet of self-broadcasting antiques. They had sent their men to attack the Air Force base and left their base of operations unguarded.

I had never seen the spaceport from the outside, at least not from ground level. It was a civilian structure, built during an era of peace, at a time in which the Unified Authority knew no neighbors and faced no threats. Hundreds of doorways dotted the lower walls of the building, hatchways through which mechanics and luggage handlers could pass.

The architects who created this building had designed it without any defenses. Any hostiles already in place would have no fortifications as they tried to stop my Marines from capturing the building. Assuming we captured the spaceport, we would have no fortifications when Martin Riley and his security force returned.

Assuming we survived Riley and his five thousand men, we would have the same problem all over again when Second Division arrived with twenty thousand reprogrammed Marines.

When my ships arrived with twice that many troops, Tarawa would face that problem all over again. By that time, though, there would be very little left of the spaceport to defend.

Colonel Ritz orchestrated the invasion while I carried out my own personal mission.

We approached the building from the west, the side facing the Air Force base, expecting no more than token resistance. More by the book than he liked to let on, Ritz still assembled his men into fire teams and sent them in by the numbers. Grenadiers carrying flash grenades and low-yield pills opened hatches, automatic riflemen took point position, riflemen and team leaders followed.

When push comes to shove, the Marines fall back on the same strategy almost every time—the main force attacks the enemy straight on and pins him down while a secondary force flanks and destroys. It's a strategy that has worked for a thousand years.

The outer hatches led into air locks, thirty-foot-long atmospheric antechambers in which Mars's native carbon dioxide was pumped out and replaced with oxygen.

I entered an air lock with one of Ritz's fire teams. It was a long, dark tube with circular walls and a floor wide enough for an automobile or one of those trailer-pulling buggies the spaceport used for hauling luggage.

A few recessed lights shone down from the low ceiling, air poured in through vents along the top, forcing a convection that expelled the indigenous carbon dioxide through openings along the base. It was a quick process, lasting less time than it took us to cross from the outer hatch to the door leading into the building.

The automatic inner doors opened, revealing an empty maintenance floor.

"General, we are leaving for the Mars base." It was Hines, my pilot. He said, "Good luck, sir."

I said, "Good luck, Major."

The next person to speak was Colonel Hunter Ritz, who asked, "General, are we going to tangle with Spaceport Security?"

I said, "I expect so, Colonel."

I'd known Ritz a while, and he'd never struck me as the most well-informed officer. Now, all of a sudden, he spouted all kinds of data. He said, "There are five thousand of them and three thousand of us, wouldn't it be easier to let them through the outer hatches and shoot them as they file through the door?"

Neutralize their numerical advantage by creating a bottleneck, good thought. I said, "We need to keep the damage to the building at a minimum. We're here to protect a civilian population."

Ritz asked, "Do you have an ETA on Second Division?"

"They're already up there, but they won't launch with the *Churchill* harassing them," I said. "Admiral Cutter's got his hands full dealing with the *de Gaulle* and two U.A. battleships."

"U.A. ships? The Unifieds are in this?"

"What's left of them," I said.

I could imagine Ritz nodding and bracing himself for the fight, as he said, "We'll keep the specking trash outside as long as we can."

I said, "Do what you have to do. Semper fi, Marine."

64

This was my day for taking risks.

The last time I had visited Mars Spaceport, I steered fifteen hundred men into the grand arcade and started a riot. Of the 3,104 Marines I brought on this mission, I left 3,004, including Ritz, to guard the doors while I took a hundred men into the spaceport's more populated areas.

The lay of the land was straightforward: one large continuous baggage area along the outer walls filled with conveyor belts and walkways. We crossed the gloomy empty space and passed through a doorway that opened to an inner hallway. As we entered this hall, I repeated the all-important directive, "Do not remove your combat armor. If you need to shit, shit in your armor. I will personally shoot any man I see removing his helmet. Do I make myself clear?"

I did not bother telling them why they could not remove their helmets. They did not need to hear sketchy information and paranoid theories about reprogramming. Once the fighting started, they would have plenty to worry about.

The cargo area was not used as a living space for one obvious reason—it opened to an outer world. If a single seal failed, the area would fill with toxic Martian air.

As we marched through the service halls, however, we came upon civilization. Mars Spaceport was just as I had left it: overcrowded, grimy, lacking hope. Picnickers lined the unadorned walls of the corridor. They watched us and hardly responded. Some people stared. A few kids pointed at us.

"Move out," I told my men, and I led the way. Most generals avoid the battlefield. Those who do, seldom take point. If I had my way, I would trade my general's stars in for the stripes of an enlisted man; the problem was that I did not trust in the abilities of the men who might replace me as commanding officers.

A spaceport map showed in a corner of my visor. We were close to our destination as the crow would fly, if that crow could fly through walls. We were below the outer gates of the Perseus wing of the complex. We needed to climb two flights of stairs to reach what had once been the general boarding level, then we needed to wind our way to the hub of the spaceport and descend into its bowels.

If we could have walked through walls, we would have had a few hundred yards to go. Observing the laws of physics and not destroying the walls around us, we had a half mile to cross.

I kept my men marching at a fast pace. We ignored locals as we sped past them. Easy to do; most people leaped out of our way, some ran.

The area was not brightly lit, but that mattered very little. We could see more than a hundred feet ahead of us in the ambient lighting, and our visors would automatically switch to night-for-day vision in the dark areas.

"Sir, I don't get it," Colonel Ritz said over the interLink. That was Ritz. Starting out by asking for permission to speak would have been too much like following protocol for the son of a bitch. He'd managed the "sir" part, then launched right into his conversation.

He asked, "You say we came to protect the New Olympians?"

"Affirmative," I said.

The corridor curved ahead. The stairs to the next level would be visible once we turned that corner.

"Last time you came, you massacred a few thousand of them." When I did not respond, he said, "You killed off their army, and now you're back to protect them?"

"Affirmative," I said.

"So, they were the enemy last time, and this time it's the Unified Authority?"

"Renegade leaders from the Unified Authority, Colonel. The Unified Authority no longer exists."

"And you say they are here to kill the New Olympians?"

"Affirmative."

"I don't get it, sir. What would holdovers from the Unified Authority have against New Olympians?"

"They don't have anything against the New Olympians. They're after us."

A long, silent pause... something I seldom got from Ritz. Finally, "Just to make sure I have this straight, sir, a mysterious group of Unifieds who have nothing against the New Olympians is going to kill them to make trouble for us."

"That just about sums it up," I said.

"Why would they attack the New Olympians, sir? Why not attack us?"

I said, "We would be a military target. They'd need an army to hit us. The New Olympians are an unarmed population occupying an unprotected facility." Yeah, I was using military-speak. I was speaking in the language that Ritz both understood and avoided.

"Ritz, you are going to have to trust me on this one," I said.

"If you say so, sir," said Ritz.

The hall was dark and packed with people, some standing in the center and some sitting along the walls. I could see the stairs in the distance.

A muzzle flared in the distance, above the crowd. An assassin with a lowly M27 waited for us on the stairs. I did not see the man, just the flash from his gun.

A sniper with a precision rifle and an excellent scope might not have hit innocent bystanders. This asshole sprayed into the crowd and hit nothing but innocents. A man screamed in pain. A moment later, a woman began screaming about her child. The panic began. People ran for their lives. A flood of people stampeded toward me and my men.

Some of the people running along the walls tripped and were trampled. No more aware of me than he was of the oxygen in his lungs, a man dashed in my direction. As he came in range, I hit him across the jaw with the grip of my M27, and he crumpled. I heard more firing and stepped back behind a wall for cover.

The people giving the orders for the enemy were in the spaceport, trapped. Freeman must have done something to disrupt their plans. Maybe Freeman had liberated Howard Tasman, maybe he had taken something or someone else.

"General, you're saying that these Unifieds want to hurt us by killing Martians?" Ritz asked. He did not hear the gunfire. He did not know that the fighting had already begun.

I said, "Shove off, Ritz. I'm busy at the moment." Then, on an open frequency that every man would hear, I said, "We have hostiles in the spaceport."

The assassin continued to shoot, brief bursts fired into the tail end of the scattering crowd. People screamed, and, in another minute, the junction was empty except for the wounded, the dead, and the sniper. He fired one last burst into the empty hall, but my men and I were safe behind a wall. I waited a few seconds. By the time I swung around the corner, the bastard had already run away.

Using my commandLink, I listened to the chatter of the Marines I had brought with me. One man said, "I wish I had a grenade." Another said, "Speck! It's so specking crowded. There's no way we can shoot back."

One Marine said, "It's not the shooting that scares me. I don't want to get trampled." Someone answered, "You're wearing combat armor, dumb ass. Half the specking planet can walk across your back, and you won't feel a thing."

"Armor isn't bulletproof," the first guy said.

The second guy said, "So don't get shot."

I waited for our gunman to return. He never did. While I waited, I checked back with Ritz.

"Any sign of hostiles at your doors?" I asked. His men had placed sensors that would warn them when anyone came within two hundred yards of the perimeter.

"No takers yet, sir. Why would the Unifieds want to kill Martians, when the Martians don't like us?"

I said, "This is just guesswork, okay?"

"Yeah."

I started toward the stairs, knowing that the man with the gun would not be there. He didn't want to fight; he wanted to slow us down. At that moment, we had a huge numerical advantage; but in another few minutes, Riley's security troops would return, and the scales would turn against us.

I said, "The New Olympians like us."

"Then why did they send martyrs to kill us?"

"They didn't send the martyrs, the Unifieds did."

"The martyrs came from Mars."

"The Unifieds recruited them. They sent evangelists here to start a religious revival. That was where the Martian Legion came from, the Unifieds were trying to play us and the New Olympians against each other while their black ops teams carried out the real work."

Ritz said, "Reprogramming clones?"

"Reprogramming the clones in Spaceport Security."

"Son of a bitch," said Ritz. "That almost makes sense."

"From what we've seen so far, the Unifieds have a few busted-up battleships, and they might have some ground troops. They can't take us on head-on..."

"So they sent recruiters to Mars," Ritz said.

"Evangelists," I said. "They started a religious revival. The goal was to recruit fanatics who wanted to believe God could deliver them from Mars."

I had my men fan out. There were only one hundred of us, but the section was small and empty now, thanks to the gunfire. Seventeen bloody people lay on the ground, most dead but not all of them. A few moaned and moved.

My riflemen took positions along both sides of the stairs as the first fire teams dashed up the stairs and secured the way.

I said, "If you wanted to bring back the Unified Authority, you'd need to get a lot of people on your side, and the best way to do that would be to turn them against us."

"The Martians?" Ritz generally referred to the New Olympians as "Martians."

"They have numbers, but they are powerless. They're meaningless, except from the humanitarian point of view... and these Unifieds are not interested in humanitarian efforts.

"They want to cause unrest on Earth..."

"So they kill off the Martians and make it look like we did it," said Ritz. "But they still wouldn't have enough of an army to beat us."

He knew about reprogramming, but he did not fully understand the implications... neither did I. "That's where the reprogrammed clones come in," I said as I walked up the stairs.

I was still at the top of the stairs, my men all around me, when an explosion rocked the area around us. It felt like an earthquake. We were in a hall that led into the grand arcade; there were thousands of picnickers. A hole formed in the middle of the floor. I didn't see it at first. Then the screaming started, and the panic, and people slid into the hole as the floor crumbled into dust.

On the upper floors, people were able to run to safety. The main floor gave way around that hole, and the disintegration spread. It looked like the floor was made of water, and that water was being drawn down an enormous drain, and the drain sucked in thousands of people as well.

A thick cloud of dust and smoke rose out of the floor. Tactical and night-for-day showed me nothing; but switching to heat vision, I saw the specters of people running, people falling, and the bodies of the trampled.

"What the speck is happening up there?" Ritz shouted over the interLink.

The floor continued crumbling until it nearly reached the outer walls of the court. Picnickers who stayed near their blankets survived, those that weren't trampled.

"General, what just happened?" Ritz said.

I looked around the area. I had not lost any of my men. Had we been a little quicker up the stairs or sent some men ahead, we would have taken casualties. We had played it by the book, leapfrogging our positions, covering the top of the stairs, then setting a perimeter. Entering an area methodically takes time.

Not everyone who fell through the floor was killed. I could hear people screaming from below.

"They detonated a bomb, but they didn't get any of us."

"The hell they didn't," said Ritz. "Whatever they did, it blew doors off hinges down here. I lost men." A moment later, he said, "I've lost forty-seven men."

I had forgotten about the shock wave. The bomb exploded under the floor, in the halls we had just traversed. The force of the shock wave would have channeled through those corridors like medicine in a syringe.

"Forty-seven dead?" I asked. During battle, I analyzed losses by the numbers. I thought, *Forty-seven men, that's more than a platoon.*

"Yes, sir."

"How many injured?"

"The men near the doors were killed, everybody else walked away."

The men by the doors were killed, I repeated in my head. Men in combat armor don't worry about flesh wounds.

"There are going to be injured civilians, Colonel. See if you can run some triage in the halls," I said.

"I'm already out there, sir. Euthanizing them would be more humane."

"That bad?" I asked.

"General, I have never seen anything like this. It's like somebody painted the walls bloodred."

65

As he watched the explorers on the tactical screen, Watson tried to decipher Harris's strategy. He knew Harris had to be the one in charge of the explorer fleet. Cutter would never have considered using unarmed antiques in a battle with modern ships.

If I were Harris, what would I do next? Watson asked himself. He looked back at the screen, expecting to see a few of the explorers traveling toward the Air Force base. *That's what I would do,* Watson told himself. *I would send a few ships on a rescue mission.*

On the screen, all 207 explorers were pressed between the spaceport and the base. *What the speck are they doing?* Watson asked his internal Harris.

"Who are they?" asked Dempsey.

"Doesn't matter, they're on our side," said Freeman.

While Dempsey speculated and Freeman didn't, Watson returned to the observation deck and its panoramic view of the Martian frontier. He could see the tiny silver ships flying in high off the ground to avoid gunfire. They did not look like spaceships to him. With their broad disc-shaped bows, the explorers reminded Watson of flying saucepans.

He remembered the day he and Harris had visited Smithsonian Field.

The explorers' thrusters worked better than wings in Mars's thin atmosphere. The ships traveled the short distance from the spaceport to the base a thousand yards above the ground. As Watson watched, the silver ships dropped out of the sky, but they did not land. Still flying in a loose formation, they buzzed around the Air Force base.

Watson heard one of the bodyguards shout, "They're going to the landing field in the back." Another one said, "I'll let them in."

He followed the second bodyguard, probably Dempsey, across the base. It was a large building but less than a quarter the size of the massive Mars Spaceport. They passed office areas and living quarters, hangars and equipment rooms. The building was mostly dark except for the soft-glow emergency lights.

Sore all over and tired, Watson had to fight to keep up with the bodyguard. After ten minutes walking, they reached the other side of the building, where they found men in soft-shell armor passing through the locks.

Some of the armor had Navy insignia, but the vast majority had Air Force. Seeing this, Watson realized that the fighter and transport pilots had come in with the men who flew the explorers.

Still hoping the explorers had come to evacuate the base, Watson walked up to the first Air Force pilot, and asked, "How soon can we leave?"

The man shook his head, and said, "There are battleships up there."

"Don't you have self-broadcasting ships?" Watson asked, a real effort with his jaw set.

"Not as self-broadcasting as I would like. Those are hundred-year-old ships out there, it takes 'em an hour to charge their broadcast generators. We're charging 'em now, but they won't be ready for another fifty minutes."

66

The U.A. battleship had impenetrable shields and a small fleet of fighters. She moved through space like an injured turtle swimming against a tide, stopped and lowered her shields to launch the fighters, and then she stayed in place, waiting to lower her shields a second time when her fighters returned. Once they were on board, the ship fired her engines and resumed the laborious ten-thousand-miles-per-hour chase.

Lieutenant Nolan said, "She's coming after us again."

"Admiral, we could outwalk that wreck," said Captain Hauser. A sly smile spread across his face. He said, "Put twenty thousand miles between us and drop a few mines in our wake. Let's give her a bumpy ride and go after her sister."

His words sounded optimistic, too optimistic in Cutter's opinion. They had attacked and outmaneuvered the crippled battleship, but they had failed to hurt her.

"Do you have an ETA on the *de Gaulle*?" asked Cutter.

"Eight minutes, sir," said Nolan.

"Eight minutes," Hauser replied. He looked at the holograph.

They were between the two U.A. ships now, spreading the distance from the crippled ship, closing the gap with the one circling Mars.

In another eight minutes, they'd be the lone EMN ship fighting two Nike-class battleships and a Perseus-class fighter carrier. The *Churchill* and the *de Gaulle* were evenly matched in every way except their crew. Cutter liked to think he could outthink the officers below him.

Admiral Cutter said, "Captain, that second ship must have a very compelling reason for staying away."

"She's keeping Harris pinned down," said Hauser. "She's the cat waiting for the mice to poke their heads out of the hole."

The battleship hovered a few thousand miles outside the atmosphere. The orange glow around her hull proved that her shields worked. A couple of questions lingered in Cutter's mind: *Why didn't she shoot at Harris's explorers as they crossed from the spaceport to the Air Force base? Why didn't she shoot them as they broadcasted in?*

He asked, "Is she leaking radiation?"

"No, sir," said Lieutenant Nolan. "Not this one."

The explorers would have been such easy targets, Cutter told himself. Then, out loud, he said, "She's a feint."

"What?" asked Captain Hauser.

Excitement showing in his step, Cutter walked around the display, examining it from every angle. He said, "We need to make a run at that ship. Let's take her head-on."

"Attack her head-on, sir?" asked Hauser.

"If I'm right, Captain, we won't need to attack her," said Cutter. "She's a feint. She's a bluff. She didn't fire on the explorers because her weapons don't work. That's what they're hiding from us."

The cat has a mouth but no teeth; that's why she isn't chasing the mice, he reassured himself, willing to risk everything because he believed it was true.

Captain Hauser did not share his confidence. He said, "Admiral, do you know what she will do to us if she's carrying shield-busters?"

"If that is a working battleship, we're already dead," Cutter responded.

"Yes, sir," said Hauser, though he did not sound enthusiastic. He turned to Lieutenant Nolan, and said, "You heard the admiral."

"Aye, aye, sir," said Nolan.

Cutter looked at the display. He watched the injured ship, now dragging twenty-five thousand miles behind them. Even as he watched, a mine struck the ship, knocking her slightly off course but unable to penetrate her shields. Those shields could be penetrated, Cutter had seen it done; but it took an ungodly amount of firepower to accomplish it.

One ship is lame, and the other has no weapons, he thought. *What happened at Terraneau?*

On the display, the icon representing the *Churchill* changed course so that it now headed directly toward the U.A. battleship, a maneuver generally performed by fighters, not fighter carriers. The *Churchill*'s standard attack speed was seventy thousand miles per hour, offering enemies a mere three-second window to track, target, and fire weapons.

Klaxons blared, warning the crew to brace for imminent attack. Warning lights flashed. In the bowels of the ship, emergency crews prepared for doomsday scenarios.

On the bridge, sailors locked themselves into their chairs. No one spoke.

Cutter watched the display from his seat ten feet away. His lips pressed against each other. His heart pounded in his chest so hard he could feel its pulse in his ears.

The U.A. ship traveled at just over one thousand miles per minute with no acceleration. She sat dead ahead of the *Churchill*, five thousand miles away...

Four thousand miles...

Three thousand miles, and the enemy would have launched her

torpedoes. It was too late to turn around now. Even emergency maneuvers would not save them.

If they fire, will the computer warn us before we die? Cutter wondered. The *Churchill*'s shields were up, but they would mean nothing against shield-buster torpedoes.

Two thousand miles. If torpedoes were coming, they should have already hit.

One thousand miles. The Klaxons continued to wail, and the warning lights flashed as the *Churchill* flew over the top of the enemy ship. Some of the sailors on the bridge shouted.

Cutter let out the breath he'd been holding for over a minute. Something had finally gone right.

And then the *de Gaulle* appeared on the display.

67

"Harris, we're falling apart down here," Ritz said.

Colonel Hunter Ritz was an officer who lived to complain, but he never backed down from battles. Using a commandLink option, I peered through his visor, then through some of the visors of his platoon leaders.

The fighting had begun.

Unbeknownst to me, Ritz had smuggled trackers into the spaceport. Trackers were motion-sensing robots. They were little more than a pole with a motion-tracking aiming device and an automated trigger. You could attach anything from an M27 to a missile launcher to a tracker. Ritz had armed his trackers with particle-beam pistols, a decidedly short-range weapon. He'd had his men place the trackers in the air locks, which were thirty feet across, slingshot range.

The particle-beam weapons blew people apart. The entrances to the locks were covered with sleeves and boots and other bits of combat armor. The blood on the walls meant that there were arms in the sleeves and feet in the boots and heads in the helmets.

Looking through different Marines' visors, I saw locks in which the trackers still worked and locks in which the enemy had managed to overwhelm our defenses.

Colonel Ritz ran to help a faltering platoon. Looking through his visor, I saw bodies piling up on our side of the lines. An RPG sailed through one of the open locks and exploded, tossing bodies in the air. Ritz turned in the direction of the blast, saw two security clones coming out of an air lock, and shot them.

"Are any of you sniper trained?" I asked the men I had brought with me.

"Yes, sir," two men answered my call. I kept my snipers and sent the others back through the rubble. At this point, Ritz needed warm bodies and trigger fingers more than I did.

Using the commandLink, I marked a map of the spaceport. I highlighted the tunnel that led to the Spaceport Security barracks, the oxygen generators, and the reactor, and I sent the map to my snipers over the interLink. I said, "You're on recon now. You take the edges and neutralize any and all threats. You got that, Marines? I will march straight ahead. You will flank the enemy and neutralize his ass." I added, "Keep an eye out for bombs. These guys don't care about collateral damage."

They gave me my "Sir, yes, sirs!" and I gave them thirty seconds to work their way into the shadows.

The area was empty now. What had been a large hall was now a crater, the floor mostly destroyed, leaving heaps of rubble and bodies in the ravines twenty feet below. For the last year, the New Olympians had lived like rats, and now they were dying like rats as well.

If we make it out of here, the airlift begins today, I told myself.

Ritz's voice came in over the interLink, shattering my meditations.

He asked, "General, did you send your men back?"

"Affirmative," I said as I ran the gear in my visor, opening a window to peer through Ritz's visor. I saw bodies. The air locks were choked with bodies. They littered the floor. I said, "Scan the area, I want to see your line."

"Are you voyeuring me, sir?" he asked.

I had never heard the term before, but I understood it. My patience was running out. Ritz was a good leader and a good Marine, but he tried my patience. I said, "I am tired of repeating myself, Colonel."

"Sir," he said as he panned to his left, and then to his right.

The fighting had slowed. I watched one of Riley's clones wading through a knee-deep quagmire of armor and corpses, firing his weapon blindly ahead. He made it all the way to the end of the air lock before bullets struck him in the head and chest.

Off in the distance, a company of our men hustled into an air lock. "Where are they going?" I asked.

"They're making sure Riley's men don't flank us," said Ritz. "It's a big spaceport, sir. There are other ways in."

Mars Spaceport had seventeen linear miles of exterior walls and passenger gates. We barely had enough men to guard the outermost wall of the Perseus Wing, the wall that faced the Air Force base. What would we do when the *de Gaulle* arrived with twenty thousand Marines?

Riley was a glorified MP, a man with no experience in troop deployment and strategy. It might not have occurred to him to flank our position. But when Curtis Jackson arrived, he would not make the same mistake. Jackson would land his transports all around the building.

68

I entered the main "trunk" of the Perseus Wing, a deserted pedestrian superhighway once traversed by as many as one million people per day. During the era when the Unified Authority owned the galaxy, every passenger traveling between Earth and any planet in the Perseus Arm had passed through this corridor. This was the hall that connected the Perseus Wing to the grand arcade, the central hub of the spaceport.

The area had gone pitch-black. It was possible that the bomb had damaged the wiring, though I doubted it. It seemed more likely that somebody had cut the electricity to this part of the spaceport.

The hall was wider than a football field. Its ceiling was twenty feet up. Had I stopped and stared straight up, the ceiling would have looked relatively high; but taken in proportion with the size of the hall, I felt like I was walking through the center of a sandwich.

A balcony ran the length of the hall. One of my snipers stood on the balcony a couple of hundred yards ahead of me. Not expected to play sniper on this mission, he only had an M27; but a skilled marksman with an M27 was still dangerous.

"Are we secure?" I asked.

"The area is clear, sir," said the first sniper.

"Secure," said the second.

I crossed the floor quickly.

There were no bodies here though the floor was littered with clothing, blankets, suitcases, and other small possessions.

No one had been trampled, and no children had been left behind, but a few people too old or too sick to run with the herd remained.

As I reached the halfway point across the long hall, a light flashed on, then off. From this distance, it looked no bigger or brighter than the flame on the head of a match.

One of my snipers fired off five shots, not a burst, but five individual shots. *Bang... bang... bang... bang... bang.*

I stopped running, and asked, "Am I clear?"

"Clear, sir," said the sniper.

"Are you sure?" I asked, not happy about the uncertainty in my voice.

"Yes, sir," he said.

As I began jogging again, he fired off two more shots.

I asked, "What was that?"

He said, "The area is clear, sir."

An old woman screamed when she heard the shots—a tiny and frail woman, sitting on the blanket that had become her home, with her legs tucked up under her chin. She quieted down for a moment as she struggled to breathe.

Dressed in my dark green armor, I was next to invisible; but she heard me, then she picked me out of the shadows and started shrieking again.

As I ran past the old banshee, I spotted the second of my guardian angels. He was on the balcony. He had leapfrogged the first sniper's position and stood at the corner, looking down into the grand arcade, with its masses and desperation.

I slowed to a jog as I reached the corner and used my commandLink to take a report. "Ritz, give me an update," I said.

"They're spreading us pretty thin," he said. Then he added,

"We've hit them hard. I think they're going to back off until their reinforcements arrive."

The *de Gaulle* would not be far away.

69

Since he did not know the names of the two U.A. battleships, Don Cutter thought up derisive names instead. The ship circling Mars had no weapons. Cutter called her the *Toothless*. The second ship had working weapons systems, but her engines sputtered. Cutter called her the *Cripple*.

The *Toothless* continued to circle Mars from just outside the atmosphere, her weapons silent, as the *Cripple* limped in from the dark side of Mars. The *de Gaulle* flew in from the side facing the sun.

One's out of ammo, and the other is practically landlocked, Cutter thought. *Practically landlocked.* He could play with them all day, maybe try to trick the *Cripple* into firing a few shield-busters into the *Toothless* once the two ships came into each other's range; but with the *de Gaulle* less than a minute away, he had no time for games.

The holographic display showed all four ships: the *Cripple* rolling in across the planet, the *Toothless* making another meaningless circuit, the *de Gaulle* coming from yet another angle, and the *Churchill* trapped in the locus. The three ships looked like the corners of a triangle, with Mars Spaceport and the *Churchill* in the center. In the background, Phobos and Deimos, Mars's potato-shaped moons, loomed on the outskirts of the display.

"We should go after the *de Gaulle* first," said Captain Hauser. "She's the healthy one. They won't expect it."

Hauser's strategy made sense. If they could stop the *de Gaulle* from landing Marines, they could accomplish their mission. He asked, "Do you have a plan of attack?"

"No, sir," Hauser admitted in a soft voice.

"They have everything we have. It's going to be a slugfest unless the *Cripple* creeps up behind us during the fight. If that happens, it will be a massacre."

Lieutenant Nolan said, "If we wait until they launch their transports, maybe we can stop their Marines in the air."

"We won't have time, not with that ship on our tail," said Nolan.

There was a silence between the officers, which Lieutenant Nolan ended. He said, "She's too low and too slow." He pointed at the *Cripple* on the display, and said, "Captain, we might just be able to take her out if we move quickly."

"How? We can't get through her shields," said Hauser.

"It would even the fight," said Cutter. He did the calculations in his head. Eliminate the *Cripple*, and they might be able to chase the *de Gaulle* or at least destroy her transports as they launched. "What do you have, Lieutenant?"

Nolan swallowed, and said, "We know her engines are bad, and her thrusters are worthless... That's why she can't turn. She slid like she was on ice when we hit her with missiles. What if we hit her from out here and try to knock her into the atmosphere." He pointed to the spine of the ship.

"We won't get through her shields," said Hauser.

"I don't think we need to get through her shields, sir," said

Nolan. "If we can knock her into the atmosphere, gravity will bring her down."

Cutter looked at the display. He watched the way the *Cripple* seemed to dog-paddle outside the Martian atmosphere. *Eliminate the* Cripple *and they would have an even fight with the* de Gaulle, *because that other U.A. ship was just for show.* He said, "Captain Hauser, commence that attack."

Hauser said, "Aye, aye, sir," but he did not sound confident. He shouted the orders and rejoined Cutter at the display.

The *Churchill* veered out, into open space, building such rapid acceleration that without internal generators manipulating the gravity inside the ship, the crew might have been crushed by their own weight.

She flew ten thousand miles traveling along a rigid trajectory that brought her straight out from Mars, then looped back. Had it not been for the artificial gravity, the crew would have been thrown against one wall of the ship, then another, only to be tossed back again as the ship settled into a collision course with the *Cripple* and the planet.

Intellectually removing himself from the equation as if he were watching an exercise instead of his own life-and-death struggle, Cutter followed his ship on the display. In his mind, the *de Gaulle* no longer existed, would not exist until this fight ended one way or another.

On the display, the *Churchill* and the *Cripple* were already touching. The *Cripple* moved so slowly, she appeared to float on the outer edge of the atmosphere. Still building momentum, the *Churchill* skipped quickly across the display.

"Captain, she's firing at us," Nolan warned.

Hauser ignored him. He stood sentinel still, his eyes locked on the tactical display, his skin and lips so pale they looked bloodless.

He shouted, "Fire particle beams!" Two seconds later, he shouted, "Torpedoes, all forward tubes."

"Captain, they fired..." Nolan repeated.

The green beams from the particle beams fired and vanished so quickly, they never showed on the holographic display.

They destroyed any torpedoes that had fired from the U.A. battleship and battered her shields. Showing as fast-moving motes of glitter on the tactical display, the *Churchill's* torpedoes crossed the no-man's-land between the ships.

"Lock on missiles! Fire missiles!" Hauser shouted. "Pull out! Get us out of here!"

The torpedoes hit the *Cripple* like a strong wind. They did not break through her shields, but they knocked her off her course, battering her toward the planet below. The missiles followed, knocking her even farther into the atmosphere.

"Sir, incoming torpedoes!" yelled a weapons officer.

"Active defenses!" yelled Hauser. The defenses had already been activated. The ship's computers tracked and destroyed incoming torpedoes automatically.

On the display, the *Cripple's* nose lowered as her trajectory took her down toward the planet. She was ensnared by Mars's gravity as securely as any fly had ever been tied in a spiderweb, and her weak engines lacked the power to take her out of the gravitational pull, and her damaged thrusters offered next to no resistance. She lowered toward the craggy surface like a plane coming in for a landing, but she had no wheels because she was built to remain in space. For the U.A. battleship, entering Mars's gravitational field was a death sentence.

On the tactical display, the U.A. ship came to a smooth stop.

Lieutenant Nolan said, "There's a spike in radiation... She's gone nuclear."

The bridge crew screamed in triumph.

Cutter slumped back against the rail, a tired smile on his face. Hauser had reached to shake the Admiral's hand, when Nolan said, "Captain, sir, the *de Gaulle* has launched her transports."

70

All of the explorer pilots were Air Force officers, and several had served on Mars. They knew how to power up the lights and the computer systems. Freeman and the bodyguards had managed to get some of the radar system working. With Air Force personnel behind the controls, the base lit bright, and the communications console began working.

One of the pilots entered the nerve center and sat beside the radar display. He typed a code on a keyboard. The screen that lit up was nearly a yard in diameter. On that display, the U.A. ships appeared as triangles with names emblazoned beside them. One of the ships circled the area above the spaceport and the base. The radar system identified her as the UAN *Abner*.

As a crowd formed around the screen, one of the Air Force pilots said, "It looks like the *Churchill* is going to make a run at that ship."

"The *Abner*?" asked a fighter pilot. "Cutter wouldn't do that, man. That's a Nike."

"Both of those ships are Nikes," said the first pilot.

On the screen, the icon marked *Churchill* dashed straight at the icon marked *Abner*.

"Doesn't look like *Churchill* is firing anything," said a fighter pilot.

"They aren't," said the Air Force pilot who had powered up the display.

"Have they launched their fighters?" asked Liston.

One of the pilots sneered, shook his head, and asked, "Do you see any fighters on the screen?"

Liston said, "I don't know what I see on the screen."

The pilot laughed. He said, "See that ship there?" He pointed to the only fast-moving shape on the screen. It was about five inches from a circling triangle labeled *Abner*. "That's the *Churchill*."

"The triangle?" asked Liston.

"Shhhh!" a pilot hissed.

In a quieter whisper, the pilot said, "Those other two are U.A. ships. That one way over there is the *de Gaulle*."

"A clone ship?" asked Liston.

"General Harris says the Unifieds got ahold of her. That's why we came in the Explorer fleet. We had to get here before the *de Gaulle*. She's got a full load of U.A. Marines."

"Damn," said Liston.

"Got that right," said the pilot.

Watson listened to all of this in silence. His body hurt, and he knew he needed to sleep, but he did not feel tired. Whether it was the patches or the danger, he did not care.

The icon representing the *Churchill* practically merged with the icon representing the *Abner*. It passed so close that the two triangles seemed to merge, then the *Churchill* continued past and the *Abner* continued to circle.

"What the speck was that?" asked one of the pilots.

"Damn if I know."

"What happened?" asked Liston.

"Neither of them fired," said the pilot who had explained the icons on the monitor.

"Why didn't they fire?" asked Liston.

"Shhhhh!" hissed the pilot closest to the display.

"*Churchill* doesn't have anything that can get through those shields, that's why she didn't fire," the pilot whispered to Liston. "I don't know why *Abner* didn't fire."

"That one over there... the *Carmack*, is that a U.A. ship, too?" asked Liston. "Why is it moving so slow?"

"I don't know."

Sharkey returned with Freeman and Emily. Freeman was still and silent. Sharkey and the others asked questions. Liston explained the icons on the screen as if he'd known how to read the display his entire life.

As he pointed to the icon representing the *Churchill*, it made a sudden movement. Liston said, "There it goes again."

This time the *Churchill* flew away from Mars. Dynamic tables along the base of the screen charted her speed, the numbers changing so quickly that no one could read them.

"Shit, she's really hauling," said one of the pilots.

"Is it running away?" asked Liston.

The question went unanswered.

On the screen, the *Abner* continued circling her territory above the atmosphere. The *de Gaulle* approached.

"Are they leaving us here?" Emily asked.

A second later, the *Churchill* changed her course. She turned and headed straight back to Mars, still building speed as she went.

"What the hell are they doing?" asked the pilot who had tutored Liston. He stood with his hand across his jaw, his fingers stroking his cheek.

Watson quietly stepped back from the screen and moved beside Emily. Freeman stood a few feet away, towering above everyone else, able to see the screen over the other people's shoulders. No emotion showed on Freeman's face. He stood silent, his eyes hard and focused, his expression a mystery.

The icon representing the *Churchill* continued building speed as it headed directly toward Mars and the slow-moving icon that represented the *Carmack*. If the display was accurate, the *Carmack* was barely moving, lying like a carcass on the side of the road while the *Churchill* swooped in like a hawk.

"Is it firing?" asked Liston.

"Oh hell yes," said one of the pilots. "There go the cannons."

A moment later, he said, "There go the torpedoes." Another moment and, "There go the missiles."

Having fired particle beams, torpedoes, and missiles, the *Churchill* changed course, flying back out to space and still gaining speed. As the icon representing the *Churchill* flew away, the icon representing the *Carmack* dipped into the backlit area of the screen that represented the atmosphere.

"What happened?" asked Liston.

"*Carmack* entered the atmosphere."

"What does that mean?"

"She's a battleship," said the pilot. "She's made for space."

On the screen, the icon representing the *Carmack* continued to lose altitude. One of them hooted and yelled, "Hell yeah!"

"She's going down! She's going down!" screamed another.

"Oh, thank God," whispered a third.

A moment later they felt the shock wave. The ground shook, and the building trembled, and the revelry came to an end as people rode the rolling floor in silence. The tremor lasted an eternity of twenty-three seconds.

That was when Dempsey, a bodyguard who had been a SEAL as a young man, watched the *de Gaulle* on the screen.

He said, "If your ships can fly, you better get us out of here."

The lead pilot said, "That carrier will pick us off with her particle beams the moment we launch."

"Yeah?" asked Dempsey. "If they got Marines on that ship, then Mars is about to become a hostile environment."

"Maybe you've never ridden in an explorer," the pilot said, his irritation obvious. "It's not a flying brick like your military transports. Those bitches stand up to anything. These explorers, I figure a nasty thought could bring one of them down."

Another pilot said, "Speck, here come the transports."

That was when Watson finally spoke up. He said, "We need to fly in two groups."

71

The snowball effect. Ten thousand panicking survivors had run out of one relatively minor hall and scared fifty thousand people in a larger hall, who then caused a riot in one of the spaceport's major trunks, a riot that then spilled into the grand arcade. Once the panic reached the grand arcade, it spread throughout the complex.

The trunk that led to the grand arcade was nearly empty, but screams and thumping echoed from the intersection up ahead. When I looked in that direction, I saw no people.

The first of my snipers entered the grand arcade on the third floor, and somebody shot him. My second sniper spotted the assassin. He was up on a catwalk, about ten feet below the atrium's glass cathedral ceiling. My sniper aligned his shot and fired, hitting his target.

If he'd asked permission, I would not have allowed the shot, not with an M27.

The man dropped his rifle and fell over the edge of the catwalk and into the roiling mass of people below. This had about as much effect as throwing a lit match into a blazing furnace. The already hysterical mob remained hysterical.

My sniper was three floors up, standing near a corner, hiding behind a rail. I could see him standing by himself, and I could see a flood of people fighting and shoving to enter the trunks leading to the other wings of the spaceport. They were as crowded together as the sand in the upper funnel of an hourglass.

Using my visor, I marked the entrance to the service tunnels that led to barracks and the power plant. It was several hundred yards ahead of me... several hundred very exposed yards.

The men who blew up that first corridor would not repeat that act of sabotage. If they detonated a bomb anywhere near the reactor, they would die along with me and the New Olympians. If the power plant below the arcade exploded, it would take half the hemisphere with it.

"You see anything?" I asked.

"Looks clear, sir," he said.

Before stepping out of my hiding place, I asked myself how much I trusted this Marine. I trusted his marksmanship. He'd proved himself several times. I trusted his reflexes, too. He was quick.

I wouldn't need his protection once I reached the tunnel. I would be in a winding, tight environment, with low ceilings and no room to maneuver. Any fighting I did down there would be close-range.

I said, "Just get me to the tunnels alive."

"Not a problem, sir," he said.

I scanned the area. Far ahead of me, the vanishing mob continued to scream and fight and push. The upper decks of the grand arcade had emptied. Thousands of bodies lay motionless on the hard ground. I'd been in battles with smaller body counts, and there were hundreds of living casualties as well.

A lone voice resonated through the cavernous space. It was the keening of a child.

I scanned the area ahead of me and spotted a little girl crawling between two dead bodies. I did not know enough about children to guess their ages accurately, but she was no bigger than a backpack. There was blood on her face and her clothing.

I searched the upper decks of the atrium and saw no traces of people hiding behind walls or rails. Not that heat vision always spots them. There are limits to heat vision. Thick walls and stealth armor can mask heat signatures.

I ran half the length of the grand arcade, passing defunct stores that had been converted into cave dwellings, passing the abandoned bric-a-brac of an abandoned people, and passing the lifeless remains of the dead. My armored boots clacked across the floor. I held my M27 out and ready, my finger across the trigger instead of along it. Anyone or anything that stepped in my way now was forfeit.

Ahead of me, I saw the doorway that led down into the spaceport underground. I scanned the area around it, then used a sonar locator to ping the entrance.

There were people in the tunnel, hiding in the darkness. They might have been refugees trying to escape from the panic, but I doubted it. They hid along the sides of the tunnel, lurking in the shadows. As I approached, I switched to night-for-day lenses and spotted one of them, a man in civilian clothing holding an automatic rifle. As I started down the ramp, I fired a burst and killed the man. His partner swung out from the other side of the tunnel. I shot him before he could aim his gun.

"I have it from here," I called to my sniper. He didn't answer. I didn't think about that. I didn't think about checking in with Ritz to see how the battle outside was going.

I was a fool.

72

Colonel Hunter Ritz pushed through an air lock, stepping over limbs and bodies, wading through the dead. His visor identified the names of casualties. They were all still listed as active members of the Enlisted Man's Marines even though they had changed sides.

He reached the far side of the air lock. His gun up and ready, he leaped over the last of the bodies and stumbled onto the runway. The spaceport's artificial gravity did not extend outside to the runway. Ritz leaped out of the building as a 186-pound man in ten pounds of combat armor; he landed as a 63-pound man in just under four pounds of armor.

Ritz saw four Marines in white armor running along the edge of the runway. They stopped. Two of them fired at him. He fired back. They used M27s. He used an RPG. Their bullets hit the ground near his feet. His rocket hit the ground near their feet as well, killing all four of them.

"Assholes," Ritz said as he tossed away the empty tube. He pulled out his M27.

He did not know if he had just killed the last members of Spaceport Security or if more lurked around the runway. He'd lost a third of his men, but he'd defeated an enemy with superior numbers.

Ritz saw a man in white armor—security armor—limping. Without waiting to see if the man had a gun, Ritz shot him.

Scattered bodies littered the runway. The corpses weren't stacked three high as they were in the air locks, but the signs of battle were unmistakable. Out here, they looked like the debris around a crash site. Some lay in groups, some lay scattered. The farther down the runway he looked, the fewer bodies he saw.

"You out here Riley? You still alive?" Ritz asked over the interLink. In his head he added the words, "you dumb bastard."

No one answered.

Ritz used the interLink to contact Wayson Harris. He said, "I have a battle report for you, General. Do you want the good news or the bad news?" He didn't wait for Harris to respond. He said, "We beat Martian Security. We're still mopping up strays, but it's over. I'd be surprised if we lost another man."

Ritz gave Harris a few seconds to respond and went on talking. He said, "Here's the bad news, General. I hope you're getting this. The *de Gaulle* is about to crash our party. She's launched her transports. Want to know how I know so much?"

He waited for Harris to answer but heard nothing.

"I can see them in the sky. You can see them, too, if you voyeur me."

There were no clouds above the spaceport, but cloudlike trails of smoke or steam laced the tea-colored sky. From this distance, the trails looked as tiny as raindrops. There were hundreds of them.

It was the end. The transports would land twenty thousand infantrymen. They would have tanks and mortars and gunships and fighters. Ritz toyed with the idea of not warning his men… letting them die celebrating victory. The moment he warned them, they would dig in for a fight they could not possibly win.

They're good men, he thought. *They won't go down without a fight.* But how much of a fight could his remaining two thousand Marines put up against an entire division?

"Are you getting this, General?"

No answer.

"Tell you what, Harris," said Ritz. He laughed. It was the end, he might as well go down smiling. He repeated himself. "I'll tell you what, Harris. Me and my men are going to go down fighting. We'll hold those bastards off as long as we can."

The transports dropped through the atmosphere quickly. The commanding officers on those birds would give their men one last speech in which they would instruct them to take no quarter.

"Good luck, Harris," said Ritz. He didn't worry about Harris, nothing short of a nuclear explosion would kill that clone. *No person alive could kill Harris, not even Ray Freeman*, he thought.

Colonel Ritz used the interLink to contact his Marines. He said, "I hope you boys saved some spare rounds." That was all he said.

Something caught his attention.

Two swarms of ships launched from the direction of the Air Force base. They were small ships. From where Ritz stood, they looked like the tiny silver fish you could catch in a stream. He knew they were the explorers, of course. Those were the ships that had brought him and his Marines to Mars.

They emerged from behind the horizon. A few of them flew up into space, but most of them flew in an arc that led toward the transports from the *de Gaulle*. That was when the explosions began.

Had Ritz been a few miles closer, he might have gone blind.

73

Cutter saw that the explorers had launched. He shouted, "What the hell is wrong with them!" He was an officer who prided himself on remaining calm in battle; now he was watching a suicide. The *de Gaulle* had not only entered the battle, she had launched her transports.

"Scramble every specking fighter!" Hauser shouted. "Attack *de Gaulle*!"

As the fighters launched, Hauser fired torpedoes even though the target was too far away.

If the explorer pilots want to commit suicide, there is nothing we can do, Cutter told himself. *Maybe they have it right. The* de Gaulle *is launching transports. With two hundred ships in the air, some might escape. No one will escape on the ground.*

He watched the display. Five of the tiny ships rose straight up, 202 explorers followed a path that took them high above the spaceport, where they would run into the transports.

The display showed the explorers as tiny specks, little helpless motes of silver that looked no more capable of defending themselves in holographic space than they were able to defend themselves in reality. The transports had powerful shields and hulls designed to withstand missiles. They did not have guns or torpedoes, but they would not need them to destroy a fleet of explorers. The transports could ram through them as if they were made of smoke.

On the display, the shining silver dots approached the red boxes that represented transports. When they were within a mile of each other, the explorers dissolved in miniscule flashes of light.

"Holy hell, they're broadcasting," said Hauser.

The explorers had risen in a swarm, and they disappeared in a swarm. Two hundred tiny broadcasts erupted. Transports were made for war and able to withstand missiles and particle weapons, but not the sheer volume of energy unleashed by broadcast engines.

Cutter looked up from the display, and said, "Satellite view."

Beside the tactical display, a large screen showed a video feed. A ghostly green ribbon wavered and shimmered in the Martian atmosphere. The sudden release of unbridled energy had triggered an aurora effect. On the dark surface of the planet, tiny sparks glowed like embers, the carcasses of fallen transports.

Cutter looked back at the holographic display. The ship he called the *Toothless* had broadcasted out. He had no idea where she had gone and no way of tracking her. She might have broadcasted to Terraneau, in the Scutum-Crux Arm. He did not air his suspicion.

About one hundred thousand miles away, the *de Gaulle* stood her ground, but not for long.

Cutter asked, "Who is the captain of the *de Gaulle*?"

"Meade, sir. Alan Meade," said Lieutenant Nolan. He had looked it up on his computation pad.

"Send Captain Meade a message. Tell him that I don't give a damn if he and his men want to commit suicide, but I want my ship back. Tell him if he surrenders the *de Gaulle* now, he might be out in time to enjoy his grandchildren."

The sailors on the bridge who heard Cutter laughed. Meade was a clone, incapable of reproduction without the use of test tubes and lab equipment.

Everybody laughed; but the sailors who suspected they might be clones themselves laughed more nervously than those around them.

"They're not responding, sir," said Nolan.

The *de Gaulle* sat silent and still until the *Lancet* and the *Christy* flew into tracking range.

"Give Meade one last chance to surrender," said Cutter.

Before Nolan could relay the message, the *de Gaulle* launched into space at maximum acceleration.

Hauser started to instruct his helmsmen to follow her, but Cutter silenced him. He said, "The *de Gaulle* does not have a broadcast engine. She isn't going anywhere."

Earth was surrounded by the fleets of the Enlisted Man's Navy. Jupiter was five hundred million miles away and uninhabitable. At the speeds the *de Gaulle* could travel, the closest planet of strategic value was over a century away.

Cutter said, "We need to stay here in case more guests arrive." He settled back in his seat, then added, "Let me know when we have contact with the spaceport. If I know Harris, that could be anytime now."

74

LOCATION: MARS SPACEPORT
DATE: MAY 2, 2519

Someone had turned off the lights. That didn't change things, I had night-for-day lenses in my visor. I had heat vision that allowed me to peek through corners when I could not see around them. The walls down in this area were made of steel and cement, thick enough that they might mask a heat signature, but they would not hide it entirely.

The night-for-day lenses in my visor showed the world devoid of depth and color, with everything in striations from black to white with a bluish hue. Emergency lights glowed so brightly over signs that they rendered them unreadable through my visor. Halls that stretched unlit for more than two hundred feet looked like black holes. The pipes and fixtures that lined the ceiling looked all to have been painted the exact same color. Seen with the naked eye, they might have been yellow and white and pink for all I knew; but through night-for-day vision, they all looked bluish white.

I searched the first hall at a slow speed, coasting ahead

carefully, searching open doorways and finding no one. I'd been in the underground for maybe five minutes before noticing Ritz's prolonged silence. His name appeared on my commandLink; but when I tried to reach him, I did not connect.

Somebody was sludging again.

Whoever was doing the sludging, I thought he would also be the one who sent Riley and all of the security force after Watson and Freeman.

Walking alone through dark, empty halls, I had an odd sense of déjà vu, and not a kind one. I felt the same crippling sense of dread I had felt when I stared into the ocean back in Hawaii.

The spaceport's water and a third of its oxygen came from the same source. Beneath the spaceport sat huge veins of underground ice. The Unified Authority had created a robotic underground mining operation that harvested that ice and shuttled it into the building using subterranean tunnels. The ice was melted and filtered. Some was sent to a plant in which the hydrogen and oxygen molecules were separated. The Os were fed into the spaceport ventilation system while the Hs were released into the atmosphere.

The machinery in those plants was old, powerful, and as reliable as a chemical latrine. I had heard somewhere that the Oxygen Separation Plant was fifty years old and still used the same machinery. A low thrumming rose from the blast chambers in which the Hs were separated from the Os. I was a thousand feet from the plant, but I could feel the vibrations in the floor.

A man hid behind a doorway up ahead. I spotted him with my heat vision. All I saw was his specter, a figure in glowing orange and yellow, crouching, holding something long and straight. It could have been a rifle, it could have been a pipe.

He was a smart man. He would be in the door of the oxygen plant when we met. I would not fire my weapon into those old relics, not unless I wanted to risk killing millions.

I thought about the toxic atmosphere leaking into the spaceport through the air locks. I thought about...

That was when I saw his friends. In all, four men attacked from four different directions, a classic ambush. I would have seen it was coming had I read the lay of the land.

Three of them came at me from behind as the fourth man swung around the corner. I heard the footsteps, spun, fired my M27, and dropped two of them. The third man fired his pistol, grazing my left shoulder, causing a moment of numbness followed by fire. I fired at the bastard, hit him in the face with three bullets, hollowing the back of his head with the first. The guy coming from the Oxygen Separation Plant slammed the butt of his rifle into the back of my head. Bullets and shrapnel could penetrate my helmet, but knives and rifle butts never got through. He hit me a good one, though. Had I not been wearing combat armor, he would have broken my neck and shattered my skull.

Despite my armor, the force of the blow sent me face-first into a wall, and I dropped my M27.

I hit the wall, slumped to the floor, and recovered my senses all in the same second. My head hurt, and my shoulder burned, and my combat reflex kicked into full gear. I no longer gave a shit about pain or shoulder wounds or blast chambers. The haze went from my thoughts, and the need for violence returned.

The man spun his rifle around and aimed it at my head. At the same time, he clipped a foot across my M27, kicking it backward so that it slid across the floor toward the door of the oxygen plant.

Bastard, I thought.

"Get up," he said.

I did. And as I did, I did something he did not expect. I pulled a grenade from my belt and let it roll off my fingers. He looked down to see what I'd dropped, identified it and instantly knew I had not pulled the pin, but the grenade had distracted him long enough. I sprang to my feet, knocked the barrel of his rifle aside, and flew into him as the back of my armor shattered into fragments.

There had been a fifth man. He'd lurked like a spider, hiding somewhere in the shadows, someplace I had not thought to look. I did not see him, but the force of the blast from his shotgun lifted me off my feet and tossed me like a toy, while the pellets shredded my armor and punctured my skin. The hormones from my combat reflex raged hotter than ever; but from the small of my back to the base of my neck, my body would not respond.

I leaned helplessly against the man I had just disarmed until he shoved me backward. I dropped to the floor. There was liquid in my mouth. I felt like I would drown any second. I wanted to roll over so I could see the man who had shot me. My legs swung, but my torso did not follow.

Taking lazy steps, the unseen assassin sauntered beside me. He pointed his shotgun into my face, tapping the muzzle against my visor. He asked, "Are you still alive in there?"

I did not answer. I couldn't speak. I felt like I was drowning, but my combat reflex kept me cognizant. I did not know the man, but his face was familiar. He had a scar, a circular dent in the center of his forehead. I focused on that scar and struggled to clear my thoughts.

He cocked his shotgun, and said, "You're pathetic, Harris; and it's your own fault if you die. You walked right in. Mister Liberator Clone... Mister Super Marine... Pathetic.

"I should finish you off. You'll probably die anyway, but it would mean more if I had done it on purpose."

He laughed, and added, "You have fans in Navy high command, people who think you'll be useful. Me, I think we should have killed you the first time. I bet you don't remember the first time, do you?"

He kicked his boot across my visor. The blow did not break the glass, but the jolt spun my body a quarter turn.

The man laughed. He turned to his partner, the man I had disarmed, and fired his shotgun into his face. The man's head vanished in a red spray that decorated the wall behind him.

The bastard lowered his shotgun and smiled down at me. He said, "If anybody asks, Harris, do me a favor and tell them he shot you." Then, still smiling, he knelt beside me.

"Harris, if you survive this one, you should know that I'll come back for you. I'll keep coming and shooting you until you don't survive." He smiled, tapped the muzzle of his shotgun to my visor, and said, "They don't even need to pay me. You just go ahead and survive, Harris; I'd love to go another round with you."

He rose to his feet, stared down at me for a moment, and I realized that this was it—this was the face of evil. "In case you were wondering, the name is Franklin Nailor," he said. "Now you can tell your friends you met me... if you live."

This was the man the Unifieds had sent. He said I had fans in the U.A. Navy, people he must have known. The Night of the Martyrs, the bastards who chased me in Hawaii, whatever reprogramming had happened in my head, this son of a bitch was behind all of it. Here he was, standing over me, and all I could do was lie there helplessly and wonder if I would even live to fight another day.

Nailor dropped his shotgun on the headless corpse of the man he had shot. After that, he started down a hall and vanished into the complex. I struggled to watch him as long as I could, but I blacked out.

EPILOGUE

LOCATION: BETHESDA
DATE: JUNE 7, 2519

Our combat armor was designed by a committee that included physicians, engineers, and politicians. The physicians made sure the armor shielded our vital areas. The engineers wrestled with finding a balance between weight and durability. The politicians made certain that the physicians and engineers stayed within the budget.

Given sufficient funding, the physicians and engineers would have produced graphene armor, stronger than shielded steel and lighter than helium, in which soldiers could have pranced like ballet dancers without fear of bullets or lasers.

Unlimited funding, honest politicians, perfect worlds... fairy tales.

The budget-constrained physicians and engineers made intelligent compromises that enabled me to walk out of the hospital. Hoping to protect our spines, they placed extra plating down the center of the back of our armor.

Surgeons removed pellets from my shoulder blades, my ribs,

and my lungs; but my spine was untouched. After four days of operations, reconstructions, and soaking in tissue baths, I went home with a robotic joint in my right shoulder. I didn't care. Why should a clone care about synthetic implants?

Putting me back together took a few days, but my rehabilitation was an ongoing concern. Doctors prodded my muscles and bade me walk along an endless pathway of lines and risers. They kept me in a naval hospital and told me to use a wheelchair whenever I climbed out of bed. When I refused, they gave me a walker. When I said no to the walker, they gave me crutches. We finally agreed on a cane.

My body was on the mend. I wasn't so sure about my head.

My doctor found new ways to torture me on a daily basis. He dug his fingers into shredded muscles and called it a massage. He stuck me with needles, wired my ribs, stabbed electric prods into my joints, and stimulated my blood circulation with chemicals. The man was my enemy. I spent many happy nights planning his death.

My physical therapist was not my worst enemy. That title belonged to the psychologist who dug his fingers into my shredded head, stuck needles into my brain, stabbed electrodes into my scalp, and pumped me full of chemicals... all in the name of repairing my mental health.

My physical therapist frequently updated me on my progress. The psychologist simply nodded and scribbled notes I would never be allowed to read. I hated the bastard.

"You have fans," Franklin Nailor had said. "They think you will be useful."

If I had fans, they never visited. Not Cutter. Not Watson. Not Freeman. Colonel Hunter Ritz came to see me one day. The psychologist interviewed him and sent him away. He sent a message to Cutter recommending that Ritz undergo therapy as well.

The psychologist told me that Cutter had watched my meeting with Franklin Nailor. I later learned that Freeman and Watson watched it as well. The equipment in my visor had dutifully recorded the entire conversation. Combat visors record everything.

In the Marine Corps, privacy is a low-priority concern.

"This Franklin Nailor fellow, he says that he met you before," said the psychologist. "Do you recall when you might have met?"

"No."

"He seems to have a grudge against you. Do you have any idea why that might be?"

"No." I was lying. If Nailor was an officer with the now-defunct Unified Authority, he'd have plenty of reason to hate me. Then again, my instincts told me that Nailor's anger toward me was of a personal nature.

"How do you feel about Nailor?"

"I want to kill him."

"I see."

I want to kill you, too, you specking bastard; and I want to kill my physical therapist and my physician, and I certainly wouldn't mind injuring Don Cutter if I got a clean shot at him, I thought. That thought did not bother me. Another thought did.

I was scared of Franklin Nailor. Just the mention of his name raised my pulse, and the psychologist knew it; equipment in the chair read my heart rate, pulse, temperature, and probably any changes in my sphincter dilation. *Could the chair tell the difference between hate and fear?*

When I was finally released from the hospital, no one told me about my status in the Marine Corps.

LOCATION: WASHINGTON, D.C.
DATE: JUNE 11, 2519

I felt some trepidation as I drove myself to work that first day. I did not know if I was entering the Pentagon as a three-star general, a civilian advisor, or a pariah.

My ID and uniform got me into the underground parking, but civilian workers parked in that structure as well. I climbed out of my car and walked to the elevator, my back straight, my chest out, my shoulders back, every bit the proud Marine. I took the elevator to the lobby and joined the queue through the security station.

I was not scared as I slowly marched toward the posts, a security device that checked identity using DNA. I still did not know what was going on inside my head, but I knew I was Wayson Harris, a Liberator clone, and that any identity I had was associated with the Marine Corps.

That much I knew.

In order to enter the Pentagon, I needed to walk through posts for a DNA reading. The person ahead of me stepped through, and the guards sent him on. I stepped through.

The MP reading the computer signaled the one ushering people through. He said, "Sir, I need you to step this way."

"Is there a problem, Sergeant?" I asked.

"No, sir. No problem. I just need you to come this way."

The MP was a clone. All the MPs were clones. I suppose they all looked like mirror images of each other to the untrained eye, like goldfish in a bowl all look alike to the casual observer. I noted differences. I noticed age, weight, muscle tone, scars, and posture.

The MP did not reach for his weapon, but three others standing about ten feet away had their hands on their pistols.

I had not come to make trouble. I came because, in my mind, I had no place else to go. "Where are you taking me?" I asked.

"There was a message to bring you to the security office."

"Are they arresting me?" I asked.

"No, sir. No, sir," he said.

I followed him through a path that led between two sheets of bulletproof glass. Behind us, a new MP took his place behind the posts, and people continued filing into the building.

The sergeant led me into a little room with a metal table and a metal chair, both of which were bolted into the floor. He asked me to wait inside the room. I did not take it as a very good sign when he locked the door behind me.

A few minutes later, there was a knock at the door. A voice

called, "You in there, Harris?" and the door swung open. Travis Watson stood at the door. So did four MPs.

As I climbed out from behind the table, Watson asked, "Where are your stars?" When I left the hospital, I found a uniform, but I never did find my stars. I explained that to Watson. He nodded thoughtfully, and said, "I'm sure it's only an oversight."

I wasn't so sure.

Watson and the clones escorted me deep into the Pentagon, to Admiral Cutter's domain. He didn't just have an office, he had his own security detail, a bank of secretaries, and an accounting office. He had one set of rooms for meetings regarding civil issues and another set of rooms for meetings regarding martial problems.

Cutter met me at the door to his office. He and Watson walked me in. They checked the MPs at the door. We all sat down, Cutter behind his carrier-sized desk, Watson and me opposite him.

"How are you feeling?" Cutter asked. Given a choice between being probed by a psychologist and questioned by an overly sympathetic friend, I'd go with the psychologist.

The expression on Cutter's face suggested he thought of me as a cripple, and I did not like it.

When I said, "I want to go back on active duty," Cutter and Watson exchanged glances.

"Are you up to it?" asked Cutter.

"I'm not setting any speed records, but I'm running a couple of miles per day."

"I meant, are you mentally up to it?"

"I have a score to settle," I said. "That bastard shot me in the back."

That made Cutter smile. He said, "Glad to hear it. I have three stars waiting for you. I also have a letter giving you a clean bill of mental health."

"From the psychologist at Bethesda?" I asked, feeling genuinely surprised.

"Oh speck no," said Cutter. "He thinks we should lock you away for good, says you're a sociopath; but Howard Tasman doesn't think you are a security risk. Do you remember anything about Tasman? He was the one Freeman went to rescue."

"Yeah, I know about him," I said. I'd never actually met the man, but I knew all about him. I knew about Freeman and Watson and the history of neural programming.

"Tasman says there is only so much the Unifieds could do with you," said Cutter.

"With me?"

"With Liberators. He did a little tinkering with neural programming during the Liberator program, but it didn't get far," said Cutter. "Do you know why we kept you isolated in the hospital?"

"To see if I was a security risk?" I asked.

Cutter nodded, and said, "Tasman says the only thing programmed in your brain is the inability to commit suicide."

"That's it?" I asked.

"That's it."

"I could have committed suicide," I said. "I pulled a pin from a grenade."

"We found the grenade," said Watson.

"You searched my billet in Hawaii?"

"We knew it was there from the start," said Cutter.

"I think there are other problems," I said. "I've got new fears."

Cutter laughed, but Watson didn't. Cutter said, "You have a lot of new fears. I looked at your psychological profile. If I hadn't known it was you... Scared of water?"

"You know about that?" I asked.

Cutter nodded. He said, "Tasman says it's classical conditioning, not reprogramming. Face it, Harris, you were an obsolete model. You were the no-frills, stripped-down version of cloning. They couldn't reprogram you because there wasn't enough programming in your brain for them to corrupt." He laughed.

I did not think it was funny.

Watson said, "It might have been worse for you than for the others. They couldn't reprogram you, so they tried to brainwash you instead. They tortured you. That's what the psychologist found, evidence of prolonged torture."

"I see," I said. "But you still trust me."

"I do," said Cutter.

"So why did you have security stop me?"

"Are you crazy?" Cutter asked. "Harris, you're a killing machine, and I have a letter from a licensed military psychologist warning me that you're insane. I'm giving you back your stars, but that doesn't mean I'm not scared of you."

Cutter dismissed me, and I went to my office.

I tried to find Freeman, but he had disappeared. I spoke with Hunter Ritz as well. He had moved into Camp Lejeune. He wanted to rename the place Fort Roanoke.

"Roanoke, that's Virginia," I said.

"Yeah. Before it was a city it was a colony. All the colonists disappeared," said Ritz.

"The Marines in LeJeune didn't just disappear, they switched sides," I said. "They were reprogrammed."

Ritz said, "Don't get too technical, General. You'll give yourself a headache."

At five o'clock, Travis Watson came to visit. He asked, "What do you plan to do about Franklin Nailor?"

"I plan to kill him," I said.

Watson rubbed his jaw for a moment. He said, "Well, that's good to hear. I have a score to settle with that man, but I think you might be better at settling old scores than I am." He smiled, and added, "I'd trade a year's salary for a ringside seat."

"Have you met Nailor?" I asked.

He said, "Yes," and nothing more.

We talked about other things. In the month I had been gone, Watson had given up prowling. He was engaged to a woman. He asked me if I wanted to go to dinner with them that evening. I said I did.

I went home. I showered. I shaved. I dressed in my best civilian clothes, a pair of khaki slacks and turquoise shirt. It was either those pants and that shirt or my uniform. I brushed my hair and ran the blue light over my teeth, then I drove back into town.

Watson and his fiancée met me at a restaurant named Don Francisco's. I'd heard of the place but never been there before. It was a trendy bar and grill meant for people my age, but I felt out of place. I was a Marine, not a politician or a lawyer or a businessman. I ate in mess halls and drank in officers' clubs. The dim lighting and soft music did not put me at ease.

When I mentioned my name, the hostess said, "Your friends are waiting for you."

She led me to the table.

Watson and his fiancée sat in a booth way in the back. They sat on one side of the table, leaving the bench on the other side for me. The rest of the restaurant was dim, but the candles on the tables sparkled like stars in this dark corner. Even by that flickering, glowing light, I recognized the girl Travis Watson had an arm around.

"Wayson, this is Emily Hughes," he said as I sat down.

"We met on Mars," I said.

She smiled. The girl had a dazzling smile. She said, "There's nothing wrong with your memory, General."

"Call me Wayson."

"Wayson," she said.

"I heard about your grandfather this afternoon," I said. "I'm sorry. He and I had a long history."

"He told me about it."

After that, we sat in an awkward silence, which Emily finally broke. She said, "Thanks to you, he got the thing he wanted most before he died. They're finally evacuating Mars."

"Did you know about that?" asked Watson.

I didn't know about anything. I said, "They kept me pretty far out of the loop at the hospital."

"Cutter is closing down Mars Spaceport," he said. "We're going to close it down and blow it up."

I started to say, "No shit," but I caught myself. I said, "No

kidding. Blowing it up? I guess he isn't taking any chances."
Good move, I thought. As far as anybody knew, Mars and Earth
were the only planets in the galaxy with buildings and life-support
infrastructure. If the Unifieds were out there and building an army,
Mars was the only place they could do it.

As we sat and talked, a woman approached our table. Sitting
with my back toward the restaurant, I did not see her coming; but
Watson went quiet in midsentence, and Emily seemed interested
as well.

A familiar voice said, "I'm sorry to interrupt you, but…"

I recognized the voice before I turned to look.

"General, it is you!" Sunny Ferris said enthusiastically, and she
illustrated her sincerity by placing a hand over her left breast. "I
thought I recognized your voice.

"We met several weeks ago. I'm Sunny Ferris. I represented…"

"You represented Arthur Hooper," I said.

Apparently glad to be recognized, she gave me a wide smile.

She said, "Well, actually the Arthur Hooper thing was a
mistake, he really wasn't our client; but we did represent the New
Olympians, and now they are being repatriated. I didn't think it
would ever happen."

She was so beautiful. I turned to Watson and saw that he
appreciated her as well. Emily looked a little less impressed.

I said, "Travis, Emily, this is Sunny Ferris. She's a lawyer."

Watson said, "It's good to meet you."

Emily only smiled, and there was something frosty in that
smile. Watson had been a player, and Emily had been a player,
and I suspected that Sunny might well have been a player as well.
Maybe members of that society could recognize their own. If that
was the case, perhaps Emily did not welcome the competition
now that she had removed Watson and herself from the game.

Sunny had come to the restaurant with friends from her office.
She said that they'd been headed toward the door when she'd
heard my voice. Watson, Emily, and I were about to order dinner.
There was no point in inviting her to sit down.

Sunny said, "I just wanted to come and say hi."

In a soft voice meant only for Watson, Emily said, "Hi."

I said, "It's good to see you again."

Sunny said, "I heard somewhere that you were injured on Mars."

"I'm better now."

"You were shot?" Concern showed in her face. She had such an expressive face.

"Something like that."

I did not invite her to join us.

She said, "Well, I better go."

She was about to leave, and I did not want that to happen. Given a free hand, I would have ditched my dinner and asked her out for a drink. I wanted to ask her about dinner, about lunch, about going out for drinks; but I could not bring myself to speak.

Perhaps I was obvious. A girl with a face like Sunny's probably got that kind of attention all the time. She gave me a smile and started to leave. Then she turned, and asked, "Would you like to go out for a drink sometime?"

AUTHOR'S NOTE

I'm relatively certain this is an urban myth, but I once heard that Pope Sylvester II declared that Christ would return to Earth on New Year's Eve 999. If that is true, and I doubt that it is, he must have been a tad embarrassed as he delivered his annual New Year's address the following day.

If the story is true, I can identify with the pontiff.

Last year I declared that *The Clone Redemption* would be the last Wayson Harris novel in the series, and I have gone back on my word. Not only have I written a new Wayson Harris novel; I have agreed to a sequel.

While *The Clone Sedition* takes place in the same universe as my past novels, it does begin an entirely new, Avatari-less story line. At least to that point I was correct.

I want to thank my agent, Richard Curtis, for putting this deal together. I want to thank the lovely and talented Anne at Ace for taking my book and for extending my deadlines.

And, of course, I want to thank my readers. Without you, there would be no point in writing my books.

Steven L. Kent
February 22, 2012

ABOUT THE AUTHOR

Steven L. Kent is an American author, best known for *The Clone Rebellion* series of military science fiction and his video game journalism. As a freelance journalist, he has written for *The Seattle Times, Parade, USA Today*, the *Chicago Tribune, MSNBC, The Japan Times*, and *The Los Angeles Times Syndicate*. He also wrote entries on video games for *Encarta* and the *Encyclopedia Americana*. For more about Kent, visit his official website www. SadSamsPalace.com.

READ ON FOR AN EXCLUSIVE SHORT STORY
BY STEVEN L. KENT

GENES MODEL
(THE FITTING END)

If I could choose any way to introduce myself, it would be with one of those old American Express commercials. I'd be dressed in blue jeans and I'd look into the camera and say, "Do you know me? You've seen me before." The camera would slowly pan down my back as I entered a locker room. Of course no one would recognize me, not yet.

In the next scene, I'd be dressed in green and white Speedos standing beside a swimming pool. I'd say, "Well, maybe you've never seen my face, but I'm in all the magazines. I've done movies, and lots of television." I'd turn to dive into the pool, and the camera would close in on my trunks.

In the final scene, I'd be getting dressed in a pair of BVDs. I'd give the usual spiel about American Express, but the camera would never show my face. Then they'd superimpose a credit card over my ass and type my name, T.A. Simpson. Some people would recognize me; I've got the most famous buttocks in the world.

* * *

I am a parts model. That means that while no one is impressed with the entire package, God blessed me with one special asset. I make as much as $2,000 a day loaning out my buttocks.

Calvin Klein, BVD and Fruit of the Loom pay me money to display their wares on my real estate. Through the magic of motion pictures, Tom Hardy, George Clooney, and Ben Stiller have rounded out their images using my cheeks. Lord knows how many rock stars have attached me to their backsides in music videos. I've lost count.

I wasn't always destined for stardom. Someone had to discover me.

Ever visit a Los Angeles construction site? First man on the job has to scare out the homeless folks. Now that's real man's work; and all too often, it was my great and good fortune to perform that service. Three mornings a week, I opened the construction site, grabbed a crowbar, and made my rounds.

On the day in question, the sun had reached the zone—that's what I call that layer of clear air and white clouds between the L.A. hills and the smog. I had just started making the rounds when I spotted an empty wine bottle glistening in the morning sunlight. Gently tapping my crowbar to the steel-reinforced toe of my boot, I set off to evict our guest.

I found the happy camper wrapped in a dirt-matted Army blanket that hung like an old fashioned tent from our fence. He'd spread all of his worldly possessions spread beneath the blanket, then washed his clothes in a cement trough and hung them out to dry, leaving him naked on old newspapers he had spread for a floor.

"Hey, you, Bud," I said, nudging him with the toe of my boot.

He rolled over as slow and elegant as a princess. His pillow, a garbage bag full of rags, smelled like road kill. "Whad do you want?" he grumbled, his lips drawing back into a sneer. He still had a couple of moss-covered teeth, but his lips were cracked and his gums were the color of Nestlé Quik.

"You gotta go, Bud," I said.

I noticed that his wine bottle was empty and felt sorry for the old Skid. Judging by the dirt and the peeling label, the bottle had probably been half empty when he found it.

He rolled so that his back faced me and I noticed twigs and pebbles tangled in his hair.

Tapping the crowbar against the empty bottle of Thunderbird wine, I caught his attention a second time and said, "It's check out time, Bud."

He sat halfway up for a moment, started to say something and waved me off. "Go 'way!" he said as he fell back on his rags.

By this time I was getting tired of seeing his shriveled up nether parts, so I stepped closer and prodded his back with my toe. He snapped around. At first I thought he'd flipped me off, then I saw the blade in his hand. He growled like a junkyard dog and said, "I tol' you to go 'way!"

I brandished my crowbar, holding it with my right hand and slapping it against the palm of my left. This time the old skidder's smile faded. Knives trump fists; crowbars trump knives; guns win automatically.

"It's check out time. Now get dressed and get out," I told him.

"I'm leaving. I'm leaving," he grumbled as he pulled his pants from the fence. Let me tell you, his knife didn't bother me much but the sight of what age and hard living had done to his manhood turned my gut inside-out. So the old Skidder finished dressing and packed up his campsite. He stuffed all of his possessions into that dirty sack of rags he used for a pillow, and he slipped a tattered pair of Converses over his feet.

Of all the people in my life, it is that vagrant who I credit for getting me out of construction and into modeling. As he walked across the street, I noticed a soggy pack of Marlboros fall out of the folds of his blanket. Normally, I wouldn't have cared, but there was a rolled up dollar bill poking out of the top of the pack. That dollar wasn't worth one hundred pennies to me, but to a Skid Row regular, losing that buck must have meant bankruptcy.

I called after him, "Hey, Skidder, you dropped your smokes." When I bent over to pick up the moldy pack, I noticed a man in an expensive-looking suit staring at me from across the street. He continued watching me as I stood up and handed the cigarettes to their rightful owner.

"You don' get none o' dis!" the Skidder snarled, and he walked off as dignified as the Queen of England.

But the day's weirdness had only begun. The guy in the suit trotted over to me. "Do you work here?" he asked. He was short and bald, with a ring of black hair and powdery-smelling cologne. Though he tried to look me in the face, his eyes kept dropping to my pants.

"You some kind of queer?" I asked.

The man flushed red and said, "Well, yes, but that's not why I'm asking."

I almost decked him.

At that very moment, Jack Lawson strutted past and said, "Hey, T.A., nice fairy!" Lawson was a welder. He had a real mouth on him and he liked to give me grief.

Now that Lawson had seen us, I felt annoyed. All I needed was a site full of guys ribbing me for talking to some queer. "What do you want?" I snapped.

The man looked around nervously. I scared him. He stood a foot shorter than me. On his toes he might have cleared five-three. "Let me give you my card," he said.

Instead of taking the card, I scowled at him and said, "I ain't gonna call you." When I want to sound really tough, I talk uneducated; it scares the hell out of the three-piece-suit crowd.

The man shifted from one foot to the other nervously and said, "I noticed you from across the street."

"You're getting yourself in deeper!" I warned him. Then I realized what Lawson would make of my telling a queer he was "getting in deeper" and realized I needed to watch my ass.

The man said, "Look, Mister…" He looked up expecting me to give him my name.

I said nothing.

"I believe there's a place for you in an advertisement that I'm putting together." He looked at my crowbar. Cautiously, he reached into his coat and pulled out a business card. "Could be worth a couple hundred dollars."

I said nothing.

"You might think about it," he said. "I'm doing an advertisement for Levi's Jeans." With that, he turned and scurried away.

When I returned to the site, Lawson pointed me out to some of his buddies and laughed. He yelled, "Hey, T.A., you set up a hot date for the weekend?"

"I always wondered what T.A. did with them old hobos first thing in the morning!" joked one of the shop foremen.

Lawson laughed himself hoarse and asked, "D'you say hobos or homos?"

Needless to say, that day was the shits.

The man's card said that he was Mars Phelps of the Kettlesworth and Phelps Advertising Agency. I didn't call him that day. If the guys knew I'd even kept his card, they would have ragged me to my grave. The guy had said that he'd give me a couple hundred dollars for a few hours' work, and unless he had a death wish, he was talking about work with my clothes on.

The next day, I called his office. His secretary said he was busy and took my name. I gave her my home phone number. If he called me at the job site and Lawson figured out who he was… When I got home, I found no messages on my answering machine.

Two days later, I called again. The same secretary took the same message. She acted as if we had never spoken before. Again, I got no response.

One week later, I decided to give old Mr. Phelps one last try. This time I told the secretary to tell *Mars* that we met at a construction site. That night he left a message on my answering machine.

It began with, "Sorry I didn't get back to you sooner. It's been hectic around the agency," and ended with, "Mr. Simpson, we'd like you to come down for a screening tomorrow at three o'clock. My address is on the card. If you have a problem, call my secretary. She can give you directions."

The next morning I called Mars from work. The secretary answered, "Kettlesworth and Phelps, can I help you?"

"I have a *screening* today?"

"You must be Mr. Simpson," she said.

"Yeah. I can't come at three. Look ma'am, I work. It's June, we don't get out of here till 7:30 or 8:00."

"I see. Please hold."

"Oh, lord," I thought to myself. "She put me on hold. She's going to leave me hanging here until someone walks by and figures out who I'm calling. This is stupid. This is so damned stupid." I almost hung up. Then Mars Phelps came on.

"Mr. Simpson, this is Mars Phelps. Is there a problem with you coming in?"

"Damn straight there's a problem. I work for a living."

"I see. What time will you be available?" His voice sounded so calm, like a teacher explaining the facts of life to a first-grader. It made me so pissed.

I asked, "Look, what do you want me *for* anyway?"

"It's a modeling job, Mr. Simpson. I thought I explained that to you when we met. I am putting together an advertisement for Levi's Jeans and you have just the right look."

"Modeling," I laughed. "You want me for a model." How can I put this delicately? When I was in school, no one ever suggested me for homecoming king. My mother once told me, "Sonny, you better work hard in school; you're not going to get by on your looks." You get the picture.

"It so happens that your... um, build is just about perfect for the shot we have in mind."

I said, "Listen here, you little faggot." Had I not been on the site, I would have said a hell of a lot more and been a hell of a lot louder.

"Look, Mr. Simpson, this is legitimate work. We want to fit you in a pair of 501s and snap a couple of pictures. I'm willing to pay you $300 for your trouble. If that works for you, be here at three. If that doesn't work for you, we can hire a professional."

"I see." His sudden show of backbone caught me off guard.

"Is there anything else I can do for you, Mr. Simpson?" Mars asked.

"No," I said.

"Fine. I hope to see you this afternoon." He hung up. I stood numb listening to the silence of dead phone line. Across the job site, pile drivers mashed concrete posts into the ground. Riveters fastened girders together.

Looking over the lot, I decided that the building could survive a day without me. I told my boss that I had the runs and he sent me home, no questions asked.

Mary, the receptionist, looked like a goddess behind her telephone. She was a black woman with soft, straight hair and smooth skin. She looked me over as I came to her desk, and she wasn't impressed by the results. "Can I help you?" she asked.

"I'm here to see Mars Phelps," I said.

Her eyes ran down my body and fixed somewhere around my belt. She smiled and said, "You must be Mr. Simpson."

I still didn't know what was going on. I worked at a construction site where I got a lot of ribbing, but that's how my kind of guy relates. Nobody tells anyone else they look good.

Maybe I had better looks than I thought, I thought. I was wrong, of course. It wasn't about my face; this visit was all about my butt. See, with a face like mine, I never held anyone's interest long enough for them to take in my ass. Mars didn't consider me ruggedly handsome. The first thing he saw of me was my behind as I reached down for the bum's pack of smokes. By the time he saw my face, he'd already made up his mind about my ass.

Mary pressed a button on her phone. "Mars, Mr. Simpson is here to see you."

"Tell him I'll be a moment, and have Matt join us, would you?"

"He may be a while," Mary apologized. "Would you like some coffee?"

"No thanks," I said.

"Why don't you have a seat," she suggested.

Almost an hour later, Mary said Mars was ready for me. By that time, I had thumbed through four issues of *AdWeek* and found nothing more interesting than an article explaining why LeBron had stopped pimping Sprite.

"Mars will see you now," she said. Away from her desk, Mary stood almost as tall as me. It looked like those long legs of hers started somewhere just below her shoulders.

From the outside, the building looked like a dilapidated hotel. The reception area was nice enough. I liked the glass brick wall that surrounded Mary's desk. But nothing prepared me for Mars' office. It was the size of a small warehouse with a 20-foot ceiling. He had living room furniture at one end of the room and office furniture at the other.

Mars and another man sat on the couch in the living-room end. They both wore designer jeans or a reasonable facsimile. Mars wore a green shirt with a fox or a polo pony. The other guy had on a Hawaiian shirt.

Me, I was dressed in the gray suit I'd pulled off a rack at Sears and feeling out of place.

"Love the suit," the guy in the Hawaiian shirt quipped.

I already regretted coming.

"Ease up, Matt. I told you, T.A. is new talent. He's working at a construction site over in Santa Monica."

"I see." Matt pulled a pencil from his shirt pocket and tapped the eraser against his chin. He stood up and walked around me. Like Mary, he inspected my pants. "Might as well have him drop the slacks. Let's see what he's got."

I snapped around. "You little..."

"Don't flatter yourself," Matt said. "Mars may be right about your ass. But the rest of you belongs out laying bricks."

"Listen, T.A...." Mars paused. "Can I call you T.A.?"

"I'm not dropping my pants," I said.

"I don't think I explained what kind of modeling we have in mind," Mars said.

"The pants stay on." Thinking for a moment, I added, "This isn't for some kind of queer magazine?"

"He's awfully raw," said Matt. "He'd better be good if I'm going to put up with that attitude."

Matt, by the way, turned out to be Matt LaBelle, a $1,000-a-day fashion photographer who was no more attracted to men than I am to rutabagas. He wasn't about to tell me that, though. He was a straight guy in a gender-tolerant world who got a kick out of making Neanderthal homophobes uncomfortable.

Seeing my confusion, Mars explained parts modeling. Strange as it sounds, I took it hard. Here I had begun to wonder if I *was* an undiscovered beauty, but with a few well-chosen words, Mars reduced me to a couple of well-formed buns.

"I don't need this," I said as I turned to leave.

"He really has good structure," Mars said.

"Just can't tell through those baggy slacks," Matt said.

By this time I was almost out the door.

"Did I mention that we'll pay $300 for the shoot?" Mars called out.

"Yeah. You said that already," I said.

"Five hundred dollars. Five hundred dollars and I promise you can keep your clothes on... and the advertisement is for *Sports Illustrated*. Strictly legitimate."

"Five hundred dollars!" Matt gasped. "A first-time shoot for $500? He'd better have the Marilyn Monroe of all asses."

Mars's money brought me back. "I keep my clothes on?" I asked, trying to sound in control.

"I need to know what I'm dealing with," Matt said.

I looked across the lobby and saw Mary glance back at me. That hair, that dark skin; for a moment I lost my train of thought. What would she think of a man who had only one photographable asset?

"Matt's right. He needs to screen you."

I stepped back in and shut the door. "So I drop my trousers, and your horny little friend..."

"Simpson, you make me many things, but horny is not one of them," Matt said.

"...and your horny little friend says he doesn't like me. You guys get your thrills and I'm out my money. You've got to be kidding!"

Mars whipped out his wallet. With snappy little movements he counted out five bills. "You know, T.A., you are a real pain in the ass, but I think you're worth it. Here is your $500. I'm paying in advance. I'll even look in the other direction if you like. As for Matt, he's straight."

"Wife and three kids, Babe!" Matt chimed in.

Taking a deep breath, I undid my belt. It took real effort to unhitch my trousers and let them slide to the floor. Underneath, I wore a pair of dark blue BBDs with a crisp, white elastic band.

"Good lord! What architecture!" Matt gasped. "If David Beckham had an ass like this he'd still be on billboards."

"Mary, you'd better come see this. He's even better than I thought!" Mars said.

I tried to spin around to see what was happening, but I got tangled in my pants and lost my balance. As I fell, I saw Mars speaking into his intercom. A moment later, Mary opened the office door.

I scrambled back to my feet and pulled up my pants.

"He is good," she said. "Mars, you really have a knack for finding talent." Two guys peered in behind her and nodded their approval as well.

* * *

I'm not going to waste time talking about the photo shoot, why should I embarrass myself? Three weeks later, *Sports Illustrated* came out with Kevin Durant on the cover and my ass on page seven. And that's not all. The same picture appeared opposite an article about the Oakland A's in *Inside Sport*, near the movie reviews in *GQ*, and beside Mila Kunis's beauty secrets in *Cosmopolitan*.

I never told anyone at work what I had done, but that didn't stop the subject from coming up. The ad itself was just a close-up of my ass in 501s with the Levi's logo showing prominently above my right cheek. No slogans, no prices, no coupons; nothing but my denim-covered cheeks cluttered the page.

Richie Freeman, the city inspector assigned to our site, brought a copy of that *Sports Illustrated* to lunch. When I noticed him reading looking at my picture, my stomach tensed. A group of rebar welders sat near him. He showed it to them and said, "You see that? That there is a black man. Ain't no white boy got an ass like that."

Richie liked talking street. He'd earned an engineering degree at UCLA, took home a solid six figures each year, and sat on two boards with the mayor. Dressed in a suit and tie, I'm sure he could conjugate sentences with the best of them, but out on the construction site, he spoke uneducated like everybody else.

Jack Lawson smirked. A wiser man would have known better, Richie being black and all, but Lawson took the bait. He said, "You don't know he's black. The picture doesn't show any skin."

"Oh, he's a brother. Ain't no white man got a round ass like that." Richie tapped the picture with his knuckles.

"Bullshit," said the guy sitting next to Jack.

"Maybe he's Chinese," I offered.

Freeman glowered at me. "T.A., you don't know shit from Shinola. That ain't no Chinaman, and that ain't no Chicano. Now that there is a proud brother."

From there, the conversation strayed off to World Series predictions and the upcoming football season.

* * *

By the way, the name T.A. stands for Theodore Andrew, not "Tight Ass." A lot of people refer to me as "Tight Ass" around the industry, but that couldn't be helped.

My rise to stardom came quickly. The construction site wasn't the only place where my photograph caught people's attention. Within a week, Mars had received calls from several modeling agencies asking for my identity. They all had a sense of urgency; apparently perfect butts don't last much longer than ripe apples.

Mars gave my name to Ford Models. Within a month, I quit construction to dedicate more attention to my burgeoning modeling career. Through aerobics, swimming, and a little modern science, I've managed to stay on top for a couple of years now.

I could tell you what I plan to do when the law of gravity finally puts an end to my career. I could, but then, that would be another story.

AUGUST 30, 2453
WASHINGTON, D.C.

Commander Bryce Klyber didn't take the other men on the panel entire seriously. There was Howard Tasman, the scientist in charge of forming the clones' brains. Next to Tasman sat Bill Driggs, who knew nothing of science or the military. He was an accountant. The Linear Committee had sent him to keep an eye on the bottom line.

Jennifer Gilchrist, the scientist making the report, was the best of the bunch as far as Klyber was concerned. Having worked on past cloning projects, she understood the military's needs better than the others.

Tasman interrupted her. He said, "Wait, you're saying you can splice DNA. Are you telling me you can extract genes from multiple donors and string them together?"

"Why is that such a big deal?" asked Driggs. "What did they do in the past?"

"We've always chosen a top candidate and extracted his DNA," said Gilchrist. "In the past, we've looked at athletes and soldiers. The last line of clones was based on a decathlon champion... is the proper term a 'decathalete'?"

"What's wrong with that?" asked Driggs. "Those clones worked well."

"I'll tell you what's wrong with it," said Klyber. "Those clones were policemen. They guarded colonies and helped little old ladies cross the street. We don't know what we're up against now. Running, jumping, and throwing discuses may not cut it after this."

"That's why the Committee approved the combat reflex," said Driggs. "We've spent a lot of capital developing a gland and a hormone. I'm not sure the Committee will approve additional monies spent splicing genes."

Gilchrist was in her late forties or early fifties, and she probably wasn't much to look at when she was young, Klyber thought as he watched her. She was trim and athletic. She spent hours in the complex gymnasium. The people working on the Liberator program weren't allowed off-campus, that was one of the rules of the game.

Tall and almost comically skinny, Klyber never forgot his own shortcomings as well. Still in his twenties, he had thinning hair over his temples. He had the physique of a praying mantis—tall, long arms and legs, a stick of a body with no shoulders to speak of.

Gilchrist said, "Mr. Driggs, in theory we could give our clones Commander Klyber's military-oriented brain. We could give him arms like a boxer's, and legs like a swimmers, and the eyes of a sniper."

"Yeah, and maybe we could give him your finger muscles," said Tasman.

"I don't understand," said Driggs.

"A penny-pincher like you has got to have strong fingers," said Tasman.

Gilchrist stifled a giggle. Klyber, who had learned how to stand stone-faced after thousands of inspections, sat stone-faced in his seat. Driggs fumed. His face turned red. He said, "That's uncalled for. I have a job to do. If you prefer that I didn't do it, you may take it up with the Committee. I'm sure they'd welcome your input."

Klyber stepped in. He said, "I'm sure we can all remain civil."

"What about animal DNA?" asked Driggs. "Can you give them cat eyes so they can see in the dark? Can you give them gills so they can breathe underwater, maybe give them sonar like a bat?"

The question was ridiculous, but Gilchrist fielded it well just the same. She said, "Human DNA and animal DNA are not compatible. We've just developed the ability to identify and extract genes that go into certain muscle groups in humans."

Tasman added, "This is genetic science; it's not mix-and-match."

Klyber glared at him. Hunting for the best genes would be a costly procedure. Bill Driggs may have been a bureaucratic asshole, but the Committee listened to his recommendations.

Driggs said, "So, in theory, you could create a soldier with the hands of Martin Stoner, the legs of Alexis Cantrell, and the brain of Genghis Khan." Stoner was a heavyweight boxer; Cantrell broke the three-minute mile.

"If we could find a suitable sample of Khan's DNA," said Gilchrist.

"Biggest, strongest, smartest, and fastest don't necessarily mean best," said Klyber. "You can make a man so bulky that he's useless by military standards. Too big, too small, too anything and you miss your mark.

"It's all a question of architecture. We need to go through recent history in search of all the right genes, and then we need to figure out how to make them all fit together."